# SWORDS
## OF
# GOOD
# MEN

# SWORDS
## OF
# GOOD
# MEN

## SNORRI KRISTJANSSON

Jo Fletcher
BOOKS

First published in Great Britain in 2013 by

Jo Fletcher Books
an imprint of Quercus
55 Baker Street
7th Floor, South Block
London
W1U 8EW

A CIP catalogue record for this book is available
from the British Library

ISBN 978 1 78206 332 2 (HB)
ISBN 978 1 78206 331 5 (TPB)
ISBN 978 1 78206 333 9 (EBOOK)

10 9 8 7 6 5 4 3 2 1

Typeset by Ellipsis Digital Limited, Glasgow

Printed and bound in Great Britain by
Clays Ltd, St Ives plc

To my wife and family.
Thank you.

# Prologue

A line of pale grey moonlight crawled across the water. The heavy clouds drifted apart and a faint outline of the coast shimmered into view.

The man at the rudder broke the silence and pointed to shore. 'That's Stenvik there.'

Ulfar heard it before he saw it. Voices, shouts and cries carried across the sea, skipped past the line of moonlight, over the deeper, darker swathes of water and blended to form the noise of a town at night. A year ago his heart would have lifted to hear it. Now he just ached and stretched, moving slowly to work the cramp out of his long legs. When he'd sat up he nudged the man who slept in the boat next to him. 'We're here.'

'. . . What?' his cousin Geiri mumbled and rubbed his face, still more than half asleep. 'When do we land? Where are we?' He clambered to a sitting position and winced. 'Next time I suggest sailing because it saves time—'

'— I'll just punch you in the back a couple of times and find a horse, shall I?' Ulfar replied. Behind them the quiet sailor smirked. The merchant who owned the boat was sound asleep on all the furs he intended to sell in Stenvik. He'd left the two young men to squeeze in between sacks of wheat, planks of carved wood and blocks of amber. Geiri was shorter, so he'd had an easier time finding a comfortable position. Ulfar had retaliated by poking him in his sleep. Still, they couldn't complain. Geiri had negotiated free passage from Hedeby all the way to south-west Norway just by mentioning his father and hinting at some undefined favour in the future. They could have navigated most of the way just by the blaze of greed in the merchant's smile.

Tiny dots of fire caught Ulfar's eye. He pointed them out to his cousin and they watched as Stenvik grew out of the dark.

'Doesn't look like much, does it?' Ulfar muttered.

'After Hedeby? Not really. But we still need to go there. Cheer up, you miserable goat. It's the last one. After this one we go home.'

'Good,' Ulfar replied, and thought of Svealand. After the . . . accident, after Geiri's father had intervened on his behalf and suggested – no, forced him – to go travelling with his cousin, he'd spent the first six months of the journey cursing his own stupidity, the next year or so enjoying the travel and the last four months being thoroughly done with the road. He touched the rune on the string around his neck. After Stenvik he was going back home no matter what.

'Who's there?' someone cried from the docks.

'Friend,' the sailor yelled back. 'Bringing a merchant with goods to trade and two passengers.' At that the merchant awoke with a start, grabbed for his chest and fondled for his pouch. Satisfied that he had not been robbed at sea he sank back down, mumbling to no one in particular.

'Dock over here,' yelled another voice. The sailor pulled on the rudder and the boat changed course. A torch flared on the jetty and a big, grubby dockhand's face emerged from the dark. 'You're out late, sailor,' he barked.

'Caught calm seas and tide out of Hedeby, thought I'd push it. Out late is better than out cold,' the sailor replied.

'That's true,' the man on the dock grunted. The two men went about the business of mooring the boat with easy, practised movements, and before long Ulfar and Geiri stood on the pier. Ulfar glanced at his cousin, who was still rubbing the sleep out of his eyes. A full head taller than Geiri, right now Ulfar looked nothing like the son of a lesser noble. He brushed a strand of long black hair away from his eyes. Geiri was a good man, there was no doubt about it. They'd practically grown up together, and Geiri's father was a great man, Ulfar knew. It was just frustrating to watch his cousin sometimes. He simply wasn't . . . sharp enough. He hadn't realized that the dockhand was going to offer them a place to stay, for one. Ulfar sighed and counted. One, two . . .

The grubby-faced man turned to Ulfar. 'If you boys need somewhere to sleep I reckon I could help you out,' he wheezed.

Ulfar would have brushed the man off, but Geiri spoke. 'Thank you,' he replied. 'Stenvik impresses with its kindness to weary travellers. We'll be glad to take you up on your offer.'

Wincing inwardly, Ulfar resisted the temptation to elbow his cousin and instead took the time to look around. Truth be told, the town of Stenvik didn't impress with much apart from its gap-toothed hospitality. The jetty was serviceable enough, which made sense for a town this far west. He knew they raided the isles from here, and even down to the land of the Franks, but for all the stories he'd heard of their chieftain he'd expected . . . more. Something fiercer, maybe. Dragons' heads and huge raiders on watch. The big, paved half-circle in front of them must be some kind of market area, he reasoned, but the houses around it looked rickety and run down.

'Heh,' the man replied. 'You won't be staying in the new town, so don't get too chirpy about your lot.'

'The new town?' Geiri asked.

'This is the old town,' the dockhand wheezed. 'Now we just unload the ships and such here. Nobody really lives here any more if they can help it. The new town is up there' – he pointed to some kind of hill or mound. Unsure what to say, Geiri glanced at Ulfar. As usual Ulfar took pity on his cousin and rescued him from the awkward pause.

'Yes. Very nice,' he said. 'It looks very . . . new.'

'It's good, isn't it? But you'll probably see it all in the morning. Follow me,' the dockhand said. He shuffled out of the small circle of torchlight and towards a clump of houses. Geiri made to follow him.

Ulfar sighed. He had a mind to let the boy wander into the shadowy alleys of an unknown town by himself. He didn't; instead he walked behind Geiri and looked after him, as he'd promised. As he'd been made to promise.

The man led them into the shadows between lean-tos, houses and wattle-woven shacks. Ulfar briefly felt for his shortsword, just to be sure. 'Ain't done too much to the old part since we built the new town,' the dockhand rumbled as they tiptoed along the wooden walkway between the houses. 'Still, it serves its purpose. Here we are.' He stopped outside a hut. 'Give me your packs, I'll throw them in and then I'll take you down to the old longhouse so you can get a bit of refreshment and maybe meet some of the locals.' Ulfar grimaced in the dark. He'd met enough locals to last him a lifetime.

'Thank you,' Geiri said. 'You're a credit to your town.'

'Heh,' the dockhand said. 'Not so sure about that. Not so sure at all. This way, boys, if you please,' and with that he disappeared back into the shadows. Ulfar looked at Geiri, who simply shrugged.

'We're here now,' he said. 'Might as well go see what this town's like. It'll give us a head start on tomorrow.'

'Lead the way,' Ulfar replied, and they followed their guide's fading footsteps towards the feeble pools of torchlight.

They found him waiting for them by the doors of an old long-house. 'Here you go,' the dockhand said. 'This is where we feed the workers, the traders and whatever else might be floating around. As you know we're in market season, so there might be some guests there as well. Take care of yourselves.' With that he nodded to them and shuffled off into the darkness.

'After you, my lord,' Ulfar said.

'Oh shut up,' Geiri snapped back.

'My sincerest pardons, highness,' Ulfar said.

Geiri rolled his eyes. 'One day I'll find out what I've done to the gods and why they sent you to punish me.'

'I think your majestic good looks offend Loki,' Ulfar replied.

'Probably,' Geiri said as they stepped in.

Steam drifted lazily up to the smoke-stained rafters from the pots at the far end of the hall. Sturdy tables lined the timber walls and the smell of roasted meat lingered in the air. The long-house was about half-full. Without thinking Ulfar scanned, counted and evaluated. A handful of boisterous groups, jostling and laughing. About half of the others were tired-looking workers, quietly resting. The evening seemed to be winding down and turning into night. Ulfar spotted a table where a slim young man with thinning hair and sloping shoulders sat nursing a mug. He saw Ulfar looking and shrugged by way of permission.

'I've found us a table,' Ulfar said.

'I'll go get the ale,' Geiri said.

'Wait and watch, cousin,' Ulfar said as he took a seat. 'Wait and watch. One of these days I may be able to teach you to . . . observe.' He gestured for Geiri to sit and nodded towards a big pillar on the wall halfway down the hall where a big, dishevelled man sat alone at a table, muttering to himself. Everything about him spoke of poor manners and worse grooming. Thinning, limp, dirty blond hair crept forward over a creased forehead, ending just above beady eyes and a mouth stuck in a permanent sneer of displeasure.

'You bastards!' the big man suddenly shouted, his pockmarked face beetroot-red. He squinted at the others inside the hall and banged on the table for emphasis. Snarling, he raised a battered wooden mug to his lips. 'Y'think you're so much better'n us just because you live in a stupid town! Think you're—' The rest of his words drowned in ale. He sputtered, swallowed and coughed. 'And you charge too much for this piss!'

'Shut up, pig-lover!' someone shouted.

'Who said that?' the farmer yelled back, furious. 'Who said that?' He rose and staggered out onto the middle of the floor, his big frame swaying. 'Come on then! I'll have every last one of you!' he shouted, brandishing his mug.

'What are you going to do – grab us by the tail?' someone shouted from another table. Pig snorts bounced off the walls, followed by raucous laughter.

Ulfar and Geiri watched as the farmer spun around, trying in vain to find the source of the insults. Groups of workers sat on benches up against the walls, eating, drinking and talking. No-one seemed to pay him any special mind, but his blood was up. He staggered over to a man sitting alone at a table in the corner by the door. 'You!' he shouted. 'You're in my seat.'

Ulfar nudged Geiri and pointed discreetly at the groups behind the pig farmer. Some of the men had stopped talking and were watching the exchange in the corner intently, but the fat pig farmer didn't seem to notice. The man in the corner ignored him.

'I said you're in my seat. Move.' The farmer's voice was strained but the man at the table still ignored him, as if willing the big drunkard to disappear. 'Move now, dogface, or I will break your head.'

One by one, the tables in the longhouse grew quiet. The sitting man sighed, reached for his mug of ale, drained it and rose.

'. . . oh,' Geiri whispered. A deadly silence filled the longhouse.

There was a tangible sense of mass about the man in the corner. A shock of unruly blond hair. Big shoulders, long arms, calloused hands with thick fingers. The man was short, but built like a bear. He put his mug down carefully and looked the pig farmer straight in the eye. Two steps took him to within fighting range. He stopped for a heartbeat. Then the stocky man moved past the pig farmer and walked towards the door without saying a word.

No one in the old longhouse spoke.

The farmer looked at the lone man's back and seemed to struggle with the impulse to shout something, but thought better of it and sat down in the corner as the blond man left the longhouse.

Ulfar grinned. 'See, Geiri. I am fortune's gift to you. If it weren't for me you'd have been pig fodder.'

'It looks to me like the pig farmer had all the luck tonight,' Geiri replied.

'If that's what you want to call it,' the thin man next to Geiri said curtly. 'Maybe fighting with Audun would have knocked some stupid out of him. Although if you want to pick someone for a drunken bash, maybe not the town blacksmith.'

'No,' Ulfar said, nodding. 'No. Maybe not.'

They looked over to the corner where the pig farmer sat hunched over his mug, looking even more miserable than before. 'I'm glad he didn't – I'd have to clean up the mess. My name is

Valgard, by the way. I make potions and mend wounds in this lovely town.'

'Glad to meet you,' Geiri said. 'I am Geiri and this is Ulfar. We've come from Hedeby on business.'

'Really?' Valgard said. 'You're not drunk, you're not slavering and you don't smell of sheep. Are you sure?'

'Yes,' said Geiri. 'We're here to meet with Sigurd Aegisson.'

'Ah,' Valgard said. He finished his ale, stood up and smiled. 'I wish you the best of luck.' Then he left.

Geiri gave Ulfar a puzzled look. 'What do you think that meant?'

Ulfar frowned. 'I don't know. I somehow doubt that it's anything good. But on the other hand, with danger averted and the table to ourselves, you may now fetch us that ale.'

Geiri rolled his eyes. 'You're too kind.'

'I know,' Ulfar replied, grinning.


## THE NORTH SEA

A few days' sailing further north, the cold moonlight danced on decks, slid over tarred wood, caught on edges, hilts and the eyes of hard men. Some murmured to themselves. Others touched small tokens on leather thongs underneath their armour. They looked like ghosts gliding across a sea of silver. Moving nimbly, an armed man picked his way to the prow of the foremost ship. 'We'll be at Moster soon,' he whispered into the shadows cast by the big masthead.

'Good,' a deep voice replied. 'Good. She will get what she needs.'

A sharp wind whipped the salt-caked sails and drove the twelve sleek ships forward. Above, grey clouds scudded over the waxing moon. When they passed, the pale light fell on a small island ahead of the ships. A handful of stone buildings clustered in the lee of a hill; trees shied away from the cold sea winds.

The ships landed like a whisper.

Sails fell, sixty men leapt overboard and suddenly the beach was alive with moving bodies. A big shape emerged from the shadow of the masthead and made to leave.

'Come to me.' The voice was a whisper, a breeze on a freezing winter's night, drifting in from the stern. A woman followed the voice, and walked to the mast. The big man walked to her and suddenly everything was quiet around them. 'Here,' she whispered. 'Take this.' She handed him a length of wood.

As he took it, she touched his bearded cheek and smiled.

'Burn them. Burn them as they want to burn us.'

The spar of wood burst into green and white flames, revealing three vicious scars on the big man's neck.

Screams and cries for help pierced the stillness. He jumped over the side of the ship and ran towards the house with the cross.

## STENVIK

This had to be the mother of all headaches, Ulfar reasoned. Surely nobody had ever suffered like this. His skull seemed to be bursting slowly. Even the morning sun, shining cheekily through crevices in the walls, added to the pain. As did the sound of every laughing child, every hammer blow, every squealing pig. Especially the bloody pigs.

Maybe he shouldn't have goaded Geiri into a fight last night. He liked his cousin; he was good company for travelling and had his head on straight most of the time. But they'd drunk too much, he'd been bored and Geiri was an easy target. Besides, the girl had been all right, and worth besting him for. Ulfar frowned, trying to remember. Inga, probably. Damn, his head hurt!

Ulfar smiled despite the pain. He'd always had it easy with girls. Although to be fair he hadn't really had that much in the way of competition. He was handsome, clever and quick-witted. Most men he saw were either ignorant boys or oafish lugs with the grooming skills of a blind cow, so he'd learned to feel confident about his chances. Besides, he was a man of the world by now.

He stretched on his pallet, yawned and sighed. This constant travelling was such a chore. 'I suppose it's time to go find the chieftain of this pig town,' he said to no one in particular, and got to his feet.

*

Audun sneered and spat. He did not like the market traders one bit. Idiots selling useless crap to fools. Changing things. Getting in the way. He'd been so close to letting go on one of them last night in the longhouse. So close.

'Move!'

The stocky blond blacksmith grabbed a small, nervous cloth merchant and pushed him out of the way. The autumn market seemed to bring an endless supply of them from all over the world, shouting and yelling, pitching tents around the old town, hawking their wares in the streets, in the square and anywhere else they could find room. Drinking too much and trying to get him to fight. That ugly bastard last night had almost succeeded, too.

And now they were blocking the gate.

Of course the broken cart didn't help.

He'd seen it happen, seen the driver, who was obviously another idiot, lead the cart too close to the side of the road in an effort to squeeze past another wagon and slip through the south gate, towards the harbour. He'd seen the rock and the hole, he'd seen the wheel bounce off one and into the other, and he'd heard the sharp crack when the axle gave. As the cart lurched, the man had tumbled off and banged his head. Served him right, Audun thought. Shouldn't have let them in to begin with. But the road was blocked and this would not do. It would slow people down, keep them from the smithy and cost him business. And that he couldn't afford.

He shouldered through the crowd in the market without thinking. Shouts and curses followed, but he didn't care. Never had, never would, he muttered to himself. Talk is air.

When he first came to Stenvik, he'd been awed by the sheer size of the walls. At a towering twenty-five feet, covered with turf and sloping upwards at a steep angle, they had seemed impossibly wide at the base. Audun had admired the construction as he rode through the north gateway with his travelling companions. A stone-walled corridor wide enough to take two carts and high enough with room to spare for a man to walk upright, it had still taken their caravan a decent time to get through. He'd thought highly of the stonework, although some of the logs in the ceiling near the inside had struck him as oddly placed. On both ends of the gateway massive wooden gates were suspended over the openings, secured by thick ropes used for raising and lowering. What they lacked in the craft shown in the stonework they more than made up for in reliability. The gates were essentially sturdy, iron-bound pine logs stacked horizontally and set to be lowered into grooves in the walls. A short tour of the town had confirmed that the other three gates followed the same model.

At the time he'd been pleased with the craft of it.

Standing in the shadow of the same walls nearly two years later, looking at the suspended south gate, it seemed more like a cage door. And now the gateway was partially blocked by the cart. The space around the cart was crammed with the usual group of useless onlookers that seemed to gather on every such scene to lay blame, give pointless advice and avoid taking any action whatsoever. Audun gritted his teeth. Three of them were standing around the rear of the cart looking particularly miserable and staring alternately at the wheel, the broken shaft and the placid draft horse still tied to the trace.

He grabbed the nearest shoulder and yanked, forcing the man to face him.

'You. Lead that half-dead nag on my signal.'

The man blinked and stared blankly back at him.

'Now! Move!' Audun half shoved the man towards the horse and turned his attention to the broken axle. Huge bags of feed had been piled topsy-turvy on the cart, and the jolt had proved too much. A quick inspection confirmed his suspicions. The other wheel would stay on, but this one was gone and would not carry weight. The cart would not be mended here, and there was hardly space to unload it.

Audun took up a position at the rear end, feeling under the collapsed side for a grip. When he'd found it, he spat into the palms of his hands, rubbed them together and grabbed the edge of the cart.

He bent his knees, straightened his back and growled low. Breathing through his nose, he slowly straightened his legs and lifted the corner of the cart. Moving his leg behind the wheel, he pushed it away from the wagon. The two men at the back stood by and gawped, as did the hapless farmer standing by the horse. 'You two – help me, or by Thor I'll drop it on your feet and smack you in the head!' Audun hissed through clenched teeth. He turned to the front and snapped: 'And you – get the bloody horse moving!'

After a brief moment of confusion, the farmers bumbled into action.

The two men in the back squeezed in on either side of Audun and tried their best to help bear the weight, and the third farmer started leading the horse. Sporadic cheers followed them through the gate and out of Stenvik.

'Off the road!' Audun commanded as soon as they'd cleared the gateway.

'But . . .' one of the farmers protested meekly.

Audun bit off the words, each a measured threat. 'Off. The. Road.'

A couple of moments later the wagon was off the path into Stenvik, jolting among hastily pitched tents and rickety wattle huts outside the walls.

'Down,' he commanded. 'Softly. Don't break anything else.'

The farmers complied, and slowly the cart was brought to a halt.

While the two at the rear coughed and tried to catch their breath, the farmer leading the horse approached Audun, dragging his feet and staring at the ground.

'Thank you for helping us. We could have been stuck there all day. Now we can—'

'So this is yours?' Audun cut in, bent double and breathing heavily.

'What? Yes . . . yes it is.'

'Seven silvers.'

The farmer looked at him, stunned.

'. . . What?'

'Seven silvers.' Catching his breath, Audun straightened up and looked the farmer in the eyes. 'I go get the tools and fix your cart. You give me seven silvers.'

'But . . . I've not . . . It's been a poor market for us!'

'If you've made enough money to buy and pile feed bags on your cart until it breaks, you have no cause to complain.' Audun walked over to the single wheel on the back end of the cart. He put his foot up on the axle, casually testing how much weight it supported. 'I could always convert it into a sled for you . . .'

The farmer looked at him, dejected.

'. . . Five?'

Audun frowned, then nodded. 'Five silvers it is. Stay here.'

He turned around and headed back into town.

\*

14

'Valgard! Come quick!'

The boy who poked his head in through the doorway could not have been more than eight years old. Golden rays slipped past him, casting their light on dust motes dancing in the air in the tiny wooden hut.

A slim man with sloping shoulders sat hunched over a workbench in the corner. Jars and bowls of various sizes were ordered all around him on the surface. A small carved wooden figure of a woman holding a bundle of plants looked down on the tabletop.

'Calm down. What's happened?' His voice was soothing, but he did not move a single muscle to acknowledge his visitor.

'A cart broke in the south gate and a farmer fell and hit his head. He's not moving and everybody's angry.'

Valgard kept his eyes trained on the workbench. In his hand was a short but very sharp knife, on a small slate of stone in front of him a handful of black berries. He had just pierced the skin of a berry and was pressing it into a bowl, counting the drops. Sensing the boy was still hovering in the doorway, he sighed.

'I'll be there in a moment.'

'I'll go tell!' the boy shouted as he sprinted off.

Valgard listened to the tread of the boy's feet fading into the sounds of the town. It had been a good morning so far. He was nearly done with the juice for the mixture. Just two more . . . His knife hand began to shake. Valgard clenched his teeth and hissed: 'No. No, you don't. No.' He forced himself to breathe as he'd learned. Slow. Slow everything down. He watched as the spasms in the hand died away till at last it was still and steady.

He cut twice more into the berry, collecting the juices into the bowl with practised ease and stowing the berries in a box. Then he took a satchel near the doorway and made to leave, but paused and reached for another small bag that sat on the far right of the workbench, grabbed it and left the house.

Behind him, a drop of black juice dripped from the knife point onto the bench.

It didn't take Valgard long to find his patient. The cart driver was powerfully built, thick-limbed and out cold. He came to with a shriek and a moan as the cold water hit him in the face.

'You just banged your head. It's going to hurt for a while. Chew this when it does. Try not to move too much for a couple of days.' Valgard pulled something that looked like a sliver of wood out of his bag. The driver eyed it and frowned. 'Don't be a fool. Take it. It's just willow bark. Not too much at a time and you'll be fine in a week,' Valgard said gently.

Accepting the bark with reluctance, the driver looked at Valgard, the satchel and the empty water bucket at his feet. He blinked rapidly and his mouth moved, but no words came out.

'Don't worry,' Valgard assured him. 'You drive carts; I patch you up when you fall on your head.' He stood up and headed back to his house, leaving the driver to look in confusion at a single wheel on a broken axle and wonder where the rest of his cart was.

'If I ever have a son, I will send him out with gold enough to afford better lodgings than these.' Ulfar ducked under the rickety doorframe and stepped into the street outside. The dockhand's shack looked considerably worse in daylight than it had under the stars last night. 'In fact, I think we might be sleeping in somebody's outhouse. Indeed, if I ever have a son, I'll buy him better lodgings, better—'

'— clothes, prettier wenches, better food, finer wine and a golden chariot to cart your lily arse between silk pillows,' Geiri finished as he emerged from the doorway behind the tall young noble.

Ulfar flashed him a winning smile. 'Are we a little bit prickly today, my brother?'

Geiri shot him an annoyed glance. 'Be quiet if you value your teeth, you traitor. And our fathers may share the same mother, but that does not make me your brother.'

Ulfar threw up his hands in a gesture of mock innocence. 'Am I not your brother in arms, in travel and in song?' he said, eyes glinting with poorly hidden amusement.

'Not after last night you're not. I've a mind to dump you back home and have them collect their debt of honour like they'd planned.'

Ulfar dismissed Geiri with a wave. 'Forget it. I was bored. It was just one kiss. And you didn't miss much. She smelled of sheep. Now, do you know your way around this town?'

'Of course I don't. Have you been to bloody Stenvik much?' Geiri shot back. 'Here's what I know. It's the only sizeable town this far west. Most defensible outpost on the west coast, apparently. Done. That's all. Nobody should ever need to come here and the sooner we're out the better. It's an outpost and nothing more.'

'Geiri, Geiri, Geiri. We must control ourselves.' Ulfar subtly changed stance, aping someone much older as he beckoned for his travelling companion to follow him down the street towards the harbour. 'You have been sent . . .' he began, sounding remarkably like a pompous middle-aged chieftain. Geiri could not help but smirk. 'You have been sent out into the world to see the sights, meet the men of note and let them know who you are. As a young man who will inherit the world' – Ulfar's sweeping gesture took in three wattle huts, a dirty screaming child running after a dog and a man pissing in the street – 'it is your solemn duty to get to know other and lesser peoples, find out what they eat, what they use, what they need and what they sell. Stenvik has become an important hub for trading and raiding. It may not look like anything, but there is much to be gained by connecting to their chieftain. Sigurd Aegisson. Man of reputation. Trade connections. Think forward, son.' At the end of his speech, Ulfar nodded sagely, blinked at Geiri and grunted, breathing loudly through his nose.

'I've said it before and I say it again – I hope you've never imitated my father to his face,' Geiri said with a smile.

'No. Never,' Ulfar said gravely. 'I have, however, done so to your milkmaid Hilda on occasion.' He winked at Geiri.

'What? And you never told me?' his cousin exclaimed. Ulfar shrugged and tried his best to look innocent. 'It doesn't really matter, though . . .' Geiri added. 'I seem to remember her telling me that your impressions had made' – Geiri made a suggestive hand gesture – 'little impression on her.'

Ulfar considered this then nodded. He'd have to give him this one. 'Well countered, Geiri. I'll make a man of you yet.'

'You always have to win, don't you?'

'Always, Geiri. Always.'

'Well, maybe if you'd not needed to win the fight with Karle you wouldn't have had to come here.'

'It was an accident, I keep telling you,' Ulfar snapped. 'Not my fault he turned out to be the Queen's cousin.'

'His arm broke just as much,' Geiri replied, enjoying himself.

'Well he didn't die. More's the pity. And his arm has healed now and I'm still out in the middle of nowhere playing nursemaid to clueless royalty,' Ulfar said.

'Shut up or I'll treat you like you deserve.'

'Much like a bleating ewe, you simply don't have the balls.'

The insults were comfortable and well-worn by now; something to pass the time. Their walk had brought them back down to the harbour. Behind them lay a town of hastily pitched tents, woven huts and frail wooden shacks. The old, run-down longhouse where they'd been drinking last night was visible over the tops of the houses. Ulfar's head pounded with the memory. This was what their dockhand guide had called the old town.

'Right then, Ulfar the Conqueror. Work your winning magic. Find us the way to the chieftain of this important hub of fish smell, street piss—'

'Will you cease your endless complaining,' Ulfar shot back as he scanned the area. 'I'll figure this out. We'll ask someone. Find a nice fish-girl . . . or three . . .'

She caught his eye because she seemed to be the only person in the square who wasn't moving. In fact it was almost unnerving how completely still she was. She just stood there, looking out to sea. Ulfar smiled to himself. She looked ripe for the picking.

'Now, young Geiri.'

'I'm three months older than you.'

'Yet you never act like it. Now, young Geiri, I gather you had some trouble with the women last night. Watch and learn.' Ulfar shot a meaningful glance towards the woman standing on the pier.

Geiri followed his gaze and frowned. 'That one? She's clearly waiting for a boat to come in. She's not going to—'

'Quiet, Geiri. Just watch the master.'

Ulfar ignored the bustle of the square. Instead he homed in on the girl. She did seem almost unnaturally still, though. As he sauntered towards her he wondered where the conversation would flow. Usually he was good at reading from their initial reactions what they wanted to hear, whether they wanted to be pushed or led, tempted or turned. He knew Geiri was staring daggers at his back and probably hoping he'd trip or something of the sort. Well, let him. Ulfar would never have Geiri's wealth or honour, but the girls loved him better. Always had, always would.

Only a few steps now.

He planned his route, drifting towards her and stealing a glimpse. She was very pale but he liked that. Must mean she stayed a fair bit indoors, which was strange for this kind of town. Maybe she was a craftswoman. The red hair was nice. Looked a bit Celtic. He'd been with a slave girl a couple of months back somewhere on the mainland – hadn't understood a word she said, but they'd got on well enough.

The memory made him smile.

He'd let himself accidentally happen to be near her now. Time for playing the lost traveller. In a smooth motion he turned towards the red-headed girl and put on a winning smile. 'Hello. I'm wondering if you could tell me . . .' And the words died in his throat. It was as if he didn't exist to her. She didn't acknowledge his presence. Instead she just stared at the sea. A spark shot up and down his spine. A challenge! He'd not had this before. The eyes. The eyes! Catch the eyes. He redoubled the charm, cleared his throat and moved so he was between her and the horizon.

'Hello!' He smiled. 'I just arrived in town and was . . .'

Slowly, as if waking from a dream, she seemed to register him and realize that he was there. She looked him in the eyes and Ulfar felt like he'd been struck.

'I'm . . . I'm . . . I've . . . We're . . .' he stammered, blushed and turned away. Furious heat burned his face. What? What just happened? His feet decided for him and walked him away from the pier, back towards his cousin.

Geiri looked him up and down. 'So? Was it incredible? Did she laugh? Did she cry? Did she beg to bear your children?' Ulfar found he couldn't speak. Instead his eyes were drawn past and through Geiri, out to sea. After what seemed like an age he finally found some words. 'She . . . um . . . she . . . Yes. I mean no.'

'Ulfar . . . did you hit your head? What happened? What did she say to you?'

Ulfar briefly inspected his feet and fidgeted with his hair. 'Nothing. Let's go.' He turned and walked away. Anywhere would do as long as it was away from the harbour. Vaguely aware that Geiri was shuffling behind him, Ulfar looked around for the biggest road leading out of the harbour square.

There.

A paved road ran due north, past the longhouse. As they breached the half-circle of houses around the harbour the old town thinned out around them. Ulfar drew a sharp breath.

What had looked like a hill when they arrived was in fact a fortress. The walls were massive, curving away in a perfect circle from a gate at the end of the road. They were the height of at least three if not four grown men, almost vertical and overgrown with grass. Sentries walked the walls, patrolling the gate at the end of the road.

'Slow down, will you?' Geiri muttered behind him as they walked towards the gate. Ulfar was in no mood to reply. 'So that's the new town. These guys seem to be serious about their fortifications, don't they? This is like Trelleborg,' Geiri ventured. Ulfar kept walking. The gate in the wall turned out to be the entrance into a short tunnel with a steady stream of people going in and out. They emerged on the other side and into a market square with stalls and carts wherever there was a bit of space. A road led straight north from the market to the centre of town, where a longhouse rose above the roofs of the surrounding houses. Without a word Ulfar walked towards it.

Geiri caught up with him at the door. 'Okay. So. We're here now.' His cousin composed himself, smoothed out imaginary creases in his clothing and stood up straight. 'Let's go.' He pushed at the thick oak doors, which swung open without a sound. He stepped inside. Ulfar followed.

The chieftain's longhouse was empty save for two old men on an elevated platform at the far end. They seemed to be deep in conversation. Geiri moved towards them. 'Svealand sends its greetings!' he said loudly when he'd come halfway towards them.

The two men looked up. Something passed between them and the older one, a short, wiry man with a bushy white beard, stood and moved towards them.

'Well met, Svealand,' he said. 'My name is Sven.'

'No – I mean – I send greetings from Svealand,' Geiri stammered. 'I thought – are you Sigurd?'

'No. My name is still Sven,' the old man said, hardly able to contain his amusement. Ulfar could see the colour rise in his cousin's cheeks. His own burned in response and he thought of the girl by the harbour. Nothing was real in this house because she wasn't here. He felt like he was watching Geiri and the old man through water.

'But you've not introduced yourself, Svealand. Who honours us with their company?' the man named Sven asked, eyes glinting in the half-light.

'Well met. My name—' Geiri coughed and cleared his throat. 'I am Geiri Alfgeirsson, son of—'

The old man snorted. 'Svealand, my boy. Are you about to say you're the son of Alfgeir Bjorne? Is that what you're going to say?'

Geiri deflated. '. . . Yes?'

The old man's eyes sparkled and he curbed a laugh. 'Really. All right then. Let's for a moment assume you are. What do you want, Geiri Alfgeirsson?'

'My father has sent me to—'

'Trade arms? Offer alliances? Take our gold and promise to come back with ships full of hardened Svear ready to do our bidding?'

Through the water Ulfar saw Geiri look at him with panic in his eyes. He saw his cousin beg for assistance, beg him to get them out of this mess. But she wasn't there so it wasn't real. He shrugged.

The old man looked at them then leaned towards Geiri, speaking softly. 'Now, son. Let me tell you something. If you've come into Stenvik to lie and cheat you're either very brave or not very smart. If you've come here in truth, think about this. Like a big sword, your father's name has weight. If you want to lift something heavy you need to be strong. Now go away before my chieftain gets impatient and has you beheaded.'

Defeated, Geiri slunk off and Ulfar followed, his mind still at the harbour.

'Just give me the damn flask.' The hand was outstretched, huge, calloused and scarred, palm up.

'I will, Harald. I will. Have I ever let you down?'

The big man snorted. Crammed into the little hut he looked ridiculously out of place. Like a bull, Valgard thought. Big, strong, clumsy, stupid and very dangerous. Especially when he wanted something.

And now Harald wanted his mixture.

'Give me the bloody thing so I can go see Sigurd and give an account of the trip. They're unloading the *Westerdrake* now but they'll be done soon and I need to get back. Next time I want more. I ran out four days ago. I am not happy, Valgard.'

Valgard shivered. He had seen first-hand what happened when Harald was not happy, so he spoke quickly, forcing a note of brightness into his voice. 'I understand, Harald. I do. I will make more for the next trip. Did you have much luck?'

Valgard handed over a small leather bottle.

'Luck has nothing to do with it,' the big captain spat as he grabbed the bottle. 'Luck is for the weak. Luck has no place on a raid. But you wouldn't know anything about that, of course.' He brought it to his lips and tilted the flask carefully. A big drop of black, viscous liquid trickled out onto his tongue. Then another.

He lowered the bottle reluctantly and savoured the taste. Then he sighed.

'That . . . is exactly what I needed. I will go to Sigurd and tell him of our victories and he will be pleased, I think.' Harald rose and manoeuvred himself awkwardly out of the hut without sparing Valgard another word. A breeze with a hint of autumn colds to come was all he left as a token of his thanks.

When he was sure Harald had left, Valgard dropped the appearance of fearful respect and looked again at the ingredients on his workbench.

A smile spread slowly across his face.

## VINGULMARK, EAST NORWAY

Torches set on pikes cast a flickering glow over the tiny settlement. A solid mass of armed men formed a silent ring of steel and blades, two thousand strong. Inside the metal band, confused and shivering people were being roused from run-down huts.

It was a raw night. The kind of night that bit your skin and chilled your bone. If there was a moon somewhere, it was hiding behind thick banks of grey cloud.

A blood night, Finn thought.

A small shrine to the old gods had been erected in the middle of the place. It was a pitiful thing. Poorly carved statues teetered over stains from animal sacrifices and a faint smell of rotting food lingered in the air. Just like all the others so far. He detached himself from his regiment, strode into the centre of the ring, took up a position next to the shrine and turned towards the locals.

'Who is your chieftain?' he shouted.

None of them seemed eager to move, but eventually a council of sorts emerged. Five men shuffled reluctantly from the safety of the crowd and formed a line in front of the big bearded soldier. That would be the council, then. They looked miserable, Finn thought. They were ragged and scrawny, a mismatched family of starved dogs. Filthy rag-wearing mud rollers, the lot of them. But orders were orders, and his were to draw the leaders out and keep them there until the King would speak to them. Still, their chieftain seemed to have at least a little pride left in him. He straightened his back and squared his broad shoulders. With fire in his eyes he looked at Finn and took a step forward. 'We have done nothing wrong.'

'That will be for him to decide.'

'Him who?'

Finn glanced at the man but did not answer. He looked strong. The way he puffed his chest and arched his back, Finn reckoned that's what he wanted to look like. However, experience had taught Finn the difference between strong men and fighters, and this man was a farmer, not a fighter. Furthermore he seemed angry, and angry farmers had no business being out on a blood night. No business at all.

Out of the corner of his eye he spied movement. Unlike the confused peasants, he did not need to turn and look. He knew very well what was happening.

To his side, the soldiers in the ring made way for a man on horseback.

Straight blond hair framed a handsome, clean-shaven face. The rings in his mail shirt gleamed in the firelight and the silver embroidery on the cloak slung around his shoulders seemed to come to life, flowing up and down his arms and back. A simple metal band sat in place of a crown.

King Olav Tryggvason rode slowly into the centre of the settlement, past the men and the women, the young and the old, towards Finn and the pathetic village council.

As instructed, Finn had made them stand next to the shrine. When the King saw it, he pulled the reins on his horse and stopped. Dismounting swiftly, he walked around the shrine, inspecting the crude idols of Odin, Thor and Freya in turn. Finn watched as he bowed his head and clutched his hand to his chest, thumbing that strange necklace of his, the cross that looked like a Thor's Hammer but without the head.

As Finn and the farmer watched, he turned and looked at them.

His features betrayed no emotion.

He walked slowly over to the man who had claimed to be the leader of the settlement. When he was close enough he fixed him with a cold look.

'Who is your god?'

The man seemed confused at this.

'Our god? What do you mean?' He looked at the King for explanation. None was forthcoming. Looking at the idols, light dawned. 'Oh. I understand. We sacrifice to Odin for the battle, Thor for crops and Freya for fertility, just like everybody else.'

King Olav looked straight at the leader. 'For this you will give me twenty of your strongest men.' The chieftain's eyes opened wide, and he moved to protest. King Olav silenced him. 'Choose them now. If you object, I take thirty.'

The farmer tensed his shoulders and took a step forward, poised and ready to strike. An almost imperceptible gesture from the King stopped him in his tracks.

Finn watched the fighting spirit in the man's eyes fade from a burning fire to a flickering candle flame. After a brief while he turned towards the crowd and began shouting names. The King's new men emerged reluctantly from the crowd.

'You are my soldiers now,' King Olav proclaimed over the shuffling group and motioned for them to leave. The soldiers stepped aside again, allowing the twenty recruits to leave the settlement.

Their friends, families and lovers watched them depart.

Olav waited until the recruits had left and the circle had closed. 'I will deal with them according to their conduct, and by their own standards I will judge them. Then they will know that I am the Lord,' he said softly to himself, and moved towards his mount.

'This is not right,' the village leader blurted, taking another step towards the king. His face was flushed. 'You cannot take the men away from us to fight for you. For what? For sacrificing to the gods? Who's going to defend us? Who's going to harvest? We will starve! We will . . . we . . .' the chieftain's words faltered as Olav turned back towards him, looking him in the eye. Finn watched the man wilt under the King's steely gaze.

'Are you the leader of these people?' Olav asked quietly.

'Y-yes.' The man looked around, but found little support. 'Yes, I am.'

'Are you the man they have turned to in their hour of need?' the King continued, tension building in his voice.

'I . . . yes.'

'Have you taken responsibility for their lives? Their eternal lives? And have you led them in worship of' – the King drew a breath and composed himself – 'these gods?' He gestured towards the shrine.

'Yes.'

King Olav Tryggvason looked at the man standing before him and seemed to come to a decision.

'Do you have any sons?' he asked.

'No. Not yet,' the man replied.

'Good.'

In a flash the King drew his sword and cut through the village leader's throat with one forceful swing.

With eyes wide open and blood gushing from his throat the farmer collapsed onto the ground. King Olav had already moved on to the man next to the dying leader and fixed him with a level gaze, and now he spoke in calm, reassuring tones. 'You are the chieftain of Vingulmark. This settlement will renounce its heathen ways. You will be responsible for removing the totems. You will not make sacrifices to the old gods. You will answer to me, and I will be your king. In time, I will send holy men to see how you fare, collect my due and teach you about the White Christ.'

The newly appointed leader looked from Olav's face to the blood dripping off the point of his sword, and from there down to the dead man at his feet. Then he nodded, eyes wide with fear.

King Olav turned and looked at the assembled peasants.

Gaunt faces with hungry eyes stared back at him.

Instinctively, he made the sign of the cross over his chest and turned to Finn.

'We leave now. Gather the men.'

'Do we take supplies, my lord?'

Olav paused for a second and cast a sideways glance at Finn. Then he looked again at the forlorn group of peasants, staring at their dead leader.

'There is nothing more here for me.' He shook his head almost imperceptibly, mounted up and guided his horse to a slow walk out of the settlement.

## AT SEA

Four oars sliced into the velvet ocean, making almost no sound. A small boat skimmed across the water, heading for the darkened mass of shore. Away from the rowers, two figures huddled in shadows in the bow.

'It is a good night,' a sibilant voice whispered. 'She will be pleased that we are fulfilling the will of the gods. The signs are favourable.'

'And so they will remain if you shut your mouth,' another voice replied. The oars kept up their silent work as the boat moved on towards its destination.

## STENVIK

Geiri leaned against a support beam in the corner, eyes closed, arms crossed. One hand rubbed and pinched at his brow. Without opening his eyes, he spoke.

'Let me see if I understand this.'

'Please. I know. I'm sorry. I said already.'

'No. No, I want to understand.'

Ulfar paced back and forth restlessly in the cramped hut. 'I don't—'

Geiri cut in. 'Two years. From the south of Svealand to Holms-gard, from Hedeby to bloody Aldeigjuborg and halfway to Smolensk and back. And we have only one town to see before we can go home, when your debt of honour will be repaid and we can inherit what our fathers have built. Only one town.'

'Geiri, I—'

'One town. With one provincial chieftain that we need to see and impress once, so he'll continue trading with our fathers and then with us. One stinking town. And you go and get your head all wrong over a *girl*.' Ulfar winced but Geiri didn't notice. 'Leaving your brain in your pants and your tongue on the pier. Leaving me to make some half-cooked introductions which I made a mess of—' Geiri took a deep breath, scowled and tried to control his temper. 'Your head wasn't there, cousin. Your mind was down on that pier. Because of a girl. A girl. You know, I stopped counting a year ago, Ulfar. Every port. Every market. Twice, sometimes three times. Sisters at one point. You'd have had them on the ships if you could. I wouldn't have been surprised to see a school of seal-women trailing us coming here. And then you let me down like that over one stupid cow.'

One moment Ulfar was standing a few feet away, the next he'd thrown a jab directly at Geiri's jaw.

He stormed out as his friend crumpled to the floor and stalked down the wooden walkway stringing together an impressive list of colourful curses. Fresh, cold autumn air and morning drizzle did little to improve his mood.

It had been inevitable, though. Geiri had not spoken to him all of yesterday after the disastrous meeting with the old man, and the tension had been building between them. He could understand that his friend would be a little annoyed, but he took it too far by a ship's length. It was one town. One town! Who cared? Ulfar kicked at a stone and missed. Those greybeards would not have had any time for pleasantries or trade talk anyway. Besides, he doubted that even his best performance would have swayed that particular chieftain. From the looks of it the only thing that would have impressed him in the least would have been walking in holding the man-sized jaws of the Worm of Midgard, and even then he'd probably ask what you'd planned for the rest of the day.

That being said, Geiri was right. It had been an absolute disaster. They'd looked like foolish boys. Geiri had simply not been prepared to speak for them yesterday, and he himself had been in no mood.

That woman. Girl. Woman.

Thinking of her made him shiver.

31

He had moved in, brimming with confidence, opened his mouth to speak, looked in her eyes and simply lost himself.

She'd seen right through him. At least it had felt that way. He had tried to turn up the charm, but inside he'd felt increasingly naked and vulnerable. She'd undressed and disarmed him, without so much as a word.

Those eyes.

Even thinking about her felt strange. His scalp tingled, his eyes felt blurry and his heart beat faster. What was this? Witchcraft?

Ulfar ambled between huts, trying to walk the annoyance off. His feet took him through the south gateway and into the market square of the new town. The people of Stenvik were out and about, most of them seeming intent on getting in his way. He noticed the blond blacksmith they'd seen in the longhouse on the first night. This time he was wearing a leather apron and carrying firewood into a smithy. Ulfar found himself moving away from the vendors, north towards the centre and the longhouse where they'd had that disastrous meeting yesterday. Maybe he could walk across town and away from this strange feeling. Shake it loose. Go back down to the seaside, or out through one of the smaller side gates. Into the forest to the north. Maybe he could loiter at the market, see if the merchants had something to distract him.

There had been so much sadness in those eyes. Like she'd known every trick he would use before he'd thought of it and felt disappointed that he thought he would need to. Like she knew he was going to try to deceive her. Like somehow he'd already let her down, and he would never be able to make it better. Like seeing him could mean nothing good. She had stung him more than he cared to admit with just one look.

Ulfar walked on past the longhouse, head down. He would have to apologize to Geiri. He hadn't meant to hit him, he shouldn't have and he wouldn't again. Could they make amends, maybe get to speak to the chieftain himself? Was there any way to salvage this, or should they just leave? The thought of leaving made him wince. He had to see her again. He had to.

'. . . *How* many?'

The man in the high seat leaned forward. Thick, silver-grey hair in a plait held together with bronze wire snaked down over one shoulder. Weather-beaten skin stretched taut, thin lips and blue eyes composed the features of a slim man of average height. Still Sigurd Aegisson, chieftain of Stenvik, had stared down some big men in his time, and now he was looking down on the portly friar standing on the longhouse floor.

'At least ten. There could have been more. I didn't count.' The friar shuddered but did not seem to notice. Wearing a simple brown robe with fresh rips, he looked likely to collapse on the spot. The left side of his face was covered with bruises and his shoes were badly torn. 'They came at dusk. Howled like wolves, they did. Creatures out of the very pit of Hell, abominations on our Lord's earth.' He made the sign of the cross. 'All with the claws of the evil one on their necks. Axes and swords and the green fire of the devil himself—'

'Spare me your Christ-babble.' Sigurd shook his hand dismissively. 'You settled in Moster, we've left you alone, you've kept to yourselves. That's the arrangement. And now you're here and you'd like me to believe that there is an army coming from the north.' The man nodded. 'An invincible army of raiders.' The man nodded again. 'On ten ships.' The man nodded again, hesitant. Sigurd continued. 'Did they have Jotuns with them, maybe? Fire-breathing giants? Was the lead ship possibly made of nails, ripped from the fingers and toes of the dead?'

To Sigurd's right, Harald snickered and shot a glance at Thorvald on the left. The tall, wiry scout frowned back and motioned for the captain to be quiet. The friar standing in front of Sigurd scowled. 'Don't mock me with heathen stories of your barbarian end of days, Sigurd son of Aegir. I saw what I saw.'

'And what would you have me do then, Friar Johann?' Sigurd snapped. 'Unlike you, I don't need to move around until I find an island small enough to hold only people that agree with me. What I do need to do is keep the people of Stenvik as alive and well as I possibly can. That is why I am here' – Sigurd slapped the solid arm of the high seat for emphasis – 'and you're there.' He gestured down to Friar Johann. 'So consider my options. What happens if you're correct? Stenvik has maybe twelve hundred men who could hold a sword, five hundred of whom are fighters. Damn good fighters, but just five hundred. Ten ships is not much but it still means two hundred raiders, possibly three hundred.' Sigurd motioned at Harald, who shot the friar a filthy look. 'Do you want me to ready our twenty ships and send them to the sea searching for ghosts? For creatures from Hell?' Sigurd gestured to Thorvald then continued: 'Or perhaps send a party of our finest hunters to search for tracks? Should I send half my men into a battle that is at best evenly matched or send all of them out on a wild chase after a phantom raiding party, which will either leave me looking like a fool with no defences or a wise man with a score of dead brothers and warriors, sent to their deaths for your beliefs and your insistence on having your own settlement? Would you like me to decide on one of those choices?'

The friar looked down. 'I cannot ask you to do that.'

'No,' Sigurd said. 'No you damn well can't. So why are you here, Friar Johann? And how did you get here? I am an old man, but unless memory fails me you were a member of the council and a man of name and responsibility in your settlement. Why did you not die defending your people, Johann?'

'We do not believe in fighting,' the friar muttered.

'Yet you are asking me to believe in your stories of a horde of mystical northerners, raiding and ravaging just up my coast. You're asking me to believe that they've somehow raised a party that has advanced within four days' journey of Stenvik without any word getting back to anyone, and that they have razed just your little pile of rock and nothing else. And that nobody has spotted so much as a sail of theirs. I'll tell you what I am going to do with you. I'll—'

There was movement in the shadows behind the dais. Sven emerged, moved towards Sigurd's seat, leaned in and whispered a few words in the chieftain's ear.

Sigurd looked thoughtfully at the dejected friar. 'Tell me about this so-called Devil's Fire. It sounds like fun.'

The friar shuddered. 'I was sleeping soundly when the screams started. When I got to my feet there was a noise . . . like a . . .' He looked at his audience. '. . . Like a giant drawing a breath. Only it wasn't. I went outside, and our church was on fire. And it wasn't regular fire. It was like someone had draped our church in northern lights.'

'They burned your roof? You Christians should be used to that by now,' Harald smirked.

The friar turned to the burly captain as if noticing him for the first time. 'No. Not the roof. The church.'

'The church on Moster was built of stone, was it not?' Sven asked.

'Yes.'

An uneasy silence filled the room.

'So . . . they set fire to the stone?' Sigurd asked.

The friar winced at the edge in his voice. 'I'm telling you what I saw.'

Sigurd stared at him for a long time. Finally, the chieftain leaned back in his chair. 'You're a lucky man, Friar Johann. My charity is such that I would happily have had your head mounted on our wall so you could scout your army of mysterious demons for yourself, but wiser men than I look to your fate. Go now, get out of my sight and try to make yourself useful somehow. Go to Einar in the old longhouse and tell him I said he should feed you.'

The friar made to speak but thought better of it, turned and walked away from the high seat. Sigurd and his men watched him leave without a word.

Silence descended upon the chieftain's longhouse as the large wooden door closed. Sigurd seemed lost in his own thoughts. Thorvald watched him intently. Harald leaned back in his chair and stifled a yawn. The mounted weapons, elaborate tapestries and gilded wooden carvings did little to relieve the oppressive silence.

Finally, Sigurd spoke.

'So. What do you think?'

'We cannot be certain of anything,' Thorvald said. 'Common robbers? Or do we think he's telling the truth?'

'A couple of stinking northerners decided to do away with the simpering cowards on their little island. Why do we care?' Harald spat for emphasis. 'Stupid place to put a church anyway, stone or no stone. I can't say I blame whoever did it – I just hope they got loot to show for it. Less use than tits on a duck, those Christians.'

'Still, we cannot ignore this,' Sven said. 'You heard the man.' He walked off the dais and sat down by the long table that stretched almost all the way from the dais to the door.

'I heard a lot of moaning, some nonsense about burning stone, and I saw a fat friar about to piss himself like a child. What do you mean, Sven?' Sigurd snapped.

Sven's voice was measured.

'Scars of the evil one. On their necks.'

A grim silence descended.

Then Thorvald spoke.

'He really did say that, didn't he?'

'Could be anyone or anything. It makes no sense,' Harald interjected. 'And why would *he* raid to the south? They'll get nothing here. Much better to carve the belly of the pig and go west. Better loot, more women, less trouble.'

The old, bearded man shot the big sea captain a cold look. 'And have you ever known him to be averse to a spot of trouble, Harald? We all knew that church would not sit well with the northerners.'

Sigurd sighed. 'But why now?'

'I don't know, but I doubt he would move without reason,' Sven replied.

Thorvald frowned. 'I have heard and seen nothing of this, Sigurd. Nor has Sigmar or any of our men. You would think that word would have reached us if he was on the move, especially during market.'

Sigurd ignored the captain and the scout, looking directly at the old man. 'What would you have done, Sven? It's plain to see that King Olav can't march in winter. If he waits until next summer the chieftains up north will be able to band together and give him a proper fight. He needs us as a wintering base. Would you have signed the treaty or would you have had the homestead of our fathers and our fathers' fathers razed for being a centre for heathen worship in the west? Those were my choices.'

'I know,' Sven replied. 'You did the only thing you could do. But think on this. We have already heard talk of the King sweeping across the south and east, much faster than we thought he would last year, and he is a good eight days away. We all know by now how he rules and what he does to those who go by the old ways. Who else would stand against him?'

'Hm.' Sigurd's eye was drawn to a hunting dog lying under the table, gnawing on a large bone. A half-grown bitch approached, sniffing for the meat. The big dog growled, a low, steady sound. The smaller dog slunk away with its tail between its legs.

'Thorvald, send out three of your men. Tell them to watch, listen and stay out of sight at all costs.' Sigurd turned to Sven. 'Your counsel is wise as always, but I feel I have to know for myself. Even though I think anyone – even him – raiding in my back yard would be unlikely.'

'Very unlikely,' Harald chimed in and spat on the floor.


## NORTH OF STENVIK

The two men leapt over the side of the boat. The younger one waded onto the beach carrying small packs, while the older pushed the boat off. The oarsmen deftly reversed and disappeared out of sight almost without missing a beat.

Wading to shore, Ragnar looked to the skies as he'd done every single time at the start of a mission since Saxony, many years ago. He'd learned then that a man who looks for rain going in doesn't get stuck in mud coming out. Clouds were gathering in the north, much as he had expected. They were still white, but given time they'd grow thick and grey. He shivered. In front of him Oraekja was already opening packs, taking out dry boots, trousers and animal skins.

'The moon will be full soon,' he muttered to himself.

'She said—' Oraekja piped up.

'I know full well what she said,' Ragnar snapped, cutting him off and turning away. He started his preparations in silence and allowed his mind to roam, ignoring the youngster. He had led advance parties for raids more times than he wanted to remember and sometimes he felt he should count each of his forty-two years twice. He felt old, and he certainly had the scars and the bald spots to prove it. He hadn't told anyone, but recently he had aches and pains to match. He had always been a scout – slim, light, quick and slightly below average height – not the best for a wild charge but just right for slipping in under cover of darkness and doing the dirty work. And it had been all right, too, in the old days. Back then you knew what it was about. It was different now. Had been ever since she came along. Suddenly everyone jumped to her tune, even his very own brother. He could understand that the men were frightened of her – he'd seen what she could do with her fire and her spells – but he'd never seen his older brother afraid of anything. She just seemed to . . . own him. And on top of that she'd saddled him with the puppy – Oraekja. The boy was obviously smitten with her, but Ragnar could not help but feel that the little runt was a bit . . . different. He didn't look like much, but he moved and listened well. There was something about his eyes, though. They were always glancing, looking, scanning, moving. One of them would slide to the side from time to time. Ragnar hated to admit it, but the boy made him uneasy. He could just about sneak and fight, sure enough – but Oraekja had none of the *sense*. The kind of sense that got you out of trouble before you got yourself into it. The kind of sense that was telling Ragnar in no uncertain terms how this particular mission was going to go. 'Fenrir take their bones. All of them,' he muttered to himself, spat on the ground and turned to the young man.

'Right, puppy,' he said in a voice laced with menace. 'Ready?'

The fervour in the boy's eyes worried him.

'Yes.'

He motioned for quiet and pointed towards the treeline, towards the road he knew would be within walking distance from the beach. They set off, moving in tandem and looking exactly like two hunters heading to market.

Underneath the bundle of skins strapped to his side, Ragnar could feel the cold, hard fire-steel against his hip.

## STENVIK

The sounds of children running, shouting and playing outside in the crisp morning air were anything but joyous to Valgard, hunched over his workbench. In his head they still pursued him, after all this time. The memory of their faces, feral and twisted in cruel anticipation, exploded in his head, their cries cutting him to the bone even now.

A tingling sensation spread from the back of his head. His heart started beating faster, harder. Tremors shook his shoulders and his breath caught in his throat. 'No,' he muttered to himself. 'Not now. No. No. No.' He could feel the muscles in his back locking. The cramps spread to his hips, down to his legs. His hands twisted and turned, resembling the claws of a tortured bird.

Gritting his teeth through the spreading pain, he thought of the pond. A quiet pond surrounded by tall trees and steeped in dark, green shadows in the middle of a forest. He envisioned the surface of the pond swelling slowly, a horrific beast rising from the depths. Around it, birds took off from nearby trees and cried out in warning. He imagined himself, powerful and muscle-bound, vibrant and strong, stepping out of the forest, striding towards the water's edge and spreading his hands. Breathing slowly, he halted the rising of the water with the power of his mind. The beast snarled and strained against him, scales and teeth and a baleful, malicious eye visible under the translucent sheen of the water.

He regained control.

Slowly, the beast retreated back down into the dark waters, and Valgard came back from the lake in his mind to the workbench in his hut. He had to use the left hand to pry the right away from the edge, where white knuckles had grabbed hold and would not let go on their own.

'Not now,' he mumbled as cold sweat broke out on his forehead. 'Not now. Maybe later, but not now.'

Shaking out the pain from his hands, he swallowed and composed himself, dried the sweat off his forehead with his sleeve and turned his attention to the workbench.

An array of jars, bowls and bags were arranged in a seemingly haphazard fashion about the surface, but there was a very particular system to it. His system. There had to be. You had to have access to the right things and in the right amounts, or the results would be . . . unfortunate. Spectacularly so in some cases, he mused. A healer that didn't know his plants was no healer at all. At the time he had seized the idea of plant study just to get away from the other children and their relentless attacks, but he had to admit the old man had taught him well. He'd taught him all he knew about plants, in fact. This was why some of the plants on the table would have to be stored elsewhere, because if his mentor saw them there would be questions. Questions that Valgard had no interest in answering.

He clambered down from his stool and shuffled over to the doorway, stinging pains in his back reminding him of how close that had been. Wincing, he peered outside. A quick look satisfied him that he would have his privacy for a little while longer. Moving back over to the workbench, he quickly collected the bowls and bags that he needed. The wooden figurine stared at him impassively. 'Shut up,' he snapped, and turned the figure so that it faced away from the workbench.

He crawled under the bench, reached behind a bundle of wood and pulled out a small, intricately carved box. He made sure everything was in its place, felt for the plants, felt for the cool touch of metal, deposited the ingredients and returned the box to its hiding place. 'Just in case,' he muttered. 'Just in case.'

Straightening up again, he sat down at the workbench. His hands started working seemingly of their own accord, tidying and ordering as he had been taught to do.

His brow furrowed in concentration as he gauged the situation. He knew full well what he wanted and how he was going to make it happen. He was going to make Harald the chieftain of Stenvik, whether the stinking brute liked it or not. Then he'd be Harald's councillor and no one would ignore him. The foreigners were an interesting twist, though. Surely there must be some way of making that work in his favour. Speed things up a little.

He frowned and wondered if he'd made the right move.

There were many pieces on the board.

As his heart threatened to burst out of his chest, Ulfar's brain scrambled to catch up.

'Erm . . . thank you for the directions yesterday,' he mumbled. Houses. He was in town somewhere, but he was not quite sure where. They were standing on a walkway between some sturdy wooden houses. Better than the ones outside the walls, anyway. He'd been staring at the ground, had rounded a corner and almost walked into her. Her curves led his eyes up a simple, light blue apron dress fastened with an elegant silver and black brooch, but now he could see nothing but eyes. Eyes that flickered between grey and blue, scrutinizing him, reading information out of every detail of his face.

He felt the heat spreading on his cheeks and realized to his horror that he was blushing. Embarrassment and fury sent his insides churning and he felt a little weak in the knees. He looked back at her.

She wore a crown of thick red hair, flowing in wild and unruly curls that seemed to leap and dance and have a life of their own, in stark contrast to her smooth and unblemished skin, the line of her jaw, her lips. Only her eyes seemed alive and seeking, the rest of her face could have been carved in marble. But the eyes looked at him and through him and he felt stripped of everything but the one thing he had to know.

'What is your name?' He blurted it out and wanted to kick himself. What is your name? What was he, twelve? What next? Run away and giggle? He was getting worse than Geiri, and he cursed himself inwardly for his own stupidity. Around them, Stenvik life eddied and swirled, taking little note of two young people talking.

Ulfar saw nothing but her.

He felt the ground slip away from him, so much so that he had to look down to make sure it was still there. Where were his words? Even her shoes were pretty, Bragi be damned. Her foot was pretty. The hem of her skirt was pretty. He felt as big as a field mouse, and made to turn away when a quiet voice broke the awkward silence.

'Lilia.'

His heart stopped for a beat, then restarted with a flush of blood to his whole body. Stars burst inside him, and her name rang out in his head. Lilia. He turned and looked up at her.

An eternity passed.

'Ulfar.'

He dared not blink, and noticed that she didn't either. But neither of them looked away.

'I . . .' he started. Completely unbidden, the words marched to his mouth. 'I did not know they had such precious gems in Stenvik.'

It happened in the blink of an eye. The first tear, the first tremble of the lip. Then she turned and ran.

He wanted to give chase but his legs wouldn't obey. He noted through the haze that she rubbed her eyes with the sleeves of her shirt as she ran away.

He stood rooted to the spot for a long time afterwards, wondering what had just happened.


## RAUKVIN, EAST NORWAY

Finn tasted blood as his head was knocked back. Two soldiers rushed to his aid and grabbed the arms of the farmer who had landed the lucky swing. Recovering, Finn threw a series of savage punches to the man's face until he stopped struggling.

The soldiers dropped him to the ground.

Angered, Finn spat a glob of reddish spittle at the feet of the man and aimed a vicious kick at his ribs for good measure.

King Olav's soldiers were fighting all over Raukvin. 'Bloody pig-headed farmers and valley clods,' he thought. 'I hope the next batch does as they're told.' They were overwhelming the small village easily enough, just like they'd ploughed through the rest of the east, but Finn found himself wishing they could have bypassed it. There was nothing here. Woven huts, mangy cows, stinking mud-rollers. There was nothing to be had, and they'd picked up too many recruits from various places as it was. He'd heard rumours of dissension already. The young King would have his work cut out controlling the army if he continued like this.

A cheer went up to Finn's left. In the middle of a dirt road four soldiers circled around a frightened girl. They shoved her back and forth between them, grabbing and tearing at her clothes. One of them had managed to get hold of her neckline and rip, exposing a breast. She tried to cover herself up but strong hands tore and pushed at her, grabbing and squeezing. Snarling, the soldiers circled. She looked about desperately for help, and her eyes met Finn's.

She pleaded wordlessly with him to make them stop.

The tears made her eyes sparkle and shine like stars.

Her mouth started moving, but no sound escaped her lips.

Her full, young, beautiful lips.

He wanted to move. He wanted to help her. He wanted her.

But he couldn't.

He was stuck to the spot. His legs wouldn't move.

The hope in her eyes turned to despair, then resignation.

And just as quickly as it had been cast, the spell was broken. One of the soldiers, a big, burly man with a crooked nose and a split lip, decided that he would no longer be denied his spoils of war and yanked her to him by the hair. A coarse hand squeezed her breast roughly, then pushed up under her skirt.

She screamed then.

Screamed and squirmed and kicked out at her attackers, trying to dislodge their clawing hands.

Energized by her sudden reaction, the soldiers grinned at one another. One of them, a fat man with wobbling jowls, squeaked: 'Hold her still, Birkir!' He brushed a strand of greasy hair from his face and fumbled excitedly with his trousers, pushing at his belly to get to his belt, eyes alight with anticipation.

'Stop.'

Suddenly King Olav was there, next to Finn.

The two men that saw him ceased immediately. The fat man and the brute kept pawing at the girl, who struggled with renewed vigour. The large man with the split lip grabbed her hair and pulled hard. She screamed again.

'Let her go.'

One of the soldiers, a slender, dark-haired young man with an easy smile, stepped in front of the group. He was better dressed than the others and his eyes were alert. He held up his hand. The others stopped their groping, but the big man did not let go of his prize. The dark-haired soldier spoke.

'My King, my name is Jorn, son of Ornulf Dale-Lord, and I am your humble servant. We joined your army two weeks ago when you swept through the valleys with this mighty host. The men are just taking their share of the glorious victory that you've wrought here with bravery and—'

'No.' King Olav did not take his eyes off the girl, who stared back at him, transfixed. 'These are the old ways. We follow the word of the White Christ. You do unto others as you would have them do unto you.'

Jorn looked incredulously at the King. 'Do unto others . . . ?'

King Olav turned to him. 'You are not allowed to do anything you wouldn't want them to do to you. No taking of women, no stealing, no unnecessary killing.'

Jorn frowned.

'My lord, I do not understand. We signed up because the army is big. It's the biggest in a long time. Nothing will get in our way. And now you're telling us that we can't take their things, and the occasional stray cat that wanders onto our path?'

'No, you cannot. You shall adhere to my word, the word of the White Christ, and do unto others as you would have others do unto you.'

The man with the split lip grinned and rumbled, 'So if I tell this bitch to fuck me, then I can fuck her? Sounds good to me!'

The fat man next to him giggled.

King Olav did not.

Instead he turned to the girl's captor, who stood his ground and flashed an impudent grin.

Finn was petrified. He'd been in too many scraps with and against men like these, and he knew that they would kill before backing down.

King Olav did not seem to realize this.

Instead he fixed the brute with his gaze and said: 'Let me repeat, my friend. The book of God tells us how it is.' His voice became rhythmic, strong and soothing. 'If a man hurts a woman, he shall be surely punished, according as the woman's husband will lay upon him, and he shall pay as the judges determine.'

The soldiers watched him warily. While reciting, the King had walked slowly up to the large man. Balanced and strong, he carried himself like a fighter. At the moment Finn reckoned that was the only thing keeping him alive. The King continued talking.

'And if any mischief follow, then thou shalt give life for life.' He gently removed the mesmerized man's hand from around the girl and extricated her from his grasp. She ran away, clutching the front of her shift to her breast. King Olav never lost eye contact with the big brawler. The silence was electric as they squared off. 'Eye for eye, tooth for tooth, burning for burning, wound for wound.'

None of the soldiers moved.

King Olav continued: 'Now go. Follow Finn. I need you to find me at least twenty men from this miserable place so we can keep moving.'

In the stunned silence, Finn found his voice. 'Move!' he barked. 'We're going to round up some bleating peasants. Now!' He turned and walked towards the centre of the village.

Jorn turned. 'Birkir, Havar, Runar. We're moving.' As one, the three men followed Jorn.

When Finn looked over his shoulder King Olav was gone.

## AT SEA, SOUTH OF MOSTER

The dragon's eyes scanned the horizon.

Fierce, gleaming, flint-tipped fangs caught the spray as it flew low over the waves. Intricate carvings slithered away from its jaws, flowed down along the prow of the *Njordur's Mercy* and disappeared into the foaming sea. The menacing figurehead seemed to eat up what little moonlight there was.

A figure crept up to it and stood to attention.

'Is she awake?' Skargrim stepped from the shadow of the figurehead. Faint moonlight caught on heavy gold rings woven into his thick grey beard. A bearskin cloak draped over massive shoulders almost covered three angry red scars on his neck.

'No,' the sailor replied. 'She seems to be with the voices again.'

'Good. Make sure she's warm and that she has broth when she wakes. She'll need her strength.' The soldier turned and started moving towards the stern. The big captain watched him leave. Erik was nothing if not dependable. He'd been on the boat for the best part of a decade now. He had two sons back home and would probably soon be asking whether one of them could take his place. His brother had died on a raid in Friesland last year, and Erik had been subdued since.

Odin had a time for them, one and all.

Skargrim thought of the advance party. Ragnar had not wanted to go. He'd suggested that they should hit Stenvik at an hour like this, just before dawn. Go in quiet and strike while the people were sleeping, set the houses on fire and raze it like they'd done countless times to countless towns. They'd scale the wall in the dark, come down quiet and hit them hard.

She had refused.

She said the pole needed to be raised to tell the people of Stenvik that the old gods were angry, to tell them that they were on the wrong side. They needed to make absolutely sure that the men, women and children of Stenvik were scared, she said. Skargrim remembered arguing that they'd be just as scared if they were being killed while their houses burned – and then she'd looked at him.

It was a mild night but Skargrim still shuddered.

Those eyes.

When she wanted something, she would fix him with those pale blue eyes and he would feel like he did when he was a boy getting ready to jump off the cliffs into the deep and chilly water for the first time, and something would lurch inside him. His limbs would go weak. And then the faintest echo of voices inside his head. Voices that went with cold, dark nights . . . Skargrim shook himself.

How had it come to this?

She'd just . . . appeared, one night last winter. Walked in from the cold wearing nothing but a shift, straight into Ormar's long-house. His crew had been there with Ormar's men, all of them drunk on strong, sour mead. A sizeable hoard had been brought back from across the ocean, and they'd been swapping heroic stories that grew bigger and more heroic with every retelling. And then she'd entered, wisps of fog swirling around her ankles, and the whole house full of hard-drinking men had gradually fallen silent. The dogs had slunk away. She'd stood in the doorway and said that an army was coming with a young king at its head. That the king brought a new god – one god to rule all, the White Christ. Ormar had roared with laughter and said that Thor the god of Thunder would wipe his arse with this White Christ.

None of Skargrim's men had laughed with him.

She said that the old gods had visited her in a dream. She said they were not pleased, and that she would lead everybody in this room to victory over the young king and the new god because the old gods had shown her what she needed to do. She said she was Skuld, one of the Three.

That got Ormar's attention. He had laughed again, but this time at her. Straight to her face. Thinking back on it, Skargrim thought that showed how much Ormar knew about people. He and Ragnar had known from the moment she stepped in that she was fey. They'd both felt that other, older powers had walked with her. They'd kept their heads down, glancing only briefly in her direction. Ragnar told him later how he'd seen when her mouth started moving, whispering quietly.

Ormar was neither so smart nor so humble.

He looked her straight in the eye and started saying something about she was just a deranged bitch and how she would be good for one thing and one thing only. He started saying he'd do her right there, on the table. And then he stopped, mid-sentence, and watched his own hand in surprise as it slowly reached for his dagger. Then he stabbed himself. Hard and fast. Stomach, chest, thighs, chest, throat, face. Blood blossomed on his clothes. His screams choked on it. They watched, horrified, as his life drained away before their eyes.

The hand stopped moving only when he was dead.

Skargrim remembered the cold, clammy silence in the long-house as Ormar's corpse tumbled out of the high chair with a dull wet thud. How a hall full of hardened fighters, raiders and murderers had sat quiet as mice and tried not to be noticed as she picked her way daintily to Ormar's seat at the head of the table. How she'd sat in it and looked as if it was made for her. How two of Ormar's thralls – two of his own thralls! – had quietly lifted him up, carried him out of the house and fed him to the crows. A few moments later one of Ormar's champions had stood up, stormed to the centre of the hall and challenged her for leadership. She'd looked at him, smiled and moved her hand in a gentle swaying motion. The hardened fighter's eyes had opened wide, and suddenly he was struggling for balance. He started retching. Her hand slowly contracted into a fist. Ormar's champion had vomited blood and collapsed on the floor, as dead as dead could be. Since then the men, the ships and the blades had been hers. No council, no ruling, no committee.

No bloodstains on her shift.

In a sense, maybe the strongest had taken over like it was sup-posed to happen. Maybe Ormar had been growing old and fat. He'd always been a stupid brute. But to die like that? There was little honour in it, that much was certain. It did improve the men's loyalty, though – there had been no argument whatsoever. That night she had delegated day-to-day command of all the men to Skargrim. She had also given him his orders. He'd not known what to say, but it was not as if he'd had any choice. He'd fol-lowed them to the letter.

A bitter smile played on Skargrim's lips as he went back to his post. He liked standing in the prow. At least then he could see where he was going.

## STENVIK

Iron didn't lie.

It obeyed simple laws.

Heat, then separate.

Then bend it to your will.

And if you listened, it talked.

The water hissed and sputtered as Audun dunked the white-hot blade in the trough. In time it would become a sword to split some poor bastard's skull, but that was not his fault. Nor the sword's, for that matter.

The sword hadn't asked to be made. Someone had asked for it. It was always about the people. And if they didn't have swords, they'd simply kill with their bare hands. Like animals. Animals that fed on blood. The smell came back to him, the heady rush of it. He grimaced and spat into the furnace. The heat in the smithy forced Audun's thoughts away from the past and back to the task at hand. He judged the colour of the metal.

Three more breaths.

The blade emerged from the hissing water, cherry-red in colour. He turned it with the tongs, felt for the weight, inspected the line and the edge.

This would be a good blade. It would do what it was made for and do it well.

And if it got stuck in some idiot's head, he'd probably done something to deserve it.


The people in the market milled about, uneasy and curious.

'So you're saying she's not worth you looking at her, pig man?' Harald said, gruff voice ringing out over the square.

'No! I think your wife is very beautiful.'

'So you were looking at her.'

The big pig farmer looked frantically around the market square for support, but no one would meet his eye, let alone step into the ring that had suddenly emerged around them. Clouds drifted across the morning sun, and the temperature dropped.

'No, I wasn't. I swear. Not like that. I simply saw her, that's all,' he simpered.

Harald looked him over with a mixture of anticipation and contempt. He circled the prey slowly, moving with the economy and practised purpose of a brawler. 'See, I say you're lying. I say you were looking at my wife and thinking filthy, disgusting thoughts, pig breeder. And I say that's not the right sort of behaviour for a visitor in my town.' Behind him two large young men stepped into the ring, smiling wolf smiles. Harald continued, addressing the crowd as much as the pig farmer.

'I reckon we have been a bit lazy in showing our guests how we do things around here.'

Harald's hands turned into fists. He smiled, took two quick steps towards the big ungainly farmer and set to explaining the Stenvik way.

'Look. It was a cowardly thing, I know and I regret it. You are like a brother to me, and I ask only that you treat me as such. I was confused and I—'

The back of Geiri's hand hit Ulfar's cheek with a loud slap that bounced off the walls of the tiny hut.

'What the—' Ulfar slipped on reflex into a fighting stance.

'You just said I was to treat you like a brother.' Geiri grinned. 'And if my brother had acted like that around his elders, I'd have

slapped him. And you should see your face right now, cousin,'
he added with a laugh.

The pain in Ulfar's cheek made him blink. Looking at Geiri's
grinning face took the fight out of him.

'Yes. I probably deserved that one.'

'You did.'

'So what now?'

'Well,' Geiri frowned and leaned back against the support. 'We
can't ask for another introduction. We have nothing to trade and
it doesn't look like we have anything these people need or want.
So we find a ship that's leaving for home and we get out of this
hole. We have no function here and it's time—'

'No.'

Geiri stopped mid-sentence. '— What?'

'No. We're not leaving. You leave if you must, but I'm not going
to. I have to see her again.'

Geiri looked incredulously at Ulfar. 'What's got into you? Is
this the man who called himself Heartbreaker, Skirt-chaser and
Kiss-taker all through the summer?'

'This one is different, Geiri.'

'Forgive me, my friend, but she can't be.'

'What do you mean?'

'Seeing as you've had every possible type of girl and woman
since we set out, she'd have to have antlers and scales to be different. And even then I'm not so sure. Some of those Rus girls
were quite . . . interesting.'

Ulfar ignored his friend, who seemed fully ready to evade an
attack this time around.

'Believe me, Geiri. She is.'

'And how do you know?'

'I just about walked into her last night.'

'Oh, long live Freya's wiles.' Geiri rolled his eyes. 'Did she throw her clothes at you this time around?'

Ulfar did not respond. He simply looked into the middle distance, lost in thought. The silence grew more and more awkward until Geiri gave in. 'Oh, if that is how it is, I will accept that you're right. Fine. There is something special about this woman.'

'Yes.' Ulfar's voice was dreamy.

'And you want to know what it is.'

'Yes.'

Geiri looked firmly at Ulfar. 'Well then, my travelling brother. I will bargain with you. We'll go drink with the locals tonight, I'll help you inquire *sensibly*' – Geiri added a stern look for emphasis – 'and we discover what there is to discover about this magical creature of yours. And we will try as hard as we can to do this. But if we don't find anything, if she's another man's woman, if there is no hope of the gods or anyone else giving their blessing—'

Ulfar nodded.

Geiri finished. '— then we leave.'

'As usual, you are the wiser one, if somewhat less pleasing to the eye,' Ulfar said, smiling. 'Thank you, Geiri. You are a true friend.'

Geiri shook his head.

'No I'm not. I just get bored travelling alone.'

'Liar,' Ulfar said.

'Coward,' Geiri retorted.

They both grinned.


The circle had formed quickly, just like up north. They tended to do that whenever there was even a faint promise of violence, Ragnar mused. Just like animals and food. This had never been a fight, though. It was turning into some kind of display, one that seemed to be making the audience uncomfortable. The crowd shuffled nervously. Someone shouted: 'That's enough, Harald!' but nobody stepped forward to stop him.

Right. Enough of this. He sought out his travelling companion, tapped his elbow and motioned for him to follow into a nearby alley. Oraekja lingered, casting a longing eye towards the centre of the circle. When he followed at last he was smirking. 'At least there's Norse in someone in this rotten sty,' he said. Behind them, sounds of something breaking were followed by a muffled scream and someone vomiting.

Ragnar shut him up with a glare.

'I am going to say this once and only once. I couldn't care a yak's arse about whether you live or die, but the job needs to get done. Keep your neck covered at all times, stay close to me and come when I tell you to. We go in, we do what we need to, when we're done we go back to where we landed and wait for Skargrim. Stay out of the forest and watch out for the raiders in this town. Despite being born this far south, Sigurd's men know their work. That's three of them in the circle, and unless you want to end up like that poor sod in the middle I suggest you keep your wits about you.'

'If they're so proper then how come we're inside their town?' Oraekja said.

'We're here because we've used our heads. We're not storming anything nor showing off our allegiance. We look like skinners, not like an invading army. That's why we can walk through the front door. Did you look up when you went through the gateway?'

The young man gave him a blank look and shrugged.

Ragnar sneered. 'From now on you note your surroundings, or I'll be all too happy to leave you to Sigurd's dogs.'

'If they get me they'll get you too,' Oraekja shot back.

Ragnar felt a faint itch in the palm of his right hand. It would be so good to scratch that itch with a hilt, with the hilt of a knife, whose point he would happily bury in the little rat's eyeball. But he couldn't rightly do that now. It would create attention that he could do without. Instead he looked straight at Oraekja and smiled his meanest.

'No they won't.'

After a spell the little bastard looked away.

'Now come on. We have things to do.'

'Help! Please help!'

Valgard rolled his eyes. There really was no rest to be had. 'Wait.' He rose slowly and deliberately from his pallet, feeling every single pinched nerve in his back, every thread of muscle in his aching legs. He shuffled to the doorway and stuck his head outside.

'What do you want?'

Two anguished and awkward men stood by the doorway, fidgeting nervously. While the fatter one caught his breath, his red-faced friend spoke up.

'It's our kinsman—'

'He's hurt—'

'In the market in the middle—'

'Got in a fight—'

'We heard some seaman said he'd looked at his wife—'

'Big man, reddish beard?' Valgard interrupted.

'Yes.'

He sighed and shut his eyes wearily. 'Don't worry. I'll come as fast as I can. Run to the market and try to make sure your kin survives.'

The men took off south, towards the market square. Valgard watched the two ungainly farmers shuffle away and smiled to himself. Harald had a remarkable talent for causing trouble and pain. He ducked inside and quickly readied his emergency equipment. While his hands worked, his mind assembled the board and moved the pieces. He tried some combinations in his head and then a new possibility presented itself. Unexpected elements suddenly fell into place.

Valgard chuckled as he headed out of the hut and towards the market. There were some interesting moves to be made.

The intricacies of the game occupied his mind all the way to the market square, but when he saw Harald's handiwork he had to push it out of his head.

It was hard to know where to begin.

At some point the pig farmer had vomited and soiled himself. Now he lay on the flat stones in a puddle of his own blood, bile and shit, shaking and crying, a shell of a man.

His nose was broken and blood trickled from his mouth. Three broken teeth lay on the ground. He was curled up in a ball, coughing and clutching his side. His left hand was grotesquely swollen, and Valgard casually guessed that Harald had stomped on it a couple of times. There were bound to be some broken bones in there.

He knelt down and inspected the miserable wreck.

'Looks like you finally got the beating you were asking for,' Valgard muttered to himself. Then he turned to the pig farmer. 'You've had a bit of a rough day, haven't you?' The farmer just whimpered. 'Right. This is going to hurt.' With a firm hand Valgard started pressing on joints and bones, creating a road map of injuries, drawing lines by the volume of the patient's screams.

Three broken ribs. One badly sprained wrist. Possible bleeding inside. Four teeth gone, as it turned out. Bruises from kicking, face would be colourful for a week. One knee twisted. Possible fracture of the shin. It was not good, but he'd seen worse. The man would live.

Valgard quickly searched his bag, bringing up bandages and a small leather bottle. Beside him lay what looked like two rods bundled together.

'Straighten him out.'

The victim's two nervous friends started gingerly moving their kinsman.

He screamed.

Valgard sighed. This was always the least pleasant part of the process. Bundling up a chunk of cloth, he stuffed it in the farmer's mouth.

'How will that make him better?' one of his newly recruited helpers asked, straining to keep the farmer still.

'It will shut him up, which will prevent me from getting distracted and killing him.' The man looked shocked. Valgard smiled sweetly and added: '... by accident.' Working quickly, he produced another cloth from his bag. He doused the cloth in liquid from a small bottle and held it over the farmer's broken, bloodied nose. As the man's eyes flew open and he started to struggle, Valgard looked straight at him. 'You will not die. You will not suffocate. You will simply sleep.' At that moment the pig farmer's eyes rolled back in his head and he passed out.

Valgard reached for the bundle and unravelled it. A length of cloth joined the two sticks together, forming a stretcher.

'You two – lift him onto this then grab an end each. Gently. And follow me.'

The two hapless farmers scrambled and strained to lift the big man quickly enough to follow Valgard, who was already heading back home.

Oraekja threaded the walkways of Stenvik, trailing Ragnar and staring at his back. *No they won't. No they won't.* Who did the old man think he was? It didn't matter that nobody had heard. It was a question of honour, and right now it took all of Oraekja's strength to ignore what Ragnar had said. How he'd said it. That dusty old relic had dared to put him in his place, speak to him and treat him like a puppy. Like a boy. It was almost too much to bear. The only thing that made it better was the memory of her.

He turned warm inside just thinking of it.

She'd called him to her that night. Just him. He'd been scared stiff but she'd whispered in his ear. Told him why Stenvik needed to be razed to send a signal to those without faith and to rob this so-called king of a winter base to slow his advance. She'd even told him who she really was. Told him she could see the future, that she could see that he would be crucial to the will of the gods. Told him how Loki had come to her, told her what to do, how to do it. She'd even leaned in closer and told him he was *really* important to her. He still remembered the hairs rising on the back of his hands, his whole body vibrating with longing. He'd been rock-hard, too. He shook his head and grinned.

Not as if he hadn't known from the start. She wanted him. Sometimes he just *knew* with women, even more than they did. She might not admit it – not in front of the men, especially not Skargrim – but she did. That had to be why she'd given him the special instructions. He didn't understand why, but he sure as hell didn't mind. He would do what she said, for she was Skuld, sister of Urd and Verdandi, one of the three witches of fate, the Thread Cutters. And she loved him.

Oraekja watched Ragnar's back and smiled.

## EAST NORWAY

As midday faded into afternoon and the shadows grew longer, Finn turned in the saddle and looked back.

Outriders on fast horses. Others carrying long spears and pikes. Shields of a variety of sizes. Jerkins of every colour. The column seemed to snake on for ever, over fields and through forests. Finn knew his eyes were playing tricks on him, but he also knew how quickly their army had swollen. In the last two months their numbers had grown by nearly a thousand men. The hunters kept griping to him about how nothing was enough, how they couldn't keep up with the ever-growing demand. He saw the fights break out because of too many men shoulder to shoulder in too little space.

He had to say something.

Riding beside the King at an easy walk, he cleared his throat nervously.

'What?' King Olav shot Finn a sharp look that made him stutter.

'The – the men, my lord. There's too many of them.'

Finn blinked. King Olav watched him impassively.

'They . . . they come from different places. And not all of them believe in the White Christ, my lord.' Finn did a rapid sign of the cross, looked down and folded his hands, as he had seen Olav do. When he looked up again, something in the face of the King had changed. There was a touch of curiosity there.

'Continue.'

It all came out. 'They are not happy, my lord. I have heard

them whisper amongst themselves. They say they do not know why we are going around bullying farmers, my lord. Some of them miss their families. They do not understand why we are fighting the people who believe in the old gods. There may be more like those four we saw yesterday. I think they might run away or try to take you on, my lord.'

Out of breath, Finn waited for a response, but there was none forthcoming from the King. Instead the young man seemed lost in thought.

Their horses walked on, setting the pace for the men marching behind them.

Heading west.

## STENVIK

Harald held a big calloused hand up in front of his face. 'There are lines on my fingers. I've never seen them before.' He furrowed his brow in concentration. 'It's hard to count when you're lying on your back.' He blinked, mumbled a curse, licked his lips and started again.

'I can't feel my mouth.' An idiot grin spread on his face. 'That shitty little pig farmer wasn't much of a man after all. He shat in his stinking farmer pants.' He giggled to himself, but then frowned again and looked at his hand. 'It hurts.' The knuckles were swollen and smeared with blood.

A small bottle stood on the ground next to his bed. A tiny drop of thick black liquid was making its way slowly down to the ground.

'Trying to . . . 'scape?' he slurred. 'Tryin' to 'scape, you li'l bitch?' He reached for the bottle, grasped it and brought it to his mouth. With slow, deliberate movements he licked the drop off.

'Can't 'scape me,' he rumbled contentedly. 'No one can.' He fumbled for the cork, but couldn't find it. This seemed to annoy him. 'Cork. Cork,' he muttered. He tried to prop himself up on an elbow, but lost his balance and fell back onto the bed. 'Hm. Too much. Had too much. Sleepy.'

He slowly lowered the bottle back down to the floor. His eyes closed within moments and soon he was breathing regularly.

Watching him, she could taste her own fear.

When he'd come home covered in blood she thought he'd either been wounded or had killed someone. He'd grabbed her roughly by the hair, twisted her round and taken her then, pushed her to the ground and driven her legs apart with his weight. Fumbling, grunting and wheezing. She'd gone away in her mind as she always did, but now she felt sore. Raw. Her skin crawled at the sight of him lying there. A mop of reddish hair, greying at the temples. Ruddy, bearded jowls with a net of burst veins, a thick neck and massive shoulders. His eyes were closed, so she allowed the revulsion to show on her face. She would never dare do that when he was awake. He could so easily paralyse her with just a look, a promise, a single word whispered with a smile. Where Harald was, pain was never far away.

There was so much she'd forgotten since she became his, but she remembered the pain. The first weeks. When she'd cried and screamed. He'd enjoyed that. He'd enjoyed gagging her, watching her thrash about, watching her blue-grey eyes scream at him, seeing her cry and hate herself for crying. He'd relished breaking her, reducing her to this. A spark in a shell. A spirit trapped in a woman made of stone.

And the stone woman did his bidding, out of fear. Fear of the pain. She kept his house; she tried her best to give him sons. She didn't let him see her cry. Not that he'd care. Not that he wouldn't occasionally make her do it for his own enjoyment. The stone woman watched him go to sea; the stone woman stood on the pier and waited for him to come back.

She hated the stone woman with all her heart.

But right now, the stone woman was her prison. She was forced to sit beside him, wait until he woke up, do as he wanted.

Her thoughts went unbidden to the man with the green eyes. Man? Boy. Man–boy. She smiled inside. A current of thrill or fear ran through her, crackling with his words.

He'd called her a gem. Her, a gem in Stenvik.

Wasn't that true, though?

Didn't the tiniest, shiniest jewels come from the stone?

Lilia stood up, turned away from Harald and allowed her mouth to form the word.

Ulfar.

The wolf in man's clothing.

Her spirit flew inside her stony cage and for a breath-taking moment she was alive again. She felt her skin. She tasted the air. She felt like sparkling, shining and twirling. Everything seemed new. The wooden walls, the gilt decorations, the tapestries. She turned to take it all in and met Harald's eyes.

Harald's open eyes, looking at her from the bed.

Cold.

Calculating.

'What are you so happy about, then?'


AT SEA BETWEEN MOSTER AND STENVIK

Skargrim brushed the salt spray from his face and admired the view from the prow of the *Njordur's Mercy*. In the distance, Wyrmsey rose out of the mist. The big cliff on the south end could have been a head; the long, curving beach to the north might have been a tail. The locals didn't like it because it looked like the Wyrm rising.

Let the stupid old sailors cling to whatever stories they want, Skargrim thought. He believed in the old tales as much as the next man, but in this case he knew. This was no monster, merely a rock – and Wyrmsey had what he needed. A fearsome reputation, distance from prying eyes, and a sheltered beach with room for ships.

Many ships.

He felt a feather-light touch on his arm and a tingling sensation in his body. She was behind him.

He turned.

As always when he spoke to her he was convinced that there was no one else in the world, just the two of them.

She smiled demurely at him.

'You've done well, Skargrim. We will camp here and wait. When will they come?'

'Soon,' he muttered.

'And have you sent the message I asked you to send?' she asked, still smiling.

'Yes,' he said. 'Yes I have. The men will be in place when they need to be, waiting for the signal.'

She nodded. 'Loki will be pleased. We will do his work, and he will reward us. He will reward us well.' Her smile stayed with him as she turned away and walked back to her lodgings at the stern.

Skargrim shook his head to clear the fog. Behind him, another eleven ships sailed towards the beaches of Wyrmsey.

## STENVIK

The calfskin map traced a rough outline of the coast.

Sigurd's knife pointed at Moster. 'This is where Friar Johann's church is.'

'Was,' corrected Thorvald.

'. . . was.' Sigurd amended, a hint of a grin playing on his face. 'Can't help it – brings back memories.'

'Those were different days, were they not?'

'They were. They were indeed. There were many good men who went over to stay. Many others went up to Valhalla when the Saxons fought back. That's why it seems strange to me that he's supposedly on the move. I thought he'd seen enough of it.'

'Apparently not,' Thorvald mused. 'But we don't know. So. Stenvik, Moster. If it really is him, he would be coming from Oppland' – Thorvald marked out a spot to the far north – 'and going . . . ?'

'That is the question I'd like to pose to Mimir's head if I could.'

'So where do I send them?'

Sigurd looked at the map. 'If he's coming straight . . . you go here. Sjoberg.' He marked out another spot with the point of his knife, then thought better of it. 'That makes little sense, though. If he's coming straight, he wouldn't have razed Moster.'

'Assuming he did.'

'Assuming that. So where is he going?'

'I will send Sigmar and two men of his choosing to Sjoberg, aim at having them there for midday, then tell them to go swiftly to here, here, here' – Thorvald marked out points in quick succession, forming a perimeter around Stenvik – 'and here.'

Sigurd nodded his approval. 'Just remember, let them look and learn but stay away. We need information, not dead heroes.'

'Understood.'

Thorvald hurried out of the longhouse.

'We need to know what's out there,' Sigurd muttered to himself. He sheathed his knife and rolled up the map. 'And we don't need bloody Skargrim with a raiding party.'

The last rays of the evening sun slanted in through a venting hole and caught on a worn, dully grey battleaxe, mounted behind the high seat.

The fading daylight in the little hut did the clothes no kind of justice. The trousers were of finest linen, a vibrant blue with silver thread, woven and fitted to measure. The coat had started out as simple grey wool, but was now a dark-as-night purple, shining with silvered buttons from neck to waist. The cloak was a rich dark red, embroidered with gold filament. Ulfar fastened it with a commanding, strong brooch cast in silver and gold, intricate designs flowing into and out of each other.

'You really are serious about this, aren't you?' There was not even a hint of mockery in Geiri's voice.

Ulfar ignored him in favour of his own reflection in a convex silver disc. He adjusted his hair, looked at the reflection, adjusted it again and combed his locks meticulously to the left, then the right, then the left.

Geiri's hand landed on his shoulder. 'If she likes you, she likes you. Stop preening. Let's go.'

Ulfar blinked and shook his head briefly. He noticed Geiri, made to speak, changed his mind then croaked: 'Yes. Yes, let's go.'

He half-stumbled out of their tiny hut. His cousin followed and tried hard not to laugh.

Stenvik changed with the light, Ragnar noted. Three of the gates had closed already, and the south gate would be the only one left open. Already workers and traders were streaming down to the old longhouse to eat and drink.

He looked over his shoulder. The boy trailed him reluctantly, the foul mood etched on his face like piss in snow. The old scout thought about things he could care less about and placed Oraek-ja's feelings somewhere between flies on cowshit and a bad rash.

Ah. There it was.

The horse pen.

Ragnar looked up, approximated the position in relation to the gates and committed the location to memory. He did not look forward to this, but she said it had to be done.

So it would be.

He signalled to Oraekja, turned and started making his way south.

Market season could go hang, Audun thought. The old longhouse was too crowded by far tonight. He glared at the assembled crowd to dissuade anyone from coming too close. Halfway in, a group of men had gathered around one of the tables. Sitting with his back up against the wall, old Sven looked calmly upon the black and white pieces on a Tafl board. Opposite him, his adversary looked sweaty, red-faced and in no control of his forces. Sven leaned slowly forward, made a simple move and smiled. 'And that is the end of that, my friend. I believe that's one bowl of stew and one mug of mead on you for me.' The man quickly vacated the seat and Sven's piercing eyes searched the crowd. 'Anyone else, while the last victim goes and gets food for the old and needy?' There were snickers in the crowd and one man took a step forward.

'Welcome, son!' Sven asked. 'Who do I have the fortune to game with?'

'The name is Ivar, and I'll beat you, old man. Your beard will fall off when I'm done with you.'

'My beard most definitely will fall off,' Sven agreed as he calmly reset the board. Ivar sat and Sven looked him over, taking his measure. '. . . eventually.'

Glaring, Ivar made the first move. Sven looked at him and feigned surprise. 'Oh – did I insult you? I didn't mean to. You have my apologies.' He made his move. 'I made a solemn promise that I wouldn't – last time I fucked your mother.'

The crowd roared with laughter. Ivar made to rise but got his feet tangled. Sven quickly extended his arms to calm him down. 'A joke, son. A joke.' He withdrew his arms and folded palms in a gesture of peace. 'An evil attempt by an old cheat to get under your skin and make you do something stupid. Take it as a lesson from the sad, shrivelled husk that I have become. Two, in fact. First – never play angry. Second – cheat whenever you can.' With that, he opened his hands and revealed Ivar's king. Hissing, Ivar snatched his piece from Sven's palm and put it back in the centre of the board. He made his move and Sven countered with poorly concealed delight.

Audun watched the exchange from his corner and tried to remember a time in the last year when Sven had had to pay for his mead and meat. But then again, such was life. They played, they lost, they bitched. And none of them had the sense to walk away from a fight they couldn't win.

He'd seen that pig farmer get mauled in the market today. Two of the young ones off the *Drake* had held him while Harald went to town on the bastard. There was yet another case of a fight you couldn't win, he thought. Still, the man was an idiot and a drunk. You could argue he'd been getting what he would eventually deserve.

Audun frowned into his mug.

It hadn't been a fair fight though.

Either of the young fighters would easily have been a match for the stupid farmer and Harald would have taken all three of them.

Not fair at all.

But that was what happened when you didn't keep yourself to yourself.

Trouble.

He tried to think about something else, move his mind away from the sickening spectacle, the brutality, the sounds and smells of it all.

The two foreigners entered. They scanned the packed room, their eyes coming to rest on his table.

Waves of laughter, shouts and bad singing washed over Ulfar and Geiri when they entered. Jugs of ale slammed on tables, women shrieked and cursed at men with roving hands.

'There's nowhere to sit,' Geiri said.

'That's where you're wrong again, cousin. Our quiet friend in the corner seems to have room for us.'

'Hm. Leave the talking to me, then.'

The shorter one approached and leaned in, while the other seemed to scan the room.

'Hello, friend. May we share your table?'

Audun shrugged and tried his best to look through the man, but the obvious hints seemed to go above and beyond him. The stranger sat down happily next to him and introduced himself. 'Geiri, son of Alfgeir. Travelling from Sveto see the famed and beautiful fjords. What is your name?'

'Audun.'

'Well met, Audun.' He motioned to the other foreigner, the taller one. 'Ulfar, go get us three mugs.' The one called Ulfar looked back at the shorter one for a moment longer than necessary before he left. Audun smiled to himself. It seemed quite clear who was used to giving the orders in this little marriage.

'What do you do, Audun?'

'Smith.'


'Very good!' Ulfar heard his friend exclaim as he walked away. So that was what he called sensible, was it? Blatant, that's what it was. That boy had no shame. Ulfar scanned the hall again. Full of big men, no sign of Lilia. A couple of farmers, from out of town by the look of it, sitting by themselves with mugs in hand and murder on their minds. He followed their stares to two burly fighting types and made a note of not being in the way when the time came. Getting to the mead was quick enough. He turned back with full mugs and headed for the corner table. Walking across the hall he couldn't help but catch an impressive string of curses bursting out of the middle of a small group of men by his side, followed by a shout.

'Cheat!'

Suddenly his section of the room went quite quiet. Ulfar ambled away from the confrontation and set the mugs down gingerly on Audun and Geiri's corner table. His head buzzed. They were playing Tafl! He had to sneak a look. From somewhere in the throng a deep, calm voice spoke.

72

'Now, son. We wouldn't want to make this a matter of honour, would we? Twelve men around you watched the game. Did any of them see me cheat?'

Silence.

Ulfar found himself craning to see.

The men made way for someone standing up.

'There has been trickery at this table,' the man spat.

'Now that I won't deny, my boy,' the old man by the wall said amicably. 'There's been plenty of trickery. But I didn't cheat.' His eye caught Ulfar's. A brief flicker of recognition flashed across his face. 'How about you, stranger? Would you care to sit down to a game of Tafl with a cheating old trickster?' He winked.

Ulfar nodded and occupied the open seat.

Settling, he smiled at the friendly old man.

'What are the stakes?'

'If you lose, you buy me mead. I've already had my stew and two mugs.'

'And if I win?'

There was badly suppressed laughter around the table.

'If you win?'

Ulfar concentrated and cleared everything from his face but innocence and curiosity. He smiled earnestly at the old man.

'If you win . . .' he said, 'I'll shave.'

Exclamations and laughter erupted around the table.

Ulfar took his time to consider this before he nodded. 'Accepted. Let's play.' He looked at the board. It was bigger than he was used to and the pieces looked slightly different, but apart from that it was close enough. He made the first move quite casually. The old man countered without thinking. Three moves in and Ulfar recognized a classic beginner's trap. He sidestepped it neatly and added a twist of his own – a sneaky diversion he'd discovered the hard way while playing an Arab in Hedeby. The old man went for the corner piece that would land him squarely in the trap but stopped, hand in mid-air.

Their eyes met.

Suddenly the face of the cheerful grandfather was nowhere to be seen. Instead Ulfar saw his opponent for what he was, a grizzled fighter who had survived to old age on cunning, guile and very little mercy.

Out of respect, Ulfar dropped his act. He'd spent most of his and Geiri's journey earning drinking money playing Tafl, eventually saving enough to buy the clothes he was wearing. However he suspected it would be both unfair and unwise to act the fool in this town.

The old man nodded slowly and grinned. 'Sven.'

'Ulfar.'

'It seems someone has had a very good night's sleep,' Sven said. 'You play louder than you talk.' He decided against the corner move that would have spelled his doom and instead countered with a clever spacing ploy that Ulfar had not seen before. Ulfar found he was smiling, too. After months of sweeping the floor with Geiri and whoever else, it looked like he'd finally found a worthy adversary. He looked towards the corner to signal to his friend that he was playing, but Geiri was deep in conversation with the surly blacksmith.

The pieces on the board begged to be moved.

Valgard entered the hall and frowned.

There were precious few seats left. One was available next to the two farmers who had helped him earlier – red-face and fatty. He took one look at them and decided to sit elsewhere.

Moving quickly toward the cauldrons he asked Einar for a bowl of stew and perched near a group of pedlars from the north-east.

He'd eaten four spoonfuls when a large hand landed on his shoulder.

He knew perfectly well whose hand it was, but allowed himself another mouthful before turning around and looking up.

Harald's face was hard to read.

He crouched down towards Valgard, the smell of the mixture unmistakable on his breath. Moving a little too close to Valgard's ear he whispered: 'Could you have a look at Lilia for me? She . . .'

'Is she ill, Harald?'

'Yes. She's . . . yes. She's ill. Or she may have fallen and broken something. I don't know. Go have a look.' Valgard looked at him, willing him to say more. Harald's face seemed to set. 'She's at home. Go.'

Valgard bit his tongue. 'I will, Harald. She will be fine, no doubt.' Harald shrugged and returned to his seat, tucked away in the shadows. Valgard got up, a sinking feeling in his stomach. What had that bastard done to her this time? He forced all memories of past visits to Harald's house out of his head and focused on the exit, distracting himself by looking at the patrons up against the wall.

He saw Sven sitting at the games table and nodded to him, but got no response. The old man seemed thoroughly absorbed in the game. Someone seemed to be giving him a run for his money for a change. Valgard decided not to dwell. There were more pressing things to attend to.

He pushed onwards to the exit, through the raucous crowd. The house was so crammed that even poor Audun couldn't get his privacy, he mused.

That was unusual.

\*

In the corner by the door, Audun found that much to his surprise he didn't mind the younger man's company. He suspected he'd already talked more than he'd done since arriving in Stenvik. That kid knew his way around a smithy and seemed genuinely interested in what he had to say. He was getting gently drunk now too, the mead settling in nicely.

'How did you figure that out?' Geiri asked.

'Well,' said Audun, slightly lost for words. 'When you've heated the ore enough so that it runs clear, you can mix things in. I've been experimenting, but I've found that coal dust produces stronger iron. Lasts longer, bends but doesn't break, and sharpens up easy.'

'I've heard tell of things like these, but that was in Rus, stories coming all the way from Miklagard. They have people from all over the world there, apparently – the finest blade-smiths come all the way from the Far East to hawk their wares. It's amazing that you should have worked this out yourself without any access to peers, or books—'

'Can't read.'

'— or a master.'

'Never had one.'

'That is fantastic,' Geiri gasped. 'So you're self-taught?'

Audun frowned. '. . . Yes?'

'I am impressed, Audun. You must be the great-great-grandson of Wayland himself!'

A rare surge of pride shot through Audun. He wasn't often compared to the Master Smith.

'One thing you've done wrong, though.' Confused, Audun frowned. A serious expression clouded Geiri's face. 'Yes, Audun. It seems you've failed in your smithing.'

'What did I—'

'You've left us with defective mugs!' With that, Geiri grabbed his and Audun's empty mugs and upended them with a huge grin.

Audun tried his best to scowl but couldn't quite make it convincing.

'I'd best go get more to make up for my filthy foreigner's manners and those of my friend, who should have replenished us a long time ago instead of sneaking off to play after the first round. When I come back, I need to ask you more about Stenvik. The women in particular,' and with a wink Geiri was off, shaking his head as he walked past his friend at the games table.

Ulfar struggled for breath. His head was pounding. The air in the longhouse mixed with the smoke of the cauldrons, the smell of mead and the sweat of too many people too close together.

This guy was good.

Already they'd launched stabs and jabs, feints and counter-feints, opened doors for each other that seemed promising but ended in horrific death down the line, sometimes slow and painful, sometimes quick and painful, but always painful. This was the way the game was meant to be played. At first Ulfar had been able to gauge how he was doing by the reactions of the group around them, but as the tension rose he'd blanked them out, losing himself in the symmetry of the board, the possibilities of the assembled armies. They had spent a lot of time preparing but now it was time. The forces were primed, lined up and ready to go.

'Cowards!' The shout rose above the din of the longhouse. 'You are worthless and unmanned, and we demand honour for our cousin, set upon by you two in the market today! We demand restitution!' Something in the tone of the voice made Ulfar tear himself away from the game and have a look.

Standing on a table opposite were the angry farmers he'd seen, now furious and drunk. They pointed at the two fighters he'd noticed, who summarily stood up a couple of tables away.

'Who are you calling cowards, you lamb-shit gobblers?' the broader one shouted. 'Here's payment for your cousin' – he hawked and spat. 'You might want to scrape up half and give it back to me, because I doubt he was worth that much!'

All hell broke loose.

Screaming obscenities, the two men launched themselves off the table.

Ulfar's world slowed down.

He saw Geiri making his way through the crowd towards the corner, blissfully unaware of the source of the shouting.

He saw the two enraged men charge through the crowd and storm the warriors' table. One of them lowered his shoulder and charged into Geiri. The other stepped on his foot.

Ulfar watched his friend lose his balance and fall, slowly fall, arms flailing. The panic in his eyes. Mugs flying. Geiri's head hit the corner of a table. His arms went limp and he dropped to the floor like a stone.

A cold feeling spread through Ulfar. Without thinking he sprang to his feet, stepped nimbly past one man stumbling away from the fight, spun past another and reached Geiri on the floor. He struggled for space to lift him out of the way of trampling feet.

A big hand was on his chest, pushing him away.

The blacksmith.

Scooping Geiri up as if he was a child. Placing him on a table. Two feet away, chaos reigned. Fists flew; someone wielded a chair.

'Knife!'

The brawlers on the edge pulled away. A knot of men was

locked in the middle, punching, grappling, kicking, stomping and doing their best to do their worst.

Snarling and fierce, Harald waded through the crowd of spectators and charged the fighters. The first man he reached had his head yanked back then slammed into the forehead of the next man. Dropping fistfuls of hair in each hand, Harald pushed the two men away. Both clutched their bleeding faces and sank to the ground. The longhouse grew quiet very quickly. Within a couple of breaths, screams, grunts, six men were on the floor grasping various parts, struggling for breath or curled up, moaning.

Sigurd strode into the old longhouse, face white with fury. Sven emerged from behind his table looking like a thunderstorm. Harald stood over the fighters, demonic and bloodied.

The longhouse had fallen deathly silent.

Sigurd took a deep breath. Then another. He looked at the fighters, some of whom had come around enough to realize their situation. Without looking away, he spoke between clenched teeth. 'Sven. Any dead?'

Sven looked around. 'None . . .'

Sigurd looked at Harald, then back at the fighters.

'. . . yet.'

Pushing for space in the crowd, Audun and Ulfar tried everything they could think of, but nothing worked. Geiri lay terribly still on the table in front of them. His eyes stayed closed.

## WYRMSEY

They arrived just before dawn, chased by a cold wind. Fourteen ships, four hundred and twenty raiders. Thrainn's crew. Vicious bastards to a man.

Skargrim grinned on the moonlit beach. 'Welcome to Wyrmsey, my brothers.'

He watched Thrainn swallow his pride and nod in greeting. He was a rock of a man, Thrainn. Tall, strong, able and a fighter of note. Long blonde hair was braided and crusted with sea spray, beard likewise. He had thought himself a leader of men, and at the tender age of twenty-two was already strong enough to have over four hundred raiders at his beck and call. So when Skargrim showed up with the message from Skuld and said they were to join them in the fight for the Old Gods, Thrainn had laughed in his face. Mocked him in public. Said he was a relic, an old has-been. Said that if anything Skargrim's and Ormar's men should come under his own control.

Skargrim smiled to himself.

He didn't mind being called old. He could see the grey in his own beard. But he liked to think of it as experience. And the only way to truly learn the value of experience was to get some.

He reckoned it had been quite an experience for poor Thrainn to be put on his back twice – hard – wrestling a greying old has-been. First time too, it turned out. Well, there was a first time for everything.

Already, Thrainn's sailors were pulling their ships up on the Wyrmsey shore next to Skargrim's.

Twenty-six of them, side by side.

The old Viking captain nodded to himself.

There was still a lot of space left on the beach.


### STENVIK

Trickles of light changed Ulfar's world from black to grey, but it made little difference. His eyes were used to the darkness in the hut by now. He'd extinguished the torch at some point during the night. The burning pitch had made it harder to breathe and the big bandaged pig farmer had lain in the corner whimpering and complaining that he couldn't sleep.

Ulfar didn't care.

He just stared.

Stared at Geiri, willing him to open his damn eyes. To move, moan, scream, wince. Anything.

But his friend just lay there. Faintly warm to the touch, breathing regularly.

Nothing more.

Dawn crept towards Stenvik.


### EAST OF HARDANGER HEATH

Around Finn the camp was coming to life. The early morning sun warmed the tents and teased the night chill gently out of his bones. He shook his head again. Orders were orders, but these made little sense.

After some searching he found the right section of camp, and then the right man. He addressed him as formally as he could.

'Jorn Ornolfsson, Prince of the Dales. The King requests your presence.'

Jorn looked at him with a mixture of surprise and amusement. 'Does he? Only he didn't seem to like us valley boys too much last time we met, Finn. What do you think, my brothers?' He turned to the three who had gathered behind him.

'Nope,' said fat Havar, beady eyes peering over his wobbling cheeks.

'N-not at all,' stammered Runar and went back to stringing his bow.

'Not a bit,' rumbled big Birkir behind them.

'So why do you think our lord would like to see us?' purred Jorn. 'Do you think perhaps he means to instruct us in . . . the ways of the White Christ?' Smiling, he drew a finger slowly across his throat.

'Might – m-might come back a head shorter,' gushed Runar, his slight frame shaking with mirth.

'I'd be glad of the silence,' Birkir added. There was a hard edge to their laughter.

Flustered, Finn said the first thing that came to mind. 'Truth be told, half the time I don't know what he's asking for and the other half I don't know why he's asking for it. I just carry the message.'

Jorn shot him a charming smile. 'That makes you a man of honour, Finn. Unlike these dung heaps and draft horses.' He pointed to his three men. 'Just see how they mistreat me. My oldest friends, my brothers in arms. They have none of your . . . mettle, Finn. None of your courage and loyalty. They're bastards.'

Finn struggled for anything to say. Finding nothing, he stood his ground.

'You're right to stay quiet, Finn – it's the only way these stray dogs can't twist your words,' Jorn added. He placed an arm around Finn's shoulder, smiled a reassuring smile and steered him away from the tents. 'I should know more men like your good self, my silent friend. Lead the way. Let us go see what our noble King wants.'

## OUTSIDE STENVIK

To the east, blood-red clouds heralded the dawn of a new day. Behind him, the sea was shrouded in night. He looked down on Stenvik from his vantage point high on the hillside. The walls, thick and strong, encircled the new town. The longhouse stood proudly in the centre. The market square just inside the south gate was already littered with vendors, even this early. To the east, the road stretched on out of the gateway and through the forest, hugging the coast farther on. The north-east road extended from the main gateway, through meticulously cleared farmland, past the east face of Huginshoyde, up into the big valleys and eventually the highlands. Between Huginshoyde and Muninsfjell the north-west road snaked out of the gateway, up the incline between the two hills and along the coast to the far west. From the south gateway his eyes traced the road down to the old town, the town that had grown out of a handful of hovels. It wound its way through the confusion of tents, huts and small houses scattered like a giant baby's toys around the old longhouse. South of the old town lay Stenvik harbour, where the fishermen were already working away, readying nets and preparing crates. Their cries drifted upward with the wind. A smile played briefly on his lips.

If Sigurd noticed Sven approaching him, he gave no sign.

The old man almost managed to hide his wheezing. 'I remember thinking this was a bad idea thirty years ago when my beard was only grey. But I suppose you can look on your town however you want.' He stopped to catch his breath. 'How will you rule?'

'How can I rule?' Sigurd replied softly. 'Tell me first of the boy.'

'I cannot say. He cracked his head badly and has not responded since. He walks in a dark place, but I am not ready to say he won't come back. I don't think the gods want him just yet.'

'At least that's something. If he dies . . .'

'. . . if he dies we'll have made some very powerful enemies in Svealand.' Sven stepped up beside Sigurd and looked down. 'He may not have made a good show of himself but his father knows everyone of note to the south and east.'

'So it becomes your responsibility to make sure he lives,' Sigurd snapped.

'It does indeed. The law says—'

'You don't need to remind me what the law says, Sven. I know full well. What of the pig farmer's injuries?' Sigurd crossed his arms.

'Harald made a mess of him but Valgard did good work and limited the damage.'

'You have taught your boy well.'

Sven bowed his head. 'He's no longer my boy, if he ever was. He is a man now and he has worked hard. I think he knows more than I do. And even if he does, and even if our people suspect he does, they still ask me to confirm everything he says when they think he doesn't hear. As if he can't be trusted.'

'Some people are not in a hurry to change their minds.'

'That is true.'

They stood together in silence for a while and watched the first of Stenvik's fishermen ready their boats. Smatterings of autumn colours were starting to appear in the forest beyond the town. A gentle breeze carried echoes of birdsong to their spot on the hillside.

'Harald is responsible,' Sven said finally.

'Naturally. He always is. Always was and always will be.'

'So what is your ruling?'

'We wait for two days and see how the pig farmer's injuries turn before settling damages. They're bound to look worse now than what they are. Harald pays half, his crewmen the other half. I will rule for the farmers and rule fairly. I will then charge them for their attack on the boys in the longhouse, but it will be much less.'

'Mead and anger. Not a good mix.'

'Boneheaded, that's what it was.'

'Still, now it stops.'

Sigurd nodded. 'Now it stops, as it must.'

They stood in easy silence together and looked on as their town was slowly wrapped in sunlight.

'We've made this into a good place,' Sven said after a while.

'I remember every single tree we cleared off that land,' Sigurd replied.

Sven nodded. 'Most of which went into the walls if I remember correctly, and if I've forgotten some of the logs my back remembers them for me.'

'Indeed. Something tells me we won't live to regret that,' Sigurd added with a grim expression.

## STENVIK

The sounds of the smithy soothed him. It was his world, a simple world, and that suited Audun just fine. There was no doubt. You needed to do certain things at certain times or the metal would punish you. No uncertainty. There was only failure, which you then turned into success through experience.

But this one was not going to be a failure. The sword was looking better every day. It was going to be a very good blade indeed.

Audun sighted one more time along the edge.

It was formed, pretty much.

Now it needed sharpening.


## WYRMSEY

Hrafn's men were the next to arrive. Ten ships' worth of frost-hardened raiders from the far, far north where the sun didn't show in winter or set in summer. They wore thick sealskin coats over their ring mail and carried long spears along with their swords, hand axes in their belts and shields strapped to their backs.

Skargrim nodded to Hrafn, who saluted with a grin. A skinny man with thinning hair, he had a hooked nose and tiny black sparkling eyes. He was continually on the move, fidgeting with his hands if he absolutely had to stand still. When asked, Hrafn had been all too happy to come and bring what looked like most of Finnmark with him. Now he was here, on Skargrim's beach.

'Well met, Hrafn.'

'Well met, Skargrim!'

'It's been a while.'

'That it has.'

'When did we last have a dance? Vasconia?'

'That we did.'

'Doesn't look as pretty any more.'

'That it doesn't,' said Hrafn. His smile grew into a toothy grin. Skargrim nodded.

Beneath him, many hands helped get the newcomers settled and the ships in line.

Thirty-six.

## EAST OF HARDANGER HEATH

King Olav waited for them outside his tent, watching impassively as they approached.

'My King.' Jorn bowed deeply.

'Stand, Jorn Ornulfsson, Prince of the Dales.' The King's voice was calm and commanding, his expression unreadable.

Jorn straightened up, looking honestly bewildered. 'I wish to ask your forgiveness, my lord, for the incident involving the behaviour of my kinsmen, which you saw and rightly stopped. They are—'

King Olav interrupted him. 'You think quickly and speak well, Prince. Your men obey you. A king needs men to speak on his behalf, for he cannot be in all places at once. If you can give me your oath that your men will abandon the old ways and bring honour to you and thus to me, I have a task for you.'

Jorn looked stunned. 'Anything, my lord,' he stammered eventually.

'Take four horses of quality. Ride ahead to Stenvik. Tell them of our conquests; tell them of the size of our army. Bring word that the White Christ's host marches and start work to prepare for our arrival in seven days hence. Arrange for supplies. Find a suitable site for our camp. Stenvik is a big town full of able fighters, so I want to be absolutely sure they are all on our side. In short, I need you to be my eyes and ears. I want to know who these men are, what they think, what they feel. The Hardanger Heath will slow us down. I need you to make sure the arrival of the army will be as smooth as possible.'

Jorn nodded. His face was set in a mask of determination.

'It shall be a great honour, my King.'

Without explanation the King ducked into his tent. He came back out with a thin silver chain coiled up in his fist.

'Take this and wear it around your neck. It shall mark you as my spokesman and be my royal seal, carrying my and the Lord's guarantee that any promise you make shall be fulfilled.' He opened his fist and handed the chain over.

Jorn pinched the chain between his fingers and let it drop. Exquisite silver cascaded from his hand, weighed down by a crucifix. His pupils widened a touch, but he composed himself quickly.

'My heartfelt thanks, my King. You confer great responsibility upon me.'

'I do. Accept and honour it. You leave for Stenvik at once.'

'As you say, my King.' Jorn fitted the chain around his neck, then turned and walked briskly towards his camp.

Stunned, Finn watched Jorn leave. He became aware of the noises of the camp, men shouting at each other, cheerful cursing in the distance. When he turned to King Olav he was baffled to see the King smiling a wry smile.

'My lord . . . but . . . what . . .'

'Finn – you should see yourself. You look as if you've just seen a talking horse.'

'But how . . . why?' Finn was reeling. 'I simply do not understand.'

'What do you not understand, my faithful friend?'

'The man is a viper! His followers are scum! You took away

their prize the other day, and if I was a man for betting, which I'm not' – Finn quickly crossed himself – 'I would say that you have invited your enemy into your house.'

King Olav still grinned, but there was a fierce glint to his eye. 'And if you were a man for betting – which you are right not to be because it is a sin in the eyes of the Lord – where else would you keep your enemy but close to your breast? It is the best place to keep an eye on him. I've sent him to Stenvik because it will give the townspeople time to think and prepare for our arrival. A delegation of four is easier to stomach than an army of thousands, and can tell us what to expect when we arrive. Now, if he yearns to do mischief, which he very well may, seeing that I spared his father's life but took his lands and his men, his betrayal will be far away when it happens and obvious when it comes. For now his silver-coated tongue is in my employ and far away from . . . ?' King Olav looked expectantly at his lieutenant.

And then Finn understood. '. . . the army,' he whispered.

'Exactly,' King Olav added happily. 'Where he cannot learn how to garner the support of men or become a real prince. See, we'll make a leader out of you yet, Finn Trueheart.'

Finn shook his head. 'It might take a while.'

'It so happens that time is on our side. Just remember, Finn – there's not much difference between a chain and a collar.'

King Olav's smile was cold and hard.


WYRMSEY

Skargrim knew they thought he was losing his mind, but he didn't care. He'd given the orders regardless. The ditch was to be the height of a man, twice the width of a warrior's leap, and go in a circle large enough to fit a longship any way one pleased. In addition, it was to be as far away from the camps as possible.

The men grumbled, but he didn't care about that either. He knew from experience that it was not a good idea to have fighting men from many counties sitting together doing nothing. There were always scores to settle, and if they were tired they were less likely to settle them, and he had other reasons besides. Even Skuld didn't seem quite sure what he was up to.

He surveyed the men from his vantage point up on the cliff they'd called Wyrmshead.

They'd see.

In the distance, more sails dotted the horizon.

### STENVIK

Thorvald stood by the table in the longhouse and looked at the three young men before him.

He had chosen them all, some when they were only seven winters old, and he'd chosen well. He'd taken them out into the forests, whipped them up Huginshoyde and down Muninsfjell, run them until they didn't tire and fought them until they didn't lose. He'd taught them how to move silently in the woods, how to hide anywhere, track anything, take down a deer with a single arrow, keep the speed high and the profile low.

The gangly old hunter smiled. He had never married; never needed to. These were his sons, gathered around the table. He unrolled the map he had shown Olav last night and gathered the three scouts around it.

'Sjoberg. By noon. Then to Birkedal, up the hill, check on the farmers at Gard for news, down to the south-east, find high points. I have marked some out, but leave the choice to you. We want to know if anything is moving out there. No heroics, just information. Sigmar, you lead.' Sigmar nodded gravely. Thorvald handed him the map, but did not spare the young man a smile. It would not do to grow soft in his old age.

'Off you go.'

Without a word his three scouts set off at an easy run towards the western gate.

Valgard woke with a start. His skin felt clammy, his mouth tasted like bile and his body felt like a wrung dishrag. Falling asleep at the workbench hadn't helped. It had been a bastard of a night. He'd had to go for fresh water for his patients five times. By the last time the well guard was cursing him roundly and threatening to piss in the next bucket.

But no one had died. Mostly thanks to him.

In the shed next door he had the pig farmer, who looked like he was going to recover eventually. He might even have had some sense smacked into him. The gods occasionally allowed for fantastic things.

Lilia . . . he'd done the best he could. He always did. Harald never let her out of the house when he was ashore, so she would be resting at home.

The Swede was another matter. Sven had been at him, bandaging, serving him mixtures, steaming plants to make him breathe better, but nothing had worked. His lanky long-haired friend insisted on sitting with him.

They were all pieces on the board now.

He tried his best to ignore the pain in his body and clear his head. There would be repercussions after the events of last night. You couldn't start something like that without damages. Honour demanded it.

It all started and ended with Harald. He'd succeeded in making the big oaf dependent on him to provide the mixture and patch Lilia up when the bastard went too far. Now Harald would probably be in trouble with Sigurd because of how he had abused the pig farmer. Harald was not one for authority to begin with, but would Sigurd push him far enough? If there was one thing that brute could be trusted to do it was to make a bloody mess of things. But how best to use it?

With his toe, Valgard tapped the bundle of wood under his workbench. Behind it, the box. He nodded slowly to himself. A lot of pieces were in place already.

Now he had to figure out in which order to play them.

Audun looked at the three sleeping forms in the shed.

The pig farmer in the far corner looked the worse for wear, bandaged almost beyond recognition. Still, he'd live.

In the middle lay Geiri. He looked peaceful, as if he was only sleeping. A large, purple-green bruise peeking from underneath a head bandage was the only thing that hinted at anything out of the ordinary.

In the corner his friend from the longhouse lay slumped. Ulfar, his name was. Before he could think about what he was doing Audun had walked over to him, put a hand on his shoulder and shaken him gently. 'You. Get some proper rest.'

Ulfar startled, blinked, tried his best to see. 'Wh-what?' He shook his head. 'Must have . . . fallen asleep. I'm awake now. Geiri? How's Geiri?'

Audun kept his hand on the young man's shoulder. 'He's still out. And you're going somewhere where you can sleep proper, not in a corner like a thrall. Go to wherever you're staying and get some rest. You might need it. I'll watch over him.'

Ulfar looked at him and blinked. After a while, he nodded and stumbled to his feet, standing nearly a head taller than Audun. 'Thank you. I'll go sleep for just a little while.'

He staggered out of the hut.

Audun looked around then sat down in Ulfar's place.

What in Hel's name was he doing, helping strangers?

He shook his head.

No good could come of this.


Oraekja rolled his eyes.

A lot of posturing, that was all it was. Stalking behind Ragnar, squeezing in between another pair of pointless, stupid huts, Oraekja meant to scowl fiercely. It came out as more of an annoyed sneer. He knew he had a good scowl though – the kind of scowl a hard bastard would use to silence a room. He'd been practising it for a while.

But this was just pointless.

No skulking, no hiding, no dragging people into shadows and stabbing them. He'd seen a couple of girls worthy of his attention but there'd been none of that either. Ragnar would just walk around during the day and look at things.

It was stupid.

And he was left trailing after the old man, who would walk around inside the walls like an idiot, just looking. Every now and then he'd see something, a house or a barn or a couple of men walking, look up at the gateway, close his eyes and mumble. Real advanced scout business, Oraekja sneered. He didn't seem like he was in any rush to do anything to Sigurd and his men. Earlier he'd stopped by a place with long sticks and bales of hay. Bales of hay! What was he going to do – feed them to death?

'When do we move?' he asked.

Ragnar sighed. 'Like I've told you, we wait for her sign. Did you not listen to the instructions?' He turned away and continued walking.

Oraekja spat and scowled. He reckoned Ragnar was simply scared. He was a scared old man and should make way for the younger generation. Men like him.

Ragnar was weak.

Weakling.

Bloody weakling.

The blood pumped in Oraekja's head. He wanted to shout, scream or pick a fight. There was only one thing he could do. He thought of her. Then he went over her special instructions again in his mind. He'd listened well enough to those, and now he was beginning to understand.

## WYRMSEY

'Put some cock into it, you lazy mongrel shit-witted bastard whoresons!'

Skargrim listened to Thora give the workers a tongue-lashing. As always the vocabulary of his second in command amazed him. She was nothing if not inventive. And the voice on her! Skargrim marvelled at the sheer loudness that fitted inside such a tiny frame. On his instructions she'd set the men to cutting down trees and hewing them down to planks after they were done with the ditch. To the side a platoon of workers was fashioning ropes to bind the logs together.

As he watched, one of them, a broad-shouldered rower from Thrainn's crew, threw down his axe. 'I did not come here to do farm work for a woman!' he shouted. Skargrim cringed. Thora walked towards him, grabbing a shovel on the way without breaking her stride. Swinging the shovel like a mallet, she thwacked him on the cheek as hard as she could with the flat of the blade. The dull klonk of the shovel blended with the wet squelch of splitting skin. The rower went down in a heap, clutching his face and screaming obscenities.

'Does anyone else of you worthless, rotten, slime-sucking bug-eyed dog fuckers—' Skargrim nodded to himself. He'd seen this before. Like a seasoned skald she had seized the audience's attention for maximum effect. The brief pause was punctuated with a fierce stamp on the prone man's crotch. His scream was cut short by a gasp for air as he writhed in pain at Thora's feet. '—want to complain?' He looked round at the assembled warriors. Thora was neither muscular nor large, but she was quick, deadly with a knife, and Skargrim had never in his whole life met anyone more vicious.

As he watched, a whole work squad of hardened raiders took one look at the tiny woman standing over their fallen comrade with the shovel casually balanced on her shoulder and found a surprising enthusiasm for woodwork. Thora looked his way and grinned. Skargrim nodded his approval.

Sometimes life was less about grand, heroic gestures and more about picking the right people to stand beside you.

Down on the beach Ingi's men were getting their ships stowed away next to the others, working quickly and efficiently.

Fifty-eight ships now.

He shielded his eyes and looked to sea. He could just make out a couple of tiny specks on the horizon.

Skargrim nodded. That would be Egill Jotunn, then.

## EAST OF HARDANGER HEATH

'What?' Birkir growled.

Havar turned towards Jorn and threw down the saddle. 'This smells of trickery! There's something brewing! He knows!'

Runar's eyes darted around, looking for hidden enemies around their tents. 'A-a-are you sure ab-buh-bout this?'

'Shut up, all of you. Start packing. We're going,' Jorn snapped.

Havar made to protest. 'But last night you said—'

Jorn fixed the fat man with a cold look. 'You know, Havar, for someone with your smarts you can be fairly stupid sometimes.'

Havar turned bright pink. 'But you *said*—'

'— and loud.' There was steel in Jorn's voice and he looked pointedly at the soldiers passing by. 'So how about we talk about this at a later point? When we're on our way, maybe? Hmm?' Without thinking he adjusted the chain around his neck.

Runar placed his hand on Havar's shoulder. 'Makes s-s-s-sense, you know. We m-mustn't l-lose our heads.' Havar turned away and started packing his belongings, muttering all the while. Runar looked at Jorn and shrugged. 'Eyes o-open . . . m-m-mouth shut?'

'Eyes open and mouth shut,' Jorn repeated and nodded. 'Indeed.'


## STENVIK

Harald sneered and spat. 'So that's how it is.'

Rays of evening sunlight caught dust motes circling the rafters in the longhouse. Sigurd sat in the high seat and looked wearily down on him.

'Yes, Harald. That is how it is.'

'So first you tell me we need to keep the peace, especially during market. And then you tell me to go and watch out for trouble. And then, when I decide to set an example so we don't have drunken farmers stumbling all over town starting fights and groping women, it's *my* fault?'

Standing at Sigurd's shoulder, Sven crossed his arms over his chest. 'You know the law, Harald.'

'Oh don't you start, you old turd. This stinks of your counsel.'

Sigurd inclined his head slightly and looked Harald straight in the eyes. 'So, let me see if I understand what you're saying.' He held Harald's gaze. 'I am unfair, wrong *and* incapable of leading on my own,' he said quietly. 'Is this a challenge?'

Harald scowled and spat again.

'Is it?'

Harald's eyes drifted to the axe on the wall behind the dais. He took a deep breath. 'No,' he sneered as he stood up from the table. 'I'm not stupid. It's just that in my opinion maybe the old . . . laws . . . could stand to be . . . revised. I will go and see what I have in my house to' – he swallowed hard – 'settle the debt of honour.' He turned and walked briskly to the exit.

When the dust had settled from the door slamming, Sven sat down on the dais next to Sigurd.

'How long do you reckon that will hold?'

'I don't know. The only reason he didn't challenge is that he still remembers what happened last time. I truly don't know if I could best him now.'

'He's had time to get stronger and meaner. Some of the stories I've heard from the raids are not pretty, Sigurd. Not to mention the girl.'

A dismissive wave almost hid Sigurd's expression. 'What a man does in his house is his business.'

'He's a brute. Worse, he enjoys it.'

'I didn't see you complaining when you counted the loot from his last three raids.'

The two men eyed each other. Sven broke the silence. 'There comes a time when you have to consider who goes with you on the boat.'

'Well, I'd rather have him with me than against me.' Sven smiled wanly. 'I know, I know. He's always barked, but his bite is getting worse. However, what I say stands. Two days to estimate the severity of the injuries and then I decide on compensation. Fenrir's mouth stays shut, and I get to keep my arm.'

'Then that's how it is.'

Sigurd nodded. 'That it is. For now.'

## HARDANGER HEATH

Birkir had to shout to be heard over the wind and the hoof beats. 'If you whip the horses like this, we'll be walking tomorrow!'

Squinting against the wind, Jorn eased his hold on the reins and slowed down to a canter. Havar, Birkir and Runar eased alongside him.

'I don't want to be a pest,' Havar began cautiously, 'but you've been riding like death is on your heels. Birkir is right. You're going to kill the horses. You can't cross the heath like this. And why are we doing it, anyway?'

'M-m-maybe now would be a good time to tell us what is g-going on?' Runar ventured.

Jorn slowed the horse down to a walk and looked round. 'Yes. Now would be a good time. We are going to Stenvik to talk to them for King Olav, help the villagers prepare for him and be his eyes and ears to make the army's arrival easier.' His voice betrayed no emotion but his eyes scanned his fellow travellers.

Birkir shook his head slowly. 'Still makes no sense to me.'

'Me either,' Havar complained. 'We hate King Olav. Don't we?'

Runar looked thoughtfully at Jorn.

'Th-th-that's a big job.'

'It is, Runar.' A hint of a smile flashed across Jorn's face. Runar noticed this and smiled back. Havar and Birkir looked on, confused.

'A l-lot of things can go wr-wr-wrong on big jobs,' Runar added.

Jorn put on a convincingly apologetic face. 'Sadly, they can.'

Runar's smile was positively angelic. 'It is very' – Runar nodded slowly to himself, taking his time to get the sentence out – 'dangerous when things go wr-wrong for a whole army that is perhaps made up of people who don't like each other very much.'

By now, the smiles had spread to Birkir and Havar's faces. Jorn nodded sagely. 'So what I propose we do, boys, is that we get to Stenvik as quick as we can, so that we can make absolutely sure that we've done our very best when the King arrives.'

Within moments they were all back at full gallop.

### STENVIK

Harald could barely contain his fury. Thick, yellowing nails, broken and bitten, dug into calloused palms. Oft-broken and scabbed knuckles whitened, forearms tensed. He just needed an excuse. Any excuse and he'd take great pleasure in breaking someone's face. His nostrils flared and a growl erupted from his throat. Muscles bunched in his arms and shoulders. He throbbed with the injustice of it all. How dare he? Sven, that old goat. And Sigurd. He'd just been following bloody orders. Make sure there are no fights in the market, Harald. Keep an eye out for the traders, Harald. He remembered it well. Of course the best way was to show once and for all who the biggest, meanest dog was. Everyone knew that. It was stupid and unfair. He'd been betrayed. And now, on top of everything, he would have to pay them. Those snivelling little toad-faced pansies who had never tasted the blood on the air, mixed with the smell of charred wood and the music of the screams. Fucking earth-humpers who had never gone in at night, never felt the tingle before the fight, never felt the calm before the storm. Never snuffed out the light in someone's eyes.

Images came to him. Starlight. Big, bearded men crouching in a longship, gliding silently up a river in green, lush land. Grinning to each other. Fastening axes to wrists with leather straps. Reinforcing shield holds. Checking mail shirts and helmets.

Praying silently to Thor, to Tyr. To Odin himself.

Muttering 'Tonight I may die,' but never believing it.

Feeling invincible.

Despite his mood Harald grinned to himself. On that boat, he knew the rules. He knew the game.

In Stenvik, he wasn't so sure any more.

If only someone would give him an excuse right now.

He needed it. Either that or some of Valgard's medicine. He needed something and he needed it now.

He turned and headed for home.


## NORTH OF STENVIK

Sigmar gave himself to the movement.

The ground seemed to whip past him. Bushes turned to green blurs, trees smudged around the edges. His feet hardly touched the earth. Breathe in, three steps, breathe out, three steps. The rhythm took over and then his heart was beating to the rhythm of his feet to the rhythm of the soil and he was alive, he was part of it, part of the rhythm of nature. He ran.

But anyone could run. Thorvald had taught them how to hunt. To watch. They could run through a forest at full speed and tell you afterwards how many trees they'd seen, how many bushes, where the deer tracks lay.

And now Sigmar was thinking, floating on the rhythm. Smelling, seeing, hearing. Working all his senses, searching for anything that would give Thorvald the information he wanted.

Sjoberg loomed up ahead. A sheer cliff rising some two hundred yards over the sea, it was the best point on their stretch of coast to scout the horizon.

The climb was steep and they were all sweating freely when they got to the top. They did as they had been taught and loosened up their muscles when they stopped, rubbing their thighs and shaking their legs. Only when that was done did they allow themselves two mouthfuls of water each, holding the precious liquid in their mouths for as long as they could. Too much water did nothing but slow you down and they had much ground to cover.

Sigmar snapped out an order. 'Orn. Horizon. Any ships?'

Little blond, blue-eyed Orn, at twelve the youngest recruit to the scouts for a while, settled in and shielded his eyes from the sun. Aptly named after the eagle, the boy could see for miles. After a little while he turned to Sigmar. 'There may be something out there but it is very far out. Could have been ships.'

'Go back, find them, try to see where they're headed.'

Orn went back to his post. Sigmar watched him frown in concentration. Time passed then he spoke again, voice cracking a little. 'Out. Far out,' he said without taking his eyes from the horizon. 'If I were to guess, I'd say they're raiders, heading out.

Must be out to sea. The only other place in that direction is Wyrmsey.'

'Wyrmsey,' Sigmar repeated and scratched his head. 'Why would anyone want to go there?'

## WYRMSEY

Skargrim sat on his rock and watched the last work being done on the planks. Thora walked towards him, all skin and bones and short, spiky black hair bristling every which way. She was a hard woman, Skargrim thought. There was nothing soft about her at all. He saw the nasty scar on her right cheek and smiled. One of her lovers had decided that it would be a good idea to assert his authority, show the bitch who was boss. He'd come out of it a lot worse than she did. She tilted her head back and looked up at him.

'Now, captain, would I be right in assuming . . .'

Skargrim raised an eyebrow back at his helmswoman, unable to quite take the smile off his face.

'. . . that you'd want these planks made into makeshift bridges . . .'

Skargrim's grin widened.

'. . . that could be used to cross the ditch . . . but would be real easy, like, to kick down into it?'

'I always thought I did well when I picked you, Thora. You're smarter than you look.'

'For which we thank Loki. And you only picked me because Ari had that accident.'

'Yes. That was unfortunate.'

'He stumbled onto my blade, poor man.'

'Nineteen times, if memory serves.'

'Twenty-one. But who's counting?'

Their conversation was cut short by three strangled, inhuman screams drifting over the sea. Thora shot Skargrim an unreadable look.

'Best get the men moving on those planks, then.'

'Not a bad idea,' Skargrim answered.

On the horizon, five sails billowed. Five ships, glistening black and silver, sliced through the waves and towards Wyrmsey.

Skargrim sidled off the rock as Ingi stalked towards him. Ingi was a short and in later days rather hefty captain with a reputation for cautiousness. While this alone would have labelled him a contemptible coward, he consistently brought home much more loot than any other captain on his stretch of coast, and lost a crew member once in a blue moon. His fighters were well equipped, well trained, hard and disciplined. There was no more give in Ingi's men than there was in Ingi himself. He had reached his fifties and become one of Norway's wealthiest chieftains by making plans, sticking to them and seeing them through. And now he was livid.

He peered up at Skargrim.

'You never told me he would be coming!'

'Would you have come if I had?'

'No! Of course not! Are you out of your tiny little mind, you oaf? Do you even know what you've bargained for? Do you even know what's on those boats?' Ingi stood on tiptoe to be able to scream up at Skargrim's face rather than his chest.

Skargrim looked down at the man and considered his options. He couldn't kill him on the spot, as much as he would like to. Some of his six hundred soldiers might take that the wrong way. And besides he rather liked Ingi and secretly admired his methods. There was something to be said for a commander who respected the lives of his men and wouldn't let stupid things like reputation or honour get in the way. And to be fair, he could see why Ingi would be spitting fire at him. Skargrim grinned. The screams still came in from the sea, although more muted now.

'Smile at this, Skargrim! We're leaving!' Ingi made to turn around, and almost walked into Skuld. Neither of the captains had noticed as she walked up to them.

Now Ingi faced her, with Skargrim at his back.

'I will not take orders from you either, woman. It doesn't . . .' Ingi's voice trailed off. '. . . It doesn't . . . make any . . . sense.'

She reached out and touched his forearm. Skargrim felt the cold kiss of crisp winter breeze, saw Ingi's knees start to shake gently and heard the little man's breath quicken. He observed her from over Ingi's shoulder. Straight, blonde hair framed her sparkling blue eyes, skin made from clouds and mountain snow, lips of sunset red moving almost imperceptibly. She was fragile, beautiful and desperately vulnerable. He wanted to toss the little man out of the way and embrace her, protect her, shield her from all harm. Her eyes had not captured his, so he could resist the powerful feeling that washed over him, but only just.

Ingi had no such luck.

'But it makes sense to leave us in the hour of our greatest need?' she asked, a note of tender, resigned regret in her voice. 'Leaving your brothers in arms? Denouncing your gods? Abandoning . . . me?'

Skargrim dared not breathe. He'd seen her do this to other men, and he knew what would follow. She'd use the powers Loki had given her to win him over, feel weaker for it, and then someone would have to die to give her strength. After what seemed like an eternity she continued.

'If that is how you wish to proceed, Ingi, then do. But know this – you are needed here. And not only needed – you are respected and honoured. Your counsel, your wisdom, your prudence. This is the mighty host of which you and your men are designed to be the backbone. This is where you will write your name in legend. Will you leave us now?'

Skargrim found he was holding his breath.

'. . . No,' Ingi whispered.

Her hands moved slowly, tantalizingly, towards his face. She cupped his cheeks and gazed into his eyes. 'This pleases me, Ingi. It pleases me greatly. Now go see to your men. Be the leader I know you can be.'

'Yes. Yes I will,' Ingi blurted out, and hurried down off the lookout mound towards his camp.

When he was gone, she turned to Skargrim. 'Do you trust him?'

'I do.' She raised an immaculate eyebrow. Skargrim continued. 'At heart he is a greedy coward, unable to deal with chaos and risk. That is precisely why we want him. He knows, fears and respects battle. If Ingi doesn't want to do it, we know we're taking chances that we shouldn't take.'

Skuld smiled at him. The smile did not reach her cold blue eyes. 'Tell me again. You sent the promise of gold?'

'I did. The forest around Stenvik will be crawling with every poacher, thief and blackheart in the south-west. As you instructed,' Skargrim answered.

'Good.'

The movement down on the beach broke the spell of her eyes.

The five black and silver ships had landed.

Unlike the other arrivals, nobody rushed to help.

A giant of a man leapt overboard from the lead ship and strode to shore.

'SKARGRIM!' he bellowed.

'WELL MET, EGILL!!' Skargrim shouted back from his mound. Egill looked up and raised one slablike fist in salute.

Skargrim walked calmly down towards the beach to meet the newest arrival.

Many of his men had doubted that Egill Jotunn even existed. His crew was the source of much legend, nobody knew where his ships came from or went back to, and various stories flourished, each of them less probable than the other. Now the assembled raiders had a chance to see for themselves.

The man on the beach was a specimen. Skargrim was a sizeable man himself, but Egill was at least a head taller. Some said he was half giant, others that he was Thor's bastard son. He killed his first man when he was five and legend had it he had once sunk an enemy ship by flinging a ram ten lengths from his own boat and straight through its hull.

Skargrim didn't care for stories. What he did know was that nobody had yet bested Egill in single combat. Hell, anyone who was dumb enough to take on that mountain of a man without a small army deserved to die. Skuld had told him where to find Egill and his crew, and when he'd seen them he'd decided on the spot that they would need them. As his ships ran ashore gently, they started forming ranks on the beach.

First came the fighters.

They leapt over the side of the ships, swift and nearly silent. Their mail shirts were black, as were their helmets. They wore short axes and longswords at their belts, and held long spears or nasty halberds. No shields. They were strong men who walked proud and looked at the amassed crowd of toughened raiders with a healthy amount of scorn.

Hard as nails, they looked.

But there were also only a hundred and fifty of them.

'Is that all you brought?' Thrainn shouted derisively from the middle of his camp. The men laughed. Skargrim winked at Egill and grinned.

From one of the ships came an agonized, strangled howl that sounded almost inhuman. On the beach, over fifteen hundred hardened raiders from all over the north took a simultaneous step back and fell quiet. Skargrim caught Hrafn's eye. The Finnmark chieftain was grinning like a child with a new toy, bounding up and down and craning his neck to see.

And then they came.

The Twenty.

Shuffling out of the boat, looking miserable, grey-green and seasick. All manner of men. Thick, thin, tall and short, strong and frail. Bald, hairy, bearded, shaven, scabby, clean, young and not so young. Carrying an assortment of weapons. Scythes, spikes, iron knuckles, shortswords, knives, axes, hammers and picks.

And no armour.

Instead, each of the twenty had a filthy, tattered bearskin tied around his waist, complete with gaping half-head.

Egill's raiders formed a protective circle around them. It was not entirely sure who was protecting who from what, Skargrim thought. Apprehension, even fear, clouded the faces of the men.

A loud voice pierced the tense silence. 'Welcome to Wyrmsey! Right, you furry goat-fuckers, get your stinky, boil-filled pus-spewing arses in gear and come on over. I and the boys have prepared a special sleeping place for you.' Thora strode in front of the circle of black-clad warriors, pacing back and forth. 'But mind, if you start any of that howling at the moon nonsense while I'm getting my beauty sleep I'll come over and smack all of you in the mouth!'

The tension changed the outburst of spontaneous laughter

instantly into raucous cheering. Even some of the black raiders cracked a smile. Striding towards Skargrim, Egill exclaimed: 'That's a good woman right there.'

'I know,' Skargrim said with a grin.

Hrafn nearly crashed into them. 'Berserkers! You brought berserkers! I've never even seen them! I've just heard stories! And to be in the presence of Egill Jotunn himself – it is an honour.' Hrafn bowed low.

Egill roared. 'Hah! Says Hrafn of the Long Knife, House-burner, Blood-beak, scourge of the North Seas? I am the one who should be giving you my thanks! I've heard much about you.'

'And likewise,' Hrafn said, clasping Egill's arm in a warrior's grip and looking almost comically small in comparison. 'Berserkers!' he bubbled.

'Yes indeed,' Egill said with a smile. 'These are the last ones. The Twenty. As far as I know, that's all that remains. I heard several stories a few years back of a man who murdered nearly half a village in a rage, but he's the only one who hasn't sought me out. If I ever see him I'll name him Third Seven, and he shall sail with me. Every one of the twenty has found us. They say they couldn't run with other crews because things . . . unfortunate things had a way of happening.'

'They did,' Skargrim agreed.

'Well, not with me they don't,' Egill added gleefully. 'I keep these bastards in line, and they love me for it. If we can, we beach when they're howling, so they can go wrestle a tree or a big rock or something. That way they don't hurt anyone unintentionally.'

'What happens if they go wild when you're out to sea?' Hrafn asked.

Egill looked at him and grinned savagely. 'Then they wrestle me.'

Thrainn approached the gathered chieftains. 'Skargrim. Hrafn. Egill. I am Thrainn Thrandilsson. It is an honour for a captain like me to be on the same island, let alone sail with legends such as you.' He inclined his head.

Skargrim grinned inwardly. Experience was already serving young Thrainn well.

'Tell me, Thrainn,' Egill rumbled. 'That looks like, what? Three hundred raiders in your camp?'

'More than four hundred,' Thrainn said, straightening up somewhat.

'I will tell you what I think,' Egill said, eyeing the young man thoughtfully. 'I reckon anyone can captain a ship if he's mean enough. Maybe two. But a raiding party of four hundred men will only follow a man who is on his way to becoming a legend in his own right. I have heard tell of you. You sail with us as a northern chieftain of note and I consider you my equal. I look forward to the battle and hope you will prove yourself my superior.'

Thrainn grinned and bowed his head once more. 'Your generosity is only matched by your size.'

Egill roared again. 'Hah! The whelp has a tongue on him!' Ingi approached the assembled chieftains. Skargrim stepped out and made space for him in the circle. When he introduced himself, Egill whipped around with frightening speed and squared up to Skargrim. 'You lying rat bastard!' he snarled and pointed straight at the old captain's face. In a split second the mood changed. Hands moved to hilts obvious and concealed. Feet shuffled into fighting stances. Body weight shifted and Egill continued, scowling. 'When you summoned us you didn't tell me we'd be sailing with people who hadn't lost their mind!'

The silence stretched on into tense confusion, until finally Hrafn cracked up and started giggling so hard he eventually had to lean on Egill, who was shaking silently. Thrainn and Ingi shot each other confused glances. Skargrim grinned wryly.

'Forgive me, I just had to,' Egill said, laughing. 'If you can't laugh, what can you do? These will be times of death and murder. I have heard tell of you too, Ingi. The voices on the wind call you Iceblood. Your crew is said to be the best, most disciplined and most consistently alive of all. I salute you.'

Ingi nodded. 'I take great pride in the safety of my men.'

There were grave nods all around. 'An honourable position,' Egill added. 'I do the very same.'

Ingi sneered. 'How can you? You have berserkers.'

'Yes I do. And my men are safe, because the mad dogs do what I say.'

'And can you really control them? Or will my men find themselves fighting next to spitting, snarling animals just as like to turn their swords on friend as foe? Maybe we should nail these last dregs up like all the others to be on the safe side.'

Egill leaned down until he was very close to Ingi's face. His voice quavered with fury. 'Yes I can control them. I can and will control them. You are safe and your men are safe. I know what I'm doing. And if you so much as look at me or my men wrong again, you quivering little bitch, I will rip you limb from limb and eat you.'

Ingi did not flinch. Instead, he smiled back. 'Good,' he said, conversationally. 'The last thing I would want is to find myself on the wrong side of a crazed half-giant. I would be forced' – and here he shot Egill a look no less fierce – 'to poison the food of all his men and murder him in his sleep if he ever threatened me again.'

The two men locked eyes for what seemed like an age. Neither budged an inch.

Skargrim stroked his beard. 'But wouldn't it be much better to look funny at Egill and then eat poison yourself, Ingi? That way, when he tears you limb from limb and eats you, he'll die.' The two men blinked, their gazes wavering. 'Revenge will be yours, and you'll be known as the brave warrior who killed the mythical Egill Jotunn.' Matching looks of confusion flitted across the two angry captains' faces. Skargrim continued. 'And then, when you're both dead and have hopefully stopped posturing like two young pups with a cock-size problem, I can take over both of your parties.' Torn between staring each other down and listening to Skargrim, the two chieftains slowly backed away and turned to the grizzled old captain. 'I might give Thrainn some of the skilled fighters, split the hard bastards in three between all of us and give the berserkers to Hrafn here. I'm sure he'd have fun going crazy with them,' Skargrim continued. Hrafn's eyes sparkled with joy and his Adam's apple bobbed in his throat. Ingi and Egill seemed to have forgotten their quarrel. 'So can we agree, now, that we all know what we're doing?' Skargrim added. Ingi and Egill mumbled their agreements. 'Good. Now go see to your crews, have your ships ready to fly at a moment's notice and try to keep your men alive. There will be plenty of killing to go around when we get there.'

Thrainn left at once, saluting as he moved away. Hrafn bounded along after him. Neither Ingi nor Egill moved.

Skargrim sighed and stepped pointedly between them. He turned to look at the shorter man. 'I can understand your concerns, Ingi. But I have every faith in Egill and I humbly request that you consider showing faith in me, if not him. Allow his men to prove themselves in battle. All precautions will be taken.'

Ingi peered up at Skargrim, but nodded before he turned and headed towards his camp. When he was gone, Skargrim turned to Egill. 'I am nowhere near your height, my giant friend. But one thing I share with you. I too have seen men grow furious for no cause, when the real reason is' – Skargrim marked Ingi's height just below Egill's chest – 'beyond their control.'

A smile cracked the giant's scowling face and continued to spread, impossibly wide.

'I too will have faith in you, Skargrim. Your reputation alone demands it. But you also know how to lead, and for that I will follow you, and my men will follow me.'

Skargrim gave Egill's hand as solid a shake as he dared. The giant grunted in acknowledgement, turned and headed towards his encampment.

Behind him the sun started its descent.


## STENVIK

'It's not my fault.' Harald sat and sulked in the corner of Valgard's house. 'They're being unfair, and I don't think I should be paying those stupid bastards any of the gold I've personally stolen.'

'I can see that,' Valgard muttered from his workbench. With his back turned, he could limit himself to just sounding sympathetic.

'I mean, I was just doing what Sigurd told me to, right?'

'Yes,' Valgard said, while keeping his eye on the point of the knife slicing into the root. 'They're not treating you right, Harald. I agree.'

'Damn right they're not,' Harald fumed. 'No one is. Well, no one but you, Valgard. You respect me. You listen to me. I don't have to threaten or beat you.'

'Of course I listen, Harald.' A drop of sweat broke free of Valgard's hairline and slid gently down his forehead. 'We're . . . friends.'

'Damn right,' Harald muttered, anger and frustration rising in his voice. 'I don't care what they say. A man has to think for himself. Only it seems Harald is not allowed to. Harald has to obey the rules. And then they change the rules, and Harald has to pay. Always Harald.'

Valgard felt the familiar tingling in his scalp. He gripped the hilt of the knife as if his life depended on it. Images of the forest flashed through his mind and he forced himself to breathe, to regain control. Suddenly the board appeared in his mind. The move was obvious. He steeled himself, made sure he had a voice.

'Do they have any family here?'

'. . . What?'

In his mind, he heard the click-clack as the pieces moved.

'The pig farmer and his kin. The people who started all this. Do they have any family here?'

'How the hell should I know that? Do you think I asked? Hello, I'm going to beat the shit out of you, do you have any uncles in Stenvik? Don't be stupid,' Harald snapped.

'Think, Harald,' Valgard snapped back and turned, eyes ablaze. Harald stared dumbly at him. 'Think. Do they have any family?'

'You keep asking me! I don't know! What does it matter?'

'Because if they don't have any family . . . then who is going to miss them?' Valgard left the sentence hanging in the air but kept his eyes locked on Harald's. He watched as the thought was born in the brute's head; saw the expression on that big dumb face turn from hurt to comprehension to malice.

'So you're saying . . .'

'I'm not saying anything. But sometimes simple country folk get scared in a big town and just run off home. As if they'd . . .'

'. . . disappeared,' Harald finished, whispering. The grin had spread to his eyes now. 'Valgard, you are a true friend.'

'Thank you. Now have a word with your boys. We'll see what happens tonight.'

Harald rose, an oversized troll of a figure in his little hut.

'Will do, Valgard. Now, do you have my mixture?'

'I do.' Valgard put the cork in the flask, heart thumping in his chest, and took a leap.

'But first, Harald.'

Harald's eyes darkened, his hand stretched out for the flask. 'What?'

'I know you. Have done for a long time. And I know it's hard for you to control your moods. But try and go a little easier on Lilia for a couple of days.'

'Are you telling me what to do, Valgard?' Harald's voice was a mixture of doubt, confusion and disbelief.

Now or never.

'Do you think I'm an idiot?' Valgard hissed. Harald recoiled and he pressed the attack. 'Do you think I'd ever give you an order? Do I look like a fool?' Valgard swung the bottle around for emphasis, feeling Harald's worried eyes on it.

'I just want you to think, Harald. If you hurt Lilia more now, she will break. If she breaks, Sven will take her. If he sees what you've done to her already' – Harald winced – 'he will tell Sigurd. And everyone else. Do you want that to happen?'

Harald shook his head.

Valgard nodded slowly.

'So . . . ?'

'Don't hurt Lilia,' Harald repeated as if in a trance.

Valgard handed him the bottle.

'Now go. We'll see about tonight.'

## WYRMSEY

Skargrim looked at the camps. Fires had gone up with the setting sun, casting flickering shadows over ships and men. Sixty-three ships, raid-hardened crews. Nineteen hundred men quietly attending to their murderous tools. By themselves, each of those crews would inspire fear in anyone. He'd gathered a host that the whole of the north would deem legendary if they knew it existed.

Which they would, soon enough.

This time he saw Skuld approach. He suspected it was because she let him. She stopped a respectful distance away and inclined her head. 'You have done well, Skargrim. The gods are pleased.'

He smiled a tired smile. 'They'd better be. This is a host worthy of Valhalla, with tempers to match.'

'I know. Rest, my brave captain.' She placed a delicate hand on his arm and looked in his eyes.

'I . . . will.' Skargrim felt her fingers like delicious fire. Sweet weariness spread through his whole body, and his knees threatened to buckle.

Summoning up the last of his strength, he turned towards their camp.

'Wait.'

Before he realized what had happened, he'd turned around. A brief twinge of pain on his chin brought confusion to his sleep-addled brain, but then she touched his arm again and everything was good.

'Go now. Sleep.'

Skargrim turned around again and staggered towards the camp.

She watched him leave.

As he disappeared among the men, her gaze travelled upward, to the stars, and she started speaking in a soft, low voice.

*You who are darkness*
*Swift and cunning*
*Move like the north wind*
*Old and wily*
*Drift on the wings*
*Of the wandering spirit*
*See all and know all*
*Come to your mistress.*

She waited.

A faint sound on the wind turned into the flutter of wings. A large raven landed by her feet and cocked its head at her. She looked it straight in its sparkling black eyes, all the while rubbing together her thumb and index finger. Her voice quieted down to a whisper, and she offered her hand to the raven.

In it was a single, coarse, grey hair. The raven hopped towards her, nudged her with its head and plucked the hair from her hand.

The big black bird shot up into the air with the hair in its beak and streaked eastward into the night.

## STENVIK

The words echoed in Lilia's head.

Don't move.

Don't move.

She'd pushed everything else out, allowing just enough space for those words, repeated again and again.

Her body screamed at her, but she didn't listen.

Don't. Move.

She lay on her side, curled up into a ball. Everything hurt. Her scalp, where he'd pulled her hair. Her lips, where he'd bitten them. The salve that Valgard had applied on her back felt like cool breath on the burning skin, but it was not nearly enough. Harald had been nothing if not meticulous with the leather strap. The splints on her little fingers only framed the dull throbbing. She could picture his face all too well as he'd broken them. He'd come home furious about something, furious and miserable.

She hadn't given him the pleasure of seeing her cry.

Instead she'd gritted her teeth and hid inside the stone woman, closed her heart to the world. She'd watched as his expression changed from anger to anguish.

He'd tried to take her but he had been limp, unmanned. And thinking back, she realized, he'd been afraid. Desperately afraid.

Right then, somewhere in her, something changed.

She shifted and lay down on her back.

Pain exploded like a blossoming flower in her head, filled her senses.

The tears came, flowed hot and silent.

She embraced them, embraced the pain. Wielded it, moulded it and relished it. She shaped it into a hammer and hefted it. She swung it with all her might at the stone woman, the granite prison all around her.

It bounced off, but so did a chip of stone.

Fuelled by the pain, by the soaring sensation of it, she swung again. The hammer smashed into the stone woman, sending a jarring blow through her arms up into her shoulders, making her teeth tingle.

Just before she lost consciousness, she saw the crack forming on the inside of the stone woman, reaching from head to heart.

*

Oraekja yawned. They'd been sitting and waiting since sunset. This could hardly get more boring. And Ragnar wasn't one for idle chatter.

He just sat there, completely still.

It was quite unnerving how he could do that, just sit down and stop moving. Oraekja was almost sure he stopped breathing as well. He'd watched with incredulity as the damned old goat seemed to melt into the background.

Oraekja jumped when the raven landed in front of him.

Ragnar was on his feet. His voice was calm.

'Right, puppy. That is our signal.'

As quickly as it had landed, the raven took off again.


The old longhouse was full of people. Valgard had to watch the entrance carefully, but he spotted them at last.

'Fellows! Over here!'

All he got in return was a matching set of guarded looks from the two bruised and battered farmers. He waved them over nonetheless.

'Come on, lads. Have a seat.'

The red-faced one looked at him with suspicion. 'Why do you want us to sit with you?'

'Are you in a position to choose?' Valgard countered. The sound of a heated quarrel drifted towards them from the far end of the longhouse. The farmer was about to start arguing when his cousin pushed him towards the table. 'Shut up and sit. I'll go get drink.'

'Better, better,' Valgard smiled. 'I just wanted you to know that your kinsman is recovering as well as could be hoped, even better. Our goddess of medicine is surely watching over him.'

The red-faced one scowled. 'Never should have needed to in the first place.'

'You're right, of course. I—'

'Hate this place,' he sneered, daring anyone and everyone to object.

Valgard decided silence might be the best course of action. Luckily, the fat cousin soon appeared with three mugs of mead. 'Ah, the saviour of parched throats. Sit and talk.'

'About what?' the red-faced farmer mumbled.

'I reckon you have a good chance at damages.'

'Do we?' The fat one's face lit up.

'Don't be an idiot,' his cousin snapped. 'That bastard Harald has friends all over this town. We have no chance.'

Little do you know, thought Valgard. He felt for the satchel on his hip, felt reassured by the shape. 'We shall not complain, though. That does no good. For now, let's drink to our health – and your kinsman's! As Eir is my witness, I tell you his health will soon be like it's never been before!'

The fat one smiled at that, while the other one frowned. Valgard did his best to down the sour ale. 'Come on now – you're not going to let a shrivelled town boy like myself drink you strong country men onto the floor?' he managed to splutter between gulps. The red-faced farmer took to his ale with belligerent enthusiasm.

Soon their mugs were empty.

Valgard shot a look at red-face. 'You or me?'

'Much like cock-rot, rather you than me,' he shot back.

Valgard raised his hands in mock surrender. 'You have a way with words! I think you're right. My turn now – you'll go later.' With that he left the table with mugs in hand and a sour taste in his mouth.

## NORTH-EAST OF STENVIK

The raven flew like a black arrow to its target, a hillside strewn with moss-covered boulders and pines leaning at strange angles, reaching up to the starry night sky.

It landed in a clearing and hopped two steps forward, blinking and cocking its head as if listening in on a silent conversation.

Suddenly its head snapped round. It beat its big wings and pulled towards the air, towards the stars.

Too late.

The knife took it in the chest, whipped it sideways and pinned it to the trunk of a pine, killing it instantly.

Moments later a man emerged from the shadows and walked across the clearing without making a sound. With the practised movements of a hunter he pulled the knife free and wiped it clean on his old, ragged clothes. Behind him two big, burly men stepped into the clearing.

'Good shot,' one of them mumbled.

''s always a good shot,' the other replied.

'Always.'

'Maybe next time something bigger, though. Like a . . . bigger bird.'

The man with the knife smiled. 'Now now, boys. You'll have your fill again. We fed well tonight; we'll do so again tomorrow. This'll keep you happy for a while.' He tossed the bird to the two lumbering men, who set to tearing it apart with their hands. 'That's our signal. When you're done, go tell the others.' Grunted assent was mixed in with sounds of teeth crunching brittle bones. The man sheathed the knife, untied a leather strap from his wrist and tied up his dirty, matted hair into a loose ponytail. 'It's time,' he said quietly.

## STENVIK

Valgard took a hearty swig of the mug in his left hand, passing the two mugs in his right to the two cousins. 'Round two!' he declared and set to finishing his ale. The others did their best to keep up. Soon the mugs were empty again.

'Right. Your turn,' Valgard said jovially to the red-faced man. Seeing the frown on his cousin's face, the fat one quickly volunteered, staggering towards the pots for more mead. 'They pack a fair bit of punch into this piss,' red-face slurred.

'They do,' Valgard concurred. 'About as much as you deserve, I reckon.'

The farmer nodded, his face flushed. An awkward silence settled until his cousin staggered back, mugs in hand. 'Round three.'

'In fact, boys, I think I have had enough. I declare myself defeated. Share mine if you want. I bid you farewell.' Valgard stood up and made for the door, vaguely conscious of a disinterested wave.

The night air was mercifully cooling on his skin. The full moon cast dancing shadows. Some of them seemed a little deeper than they should be. Maybe it was the mead.

And maybe not.

Valgard headed home and willed himself not to look over his shoulder.

## NORTH OF STENVIK

Sigmar had smelled it for a while now. It had met them in the forests a mile downwind from here and grown stronger as they got closer. A mixture of things, and he couldn't quite tell them apart. They had made good time up through Birkedal, but seen nothing. In fact they'd seen nothing at all, which was odd. They should have met someone or seen some kind of evidence of humans. But there was nothing. Now, approaching Gard by moonlight, they'd been slowing down.

Something was not right.

Cresting the hill overlooking the fields of Gard, the smell hit him like a wave.

It smelled like burning wood. It smelled like blood.

He looked down on the big farmhouse, saw the tendrils of smoke. Saw the yard.

The air smelled like roasting flesh.

## STENVIK

Ulfar blinked.

The light in the hut was fading.

Geiri.

What?

Where was he?

Find Geiri.

He stumbled to his feet and staggered out. The stars twinkled above him. Clouds drifted past the moon, bathing his path in a silvery ghost-light. He staggered across the quiet walkways towards the healer's hut, still more asleep than awake. When he got there he found Audun the blacksmith still on the same spot, eyes trained on Geiri's sleeping form. As the smith made to rise, their eyes met. Ulfar nodded and helped the stocky man to his feet, but just as Audun got up they heard the scream.

'FIRE!!!'

## STENVIK

Ragnar was no more than a shadow gliding silently across the moonlit walkway. Oraekja watched him open the gate and step inside. Moments later, he led an obedient old draft horse out of the enclosure.

He had to admit it. Despite the old man's stupidity and arrogance he moved well. So let him sneak and skulk. Lookout would do fine for tonight. Watch, melt into the shadows and disappear at the first sign of trouble. Oraekja smirked in the darkness. 'No they won't catch you. No, they won't. We'll see about that, old man,' he muttered as he moved to join Ragnar.

They led the horse quietly past the huts and towards the harbour. The old man had found the spot earlier on one of his many walks, a darkened corner between some storage shacks. Apparently it was not visible from the walls – not that Oraekja had ever seen any of the guards Ragnar kept mentioning.

When they got there, a long rod and an armful of thatch lay on the ground waiting for them.

Ragnar started stroking and soothing the old horse, muttering in his ear all the while. Moving slowly, he produced a short, solid club from the folds of his tunic, raised it and brought it down with all his might on the back of the horse's head, killing it instantly.

Oraekja had to hop away to avoid the falling body, which hit the ground with a muted thump. Ragnar was already crouching. He jerked the old nag's head back, exposing the neck. Then he produced a skinning knife from somewhere and sliced into its throat. Soon the ground was painted with streams of blood. Amazingly, Ragnar had managed to escape without as much as a stain. As the flow slowed to a trickle the old scout started cutting into the flesh around the neck with the skinning knife. He worked quickly, carving a path to the neck joints.

'You never were as much of a man as your father, I always said,' the red-faced farmer slurred, leaning on a fencepost behind the longhouse for balance.

Standing next to him, his fat cousin heaved and gasped for breath. 'Shut . . . up,' he managed before another surge of bile filled his mouth.

The annoyed farmer breathed in, nostrils flaring and eyes widening. He breathed out again, slowly, and swallowed. 'I'm fine,' he added. 'I'm not being sick like a little runny-ass girl.'

'Shut up, you . . .' his cousin doubled over again, a hacking cough sending up the remaining contents of his stomach.

'Shut up, shut up. Why don't you shut up so you stop' – the red-faced farmer held his hand to his mouth, burped and winced – 'spewing like a child, you wet-arse?'

Behind them the shadows changed shape.

Oraekja had to strain not to vomit.

It was filthy work.

The blood stank. The carcass stank. By now, Ragnar had finished the first stage and was on to the next, skinning knife in hand, sack at the ready. Oraekja busied himself tying together bundles of hay and touchwood from the pouch.

Soft, squelching sounds.

Ragnar's voice was calm and measured. 'Make sure you don't get blood on your clothes. When the time comes we'll be walking out of here.'

Oraekja chose not to look at him. The smell was bad enough.

And then they were done. Two full sacks, a pole almost half again the length of a man, and three touchwood bundles for each of them. Ragnar moved first, ducking between two shacks and looking towards the harbour. The square and jetty were dusted in silvery moonlight, almost as bright as day. Oraekja looked over Ragnar's shoulder and swore under his breath.

'Don't worry,' Ragnar muttered. 'The hero may charge but the wise man . . .' He looked up. '. . . waits.'

The moonlight seemed to fade. A cloud drifted in, floating on the wind like the finest silk, draping itself across the moon. Soon another followed, and then another.

Darkness descended on the square.

'Now. Go.'

On the walk to Stenvik they had mapped it out in detail so there was no need to ask, think or talk. Oraekja was glad of it. He just sprinted to the jetty. Ragnar went to the near end. Oraekja looked at the ships in the middle, seeking the right ones, the ones that would burn best. Ragnar picked a small, fat merchant boat hemmed in by larger ships.

Oraekja became aware of movement out of the corner of his eye. Signalling furiously to Ragnar, he slid down into the biggest longship he could find and lay down, flattening himself against the side of the boat and clutching the bundles of thatch in his hand.

Straining, he heard footsteps and heavy breathing. The pier creaked, the sounds coming closer and closer.

Voices.

'Which one?' Out of breath. 'Heh. Let's take Ingimar's. Never liked him. Besides, it's next to the *Drake*, and nothing should be.'

Someone spat. 'Damn right.'

Another man grunted. Wood creaked next to Oraekja's ear. They were in the boat next to his. He pressed harder against the side and held his breath.

'I say we cut them.'

'No. No blood.'

'Then what? They're out now, but they'll come to by dawn at the latest.'

'Just wait and see,' the third man growled. More grunting. The boat rocked. 'Pass me the rope.' Scuffing, straining. 'Now give me the knife.' Scraping noises. Oraekja felt the blow through the side of the ship. Then another two in quick succession. Metal on wood. 'There. That should do.'

'Oh. Oh, that is . . .' there was admiration in the voice as it trailed off. Then, grim chuckles.

'What about the pig man?'

'A couple of well-picked words in his ear and he will find pigs somewhere else. Like Rus or somewhere. I've heard there are lots in Miklagard. If not . . . well, we can always arrange for another lesson,' the growling voice concluded with smug satisfaction.

More laughter.

Creaking wood.

Oraekja's heart thumped. All they had to do was lean over the side and look down and they would be right on top of him. He was willing to bet that Ragnar would disappear, too. He'd be found alone, lying in a boat that wasn't his, clutching fire-starting equipment.

But they moved away, back up to the pier.

He felt more than heard the push as the boat next to his ship slid out and onto the tide.

'Their own fault.'

'Damn right,' the growling man agreed.

Footsteps moved away.

He peered up over the side as soon as he dared. In the distance, someone staggered along the street and disappeared among the houses. Behind him, a boat floated serenely out to sea, carried on the tide. He could vaguely make out two shapes on board, huddled close together. At the far end of the pier, he could see Ragnar. He must have sneaked across the square while the bastards were in the boat next to him, and now he stood by a shallow-keeled, speedy raiding ship, signalling him to hurry.

Oraekja glanced at the moon and could see what he meant. It was full to bursting and starting to peer at them from behind retreating clouds. He must go, and go now.

He looked around. It was a drake indeed. He counted twenty-five benches, exquisite curves, beautiful woodwork. Lost in thought, he ran a hand along a smooth and neatly tucked-in oar, a warrior's weapon in the battle with the sea. It was a shame to destroy such a beautiful ship, but Skuld had been adamant. The raiders of Stenvik needed to have their manhood taken away, they needed to live in fear of the old gods. And her word was to be obeyed.

Oraekja placed the bundles around the thick mast and had to suppress a wave of nervous giggles. This was not going to work. Trying to ignore the shaking in his hands, he found the bowline and dropped the sail. He could already see the flicker of a flame coming from the first ship that Ragnar had set on fire. The light was shielded from watchful eyes at the wall by barrels and cloth, but it wouldn't stay that way for long. Working quickly, Oraekja cut ribbons from the woollen cloth. It was a well-made sail rein-forced with leather and the cutting was hard going. Still, it yielded to his knife and slowly strips of cloth gathered in a pile at his feet.

When he was convinced the pile was big enough he added the bundles, drew his dagger and loosened the fire-steel from his belt. Striking it hard against the flint pommel of the dagger, he pro-duced a spark that flew at the touchwood, but didn't take. He tried again. No luck.

It took four tries, but then finally the spark became a flame that grew in size, devouring the thatch and the wool, sinking its teeth into the mast.

The red-hot orange dance of the flame almost got him. Trans-fixed, he had to tear himself away from its beauty. But time was fleeing with the clouds. He jumped up onto the jetty, grabbed his sack and hurried to the middle of the square, where Ragnar was busy making a small hole in the ground.

Shaking, Oraekja upended the sack at the old man's feet. The horse's head spilled out, staring with frozen eyes at the night sky. Ragnar looked round and nodded at Oraekja. The skinning knife flashed and three horizontal stripes emerged, widened and oozed blood just above the jagged cut where the head had been separated from the body.

He watched as Ragnar grabbed the horse's head under his arm, jammed the knife alongside the remainder of the neck joints and carved a hole. Then he took the pole, shoved it into the neck and gave a twist for good measure. Oraekja grabbed the bottom end and guided it into the hole in the ground as Ragnar steadied and pushed it. The damn thing seemed to rise for an age. Risking a look back, Oraekja could now see flames dancing onboard the three ships. The knarr was burning happily and the longship showed flames in five different places. Even the *Drake*'s mast seemed to be moving as fire-cast shadows caressed the timber. Finally, Ragnar let go of the pole. It stood upright, the horse's head grinning madly at the pier. He turned it so the head faced the town, muttered something under his breath, reached into his bag and tied a calfskin roll to the wood. Then he turned to him. 'We're done. Let's go.' Oraekja grabbed the second sack and the two men rushed out of the square.

The shadow had always been Harald's friend.

He'd been alive again. Focused. Like he knew what it was about. Odin's warrior, sent from above for the heads of weaklings. He had smelled the sea, the autumn in the forest, tasted the starlight in the air. It had felt good. He'd knocked his man unconscious in one. The boys had struggled with the other one, but managed eventually. Valgard had poisoned those two dirt-fuckers well enough.

The boys had wanted to gut them on the spot, but he'd said no. He'd said no because he was a good leader. Blood meant questions and they didn't need that.

Not now.

He smiled to himself.

Problem solved.

'FIRE!'

The cry carried across Stenvik, bouncing off the walls in the still night. Ulfar looked at Audun, searching for signs of a false alarm, a regular occurrence, something.

'What do we—'

Audun cut him off. 'I go. You stay with Geiri.'

And with that, he ran out.

Ulfar was left blinking in the gloom of the hut. Shaking his head to dislodge the fog of sleep, he knelt down beside Geiri. A sheen of sweat had formed on the sleeping man's brow.

Ulfar found the water barrel but it was empty. He cursed, grabbed a water skin and left.

The old man really picked the worst time to lose his nerve. Confusion and panic shone out of his every move, leaked from every line on his face. Oraekja cursed as he trailed Ragnar at a dead run past the small wattle houses, heading back towards the southern gateway. A short, fat man emerged from a hut in front of them, fumbling with the cord of his trousers. Ragnar lost his balance and stumbled into him.

Behind them, Oraekja stopped abruptly. The old bastard was going to get him caught. Caught and tortured. Without thinking, he reached for his sword.

'Watch where you're going!' the fat man snarled and gave Ragnar a hard shove. Wild-eyed, the old scout turned around. 'There's a fire! Down at the harbour!' The man frowned, suspicion etched on his face. 'Use your nose if you don't believe me!' Ragnar implored.

And sure enough, a faint whiff of burning wood carried on the wind.

Snapping to in an instant, the man ran off, shouting 'FIRE!' at the top of his lungs.

Oraekja watched in astonishment as the panic drained out of Ragnar's face. The old scout flashed him a cold, calculating grin and winked. Almost instantly the panic flooded back into his eyes, into the turn of the mouth, the stooping back. He joined in with the rising chorus of 'FIRE!' and took off at a loping gait towards the south gate. 'Bastard,' Oraekja whispered as he chased him towards the south gateway.

'FIRE!!'

Voices rose to echo the cry.

'FIRE IN THE HARBOUR!'

Suddenly the streets were full of bodies, jostling and pushing.

'THE SHIPS ARE BURNING!'

Elbows, shoulders and hands pushed at Audun.

Too slow. Too many people in the way.

A thin, greying man pushed past him going the other way, eyes wide open, panic etched on his face. 'IT'S ALL BURNING!' he shouted almost into Audun's ear. A young, shifty and rat-faced man followed him, face set in a grimace. Audun shouldered past them and kept pushing, trying to inch and squirm closer to the gateway. The gate loomed, blocked by a throng of men pushing and scrabbling to get out of Stenvik and down to the seaside. Gawkers, he thought. It was all entertainment to them until proven otherwise.

But if it broke, it had to be fixed. And if he got there first, he'd have a shot at doing it. That was the reason he gave himself for shoving harder, pushing more, receiving shouts and cries for his trouble. They did move out of the way though, he noticed with a twinge of satisfaction.

Inch by inch he pushed closer to the south gateway.

The stone tunnel was rammed full of people, pushing and shoving to get to the harbour. A surge of panic made Audun's blood rise. This was not a good place to be. An animal urge drove him past the people in front of him and he gulped down the cool night air on the other side, allowing the stream of people to carry him down the road to the old town and into the square by the harbour.

The scene before him was mesmerizing.

The flames merged with the moon rays to cast a flickering, dancing, orange light onto the square by the harbour. Skittish shadows weaved this way and that as the flames licked masts, tore at sails and bit into deck timbers. A suddenly quiet half-circle had formed at a respectful distance from the burning ships. Audun broke through the wall of milling people and stormed down to the harbour, eyes trained on the three ships burning brightly in the harbour. Waves of heat washed over him. Undaunted, he sprinted to the far right, where the flames rose highest.

The stream of villagers through the south gateway had become a trickle. Shouts and cries could be heard past the gates, but they sounded muted and far away.

Ragnar raised a clenched fist and signalled for a halt. He looked up, to the north gate then to the east, and veered to the right. Two more turns and they'd reach their destination.

As the knarr bobbed on the waves, unable to dislodge the crackling, spitting beast that gnawed at its innards, Audun's eyes whipped round. The fire could jump across to the next boat at any moment, and from there . . .

Think!

There it was. A huge whetstone sat by a metalworker's hut. Audun strode to it and took a deep breath. He bent his knees and took the time to test for the right grip. When he found it he strained, willing his muscles to cooperate. Somewhere within him a spark ignited, lighting an old fire. He growled and rose slowly, painfully, and the stone rose with him. Determined steps took him back towards the pier.

Ulfar felt it in the pit of his stomach the moment he rounded the corner.

Something was not as it should be.

The guard was nowhere in sight. Instead there were two men huddled around the well, looking down. One of them, an unpleasant-looking man with longish, greasy hair, hoisted a sack up onto the edge. The old, wiry one was busy untying a small cloth bag from his belt.

Ulfar looked around. There was nobody near him. Even the walls seemed empty. Slowly the situation became clear.

Everyone was down by the harbour.

Ulfar took a deep breath and shouted as loud as he could, 'THE WELL! ALL TO THE WELL!' The old, grey-haired man whirled around, grabbed a fist-sized stone off the ground and hurled it at Ulfar. Pain exploded in his head and his knees buckled. Try as he might, he could not remain upright. Sinking to the ground he saw the grey-haired man approach him, kneel and draw a short skinning knife. Ulfar blinked as a ghost-like form emerged sneering behind the grey-hair, steel glinting in the moonlight. The surprise on the old man's face as the dagger punched into his back matched Ulfar's.

He saw the old man go down, saw the long-haired, rat-faced devil grinning behind him. The long-haired warrior dragged the older man over to the well, shifted him quickly and grabbed his ankle. The knife flashed again, this time near the old man's heel. In one forceful motion, long-hair sliced through the tendon.

'You know what, Ragnar – I think they will catch you,' he sneered. 'Unless you can fly. Skuld sends her regards. You will no longer poison the minds of her warriors.' The long-haired man turned and disappeared into the night.

Ulfar's head felt like it was about to crack. Stars sparkled in his eyes and his skull pounded.

He passed out.

The whetstone punched through the hull with a loud crack. Water bubbled up and met burning wood, hissing and steaming. Audun was already on his way to the far end.

'Sink the ships!' he screamed at the top of his lungs. 'Sink them! Or they'll all burn!'

Sven came running out of the crowd and towards Audun. 'Right, son,' he said, eyes gleaming in the reflected firelight. 'You don't have any more big stones and we won't get her out to sea. We're going for a dip. You're front, I'll go back.' Audun wanted to ask him what he meant, but Sven was already on his way. Moving with surprising speed he leapt from the harbour to the back of the burning ship, finding a foothold on the slippery boards with ease and grabbing the graceful curves of the rising stern. 'Come on! I'm not getting any younger!' he hollered cheerfully at Audun.

Realizing what Sven was asking for, Audun raced down the pier, past the burning midsection of the ship, and searched for the right place to jump. She was rocking gently on the waves now. Sven had found a foothold facing away from the pier and started to tug rhythmically at the stern, throwing his body weight back and forth to gain momentum.

Sweating from the heat, Audun leapt onto the prow, crashing into the planks with little of the old warrior's grace.

'Cows on ice stand better than that!' Sven shouted. A flush of anger propelled Audun into place and he locked eyes with Sven.

As one, they started rocking back.

The broad, shallow hull of the longship pitched to the side but the weight of the ship righted it again, sending the keel smashing into the water. The impact jarred through Audun's arms and up into his teeth. Sparks flew, fizzed and spat when they hit the water.

Again, they rocked. This time the gunwale lay flush with the water. Audun pulled for all he was worth, hanging off the prow. Water started seeping into the boat. 'That's the way, boy!' He was sure he could hear Sven cackling.

The weight transferred, but the ship had already taken on water that sloshed with them, hissing when it met the flaming mast. The roll was powerful, almost tipping the ship over and into the jetty. He concentrated on finding footholds on the prow, inching higher up to create more counterweight.

The ship tipped over again towards them, and he launched himself, hanging off the prow.

The ice-cold water grabbed at his ankles, his calves, knees and thighs, the shock almost costing his hold.

For a heart-stopping moment the ship rested on its side, keel showing for the whole world to see, mast horizontal with the water – and then it tipped.

Steam erupted as the burning mast was plunged into the water.

Pushing off, Audun swam clear of the capsized ship and towards the harbour.

'Well done, son. Well done.' Sven's bearded face and calloused hand appeared from the pier above, helping him up. Breathing hard, Audun clambered up and stood there, wet and shivering. When he glanced at Sven, the old man didn't seem to have landed in the water at all. He blinked, shook himself to clear his head, and focused on the task at hand. The *Westerdrake*. The big ship that they moored at the central pier was by far the largest one, and while the fire had started slowly it was locked in by now. A smell of burning thatch, heated metal and blackened wood rose to meet him. The sail billowed in the hot air. His first step towards the last ship was met with a coarse, pained scream.

'NOOO!'

People scattered as Harald cannoned through the throng, yelling at the top of his voice. Sprinting towards the pier, he pulled off his shirt as he jumped onto the *Westerdrake*, thrashing about, beating at the flames. Momentarily stunned, Audun could do nothing but watch as yellow tongues of fire licked at Harald, singeing his hair, blistering his skin. He was jolted into action as the crazed man on the boat shot him a murderous look. 'Help me, you useless bastard! Get water!'

But it was too late for that. Fire had eaten its way into the mast, bitten into the yard, spread over the sails. 'Harald! We will have to sink it!' Sven shouted from the pier.

'NO! NO!' Harald screamed, cried, roared in rage. 'THIS IS THE *WESTERDRAKE*! BEARER OF ODIN'S WARRIORS! IT DOES NOT DIE!'

A shadow appeared on the pier, walked briskly past Sven and Audun and stepped onto the *Westerdrake*, into the flames.

Sigurd.


Valgard ran towards his house. He'd need more willow bark for pain and chickweed poultice for burns. Most of all he'd need water.

His bucket was empty.

Hut. There would be water in the hut. He could fill up the patients' bucket later.

No water in the hut. No friend with the foreigner either. Strange.

A filled skin from the well would have to do.

Walking the path he'd walked countless times before, Valgard only noticed the foreigner just before he trod on him.

Sigurd stepped towards Harald and put a hand on his shoulder. Audun could not hear what was said but the big sea captain's head whipped round, face feral and snarling. He smacked Sigurd's hand away, screamed 'NO!' and turned back to the fires.

Sigurd's hand came down hard on Harald's shoulder and yanked him around. Contorted with rage and grief, the bare-chested captain's face looked inhuman. He turned on Sigurd, grabbed a burning oar and swung, screaming.

Two steps and Sigurd was out of harm's way. Flickering fire lit his face, snapping and crackling drowned his voice. Behind his back he made a chopping motion. Audun did not understand until he heard the thwack of knife meeting wood. Sven had cut the moorings with a wicked curving blade. The fire danced up the halyards, sparks kissing the sky in a dozen places. Resembling a child's drawing in yellow on black, the ship soon responded to the gentle tug of the tide and started floating out of the harbour.

Flailing madly, Harald went after Sigurd with a vengeance. 'YOU OLD BASTARD! HOW DARE YOU?' he screamed. The burning oar drew flaming lines in the night sky, but Sigurd seemed to join with the shadows, always shifting, never in one place long enough for the blow to connect.

As the *Westerdrake* cleared the jetty Sigurd made his move. When Harald swung the oar, this time he ducked down instead of moving back. Then he launched himself at the big man, landing a series of fierce and fast blows to the jaw and stomach, then a vicious head butt that knocked Harald out.

'Had to happen sooner or later,' Sven muttered mirthlessly behind Audun. 'We were lucky on that one.'

Onboard the *Westerdrake*, Sigurd was lugging the unconscious Harald towards the gunwale. He rolled the hulking raider overboard and jumped after him.

Sputtering and coughing, Harald came up for air. Sigurd was already halfway to the harbour. Audun watched as the captain swam after the chieftain, powerful strokes propelling him through the water.

'Time to move, son,' Sven said at his back. 'Things could get ugly still.'

Sigurd emerged at the end of the pier, grey hair plastered to his head. Streaks of soot lined his face and he looked like something out of a tale to scare children. He locked eyes with Sven. Audun looked back and forth as something passed wordlessly between the two men. Then Sven flicked his wrist and the knife flew gracefully at Sigurd, spinning blade over hilt. The chieftain snatched it out of the air and turned to the sea. Arms relaxed at his sides, he suddenly looked less like an old man and more like a mountain cat about to pounce. The knife formed a natural claw extending from his right hand. A chill passed through Audun.

'Killing time,' Sven muttered.

Harald clambered up onto the end of the pier.

His upper body was covered in burns. Large, red patches of skin, bleeding scars, angry red welts where sparks had landed. Long reddish hair lay slick against his bull neck and square shoulders.

Sigurd's voice was hard and clear. 'Harald, son of Jormund. You've challenged me, and it's—'

'Do it. Do it now.' Harald knelt and bowed his head.

Sigurd stood for a long while, immovable.

'Do it.' There was no hate in Harald's voice. No anger. Just tired resignation.

Finally, Sigurd spoke. 'We have sailed together, Harald. Fought together. I saved your life amongst the Danes; you pulled me out of the fires in Jorvik. We are brothers of the edge. I will not gut you here and now like a sodden dog if you show me that I can trust you.' The flames from the burning *Westerdrake* outlined Harald's back, framing his shoulders and head in flickering light. The man looked broken, Audun thought.

'Swear.' There was menace in Sigurd's voice, and Audun suspected the threat had not been empty. He could sense Sven tensing behind him, inching forward.

Harald shifted imperceptibly.

'Swear, Harald. Swear your loyalty to me and to the town.'

A pause, and then Harald spoke. 'By Odin the all-father, I swear. I serve Stenvik, I serve you.'

Sigurd relaxed. 'Rise and look me in the eye.'

Harald rose and Audun caught his breath. The big sea captain's face was ashen and streaked with tears. He looked like a shell of a man, like someone who had aged by ten years overnight.

Sven broke the silence, his voice gentle. 'I've lost a ship too. But ships can be built. It takes longer to train a captain. Especially a vicious bastard like yourself.' A flicker of a smile crossed Harald's face. 'But now we've made sure we still have ships, we need to address the other matter.'

'What other matter?' Harald mumbled.

'Whoever did this also propped up a nidpole in the square.' Harald stared dully at Sven. 'There were three lines carved on the horse's neck.'

Life flashed back into Harald's eyes.

'Oh shit.'

*

139

Ragnar was warm and tired. Something was wrong with his lungs. They rattled and there was something wet in them. It wasn't so bad, though. He could just take a nap here, just rest a bit in the warmth, and then he could get going. He'd done what he was supposed to do, exactly like she'd told him. And then Oraekja had attacked him from behind. Stabbed him like a coward. He blinked, confused. It didn't make any sense. He'd done it. He'd walked into the enemy camp, set fire to their ships, poisoned their water and made them run around like headless chickens.

His leg hurt.

He'd felt the tendon snapping back up into the calf when Oraekja cut it and now there was a hole in his leg somewhere, something missing that was supposed to be there. So now he couldn't stand properly. He'd managed to crawl away from the well, towards the northern gateway. He had to get out of here. They'd be very angry when they found out.

So tired.

The muscles in his back wouldn't move, wouldn't help him get up. So he'd just have to lie down here, catch his breath and wait for Skargrim to come. Wait for big brother to rescue him, like he'd always done. He'd never hear the end of this. Fooled by a rat-faced coward.

Ragnar smiled and closed his eyes.


The fires onboard the *Westerdrake* flickered in the distance. The harbour square was once again draped in the moon's silvery rays. Torches mounted on house corners created circles of warm light.

The nidpole stood in the middle of the square, the horse's head gaping towards the town walls. Drops of blood had spattered onto the stones beneath it, coloured the rim of the hole and stained the wood reddish-brown.

Word had spread quickly.

Nearly every man in Stenvik was gathered around the pole. The square was packed with people, but none of them stepped within three strides of the horse's head. Muttered superstitions and fearful whispers swirled, and even the most hardened of warriors scanned the surroundings, ill at ease. Sigurd elbowed his way through the crowd and stepped into the circle around the pole, followed by Sven and Harald. Their faces seemed carved in stone as they looked at the crowd, daring any man to talk in their presence. Slowly the people in the square fell silent. Sigurd turned to the pole and unwrapped the scroll tied to it, reading out loud.

> *'Shame shall be called*
> *Upon the land-spirits*
> *who formed the earth*
> *where Stenvik lies*
> *That they may wander*
> *Never to rest,*
> *Until Stenvik is turned*
> *To ash and ruin.'*

The silence lasted for a couple of breaths, and then nervous chatter erupted.

The three men in the circle simply waited as the talk died down and worried faces turned to Sigurd. When he spoke, it was almost conversationally.

'Fear.'

His voice carried all over the square.

'That is what this is. That is what this is meant to make you feel.' He rested his hand, almost absent-mindedly, on the pole. A smattering of gasps could be heard.

'Fear.'

A nervous merchant made to speak. 'But Sig—'

'FEAR.' His voice rang out loud and clear. 'Fear of the strange, fear of the unknown. Fear of the dark. Fear that Loki himself came down here and raised the pole to call us out, strip us of honour and cast us down, tell us that we should cower in the dark like rats for committing some unnameable wrong.' His voice grew louder and the grip on the pole grew tighter. 'But if it was Loki, he might have done well to ask where he'd landed. Because this is Stenvik! And I, Sigurd son of Aegir, have fought with most all of you, your fathers and your sons. And I would gladly face the God of Tricks – and tell him that the men of Stenvik' – Sigurd's hand closed on the pole, knuckles whitening. He strained, the pole moved.

'. . . do . . .' Another pull and the pole inched up.

'. . . NOT . . .' The horse's head swayed.

'. . . FEAR!'

With a mighty effort Sigurd tore the nidpole free with one hand and raised it straight up, balancing the horse's head on top.

In the square, hardened raiders, merchants and craftsmen roared as one.

'STENVIK!'

Standing behind the three leaders, Audun looked at the townsfolk. A frightened, apprehensive mob had turned into a fierce, tough, angry army, ready for anything. Sigurd had won them over.

Only one face lacked the fire and the fury.

Valgard was pushing his way through the crowd, heading towards the three men in the middle.

'Silence!' Harald's voice cut through the noise of the crowd. 'We will double the guard on the walls. Tomorrow's morning watch joins night watch tonight. Keep weapons close to your beds. Stay cold and focused. We will meet again at first light. Raiders of the *Westerdrake*, to me!'

The crowd dispersed slowly as it became apparent that there would be no immediate confrontation. Fighters with their blood up returned reluctantly to their sleeping quarters, while Harald's crew gathered around him.

Valgard slipped through gaps and between bodies. He appeared at Sven's side and whispered in his ear. A frightening calm settled on the old man's face. 'Bring him,' he said to Valgard and nodded towards the town. Then he laid a hand on Sigurd's arm.

'Longhouse. You need to hear this.'

Sigurd sat in the high chair on the dais and stared into space, a thoughtful frown carved deep into his face.

Gathered around the table in the longhouse, the raiders of the *Westerdrake* looked like a pack of barely tamed wolfhounds. Torch-light turned weather-beaten faces into the masks of snarling demons. Above them Harald glowered in his high-backed seat on Sigurd's right-hand side. Someone was going to pay. Someone was going to pay hard.

'So now we know,' Sigurd said finally. 'Skargrim is on his way. They've set fire to our ships' – Harald's lip curled in a menacing sneer – 'raised a nidpole in our square . . . and while everyone was running down to the harbour, they poisoned the well.'

The assembled raiders exchanged grim looks. A poisoned well meant a full assault. It also meant no prisoners.

'They dumped horse guts in it.'

Bjorn, a solidly built blonde raider with a nasty scar on his left cheek, snorted. 'Horse guts? The water will taste like shit, but that won't kill anyone.'

Sigurd smiled.

From the shadows by the doorway, Valgard spoke. 'So we'd fish up the horse guts, count our blessings and happily drink water with a bagful of crushed foxbell leaves.'

He stepped into torchlight and a stony silence, guiding Ulfar with him.

'Tell us what you saw.'

Ulfar described the two men.

'Where are they now?' Sigurd snapped.

'I saw the long-haired one leave,' Ulfar replied. 'Not sure where the old one got to. He wasn't there when Valgard brought me back.'

'Thorvald . . .' Sigurd turned to the empty chair. 'THORVALD! Where is—' Thorvald burst through the doorway and ran up to the dais.

'Sigmar and the boys are back. They found something,' he said quickly, words tumbling out.

'Skargrim's boys? I hadn't even asked you yet,' Sigurd replied.

Thorvald stopped in his tracks. '. . . That's not what they found. Not at all.'

Sigurd sized up his scout master. After a silence that seemed to stretch for an eternity he said quietly: 'So that's not it. Tell me what you know.'

Thorvald looked wary.

'If Skargrim is also on the move, I do not think you will like this.' All eyes were on the dais, willing Thorvald to speak. 'Every man, woman and child at Gard has been butchered. There were all manner of tracks.'

'Tracks? Tracks of what?' Sigurd interrupted.

'Men. Lots of them,' Thorvald said. From the shadows, Ulfar watched the tall, slim man fidget nervously. 'You know me,

Sigurd,' he continued. 'I've never told an old wives' tale in my life. And Sigmar is the same. But this . . . this is different. He said the bodies had been . . .' The scout master blinked rapidly.

'Thorvald!' Sigurd banged his fist down on the chair arm. 'Get it out!'

Thorvald recoiled as if he'd been slapped. He shook his head and took a deep breath. 'Here's what Sigmar told me. What tracks they could see by moonlight led to the farmstead. Two sets followed by any number of them. Badly mutilated bodies. Sword wounds, broken skulls, split stomachs. Arms, legs hacked off. Fire taken to houses. Someone had taken a chunk out of some of the people.'

'Carrion?' Sigurd interrupted.

'No. The fires were still burning and there were neither crows nor bite marks. Some of them had been . . . carved. Like mutton.'

Sigurd stared at Thorvald.

'So what was it? Who did this?'

'Sigmar doesn't know. But whoever it was had nearly a good hundred men with them. Maybe more.'

Sigurd slumped back into his chair. 'So in the same bloody night I get Skargrim *and* bloody roving outlaws in the woods?'

Ulfar leaned towards Valgard. 'Why is he so angry? Is this a new problem?' he whispered.

Without so much as glancing to the side, Valgard whispered back: 'There's a handful of desperate men out thieving every now and then, but never this many. Gard is a big farm with over twenty hands and would not be troubled by a normal gang of outlaws. I've been saying for a while that we should have gone to look, but nobody listened. Now it seems there's enough of them to cause trouble, and that they're heading this way. Why they're banding together all of a sudden is anyone's guess.'

Valgard's eyes were glued to the dais, where an argument seemed to be taking place.

'No, Harald,' Sven was saying from his place by Sigurd's shoulder. 'That's rash, angry and not practical. We have events, but we don't really have information of any value yet. We have to find out where and what before we can do anything. We can't go out into the woods chasing shadows.'

Harald sneered, but kept quiet.

At the long table, the raiders of the *Westerdrake* seemed to pick up on the mood of their captain. Eyes narrowed, lips curled. Several of the men muttered among themselves. Ulfar glanced at Valgard. The thin man seemed miles away, a grin forming on his lips.

'It is such a shame that our leaders are unable to work together,' the healer muttered.

'It is,' Ulfar replied at his side.

The grin turned into a nervous smile as the healer became aware of being watched.

'They're fine really,' Valgard blurted out, turning to face Ulfar. 'I mean, they are the best leaders we could hope for. They just bicker.' The left side of his face began to twitch. Valgard's eyes closed and beads of sweat broke out on his forehead. 'No. No. No,' he hissed between clenched teeth. His eyes flew open and his breath grew more laboured as he started shaking.

Without thinking, Ulfar reached for the man's shoulder to steady him. Like an adder Valgard's right hand went for Ulfar's and seized it in a vice-like grip. He could only watch as the thin man seized up, fingers digging into his forearm, unblinking eyes glaring impossibly wide. Spasms racked the thin, reedy frame. Grimaces of pain etched on the healer's pale, drawn face. He stopped breathing.

And then, just as suddenly as it had taken hold, whatever had seized Valgard released him again. He breathed out slowly and looked at his hand, clamped on Ulfar's wrist. Comprehension seemed to dawn and he loosened his grip, stared down at his hand as if it was foreign to him.

'Are you . . . are you well?' Ulfar ventured cautiously. Valgard looked up at him and Ulfar caught his breath. For a fleeting moment hatred flashed in the red-rimmed, moist eyes of the pale, thin man. Pure, venomous, murderous hatred.

Then gratitude slid over Valgard's face like a well-worn mask, and the healer looked wearily back at him. 'Well . . . I have never been particularly well. But I am not dying.' He affected a smile. 'Thank you, my friend. Your care is most . . . touching.' Suddenly the air in the longhouse felt stifling.

'I owe you my life,' Ulfar said hastily. 'And it seems to me that in these times we should really care for each other.'

Valgard smiled at him. 'Absolutely, my friend. Take care of each other. Absolutely.' The smile did not reach his eyes.

Harald barged past without any regard to obstacles in his path. 'Fucking greybeards,' he swore under his breath as he passed Ulfar and stalked out into the night.

Oraekja swallowed hard and tried to squeeze himself deeper into the shadows. Those bastard scouts had been sniffing about town all night and it had taken all his guile to evade them. He wasn't a coward – he'd take them all on – but she'd asked him to come back, so he would. He had to.

A warm feeling spread through him when he thought of her lips, her eyes, her curves.

He'd heard the cries when they found Ragnar's body. The old bastard had actually almost managed to crawl away on one good leg, but they'd caught him. Just as he said they would.

It hadn't seemed all that right to him once the fury had faded away, but she'd explicitly said Ragnar would have to die. She'd also told him what he'd have to say to Skargrim when he came back.

If he came back.

He just needed to find . . . there. Three farmers loading an ox-cart. There'd been people streaming out since they saw the pole. They knew all too well what it meant, and Skargrim's name had already been bandied about. The people of Stenvik seemed to have the proper respect for Old Grey-hair. Oraekja decided he'd remember to tell her that. Now, however, he had to leave, and these men would be his disguise. He scanned the area from the cover of the shadows. When he was certain as he could be, he walked calmly around the hut he'd been hiding behind.

They looked at him with dull suspicion. 'What do you want?'

Oraekja put on his most charming smile. 'Me?' No response. 'I just want to get out of this stinking place, to be honest, and I wouldn't mind doing so with some company.'

None of them invited him, but the man nearest to the cart relaxed his stance a little. Oraekja did not wait for permission. He stepped to a sack of hay and hauled it up onto the cart floor. A few moments later the three men around him started again, working in sullen silence under the last twinkling stars of the night sky.

## WYRMSEY

Skargrim could smell the fresh resin on the newly felled logs. Valhalla rose before him, impossibly huge. The walls were made of majestic timbers, latched together to make a hall fit for heroes. He looked round the clearing. Around him the fir trees stood tall, lords of the forest, the treeline dark and menacing. Nature was strong here. The air crackled with raw power, the power of the old gods.

A crack and a creak behind him, and the doors swung open. Towering slabs of iron-bound wood moved as if mounted on air.

He turned.

A wave of light, sound and smell spilled out. The lusty roars of drinking men, roast meat that made his mouth water, flames from giant cooking fires. The hall was bigger than any he had ever seen. Golden light reflected in polished shield bosses, gilded spear points and goblets of finest bronze. Rows of fighters, all merrily in their cups, singing and roaring along. A dais stood at the far end, almost covered in the gloom. On it he thought he could see a tall, grey-clad figure watching from the shadows, face hidden by the brim of his hat.

The chant rang out into the starry night.

'We fight for the glory of Odin, of Odin!'

The sound of it filled his head, pumped in his veins. Soon he found himself mouthing along.

We fight for the glory of Odin.

Before he knew, his feet had taken steps toward the door. Honour, pride and joy coursed through Skargrim.

We fight for the glory of Odin.

With grim satisfaction, he noted that some of the men were sizing him up. There would be a reckoning later. In fact, there was someone that looked like Hedin the Unruly from up north, scowling at him. Big guy, braided beard, hammer at his side. Hovering behind was that dog-faced helper of his, all skin and bones and dark hair. The kind that always has a knife handy.

We fight for the glory of Odin, of Odin.

He remembered the swell of the ocean, the ships tied together

149

to create a makeshift fighting platform, the feel of his axe going through Hedin's collarbone. How his followers had scattered. That had been a good day.

We fight for the glory.

The colours, sounds and smells bled into one for Skargrim. All that was left was the thrumming pulse in his blood, the chant, the pride. The knowledge of who he was, what he was and why he was.

A beatific smile spread on the sleeping raider's form.

Skuld looked down on him, smiled back and continued her walk through the camps, past and over the rows of sleeping men. Under her breath she muttered over and over words that hadn't been heard in the world for a long time.

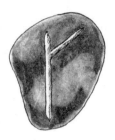

### NORTH-EAST OF STENVIK

The blood-red rays of the dawn sun broke through the darkness and shone on the hills, the stray firs and the forest down below.

'L-l-look,' Runar whispered, laying flat against the ridge, adjusting the recurve bow on his back.

Jorn peered down into the trees. 'I see nothing. You've stolen my sleep and wasted my time, you idiot. We're still far away from Stenvik,' he growled, and made to rise.

Runar grabbed the young prince by the collar and hauled him back to the ground. Struggling to get the words out, eventually he stuttered: 'St-st-st-st-stay d-down and l-lll-lllook *better!*'

Furrowing his brow, Jorn turned his eyes back to the treeline. As he adjusted to the gloom, he could detect movement. After a while he looked over at Runar, who nodded excitedly.

'Th-th-th-they're—' he began, but now it was Jorn's turn to signal for quiet.

'Noise carries, Runar,' he whispered, without taking his eyes off the forest. 'They look to be about four hundred yards away, but I really don't want to start the day with a foot race.'

Runar grinned, eyes beaming.

Jorn trained his eyes on the treeline. Indistinct figures were slowly emerging from the forest. They wore rags, carried a variety of weapons and moved with purpose. Fleet-footed hunters armed with bows set up a perimeter.

'Th-th-th—' Runar whispered, gritted his teeth in fury and gestured for Jorn to look at him. With exaggerated movements he sniffed and looked around.

'You mean they're—' Jorn's heart leapt. Quickly he checked. Through some blind luck, he and Runar were downwind.

His heart started beating again.

Suddenly the group seemed to focus on the treeline. Even the guards on the perimeter gazed into the shadows. Two big, burly men appeared, dragging a struggling, wailing farmer. Behind them a man walked calmly. He had his hair tied up in a ponytail. The farmer cried for help. Runar stirred beside him but Jorn put a hand on the young man's arm. 'No. There's at least thirty of them down there and more are coming.'

The small procession had now reached the edge of the forest and set about tying their captive to a tree. A scream of pain bounced off the hillside as arms were bent backward and lashed together behind the tree trunk. More of the scruffy forest people kept emerging from the woods.

'They just keep on coming,' Jorn muttered to himself. 'There must be at least a hundred and twenty of them.'

'A hundred and f-f-forty-three,' Runar spluttered.

Jorn smiled and nodded. 'Thank you,' he said.

'N-no problem.'

The leader had taken up a position directly in front of the captive. He seemed to be speaking but Jorn could not discern the words. The farmer shook his head repeatedly. The pony-tailed man stepped closer to the captive. A flash of metal, a cheer from the crowds and the farmer's tunic fell away.

A deep feeling of unease crept over Jorn. He looked across at Runar, who seemed to feel the same.

'Th-this is not good, is it?'

'No.'

The poor farmer was thrashing on the tree now, straining against his bonds. The voice of the leader grew louder. The numbers in his circle swelled.

'T-t-two hundred and twelve now,' Runar added.

The leader was shouting single words now. As one, his followers echoed. Jorn felt the dread in the pit of his stomach but he found he could not look away.

Suddenly the leader plunged a knife into the victim's shoulder. The screams of pain mingled with the shouts of the gathered men and dragged on as the knife moved from shoulder down to rib, towards the sternum and up to the shoulder again. With a flick of the knife the pony-tailed man carved a piece of flesh out of the farmer's chest and tossed it back to the two big men standing behind him. Red flowed down the front of the howling, weeping farmer. The knife dug in again and soon another piece of flesh came flying over his shoulder. A faint, metallic smell of blood drifted up towards Jorn and Runar.

As the farmer's body slumped against the tree, the man with the ponytail turned to address the group. Jorn strained to hear but as much as he tried he could only discern one word.

Stenvik.

Sweating despite the cool morning air, Jorn and Runar stole away as quietly as they could.


### WYRMSEY

'. . . for the glory . . .'

Another man from Ingi's camp passed him, composed and quiet.

'We fight . . .'

All around him, men were moving with determination towards the beach, towards their ships, ready for the assault.

Tall, broad-chested Thrainn's men.

Hrafn's sealskin-clad warriors.

Ingi's army, silent and well-drilled.

All of them wearing the same, glazed look.

All of them muttering the same chant under their breaths.

Skargrim's heart thumped in his chest.

Out on the bay, Egill Jotunn's five black ships already waited, tacked and ready.

Skargrim glanced up at the rock he had used as his vantage point.

The morning sun cast its rays on Skuld's back. Her silhouette looked . . . older.

He could not see her face, but he felt her smile.

## JUST OUTSIDE STENVIK

Oraekja had kept close to the side of the cart as it inched through the eastern gateway. Nobody had asked any questions. He had guessed correctly – they'd found Ragnar by now and were looking for one man, not four traders with an old, creaky cart. The guards had just wanted rid of anyone who wasn't going to stay and fight. Clear of Stenvik, Oraekja allowed himself to turn around and look.

Bathed in the rays of the morning sun, the walls around the town looked massive and impenetrable. Huge grass slopes up to the fortified walkway, too steep to charge. No way of getting to the top of the wall, which was manned by a score of spear-carriers. They'd have a lot of supplies in there, too.

Not so much water, he thought with a grin.

Still, he couldn't see how Skargrim's crew would manage this. Maybe she could. If so, then he'd know soon enough. Skuld would share her plans with him so he could offer suggestions and improvements.

He smiled.

It would be good to see Skargrim's face when he, Oraekja, gave the orders. Now all he needed to do was get to the forest, give these oafs the slip and find a nice hiding place overlooking the beach where Skargrim said he'd land. They drew closer to the treeline, in the middle of a modest caravan. Forty yards now. He wondered what Skuld would be like naked, whether she'd hold him tenderly and gaze deep into his eyes or go wild, screaming and bucking. Maybe both if he did it right. A smirk crept across his pockmarked face. Thirty yards. Thirty yards and he could break free of these plodding farmers, circle Stenvik on the north side under cover of the forest and emerge by Muninsfjell. And then – back to her. Twenty yards. The road snaked in amongst the trees, dipping out of sight. The first cart disappeared around the bend. Fifteen yards. Ten.

The wrist-thick spear hurtled silently out of the shadow of a cluster of trees and took their old ox just below its head, breaking its neck on impact. A blood-curdling yell from a hundred throats followed, and as the animal hit the ground a swarm of men in rags burst out of the forest, charging the caravan at a dead run.

Oraekja realized that his life was now measured in moments. He scanned the faces of his fellow travellers.

Wide-eyed panic.

Dismissed.

Cattle.

Going back was not an option.

Neither was sideways.

155

Oraekja filled his lungs with air, summoned up all the hardest bastards he could ever remember giving orders at sea, and screamed at the top of his voice:

'RUN! BACK TO STENVIK! RUN!'


## STENVIK

Just one.

Just one of them.

Harald clutched the leather bottle so hard that he thought the veins in the back of his hand would pop.

Please.

Let just one of them give him a reason to smash their face in. He rocked slowly back and forth on his bed, jolted awake by a dream he couldn't remember, no matter how hard he tried. Somewhere in his head he was vaguely aware of the empty place where Lilia was supposed to be.

It didn't matter.

Nothing did.

His mind didn't sit right. There was too much going on. He'd tried to sleep after the night meeting in the longhouse, but had found no peace. The move on the two pig-fuckers was small consolation. They'd drown screaming, but the *Westerdrake* still sailed to its doom before his eyes, a burning skeleton ship. In his mind Sven told him off, humiliated him in front of his men. Even Valgard snapped at him – and how dare he? Should have broken that weakling's neck on the spot. The feel of the leather in his palm reminded him why he hadn't.

Without thinking, Harald raised the leather bottle, licking his lips in anticipation. The mixture oozed out slowly. As it touched his lips vivid colours, shapes and scents seemed to blossom from the inside of his mouth, from the bitter-sweet taste of it, spreading warmth through his body like a fire in a cold house.

His eyes closed. Another world opened up.

He was inside a longhouse, finer than he'd ever seen. The echoes of a thousand men, shouting and singing drinking songs.

Three people sat by the end of the long table.

A mountainous, muscle-bound, red-haired warrior, hair and beard braided in fine lines, hammer at his side. A woman unlike any he'd ever seen, her every curve a whispered challenge to his manhood, daring him to resist her. Blonde hair cascaded down to her ample chest, curls falling over curls, adding curves and more curves. Her simple white shift nearly hid and nearly showed, and Harald found it hard to keep his imagination in check.

It was only the third one that gave him pause. His eyes watered as he tried to get a good look at him. The slim, dark-haired man seemed to slip into and out of shadow, never quite . . . there. The wiry form reminded Harald of a killing knife. Fresh, sharp and just waiting to do some damage.

They all looked straight at him. Into him. Through him.

He wanted to speak, but no words came out. Instead the colours in the hall started to fade. He heard the faint echo of a chant, but caught only three words.

'For the glory.'

He couldn't be sure, but as the image in his head disappeared, Harald thought the woman might have winked.

A powerful sense of loss tore through him and he opened his eyes again. A single room, pot in the far corner, double bed. Spikes in the wooden wall, clothes hanging on them. A chest for valuables, baubles he'd brought back to her in moments of softness. Sword, axe, shield, spear. Tools. His home.

None of this registered.

In his head the people from the dream still looked into his soul.

Thor. Freya. Loki.

Ulfar sat in the corner of the patients' hut, too tired to move. 'Well, you're not moving much either so you can't argue,' he said wearily to Geiri's still, silent form. He could hear the sound of Stenvik through the walls, but there was a different quality to it, a current of tension and fear.

The incident by the well had taken more out of him than he'd care to admit. His head still pounded and the image of the old, grey raider with the skinning knife still lingered.

Ulfar shuddered as he remembered the night before and the hatred in Valgard's eyes. There was something about the healer. Something that wasn't right. Before he could think more about it he felt his skin tingle and his heartbeat quicken. Then the door flap moved. Daylight spilled in and hit his eyes, blinding him. Someone moved into the doorway and blocked out the light from the entrance.

'. . . Ulfar?' The voice was soft, searching.

In his mind the walls of the hut fell away. Nothing mattered but him and her, Lilia, stepping from the outside into his little world. She was just a silhouette in the blinding daylight. On reflex, he brought his hand up to shield his eyes.

'Oh – forgive me.' She stepped nimbly inside and drew the door flap shut.

A sudden, embarrassed silence filled the room.

Heart thumping, Ulfar looked at her. He almost laughed when he realized that moments ago, he'd been reflecting on moments of life or death – and now he was wondering whether his hair looked all right.

But then this was also a matter of life and death. He wanted to spend his life with her, and he'd die if he couldn't. He would never touch another woman. The certainty of the realization struck him hard, and he looked at her almost in a daze.

Soft red curls framed her delicate features. She looked away and chewed her lip nervously. 'Is . . . is this your friend?' She moved to the middle of the hut and knelt over Geiri.

'Yes,' Ulfar half-whispered, breath caught in his throat as he followed her. 'Yes,' he repeated, regaining control of his voice and cursing himself. 'He had a nasty fall. Hit his head. He should be all right, we hope. Valgard says he should be fine.'

'How did it happen?'

'There was a fight in the old longhouse. This man called Harald and two others beat that man over there' – Ulfar pointed to the big pig farmer, snoring softly in the corner – 'pretty bad. His cousins then went after the two others in the old longhouse and Geiri got caught in the middle.'

Lilia went very still.

'So this all traces back to Harald, does it?' Her voice was leaden.

'I don't know. Yes, maybe so. When Geiri comes to, we might ask for damages, but I don't know. He got caught in the middle of something that this man Harald started.' Ulfar looked at her, trying to figure out what she was thinking. 'Why? Do you know . . . ?' Ulfar's voice trailed off.

Their eyes met and her smile broke his heart.

For the first time he could see the pain, the suffering. The lines and contours in her face, scars that belonged to someone a lot older.

He saw the stone woman.

She raised her hand slowly, gently. Without breaking eye contact she placed it on a bruise on his cheekbone.

Her touch felt searing hot on his skin. He winced and smiled, never looking away from her eyes. Words came to him and stopped short of emerging for fear of breaking the spell.

He watched a single teardrop run down her cheek, moving in synchrony with her hand on his face, meeting and merging with her smile, the smile that came from the whole of her.

Ulfar remembered to breathe, and a half-giggle escaped his lips. Her eyes twinkled like stars, like diamonds through the tears, and soon they were giggling incredulously at each other, blinking, crying, smiling, still touching.

A woman's whispered voice at the doorway. Urgency and fear. 'Lilia! We have to go!'

She recoiled from him, suddenly like a trapped animal, frantically searching the corners of the hut, peering into the shadows.

He reached for her arm and found her eyes. 'Sshh . . .' he whispered. The urge to soothe her, to protect her, was so powerful that he had to hold his breath to keep from fainting.

But he got through.

She blinked rapidly and seemed to come back into the room. As she saw him, saw his hand on her arm and the look in his eyes, her features softened and another tear escaped. She made to speak, then stopped herself and hurried to the door. In the doorway she cast a lingering glance at him, looking up at her.

Then she was gone.

Ulfar stood up and made to run after her, but something held him back. Something . . . He would have to think about this, regain his senses. 'Did you see that?' he asked Geiri out of habit. 'Did you see that?' He paced inside the hut, shook his head and tried in vain to make sense of what had just happened. His thoughts went unbidden to her hand, touching him. The feel of her skin on his skin.

And then he realized what he remembered, what he'd noticed. The bandages on her stiff, broken fingers.

'We're being attacked! They're coming from the forest!'

Shouts from the eastern wall echoed across Stenvik. Within moments Sigurd was at the foot of the inside of the wall, taking the steps to the top two at a time.

The caravan's rout was complete. A huge group of savage-looking forest men chased farmers running for their lives to the eastern gateway. Arrows flew from the cover of the trees.

'Open the gate!' Sigurd shouted. The guards hesitated, transfixed by the sudden attack. 'OPEN IT!' he screamed, watching the guards snap to and begin hauling on cables to raise the big, wooden gate. He bounded down the steps towards ground level.

'TO ARMS! MEN OF STENVIK, TO ME! WE CHARGE!'

In the chaos nobody noticed a solitary figure crawl from underneath an abandoned cart and slink into the cover of the trees, behind the onrushing force.

Peering out from a crack between the door and the jamb, Valgard's lip curled up in an unconscious snarl as he watched Lilia hurry away with her little blonde friend.

He thought of Ulfar, of how that . . . that *boy* was going to start looking at him with a mixture of revulsion and pity after the near-seizure in the longhouse, like he was some kind of cripple. He knew that look well. It was the look reserved for the sick and the old, and he had faced it all his life. When he was young he'd seen strong men with grim faces lead the feeble ones up the path to Hnipisbjarg on Muninsfjell and come back alone. None of the others came back down. At least not by way of the path. Mouths to feed and all that.

So he had studied to become a master of herbs. Healing the sick. Curing illness. Saving lives. His own, mostly. He was not going to let them throw him off the cliff just for being frail.

Valgard snorted at the memories.

Some healer. Couldn't even cure himself.

The fits came in his thirteenth summer. The first one was luckily in Sven's hut. The second had been in the middle of the square, and it had taken all of Sven's skills to keep Valgard alive. Some of the townsfolk – his people, he thought bitterly – had advocated sacrificing him to the gods and argued that he was clearly full of the spirits of Hel, the way he thrashed about on the ground and foamed at the mouth. One of them had drawn a dagger and tried to tear him away from Sven.

Sven had killed the man on the spot and challenged anyone in the square to single combat there and then. You'll take the boy over my dead body, he'd said. Nobody had been tempted to try.

The matter was resolved quickly, but Valgard might as well have died for all the good it did. After that day in the square, no one would as much as nod to him in passing. People would stop talking when he walked by. He became invisible, a non-entity.

It had taken years to change that. Years of herb lore, apprenticing with Sven, washing filthy bandages, holding hands and talking calmly to sick, frightened people. In the end, they accepted him – but they never embraced him. He knew they thought him weak. Unreliable. And now that foreign boy would start pitying him as well.

'We should really take care of each other,' he mimicked with a sneer. In his mind, the pieces on the board lurched to life. Harald on the dais. Sigurd. Sven. The raiders of the *Westerdrake*. Valgard moved them around then reset the position. The game was supposed to end with Harald challenging Sigurd for the chieftain's chair, winning and installing him, Valgard, as his most trusted adviser. He moved the pieces again in his mind, but reset them with an annoyed frown. The plan was in place. Now he just needed the right move.

Maybe it was time to play harder.

Still frowning, Valgard went back into his hut. He would need to examine the contents of the box for this.

## GRANDAL, HARDANGER HEATH

King Olav's reputation seemed to have preceded him. To the best of Finn's knowledge, there had never been more than a hundred people living in Grandal. Now they were all gone and it seemed they had left in a hurry.

Much like the others, the village consisted of a scattering of huts. There was a stream within walking distance and he'd seen enough game in the woods on the way here. Grandal also had a decent longhouse which had probably served as the chieftain's home.

Not any more, Finn thought with a grin.

When it grew clear that there would be no fighting here the army had set up camp. Fires were being lit in a wide circle around the town, and men from all over the east sat down to enjoy a little rest after days of marching.

A small group of fighters had gathered by the longhouse. Walking planks had been laid out in front of the house, creating a square dominated by a large sacrificial stone set some eight feet from the entrance. The stone was half a man's height, flat on top and spattered with coppery brown stains.

Standing by the stone were three wooden statues. Artful

carvings depicted Odin the All-knowing, Thor the God of Thunder and Freya the Goddess of Love. The men were gathered, however, around a clumsy effigy that lay on the altar. It was nothing more than a stick figure, but it clearly depicted a man wearing a white shift. He was adorned with pigtails, chicken feathers and a necklace of ram's testicles.

The soldiers were amused.

'Look at that!'

'He's wearing a dress!'

'And feathers!'

One of them played a chicken running around in a panic, to the whooping encouragement of the others.

Finn was furious. How dare they? He rounded on the men and roared: 'You! Back to your post! Or so help me by our lord God you will regret it!'

The men shuffled off, eyeing him with disdain. Finn scowled back, willing them to challenge his authority. None did.

When they were gone, he set about looking for somewhere to throw the effigy away. He gathered the sticks in his arms and turned around.

King Olav stood ten feet away and watched him calmly.

Finn faltered. 'My King, I . . .' He followed Olav's gaze to the effigy he was holding, and dropped the sticks as if they were on fire. 'I . . . they . . .' Finn's voice trailed off.

He thought King Olav would erupt. Shout. Curse. Maybe cut him open to set an example.

But nothing happened.

Instead, the king looked thoughtful. His eyes scanned the longhouse, the nearby huts, tools leaning up against walls. After a while, he spoke.

'Assemble the men here.' He gestured in a wide semicircle in front of the longhouse. Finn furrowed his brow in question.

'All of them. Now.'

Finn snapped to attention, turned and headed for the camp-fires. He moved quickly, singling out chieftains and men of note among the soldiers, relaying King Olav's orders. Suddenly a soldier next to him pointed towards the middle of the town.

'It's the King!'

'He's on the roof!' another echoed.

Finn could not help but stop what he was doing and gaze in wonder. More and more soldiers were looking and pointing at King Olav.

He had left behind his chain-mail jerkin and cloak, and was wearing only trousers, boots and a simple white shirt. Something that looked like a coil of rope was wrapped around his shoulder as well. His progress was swift and effective, and soon he was balanced on the top of the roof.

He took a moment and seemed to survey his troops, who had swelled from two to five thousand men in a matter of weeks. Then he invited them to do the same with a slow, sweeping hand gesture encompassing all the men that were gathering before him.

The army fell silent.

'Northmen!' King Olav's voice boomed. 'Look around you. Look at this.' He pointed to the hut, and the men exchanged questioning looks. 'You may see a village like any other. But I see hovels! I see people living in mud, feeding on mud, scrabbling in mud! Killing their own kin! Living lives of pain, squalor and death! And where has it brought us, Northmen? Have we won great glories in battle? Have we struck fear into the hearts of our enemies? No, we have not!' Some men whispered to their fellow soldiers, but none took their eyes off Olav. His voice rang out again. 'I say the old gods have grown weak! They are no longer ready for battle!' The silence was tense. King Olav continued, calm and certain. 'We need a new god.'

Angry voices erupted here and there in the crowd. Some of the soldiers were visibly furious. King Olav ignored them. Proud and defiant, he stood above his army. Like the captain of a ship in a sea of angry faces, Finn thought.

'I have travelled the world, Northmen. And if we do not change – if we are content to huddle in a cabin like the old gods that grow grey and frail and weak – we will starve and die in misery.'

One angry soldier shouted: 'So what will your White Christ do? How will he protect us? There's only one of him!' A smattering of affirmative shouts followed.

Olav spread his hands and waited until the crowd had gone silent. He looked straight back at the soldier. 'Let us examine this, my good friend,' Olav said almost amicably. 'We are brought up to believe that Odin, Thor and Freya live above us in the sky, are we not? In Valhalla?' He gestured skywards and waited. There was no immediate reply. 'Are we not?' Olav repeated.

'Yes,' the soldier replied eventually.

'Well,' said the king. 'Let us compare my god . . .' he unhooked the coil from over his shoulder, 'and the old gods.' He braced himself and started pulling on the rope. The carved statues of Odin, Thor and Freya fell over, scraped on the stone and then started rising slowly. They must have weighed the same as three grown men, and the ease with which the king pulled them up was not lost on the men.

When he had pulled the figures up onto the roof, he untied the statue of Freya. He held it in front of his chest and spoke to the men.

'My god . . . will protect me.'

He threw the statue off the roof. It hit the stone altar and split with a loud crack. The shock resonated through the ranks. Stunned looks spread on the soldiers' faces.

King Olav's voice rang out again.

'My god . . . will support me.'

The semicircle around the longhouse widened as the men pulled back instinctively. The statue of Thor was already airborne. It hit the altar's edge and broke cleanly in two.

This time all eyes were back on Olav.

He had already hoisted the carved statue of Odin above his head. He did not seem to notice the weight. Clear, strong and chilling, his voice rang out again.

'*My* god will guide me! For *my* god I will unite us all, a mighty army of Northmen! *My* god will shatter the old gods, strike them down and send their believers to Hell!'

He threw the statue of Odin down hard onto the stone. It hit and shattered. Five thousand stunned faces stared up at Olav. He continued.

'*My* god . . .'

He calmly undid the strings on his trousers.

'. . . would never have allowed this . . .'

With his trousers lowered he let forth a stream of piss onto the ground, splashing the splintered, ruined statues.

'. . . to happen.' Completely unhurried, he did up his trousers and turned to the soldier.

'Now, my friend. Has Thor struck me with his mighty hammer?' He waited for an answer. None was forthcoming. 'Do you see wolves? Do you see ravens?' The men looked up, entranced. 'Has *anything* happened?' Silence enveloped the village.

Olav looked at the gathered men. He drew a deep breath and shouted: 'So I say to you, Northmen – the old gods are weak! As I have destroyed their images, march with me to destroy their followers! March with me and I shall lead you into battle, to honour . . . to victory!'

Finn realized he'd been holding his breath for a very long time. He let it out and shouted: 'Long live King Olav!'

Almost at once, five thousand voices echoed his cry. The ground shook with stamping feet. Men banged their shields. Horses whinnied nervously.

From a nearby field two large, black birds took to the sky.

## STENVIK

'Where's the healer? My head hurts.' The pig farmer's speech was slurred and he squinted in the faint light of the hut.

'I don't know,' Audun replied from his spot in the corner.

The big man in the corner moaned. 'I can't get up. I need help. You – help me!'

Audun ignored him.

'I'm talking to you! Where's the bloody healer? I'm dying!'

Audun rolled his eyes and took a deep breath. 'You're not dying. You've been badly hurt. Valgard will be around to look at you soon enough. Just lie down and try not to move.'

The pig farmer snorted and clambered to his feet. 'Pah! You don't know how I feel. You don't know anything. I demand compensation and honour restored! I'm going to find the healer that patched me up and tell him . . .' Halfway to the door, he squinted into the corner and recognized the blacksmith. His voice trailed off and he hurried out of the hut.

Audun watched him go then looked at Geiri's prone form. 'You know,' he said to the unconscious man, 'I think maybe we'd have less trouble if more people were like you.'

\*

Patches of black and blue skin made the pig farmer's left eye seem like it had sunk deep into his skull. Both his lips were split and a large, oozing sore covered most of his jaw. Thinning blonde hair hung in greasy hanks. He hid his left hand under his arm and nursed a broken rib on the right-hand side as he staggered towards the square, but he was damned if he was going to let anything stop him.

He saw the two old men, the one who fitted the description of the chieftain and his friend the white-beard, walk purposefully towards the steps to the south wall. He tried to ignore the aches, to keep his mind on what he meant to do. March up to them, state his claim, say he wanted a tribunal, restitution.

As he set off across the market square someone grabbed his shoulder, spun him around and dragged him out of sight, in between two huts.

'I don't think you should disturb Sigurd right now, pig man,' Harald said calmly. The big farmer tried to shake himself free but the raider's heavy hand was firmly on his shoulder, fingers clawing into muscle, digging in under the shoulder blade. 'He's busy, we're under siege and he has no time for anyone, really.' Pain lanced through his side and the farmer grimaced. 'Oh, sorry. Am I hurting you?' Harald said, sounding full of concern. The grip on the shoulder tightened and twisted. The sea captain stepped towards him. Face now inches from the other's, Harald spoke in a completely level voice.

'You may think you have been treated unfairly. You may think you're owed something. Some kind of restoration of honour. Mmm?' He squeezed and pulled, and the pig farmer's knees buckled. 'You may also wonder where your cousins went. I'll tell you.' Struggling to stand, the farmer's eyes welled up and he lost control of his bladder. Harald wrinkled his nose but continued,

169

his voice sweet and soothing. 'They made claims on your behalf, you see. Then they got drunk, punched each other out, tied themselves up and went and sat in a boat without oars that floated out to sea.' The pig farmer's lip trembled and a slow smile formed on Harald's face. 'Somehow . . . somehow one of them got a hold of a knife . . . and scratched a hole in the boat. Between the timbers, you know? Not a big hole, not at all. Just big enough for some water to trickle through and wake them up when they were far enough out to sea. So they could watch the water pool in the bottom, rise slowly and sink the boat, while they were tied up safely and watching the coast from a distance.' Harald smiled at the crouching pig farmer. 'Now I don't know how close they were to you, pig man, but you know they say madness runs in families. I think the only way you can be safe from' – he twisted savagely and the farmer felt something break; he sank to his knees – 'finding yourself drowning slowly . . . is to tell Sigurd you've decided your honour has not been tarnished. How does that sound?'

The pig farmer fought for breath. The walls of the huts felt like they were closing in. The pain was intense now, his knees ached and his ribs felt like they were squeezing his lungs. He looked up at Harald and nodded, tears streaming from his eyes. The big raider looked down on him and smiled.

'Good. I'm glad we've put our little misunderstanding behind us.' With that, he turned and walked away, leaving the big pig farmer on his knees, sobbing quietly.


## BETWEEN WYRMSEY AND STENVIK

Skargrim stared down at the sea foaming around the prow of his ship, the *Njordur's Mercy*. The glow inside, the strong sense of belonging, had faded as the morning passed slowly into afternoon and been replaced with a hollow, empty feeling. He frowned and spat.

'What the hell is wrong with you then?'

Thora stood by his side, looking out at the sea.

'Nothing,' he snapped harder than he'd intended. Still – it was none of her business.

'Right,' she said amicably. 'And I regularly shit a pot of gold. A large one, too. You don't need to play chief with me, you old fart. What's wrong?'

Skargrim grinned despite himself. 'I should probably behead you for that.'

'You'd have to catch me first, and we both know that's not happening. So spill your guts. Might stop you walking around like a bear with a boil on its arse.'

He sighed. 'I really should have drowned you when I had the chance.' He shrugged. 'I always know what needs doing.'

'But now you're not sure.' He nodded. 'I've never known you to doubt, Skargrim. And you'd have their heads if any of the men doubted you, I reckon.'

'I . . . I am just not good at following, that's all.'

She snorted. 'Hah. That's dipping your oar lightly in the water, I'd say.'

'I just wonder what the gods really want with us,' he blurted out. Thora remained silent. He turned to her, but she looked resolutely away. 'Best not talk about it, I suppose,' he added. 'Best not think about it at all, in fact.' They stood together silently. For a while the only sound was the wind in the sails and the waves lapping at the side of the ship.

Then Skargrim spoke. 'However, as raids go, this is a legendary one. We are sailing with Hrafn. And young Thrainn. And Egill.

We're seeing Egill Jotunn and living to tell the tale. He is a huge bastard, though.'

'He certainly is.'

Something in the tone of her voice made Skargrim turn his head and glance at Thora. She looked back at him, raised an eyebrow and smiled sweetly. '. . . What?' The twinkle in her eye told a different tale.

Skargrim grinned. 'You must be Loki's stepdaughter.'

'Good.' She gave him an appraising look. 'Now that you're yourself again, stay like that. It makes it a little more likely we'll come through this mess.' She punched him hard in the shoulder, turned and started picking her way back to her post at the rudder, relieving her cover with a stream of expletives and a slap on the back.

He turned towards the prow and looked ahead. A day's sailing lay ahead of them.

Then, Stenvik.

Without thinking, he adjusted the axe at his belt.

Sixty-five ships drove ahead, the wind at their back. Behind them, the sun started its slow descent into night.

## STENVIK

The furnace glowed red-hot. Audun's forehead wore a sheen of sweat.

It had been a bloody affair, quick and brutal. Three men of Stenvik had died along with five farmers, and four were injured, but twenty-two of the men from the forest lay dead outside the eastern gates. Outnumbered and outfought, the enemy had turned and ebbed back into the forest, followed by the jeers of the men on the walls. Then Sigurd's fighters had returned to him with the killing tools that needed fixing.

Audun twisted the blade deftly, watching the colour shift. He hadn't wasted time cleaning the blood off, but even knowing it had been there still made him uneasy.

When he judged the heat in the blade to be right, he brought it over to the anvil and picked a small hammer from a rack on the wall. A couple of well-placed blows straightened out the dents where the sword had been used to block an attacker's strikes. With swift and assured movements, Audun plunged the glowing blade into a tub, setting off a plume of steam as the water boiled around the sword. As he waited for the metal to cool down, he looked over at the pile of assorted weapons they'd dropped on him after the clash.

Death was never as glorious in real life as in the songs, he mused. There was nothing heroic about it, really. You were just alive, and then you died. You were alive, and then you were blood and meat and bones in a slightly different order. His scalp tingled as old memories surfaced somewhere in the back of his mind. Audun pushed them away, put the sword in a bucket by the whetstone, and busied himself with heating and fuelling the furnace. He had a lot of work to do.

In the noise and heat of the smithy, he didn't notice Ulfar entering until he heard the grind of metal on stone. He turned around, white-hot blade in hand, only to see the tall, young man standing over the whetstone, sharpening a sword with easy, confident strokes.

Audun watched for a while. Catching Ulfar's eye, he nodded once and turned back to the forge. There, he set to hammering swords into shape, fixing broken axes and reattaching spear tips. They worked together without words.

As the light faded, the last sword clattered onto the pile of straightened, mended and sharpened weapons. Audun brought forward two stools and a sack with dried meat and a flask of mead.

'Thank you,' he said as he handed Ulfar the food. 'I would have been working into the night if it weren't for your help.'

'I just needed to get out of that hut. I was losing my mind,' Ulfar answered, looking unusually nervous. 'Look, there's one thing I want to ask you.' Gone was the confident young man, in his place an embarrassed, gangly boy. 'Do you know anything about a woman named Lilia? Here, in Stenvik?'

Audun's heart sank. 'Why do you want to know?'

Ulfar fidgeted, but did not answer.

'You need to learn to pick your battles, boy,' Audun said gently. 'And you need to not pick that battle.'

'So you do know who she is?' Ulfar replied eagerly.

He sighed and nodded. 'How is Geiri?'

'Nothing's changed. Being so near Geiri when he's not really there is very hard. But tell me of Lilia. Please.'

Audun took a deep breath and scolded himself silently. No good could come of this. No good at all. But he'd seen that expression before on a young man's face, and Ulfar didn't look like one to give up. Maybe he could explain the state of things to him. Make him see some sense.

'You've seen Harald? The guy who beat the daylights out of that pig farmer? Lilia is his wife.' He glanced over at the young man, who hung on his every word. Audun went on. 'He brought her over after a raid. She's his second. He had one before, but she died. No children. Some said she had an . . . accident . . . because she was barren.'

'Go on.'

'He's not a forgiving man, Harald. If he finds out you've even been asking about his wife he will challenge you to a duel of honour, and he'll take great pleasure in gutting you.'

'Does she love him?'

'What?'

'Does she love him?' Ulfar persisted.

'How should I know?' Audun shot back, stung. 'What does that mean? Does she want him? I doubt it. She's less of a wife and more of a slave, and she has no family here, so no one can do anything for her. Does he treat her right? No. There's talk, people hear things. They say he beats her, but nobody does anything. Lucky for her he's away most of the time. But she waits for him on the pier when he's gone.' The silence from the other end of the smithy was intense. He felt Ulfar's stare more than he saw it. 'Look. I don't want to tell you what to do. Just make sure you know what you're up against when you go in. Harald is a vicious bastard by all accounts, and he eats boys like you for breakfast. Judging by your work you've seen a sword before. You might even know what to do with it. But you're, what? Twenty-two?'

'Twenty-three summers after this one.'

'Harald has been raiding for twenty-five years and he's still alive. Think on that.'

'Thank you,' Ulfar said as he rose. 'For the information, and for the warning.'

'What are you going to do?'

'Me?' Ulfar thought for a while, then replied: 'I don't know. But thank you again, my friend. Your words have put me at ease. And don't worry. I won't do anything stupid' – Audun was about to protest that he hadn't worried at all when Ulfar interrupted him – 'tonight. We'll see about tomorrow.'

With a hint of a smile, he ducked out of the smithy.

Audun shook his head and frowned. 'Let's hope you hold true to that,' he muttered to himself. Looking around, his eye caught on his most recent sword. Excellent raw material, but in dire need of sharpening.

He picked up a pail of water and brought the blade towards the whetstone.

Valgard did a brief inventory in his mind as he walked. Splints, bandages, salves as far as they went. It was all ready, decked out by the station he had created by the longhouse. Sven had suggested it, said an equal distance to all the steps wouldn't be a bad thing. It was hard to fault the logic in that. It wouldn't be delicate work, though. And there would be blood. Lots and lots of it.

'Hey! Valgard!'

He turned and saw Harald bound towards him looking positively cheerful. 'Come on. Let's go to your place, you can make me some mixture and I'll tell you what I've done.' The gleam in the big sea captain's eye sent chills up and down Valgard's spine. 'What are you doing over here? You're almost at my house.'

'Am I? I guess I am. I was just . . . walking. Setting up. Clearing my head.'

''s a good idea, clearing your head,' Harald nodded. 'Now how about you make some mixture so I can clear mine? Come on, you scrawny fucker!' He grinned broadly and slapped Valgard hard on the shoulder. The sheer weight of the blow sent him staggering, but he regained his balance and managed to turn the stumble into two steps towards his own home.

'If you insist,' he replied, forcing joviality into his voice. 'You've got me all curious now.'

Beaming, Harald led the way towards the healer's hut. Valgard had to raise his pace to keep up. Something seemed to be spurring the big sea captain on. He even hummed a melody as they approached his house.

When they got in, Harald went to his customary corner, leaned back and smiled. 'Now. Do you have anything ready?'

'Yes I do,' Valgard replied. 'Give me a moment.' Shuffling towards the supplies, he found a portion he'd mixed earlier. It had turned out slightly stronger than he'd intended so he'd kept it in reserve.

Turning, he handed the leather bottle to Harald. The big man grasped it eagerly and took a swig. His eyes turned vacant as he savoured the taste, the sensation that spread from the mouth to the brain and the body, the warm fuzziness.

'No honour debt, no restitution, no nothing.' He licked his lips, tasting the last drops of the mixture.

'What do you mean?'

'I told the pig man what had happened to his cousins and explained that the same sort of thing might happen to him unless he stayed in his pen. Problem solved,' Harald said, slurring the last words slightly. 'I'm off the hook and the gods will be happy . . .' As the herbs took hold he relaxed into a happy sleep, eyes closing slowly.

Valgard looked at the big captain snoring softly in the hut. The mixture was serving its purpose very well now, giving him rest when he needed so he could stay up longer than an ordinary man would. He still remembered the first time he'd made it. Harald had been bent double with muscle ache and needed something to help him sleep. It had worked better than he'd expected. He'd slowly been growing less receptive, so Valgard had had to change the recipe. Sven had once cautioned against using too much of dried hemp flower in anything – said it turned a man's brain to mush – but what use did an oaf like Harald have for a brain, anyway? Valgard needed him to do what he was told, not to think for himself like this.

This was very inconvenient.

Now there would be no trial, Harald would not be forced to pay what he would consider an unfair amount, and there would be little chance of him taking on Sigurd in a leadership battle. Valgard was losing pieces and getting nothing in return. Suddenly nervous, he checked the box underneath the table. It contained all it was supposed to contain. The game was not finished yet.

Still – something had to be done. But what?

### STENVIK FOREST

Instinct, Oraekja thought. That's what that was. He'd made a life-saving decision, just like great leaders do. Some of the useless farmers had died, but that was bound to happen. He was alive and he was going to stay that way. He'd got to the cover of the trees, found thick underbrush to hide in and lain down, aiming to do like he'd seen Ragnar do and stop breathing.

It had worked. He'd melted into his surroundings.

He wrapped the cloak tight around himself. Night was coming. It would still be a while before Skargrim arrived. Thinking of Skuld, he drifted off into an uncomfortable sleep.

### HARDANGER HEATH

The last rays of the setting sun cast a fading light on the field. Tents were lined up in patterns, dotted by campfires being lit. Around the fires, the men of Olav's army sat and talked.

'Did you see?'

'You've asked me three times now. Yes I did. We all did. We were all there.'

'I still can't believe it.'

'I know. They should have queued up to strike the King down. What I want to know is what manner of god this White Christ is if he could outwit Odin, outfight Thor and ward off the charms of Freya. He must have either defeated them or protected our King.'

'Or both.'

'Or both. There has been no sign of thunder tonight.'

'It makes you think twice, it does.'

Finn listened to the campfire talk as he made his rounds. The events of the day clearly weighed heavily on the men's minds.

The camp looked much better now, he thought. When they started out men had just slung down their packs when it was time to stop. They would wander from their little circles to drink, argue or settle scores with old neighbours. King Olav had put a stop to that on the third day of their campaign, months ago now. 'These are the old ways,' he'd said. Finn still remembered the looks on the grizzled old chieftains' faces as the young King told them how to command their men. The King had created rules. He had told the chieftains where to camp relative to his tent every night. He had shown them where to put sentries, where to place the horses at night. Rotations were drawn up and a division of hunters and gatherers created. Some of them were plainly furious, but none had dared to go up against him. And even the stubbornest chieftain had to admit that the young King seemed to know what he was doing. A few troublemakers had tried to upset the balance a couple of days later. The King had dealt with them fast and without mercy.

Finn's musings had brought him towards King Olav's tent. The flap was open, the hide pinned back to let in air. Or display the inhabitant, he thought.

The King knelt before a small wooden box or chest of some

sort. On it was easily the biggest book Finn had ever seen, open in the middle. The young man seemed to be mouthing words, lost in thought. He fingered some sort of talisman that hung around his neck. All at once his lips stopped moving, and he reached for the book. He touched it tenderly, traced a line on the page. Reaching for the cover, he closed the book slowly and spoke without looking up.

'Good evening, Finn.'

Finn was taken aback. How could he know? He hadn't made a sound. At last he managed to stutter a reply.

'Good . . . good evening, my lord.'

King Olav got to his feet, his back turned towards Finn. He looked at the ground and seemed deep in thought.

'Tell me of the men. Are they tired?'

'No, my lord. They are well. Most of them are sitting around campfires, talking.'

'What about?'

Finn paused. What were his options? Keep silent? Hardly. Lie? That didn't seem very smart.

'They're wondering, my lord. About the White Christ.'

King Olav turned around, raised his head and looked hard at Finn. His expression was very hard to read. 'Well then. I suppose we should go and do our duty, should we not?' He strode off without waiting for an answer.

Finn followed the King. Daylight was fading fast, and he had to watch his step to keep from falling over.

When they approached the first of the campfires, King Olav slowed down and turned to Finn.

'Those men over there. Do you know them?'

'Yes, my lord. They're from the east coast. Part of the original group that rose up against Haakon Jarl. They're trustworthy.'

'So if I were to talk to them, do you think they would run around repeating what I said?'

Finn answered immediately. 'No, my lord. Not at all.'

'Then we move on.'

Thoroughly confused, Finn followed.

At a distance from the next campfire, King Olav stopped again. 'How about that bunch over there? Are they less worthy of my trust?'

Finn peered through the gloom, trying to make out faces. 'They seem to be from the south. Botolf's men are there. Some are Skeggi's. They're . . . I probably wouldn't . . . I mean . . .' He hesitated. King Olav looked at him for a second, then turned and set off towards the campfire, silently and slowly. Strands of the men's conversation lingered on the night air. What Finn heard set his heart racing.

'. . . but surely the White Christ cannot have both the strength of Thor and the cunning of Odin?'

Five soldiers were sat around a campfire. Some argued, others laughed. A fat man with crooked teeth and a bushy beard laughed the loudest.

'What's next? Does he have the hips of Freya?' he roared, taken with his own wit. He slapped his thigh, made some very sugges-tive gestures and laughed heartily.

Nobody laughed with him.

'What's wrong with you?' he shot at his companions. 'Did the King break your balls on that stone today or something?' He faced a half-circle of white faces, all staring at a point a little bit above and behind him. Slowly, confusion flowed into realization as silence spread like rings on water around the campfire. Finally, one of his friends spoke up. 'My lord . . . we were not . . . he didn't mean . . .'

'You have not understood what I told you about the White Christ today, have you?' The King's voice was steady and reassuring. The question was more of a statement.

'. . . No?' mumbled the bulky soldier.

King Olav stepped into the circle. In the flickering light of the fire he seemed otherworldly, like something carved out of the bones of giants. The men stared at him, mesmerized.

'What would you know of him? Ask and I will tell you.' He looked at each one of them in turn. None dared hold his gaze. Finally one of them, a solidly built young man with unruly dark hair and a thick brow, worked up some courage.

'See, um, we were wondering. Because the old gods, Odin and Thor and—' The young man faltered. The others seemed to hold their breath. One or two of them looked for King Olav's sword. The men to either side of the young soldier inched away. He bravely ploughed on. 'The gods of our fathers have been with us for a long time. We know what they can do. But then you broke the idols and they did not strike you down. Why?'

The question hung in the air for what seemed like an eternity. Then King Olav smiled. In the flickering firelight, it wasn't an entirely reassuring sight. 'They did not, as I told you, because my god—' He paused and corrected himself. 'Our god protects us, and he is wiser and stronger than both Odin and Thor.'

Emboldened, the dark-haired man countered: 'That must mean that the White Christ is a warrior beyond any the world has seen.'

King Olav's face was unreadable. There was an almost imperceptible pause before he continued. His voice changed subtly. 'Yes. Yes he is. He is as tall as the biggest giants. He makes Thor look like a boy.' Amazement shone on the faces of the soldiers. King Olav went on. 'He has a sword that only he can lift. He uses this as others might use a knife. In his other hand he holds a shield that only he can hold and not even Tyr himself could break. It is pierced in two places by the fangs of the Worm of Midgard . . .' King Olav paused artfully. The soldiers hung on to his every word. '. . . which the White Christ fought for sport.' The men stared at him, silent and rapt with attention. Olav's voice carried conviction and strength, and he continued. 'The White Christ lives in the sky, in a hall filled with riches that make all the gold and finery on earth seem like the contents of a smallholder's pouch. He can take wives where and when he wants, but waits for one that is worthy of him.' Some of the men seemed confused at this, and Finn noticed that more had drifted towards the spectacle, curious but wary of coming too close. King Olav continued.

'The White Christ's hall is at the very least twice the size of Valhalla. Many wondrous things are there to please the eye and fire the spirit. Shapely maids serve ale from golden urns. No man that takes the White Christ into his heart ever goes hungry or cold after he dies, nor does he have to content himself with the same pig's flesh and goat's milk every day. He can choose whatever he wants, and Christ provides.' Among the men, nods and murmurs of assent were exchanged. With increased passion and intensity, King Olav pushed on. 'The White Christ has won more battles than anyone can count. His followers toppled a mighty empire to the south, the Romans. Their armies seemed invincible, but with the might of the White Christ, the people of true belief could work miracles, things that mortal men cannot. And the White Christ performed miracles as well. He walked the earth in the guise of a man, much as Odin did.'

The audience had quietly grown from five to twenty men, most of whom hid in the dusk beyond the firelight. All eyes were on King Olav. He paused, and the silence was absolute. None dared draw a breath. When he spoke again his soul seemed to be in every word.

'The White Christ can heal the sick. The White Christ can wake the dead.' Gritting his teeth, King Olav drew himself up to his full height and snarled: 'The White Christ is good and pure. But he will *not* show mercy to those that have confessed to being his enemies. He will deal with them according to their conduct, and by their own standards he will judge them. Then they will know that He is the lord.'

As he spoke, he looked into the face of each and every man standing around the campfire, finding the eyes even of those hiding in the dark. Daring anyone to object to anything he'd said, he held their attention and their silence for a brief moment. Then he nodded to the large soldier whom he had surprised earlier.

'Get some rest. We march early tomorrow for Stenvik. Christ bless you.' King Olav left the circle and disappeared towards his tent.

Crackling fire, fading light and the measured voice of a man telling stories of his White Christ had cast a spell on the men. They sat around the fire in a stunned daze. Finn had to pinch himself to snap out of it. He ambled after King Olav, half aware of smatterings of conversation starting behind him.

When he got to the King's tent, the flap was closed.

He could hear King Olav's voice within, reciting softly.

'Our father, which art in heaven. Hallowed be thy name. Thy kingdom come, thy will be done.' The voice seemed to trail off. The last thing Finn heard before he left to inspect the sentries was a muted whisper from the tent.

'Forgive me.'

## STENVIK

The fires in the longhouse burned low as Thorvald stepped through the doorway. Sigurd watched him from his seat on the dais.

'Well?'

Thorvald bit the words off. 'There are a lot of them out there, but they keep to the darkest parts of the woods. It's murder to get any kind of estimate on their number. I've lost two scouts trying.'

'But they're staying put? They're not grouping up? Did you see their leader?' Sigurd fired the questions fast and hard.

The scout master looked wearily back at him. 'What do you want me to say, Sigurd? I don't know. I don't know how they work. We've never faced them before. All I know is there's a lot of them, ranging from the scrawny and desperate to some bastards that can really handle themselves. I also know they're here and they got two of my boys.' Thorvald's face was flushed with anger and he had to swallow hard before he continued. 'The answer to your question is no. We've not seen them grouping up in any way that I understand. Except for there being a pile of them in our own wood.' Thorvald scowled.

'Their lack of movement is not necessarily good,' Sven added from the corner.

185

'What do you mean?' Sigurd spat.

'Skargrim is coming and suddenly our forest crawls with out-laws.'

'If you mean what I think you mean, you're slipping into old age sooner than we thought,' Harald countered.

'Maybe, maybe not,' Sven replied. 'All I'm saying is that we should not be surprised if the outlaws move when Skargrim appears.'

Harald banged the arm rest of his high-backed chair. 'Shut up, old man! We should gather our fighters! Root them out before Skargrim—'

'No, Harald. It's time you shut up!' Thorvald snarled. 'I'm not risking any of my men in those woods just because you want to go bash some heads!'

'I agree with Thorvald,' Sven added.

'You would,' Harald shot back. 'None of you dare stand alone against me. You always—'

Sigurd rose slowly from his chair and the three men fell silent. 'We know Skargrim is on his way. We know that there are outlaws in our woods, and they've come in numbers.' Sigurd took his time and looked at his warriors in turn. 'Now there is only one question. When the crows come to feast . . .' He stepped off the dais, turned and looked up at Harald, Thorvald and Sven. '. . . are you going to sit here scratching your arses and yapping like old women, or are you coming with me to do something about it?'

A cold smile played on his lips as he moved towards the door of the longhouse. Behind him, the others swapped quizzical glances as they got up to follow their chieftain.

## NORTH OF STENVIK

'*Pater noster, qui es in caelis* . . .'

Finn didn't understand the words, but by now he knew them by heart. At first only a small group of men had wanted to join the King for Morning Prayer, but the number had grown steadily. Over half the army had joined in since King Olav cast down the totems.

'*Adveniat regnum tuum* . . .'

The murmured voices of two thousand soldiers sounded somehow unstoppable, like a glacier rolling over rock, crushing everything in its path. There had been a marked change in the men recently. No one dared cast snide glances at the young King now, and a core of them would gladly follow him to their deaths.

'*Fiat voluntas tua, sicut in caelo et in terra* . . .'

A smattering of red and yellow decorated the nearby trees, a sure sign that autumn was coming. When they got to Stenvik they'd be able to split the army up into divisions, go further, cover more ground and always return to a safe base. The Lord's work would go much faster.

'. . . *sed libera nos a malo. Amen.*'

The lithe young man rose and behind him, as one, a mass of soldiers followed suit. The body followed the head. It sent shivers up Finn's spine. There was no doubt about it.

These men would do anything for King Olav and the White Christ.


## BETWEEN WYRMSEY AND STENVIK

Hrafn sailed on the left flank. Ingi formed the rearguard. Thrainn's contingent covered their right flank and Skargrim's ships made up the van. Egill's men were not in formation, content to hover some distance off. Skargrim didn't mind. He'd often said that a small dose of chaos did a powerful lot of good in a fight.

'You. Get some sleep.' Thora had somehow sneaked up behind him at his post by the masthead. 'I won't say it again, and I don't want to kick you in the balls. Can't be bothered dragging your big hairy arse to your perch. Get some sleep.'

He turned away from the wind, the sea spray and the fresh rays of the rising sun. Nodding slowly, he offered a smile to his second in command and started picking his way across towards the helm. There was sense in the woman. Better grab rest when he could. One never knew when the opportunity would rise again.

Far behind him the west coast of Norway rose out of the mist, a green stripe on the horizon.

## STENVIK FOREST

The road had led Jorn and his three riders through farmland, along the coast and now towards a forest that was growing steadily more dense. A beautiful autumn morning sun shone down on trees slowly shedding their summer hues, sporting the occasional yellowing and reddening leaf. The tranquillity of the scene drew them in. There was not a single sound of any kind to be heard in the forest.

'Th-th-they're h-here.'

Birkir unwound the leather strap on the haft of his axe. It was a nasty piece of work, a woodsman's hand axe augmented to serve other, less genial purposes. The blade tapered down from the edge to a pick-like point at the back and small iron tacks had been smelted onto the head, designed to rip and tear as the axe sliced through flesh.

'Put it away, big man.'

Birkir shot a glance at Jorn. 'So we're going in like lambs?'

The smile on the young Prince's face was chilling. 'No, we're not.'

Realization dawned slowly on Birkir. 'You're saying we can't fight our way through. And we won't sneak. You're going to run for it, aren't you?' Behind him, fat Havar whimpered.

Jorn only nodded and reined in his horse. The animal, scenting something, snorted nervously. Runar lined up beside the Prince and inspected his bow. Behind them, Birkir shook his head. Starting at a trot, Jorn urged his horse forward, leaning on the animal's neck and whispering in its ear. They picked up speed gradually until they were galloping along the forest path.

Shaking in his saddle, Runar struggled to be heard over the din of hoofs. 'I-I-I hope you've p-p-picked the right p-path!' Jorn only grinned and spurred his horse onward.

The sky above the galloping riders disappeared behind a ceiling of green leaves as the forest enveloped them.

The first arrow missed Jorn by inches. Shouts erupted and the shadows in the trees took form and purpose. Colours blurring around them, the four riders could do nothing but push on as arrows and spears whizzed past. Swivelling in the saddle, Runar fired back as best he could.

Suddenly a wiry fighter broke free from the bushes up ahead and ran snarling towards Jorn's horse. Two powerful steps, a well-timed leap and the fighter was airborne, flying at Jorn.

Something blurred at terrifying speed into the Prince's field of vision. The onrushing warrior's head lost shape in mid-flight. Blood and brain matter sprayed the riders as the outlaw dropped dead and was trampled in an instant.

Jorn looked back at a grinning Birkir, reeling in his axe by the leather strap fastened to his wrist.

'You disobeyed me?' Jorn yelled.

189

'Sure did!' Birkir shouted back.

'Good!' Jorn screamed at the top of his lungs. 'For the Dales!'

'FOR THE DALES!' the three men echoed, thundering through the forest drunk on blood and danger.

STENVIK

'VALGARD! VALGARD, COME QUICK!'

The healer turned over on his pallet, pale and drawn, and began cajoling his body up into an upright position, inch by painful inch. Valgard, do this. Valgard, do that. Why couldn't these bloody peasants have the decency to get sick, break bones or die when he was on his feet?

'COME ON!' The voice was insistent and far too loud.

'Yes, yes! I'm coming!' Valgard shot back irritably.

'HE'S WAKING UP! THE SWEDE IS WAKING UP!'


The broad steps were hewn into the sloping side of the wall and paved with flat stones. Ulfar picked his way up towards the battlements. Sleep had not come to him last night. Every time he'd thought he could rest, images of her had filled his head – her touch, her smile, the feel of the rough linen bandages around her broken fingers.

She possessed him. She owned his every thought, and it felt delicious. Ulfar let his mind wander as he counted the steps. Faces of nameless, shapeless girls in long-forgotten ports floated into view and were summarily dismissed. They meant nothing to him now. He felt embarrassed about his womanizing, but then he reasoned that those girls had fallen for someone else. They'd fallen for a charming boy and nothing more. Someone who would do anything, say anything, use anything just to weasel his way into their affections. Just to win. That boy was gone, he thought proudly. Now he was a man, and somewhere deep inside Ulfar knew that it was how it had to be. He would have to be honest and steadfast. He could not – would not – toy with Lilia's emotions.

His head spun. When he reached the top of the steps his stomach lurched as well. It had looked like an easy climb from the bottom, but the way down was much longer. He was struck by the sheer size of the battlements.

On top of the massive wall Sigurd's men had formed a wide, shallow ditch, paved with planks. It was broad enough for three men to stand side by side and deep enough to cover a fighter's lower half from attackers coming over. Set in the planks on either side of each gateway were what looked like a pair of battered old shields. Ulfar ran his hand absent-mindedly over the grass on the outer wall as he walked. Suddenly he scraped it on something sharp and jerked it back.

When he saw what it was, he whistled softly.

Set in the outer walls, invisible from below and covered by only a thin layer of turf, were murderous, three-inch-thick sharpened wooden spikes, facing outwards. He'd found the tip of one of them with his palm. Anyone scaling the wall from the outside would stand a decent chance of getting a nasty surprise if they put any sort of weight on what seemed like solid earth at the top.

He took in the near-perfect circle of the wall, with the town beneath him. Then he walked along it to the east, briefly noting some men with shovels on the road to the old town. Some of the *Westerdrake* raiders manned the gates, most looking towards the woods. Suddenly the forest seemed dark and forbidding, teeming with unseen outlaws. Some of the watchmen traded nods with

Ulfar as he passed. A gentle autumn wind caressed him as he finished his circle and the smells of the sea drifted in. A dull weariness crept up on the young man and he perched on the inner wall over the south gateway, looking out to sea.

The raw beauty of the land overwhelmed him.

On his right the shady forest loomed, ready to claim back farmland and buildings at the first sign of human surrender. Towering trees gave way to fields, squares of colour in stark contrast to the soft lines of the forest. The eye led on up the curve of the hill they called Huginshoyde, coloured in shades of grass, rocks and moss. He could still see some carts on the western road, lumbering away to another haven of perceived safety. Muninsfjell rose on the other side of the road, commanding and strong, and collapsed into the sea, an endless expanse of blue with a single thin black stripe of an island in the distance.

Ulfar looked down and swallowed hard as the emotions of days past came back with a vengeance. Fear. Anger. Love. Fighting back tears, he mouthed a silent prayer to Odin for Geiri's life. The man was his cousin in name only. In Ulfar's mind they were brothers. As he looked up again and wiped his eyes surreptitiously with his sleeve, he blinked. The haze made the island seem to move.

Looking around, he saw two large men manning the guard posts above the western gate. One of them sat on the back wall; the other stood and looked down at Sigurd's group working by the harbour. A couple of strides later Ulfar was within speaking distance. The guards eyed him warily as he spoke.

'Well met.' The sitting guard, a solidly built young man with a broken nose, nodded noncommittally. The other one turned towards Ulfar. Tall and long-limbed, his black hair made a limp and greasy frame around a birthmark that covered half of his face. The look in his eyes gave Ulfar the sense that he was not necessarily invited to come any closer. He bit his tongue and forced an open smile. 'I'm just wondering,' he continued, 'what is the name of that island out there?' He pointed towards the black stripe on the horizon.

As the question penetrated, confusion spread slowly over the guards' faces.

'What island? There's nothing there but sea,' the broken-nosed one spat. 'What are you talking about, boy?'

'Look.' Ulfar turned slowly and looked straight at the thin black line, now ever so slightly thicker.

'There's never been no island there,' the standing guard grunted.

'If so, then I think one of you might want to go get Sigurd.'

The tall, black-haired man sneered. 'You're not giving us orders, you whelp. Just because you got to listen in at the longhouse doesn't mean—'

'NOW.' The authority in Ulfar's voice was the sum of all the commands he'd heard from his father, his grandfather and all his uncles, leaders of men from way before his time. It was a conduit to home, to what was expected of him. To the man he was supposed to be and become. Ulfar shivered with disgust, but the effect was immediate. The guards snapped to attention and the barrel-chested one scurried fast down the western gate steps. The lanky man with the birthmark eyed Ulfar with suspicion and malice.

Without thinking, he stared back. Do it, he begged silently. Do it. Come on. Make the first move.

The tall raider made a show of curling his lip in distaste and looking away.

Ulfar exhaled. He was not a brawler by any stretch, but he'd been ready to get into a fight right there and then, a fight he would probably have lost. A numbing wave of fatigue washed over him, followed by a rumbling stomach and cold sweat as his blood came back down. He could really use a square meal and a good half-day's sleep right about now.

'RIDERS AT THE EAST GATE! AND OUTLAWS!'

Ulfar and the black-haired guard were up and running side by side before their counterparts on the other side had finished the sentence. Looking to the east they could see four men riding for dear life, chased by a gaggle of ragged outlaws.

Sleep would have to wait.

Harald strode towards the horsemen. He was in no mood for new things. Not now. 'Dismount,' he snapped.

It had been touch and go on the forest path, but the four riders had outrun the outlaws on open ground. After the narrow escape they'd been admitted through the eastern gateway. Now they looked down on him from their lathered horses, grinning and in no particular hurry to follow orders. Harald hated them on sight. The fat one especially.

'I said dismount.'

The slim, well groomed one in front started to speak, but Harald interrupted him. 'No. Shut up. You and your men are dismounting. Right now. Or I'm cutting the legs from under your horses.'

Fifteen raiders of the *Westerdrake* moved calmly to form a circle around the riders. Understanding dawned in the man's eyes. 'Off,' he commanded. The three others obeyed at once. At least he had his dogs on a leash, Harald thought.

'Take care of the horses,' he barked to two of the guardsmen. Then he turned to the four riders. 'You – follow me.' He set a course for the longhouse. The four men trailed after him, guarded by the raiders. When they got to the longhouse, Harald ushered them in.

Quiet and effective, the raiders herded the four men onto the middle of the floor and formed a circle. The captives turned back to back instinctively. Harald saw them whisper among themselves.

'Weapons.'

He saw the four men reluctantly begin to disarm. A well-formed recurve bow from the skinny runt. Sword and knife from the leader. Daggers from the fat one – no surprise there. A mean-looking axe. He looked at the man who had put it down. Big, looked like a brawler.

All in all, an interesting group.

Harald gathered up the weapons and let his mind wander as he walked slowly towards the dais. Sometimes it was worthwhile to give people some time to consider their situation. It could soften them up a little bit. And he'd not had much rest recently. He might as well breathe while those four considered their situation. If only Freya and Thor were here, and Loki, like in that dream. It hadn't felt like a dream, though. It had felt real. A faint echo of a chant about glory drifted into his mind from somewhere, along with the smell of morning in a forest among giant pine trees.

'If I may just introduce us—'

Harald was jolted out of his trance and back into the longhouse, where he found himself facing the high seat on the dais. He lost his hold on the weapons, which clattered noisily onto the floor. A brief jolt of fear coursed through him, as if he had been caught somewhere he shouldn't. Within moments the fear turned to anger. With great effort he managed what he hoped looked like a dismissive gesture. 'Shut up,' he growled with his back turned towards the prisoners. And with that, menace bubbled to the surface and years of experience reminded him what needed to be done.

Harald turned and started walking towards the four captives. Taking his time, he allowed them to take a good look at him. He let them see him for what he was, and wore the years of hard sailing, battle, raiding and murder with pride. It was only fair to give them the chance to assess whether they really wanted him to catch them lying.

He saw the runt nudge the leader, saw the leader speak out of the corner of his mouth. Inside, Harald smiled. They were rattled all right. He could see their leader thinking, could see him work up the courage before he spoke again.

'My name is Jorn and I am but a humble emissary for our holy King Olav Tryggvason, sent to tell you of his victories and negotiate practical matters before the army arrives. His highness would like to extend his eternal gratitude for the graciousness shown by the people of Stenvik, and especially by you. You are an honourable man, a wise chieftain and a worthy leader of men. The king holds you in high regard, Sigurd Aegisson.'

Frost flowed through Harald's veins and stars burst in his eyes. He had to fight the urge to charge the four, bite, kick, tear their throats apart. Harald took a deep breath, forced down the swell of feeling and fixed the leader with his eyes.

'What. Did you. Say?'

The words escaped through gritted teeth. Fists clenched, forearms vibrated. He barely registered the shift in the middle of the circle as the little runt squeezed past his leader.

'I'm-m-m s-so-so-sorry, m-most f-feared warrior. It is m-m-m-my fault.' The words tumbled out of him almost haphazardly, an idiot's smile wobbling on his stupid face. 'It was I whuh-whu-who misinformed our leader here. Y-you are n-n-not Sigurd Aegisson at all. I r-r-realize now. S-Sigurd is . . . old. Is he not?'

A sound escaped Harald's lips, closer to a bark than a laugh. Faced with the ludicrous little man, tension drained out of him. 'Well – I am not Sigurd,' he fired back. 'My name is Harald. You'll do well to remember that. And you should know better than to listen to idiots,' he directed at Jorn.

'So should a lot of people,' Sigurd's voice snapped from the doorway, and something lurched inside Harald. A vivid and snarling vision flitted in front of his eyes, of him wading into the middle of the circle, grabbing the yappy little messenger and smashing his face in. Standing alone in a room full of corpses. Sitting on the dais, resting his feet on Sigurd's severed head. He could smell the blood, taste it, feel it – but he held on. Just.

Men started streaming in through the door. Sigurd, Thorvald and Sven headed straight for the dais. A large number of raiders of the *Westerdrake* entered. Harald hadn't seen this many people in the longhouse since before the last raid.

Sigurd caught his arm in a steely grip and half-dragged him towards the dais. 'Are these the riders? Who are they, and why are they here?' he hissed under his breath.

'They escaped the outlaws on a dead run through the forest. The dark-haired one says they're messengers from King Olav.'

Anger flashed on Sigurd's face and he shot a glance at the newcomers. 'We'll see about that,' he muttered, and strode off into the circle. Two short commands and the raiders left to take their seats up against the wall. A single sentence to the dark-haired leader of the riders and the four men went off to the corner, out of the way, where they waited patiently.

Sigurd made his way back up to the dais, sidestepped the pile of weapons and turned around to face the assembled group. The silence was absolute.

'Right. No more waiting. Skargrim is here. And he's brought some friends.'

So the Swede was not dying after all.

Valgard frowned as he picked his way to the animal pens. They'd have fresh water, or near as, in barrels there. He would have to rob Stenvik's horses of a little bit of drink to aid their noble guest. The thought of it sent the bile surging through Valgard's stomach. Noble guests. Bloody peacock boys playing chieftain, more like. No doubt that boy Ulfar would tell his friend about the fit he'd seen. How the healer was really a cripple. No doubt they'd share a giggle, shame each other for laughing and then smirk. A sneer crept across Valgard's face as he picked his way through Stenvik. They were just too perfect, weren't they? Too damn perfect. Healthy, strong and lucky with women. Those boys had perfect lives because they'd been fortunate enough to be born from the right people in the right place.

Still. Luck was a coin, and every coin had two sides.

Valgard continued his journey, the sneer fading into a faint smile.

'Sixty ships.'

The silence in the longhouse was palpable.

'That's what Orn says,' Thorvald replied. 'And I have no reason to doubt him – the boy bears his name proudly and sees farther than anyone here.'

'Good.' Sigurd nodded slowly.

Thorvald knotted his brow and looked back at his leader. 'But . . . I don't understand. Sixty ships. That could be between eighteen hundred and two thousand men. We've only got the five hundred raiders and another seven hundred either too old or too young, not counting the women.'

'Maybe so, Thorvald – but now we have something we've needed for a while. Knowledge. We finally know our enemy, we know who he is and where he is coming from.'

Ulfar looked around. The men did not appear to share Sigurd's idea of good fortune. The chieftain seemed to notice this as well, because he rose and looked down at the assembled raiders.

'What we also have – is Stenvik. We all know the work that went into the walls. We built them with our bare hands when we'd sacked so many southern towns that we needed the walls to keep our own gold safe! And what's more – there is not a stone in our walls that isn't where it's meant to be. That is why Skargrim has brought the people he's brought. He wouldn't dare try to take us on with only his own crew. That is why he sent in rats to poison our well. Because he knew that if we had water we could defend Stenvik until we got bored, fat and old. He is coming in hard, hoping to scare us, hoping to unsettle us and make us think we're doomed. And I believe Sven – I believe he's somehow gathered the outlaws out of every cave and mountain hole in the west to prowl our forest and make us believe that we're hemmed in, surrounded and trapped, and frighten us into giving up. He's probably promised them gold, meat and women. But did you see the charge they made? Did you see our men slaughtered? Did you see our fates sealed? I did not! What I saw was Stenvik steel!' A cheer went up from the assembly. 'I saw enemies of my favourite kind – dead ones!' Another cheer. 'I saw fierce hard outlaws, killers in the shadows, the stuff of children's nightmares – run away from the raiders of the *Westerdrake*!' Roars of approval. Sigurd gave the men their time to shout, and then allowed the noise to die down.

'So let him come,' he continued softly when the men had gone quiet. 'Let him. Let him surround our town, shout at the wall, offer us surrender, call us cowards for hiding. Let him send his men to scale the walls – and let them die trying.' All around Ulfar cold smiles and determination showed in weathered faces.

Sigurd looked around, catching each and every man's eye. Then he turned to Harald and Thorvald, speaking softly to both. Facing the raiders again, he spoke up, this time calmly. 'These are my orders. You are to relay them to your brothers, your fathers and your sons. When you leave this longhouse you go to war. Take food and drink when you can. You may eat in Valhalla when you're dead, but until then you eat your fill here. I will not have my men hungry or thirsty. Because when we fight, we fight for our life. We fight for our fallen dead, our sons and unborn daughters. We fight for our home.' He held his men's attention for half a breath more, then finished. 'Harald and Thorvald have orders for you. Go with them.'

Sigurd's two generals rose as one, and with them the assembled raiders of the *Westerdrake*.

When they'd left, Sigurd returned to his chair. Once seated, he leaned back, crossed his arms and touched his chin. His eyes passed Ulfar briefly and landed on the group of four men standing silently in the corner. He beckoned them casually towards him. 'You. Approach.'

The four men moved into the centre of the longhouse.

'Explain yourselves.'

A young man with dark hair, delicate features and a runner's build stepped forward. He bowed deep.

'Sigurd Aegisson?'

'Yes.'

'My name is Jorn of the Dales. I am a forerunner of King Olav

Tryggvason's army, sent here to thank you in the name of God for—'

'Yes, yes. Prove it.'

Jorn seemed flustered. 'I— but . . . I— what?'

'Prove it. Prove it to me – right now – or I cut you down with your own weapons to save me time in cleaning mine.' There was no posturing, only weariness in Sigurd's voice. The large man behind Jorn looked at the greying chieftain with contempt. Sigurd smiled back. 'Just prove it.'

Frowning at a voice behind him, Jorn shook his head. Then something seemed to dawn on the man. He reached quickly inside his shirt and pulled out a shimmering chain.

'This is a chain with a cross given to me by King Olav, proving that I am his and our Lord God's messenger.' He knelt and offered the cross up to Sigurd.

From his seat on the dais, Stenvik's leader sighed. 'I don't know if you heard what just went on here. Skargrim is on his way, we have some friends in the forest that you've met, and the last two front-runner guests we had just poisoned our well. So as it stands, when new and interesting strangers show up at our gate waving some junk and pretending to be King Olav's messengers I am more inclined to carve them up, feed them to the crows and keep their baubles than believe them. We'll just have to wait a little.'

Ulfar watched the dark-haired man stare in desperation at the chieftain who was now conferring with the ever-present Sven. The four men started talking heatedly among themselves, the fat one pointing at the cross, the big bruiser scowling and ready for a fight. Only the weedy one at the back kept quiet, and scanned the room. Ulfar turned his attention to the conversation on the dais.

The door to the longhouse flew open. In stumbled a red-faced and overweight man wearing a brown robe.

'Ah! Friar Johann. Thank you for joining us!' Sigurd exclaimed from the dais.

'I am most honoured to help you in any way, Sigurd Aegisson. However, next time you need me please send someone other than that brute Harald. He told me where you'd stick my crucifix if I didn't run here!' The friar's face was flushed with indignity.

Sigurd and Sven both stifled a laugh. 'Now now, Friar,' said Sven. 'You know Harald. He doesn't mean it.' The friar harrumphed.

'Well, not much,' Sigurd added. 'But we need your knowledge. These men claim to be messengers of his holiness King Olav. They have some kind of cross that proves it. Now I've seen a fair few Christian relics in my time' – behind him, Sven grinned an old wolf's smile – 'but I want your confirmation that it is the real thing.'

Friar Johann gazed at the four men in the middle of the floor. 'At last! My prayers have been heard! Christians, come to deliver us!'

Ulfar saw the big bruiser roll his eyes. He also saw their leader subtly kicking the big man's shin. As if nothing had happened, Jorn turned to the friar. 'Go with God, father. I would implore you to look upon this cross and verify it for us. It was given to me by King Olav, who said I was to be his voice, his ears and eyes in Stenvik, to prepare for the coming of his heavenly army.'

The friar's face lit up. 'This I can do, my son. Show me.' Jorn dutifully handed him the chain. The friar's face changed at once. Flustered anger, red-faced indignity and anguish gave way to serenity and confidence.

He turned towards Sigurd.

'These men are who they say they are, Sigurd. This cross bears the inscription of King Olav and says in Latin that he who wears it walks with God.'

Sigurd inhaled then exhaled slowly. 'That's . . . great. So, Jorn of the Dales. Welcome to our humble town. Forgive the reception, but these are rather' – Sigurd rose from his seat and interrupted Jorn, who was about to speak – 'exceptional times,' he continued in a louder voice. 'So.' Walking quickly towards the four, he swept them with him out of the longhouse. 'If you want to be the King's ears, listen.'

As the four riders struggled to keep up with Sigurd storming ahead, the sounds of metal on metal could be heard all through Stenvik. The chieftain strode towards the west gateway. 'Do you hear, Jorn? Those are my raiders, my old men and my children sharpening their knives, steeling their swords, honing their spears.' A tortured bleating cut through the sound of stone on metal. 'Oh, and slaughtering all our livestock. Every single animal. We'll eat well in the next two days.' They reached the steps up to the wall, which Sigurd mounted as if they were flat. Jorn's men had to jog to keep up. 'Now I noticed that you didn't seem to think much of it when I said Skargrim was on his way. I understand that you will be the King's mouth, but I bid you hold your tongue—' Sigurd reached the top of the wall and took his bearings. When Jorn caught up Sigurd fixed him with an intense look. 'Until you've been the King's eyes and seen *this*.'

With that he turned and pointed out to sea.

At a big, black line on the horizon.

Sixty ships, headed for Stenvik.


Now that she had embraced the pain, Lilia found the confidence to venture out of the house more. At first she was afraid, as she'd always been. Afraid that he'd be watching her, that he'd somehow catch her even when she'd left him knocked out on Valgard's mixture.

But he wasn't watching.

And increasingly, it seemed he wouldn't be. Harald had seemed different in the last few days. It was as if he wasn't quite . . . there. He'd looked like he'd lost interest in her after the last beating, when she'd seen him cry. There had been a couple of flashes of temper, but even then he'd looked like he was holding back for whatever reason. She couldn't fathom what it was that had changed him, nor did she want to. She was too busy staging her own modest escape, breaking free from her captor.

In the five years since she'd arrived she'd made few friends, but Inga was one of them. She was blonde and slim, with big blue eyes and a seldom seen, crooked smile. A little younger than Lilia, but already a widow at seventeen, she had lost her husband to a Saxon arrow on a raid last year. On the few occasions when Lilia had dared to go out – to wait for Harald, of course – Inga would come and stand beside her down at the harbour. There they'd stand, one waiting for the man who'd never come again, the other hoping that hers would not return. They had not exchanged many words in their respective vigils but their friendship was a solid thing, a quiet bond reinforced through pain and desperation. After ably serving as lookout yesterday in Lilia's daring trip to see Ulfar, Inga was her closest ally and co-conspirator by default. So when Harald did not return or demand anything of her, Lilia went outside to seek her friend.

Stenvik was buzzing.

It sounded different, though.

These were sounds of purpose, intent and intensity.

She saw young boys carry spears up onto the walls. Behind them came women with slop buckets half-full of water. She could see little girls running around, picking up stones from the side of the roads and throwing them into small sacks.

As she turned onto the road from the western gateway her stomach lurched as if she'd been hit, her vision blurred for an instant and her whole body tingled.

A moment later, her brain told her what it was.

It was him. Ulfar. Standing by the door of the longhouse. Intent, sharp, focused and beautiful. Talking to someone old, and pointing a lot. Sven, her brain whispered in the background. He's talking to Sven.

She watched them, transfixed, breathing quickly.

'Lilia?' There was a note of surprise in Harald's voice. 'Where the hell do you think you're going?'

'I—' she began, scrambling. She turned to find him standing between two houses by the side of the road, looking at her. 'I went to get some water.'

'You can't. They poisoned the well.' She stared at him, paralysed with fear. He simply looked back blankly. 'Go home. You shouldn't be out.'

With great effort she broke the hold, nodded quickly, turned and ran.

Ulfar caught only a brief glimpse of Lilia as she ran away, but it was enough to make his heart jump. He was about to set off after her when a young boy came running.

'He's awake! Your friend is awake!' The boy barely managed to stop himself before crashing into Ulfar and Sven. 'Audun says you're to come quick! He's speaking!' With that, the boy ran away again.

Torn, Ulfar cast a longing glance towards the place where Lilia had disappeared in between the houses, then turned and set off swiftly towards the healer's house, followed by Sven.

Up the road towards the western gateway Harald emerged. He watched the two men walk away, an unreadable expression on his face. When they'd gone he turned and headed south.

## STENVIK FOREST

A subtle change in the sounds of the forest was enough to wake Oraekja. His back hurt, his knees hurt and he had to try very hard to keep his teeth from chattering.

Someone was very close to his hiding place. He could smell it. Inching forward, he caught a glimpse of the man.

He was a scrawny bastard, dressed in rags and wielding a battered old shortsword. He didn't look like much, but Oraekja had learned not to judge fighters by their looks. A powerful longing gripped him then, an urge for someone to take the lead. Someone to tell him what to do. Someone like Skargrim. He thought of Ragnar and blinked furiously. Still, the scrawny man looked nothing like the people from Stenvik. That had to mean he was one of theirs, right? The people from the forest had attacked the caravan so they were on the same side. Had to be. The more Oraekja thought about it, the more it made sense. He'd explain who he was and what he'd done, and be taken to their camp where he could wait for Skargrim and Skuld to arrive.

He rose.

'Hello, friend,' he said, raising his hands.

The scrawny man twirled around, shock and surprise on his face. He bared his teeth and launched himself at Oraekja.

## STENVIK

'You bastard! I thought you were good as dead and it turns out you were just having a rest!'

Geiri mustered a tired smile. Ulfar's words said one thing but his face said something entirely different. 'Sorry about that. Next time you go get the ale.'

Ulfar smiled sheepishly. 'Maybe next time I will.'

Behind him, Sven cleared his throat. 'Now, son. Move over and let me have a look at the man. See if he's still in one piece.' Ulfar moved out of the way and Sven knelt over Geiri, touching his scalp and feeling for injuries.

'I checked. There's nothing on the outside,' Valgard said. He was standing by the door, looking down on Sven crouched over Geiri with the two newcomers. 'I think he's safe from bleeding on the inside. Some bruises, but his skull looks fine.'

'That it does,' Sven muttered, without taking his eyes off Geiri. 'You've done well with our wounded men, Valgard. And speaking of which – where is the pig farmer? He was bundled up in a heap over in the corner last time I saw him.'

'He was going to find Sigurd and talk about his . . . rights,' Audun said, choosing each word carefully. 'But that was yesterday.'

There was a brief silence in the hut. Then Sven spoke. 'It's amazing that that man isn't dead yet. Considering his sense of timing, we might see him back in here sooner rather than later.'

## STENVIK, THE OLD TOWN

'Out!' Harald banged again on the shutters of the little hut. 'Get out! Now!' Sigurd's instructions had been simple enough. Go to the shacks and huts of the old town, round up the stragglers and bring them in behind the walls.

A thin, nervous man scurried out, carrying a bag on his back. Behind him a scrawny woman holding a snotty, whimpering child manoeuvred herself out of the hut, blinking and looking around. Harald pointed wordlessly at the town walls. They got the message and hobbled towards the southern gate. He moved on. Get everyone out of there and move them into town. Those were his orders. And then there were more of Sigurd's little surprises to arrange. Already he could hear shouts and hammering sounds. Valgard had walked off into the old town with a big sack on his back, picking huts at random and disappearing inside. But Harald struggled to keep his mind on the task at hand. His head hurt. Gliding along in some kind of odd half-sleep, he felt strange inside. Like something was melting, leaking, giving way. The vision from yesterday morning taunted him and kept coming tantalizingly close, staying just beyond his reach. Suddenly a flimsy hut would grow bigger before his eyes, so much so that he felt he was knocking on the vast doors of Valhalla. Thor would pass him in the street and clap him on the shoulder like a war-brother and his heart would swell. Freya would wink at him through various women and he would feel the blood rush to his groin. And sometimes it felt like shapes in the shadows were . . . watching him. Watching and smiling.

Still, the work got done. He dispensed commands, praise and threats where needed. And it worked. The men with the shovels had done their jobs, the men preparing the huts equally so. There was a steady trickle of people with bedrolls and whatever meagre possessions they could scrounge trickling into town through the southern gateway.

He took no pride in it. He just wanted to lie down.

He wanted to lie down and sleep and wake and drink some mixture and sleep again. He wanted to go to Valhalla, to speak with the gods. To eat and fight. Go somewhere where things were simple again, where he did the right thing. Where the thing he did *was* the right thing.

'Like if you were the chieftain,' a dry, cold voice whispered from the shadows, smirking. Harald's heart thundered in his chest, but he didn't show it. You never show your fear. That much he knew. It had been beaten into the very core of him.

'Chieftains. Men with power. Mmmm.' The husky notes of a woman somewhere, gliding over him like warm honey, infiltrating his head, surrounding him. Visions of Freya's curves danced before his eyes. Harald could feel his body stirring and drew a deep breath, trying to push the images away. He was not well. There was something wrong with his head. Maybe he should tell someone. But that would mean abandoning his post. And Harald would not shirk his duties, regardless of how he felt or what he thought of Sigurd. Not now. This was war and he needed to be reliable. Reliable and solid. So he continued and tried his best to ignore it when his head changed things around him.

And soon enough the voices of the gods stopped bothering him. As Harald walked through the old town banging on shutters and ordering people into the fort, the visions became his friends and companions through the preparations. He made sure he didn't talk to them, though. Not here. Not now. But as he grew more familiar with Freya's eyes, Loki's shadow-smirk, Thor's curt nods, his head cleared again. There was nothing wrong with him. Quite the opposite. It was all beginning to make sense.

He had been chosen by the gods.

Now he only needed to find out why.

## STENVIK

Sven found Sigurd walking the wall, looking towards the woods. 'Did the pig farmer come to see you for a ruling on his rights?' he asked without preamble.

Sigurd looked at him, briefly puzzled. 'Oh. That. That's today. No, I haven't seen him. Why?'

'It seems he left the hut yesterday to go find you.'

Sigurd shook his head. 'I cannot keep track of everyone within our walls, Sven. Maybe he's changed his mind. I've seen neither of his kinsmen either since last night.' He shrugged. 'I guess that means Harald is safe.' Moving slowly among the men, he nodded at a fair few, clapped backs and clasped hands.

'Maybe,' said Sven. 'He is still responsible for Geiri's wounds, is he not?'

'He might be, yes. But if the boy lives it's not that bad, is it?' Sigurd looked at his adviser with a critical eye. 'I promise you that if we survive this we'll lean on Harald. The boys will get their worth and everyone but him will be happy. Then we'll send him out to raid somewhere else and take it out on some Saxon farmers. Is that acceptable?'

'I guess that is our only option,' Sven replied.

Sigurd smiled. 'One is better than none, my friend.'

The raiders of the *Westerdrake* had followed orders and spread the word – prepare for war. Everywhere Audun looked, Stenvik obeyed. People worked with steely determination. Harald's raiders had rounded up all the people in the old town and escorted them inside the walls. The fast-approaching line of enemy ships was spur enough.

Thorvald's men were coming in from the outside carrying pails of water quickly drawn from irrigation ditches, animal troughs and anywhere else. Some of the scouts were wounded from skirmishes with the outlaws.

The town bristled with weaponry. An old man walked past Audun, a fierce glint in his eye and a rusty sickle in his hand. Kids were running up the steps to the top of the wall, carrying bags bulging with stones. By the southern gateway Harald stood at the head of a group of ten raiders, all armed and ready to go. Audun watched as the big captain put on his helmet in silence. As the metal guard cloaked his eyes, the big raider checked the axe in his belt, the sword sheathed on his hip, and pointed silently towards the southern gate. The raiders followed him without a sound. Looking around, Audun noticed three other ten-man groups, all heading towards the southern gateway.

Up on the wall, Ulfar and Sven watched as the enemy fleet split in two. Still a fair distance out, a large group of ships seemed to double back and hold, reefing sails and working oars. Meanwhile, twelve ships in the vanguard appeared to set a course to the south of Stenvik, skirting past the harbour. Five sleek black-and-silver vessels peeled off from the bulk of the fleet and followed.

Around them fighters manned the walls under Thorvald's control. Dressed in mail shirts and helmets, armed with spears and axes, two raiders would line up on the wall. Between them an old man or young boy would stand armed with whatever he could find, several bags of small stones by his feet. Over on the far side of the wall Ulfar saw Valgard laying out cloth to use as bandages.

'This is going to be one hell of a scrap,' Sven remarked. They stood in silence for a while. Then he added: 'You're not half bad at Tafl, son. So tell me, what are they doing?'

Ulfar found to his embarrassment that the compliment made him blush. 'Well, if you're outmanned you wouldn't split up – the larger force would murder first one half of your troops, then the other. So odds are Skargrim knows he's got the numbers. Maybe that's what he's showing us. It depends on what happens with the outlaws, but I'd expect him to have his men form a loose circle around the town, focusing on the four exits. Then he'd wait us out.'

Sven grinned. 'Not bad, son. Not bad. But what do you know about Skargrim?'

Ulfar scratched his head. 'Not much, I must admit. I've heard his name mentioned, but detailed news of his conquests hasn't quite spread down my way.'

'Well – I'll tell you this for nothing. He is smarter than you'd think, absolutely merciless and fond of the unexpected. That's why he's coming in now.'

'What do you mean?'

'You'd think he'd want to approach under cover of night and hit us just before dawn, surprise us and hack us in our beds. It's the way we usually raid, it's smart and it saves on men.'

'You're right,' said Ulfar, frowning. 'So why is he coming in now?'

Sven smiled through his white beard. 'He wants to soften us up nicely first. He figures we'll be staying and fighting, so he wants us to see him coming. He wants us to know and have a good long think about it. If you add that to the poisoned well and the outlaws, you get defenders with death on their minds who are therefore twice as likely to run away or break down.'

'M-hmm,' Ulfar replied, lost in thought and examining the terrain. 'And how do you know what he's thinking?'

212

Sven's face turned hard.

'Because Sigurd and I used to sail with him.'

'But what about grain? Meat?' Jorn tried to keep pace with Sigurd, who was marching towards the longhouse.

'We have enough.' Sigurd's reply was clipped, offhand.

'For how long?' Jorn followed the chieftain as he opened the doors to the longhouse and stepped in, hardly breaking his stride. He didn't reply. 'For how long? And where do you keep it?! Tell me! I have to know!' An edge of hysteria crept into Jorn's voice. 'King Olav told me that I had to find out! Prepare for the coming of the holy army! The word of God!'

Sigurd turned on Jorn, eyes blazing. 'We have enough grain, the sheds by the animal pens are full of bloody grain, and your King Olav can bloody come here and ask me himself instead of sending some wet little boy to do the work! How far away is he? Come on! How far away? Tell me that, Jorn of the bloody Dales!' Sigurd advanced on the young man, radiating fury.

Shocked, Jorn took two steps back. 'I – I—'

'You don't know. And how could you?' Sigurd sighed and turned towards the dais. 'You're just boys who know nothing,' he muttered, stepping up to his chair. Instead of taking a seat he moved behind it, reaching for the big axe mounted on the wall.

It came down easily.

Turning towards Jorn and his men the old chieftain hefted the menacing weapon, weighing it in his hands, looking at it like he'd never seen it before. 'You were never going to stay on that wall, were you?' he said quietly, looking at the worn wood in his hands. 'You were always coming down again.' Looking up, he seemed to realize where he was. 'Stop gawping,' he snapped. 'Make yourselves useful. Jorn and you' – he pointed to Runar –

213

'report to Thorvald. Tall, skinny. Scout master. You two' – pointing at Havar and Birkir – 'report to Harald. You've met, I believe.'

'I don't mean to complain but you can't—' Havar began. Sigurd turned and looked at him as if noticing him for the first time. The fat man yelped involuntarily. Ramrod-straight, strong and lithe, holding the massive axe as though it weighed nothing, the years seemed to drop off Stenvik's chieftain. A slow, wolfish smile spread on his weathered face.

'. . . Can't?' he prompted.

'I beg your pardon. So, so much,' Havar bubbled nervously. 'I meant to say that you can't ask for more than to fight beside yourself against – against the . . . the others. The enemies. The enemies of Stenvik are the enemies of King Olav and oof—' A well-placed elbow from Runar silenced the fat man.

Jorn seized the opportunity. 'Sigurd. We're about to be besieged. If King Olav knew of this army of raiders coming in, he told us nothing. We must send your best runner out past the outlaws to alert the King!'

The old chieftain headed for the door without looking back. 'We must do nothing but survive. However, your suggestion has merit. Ask Thorvald whether he will send Sigmar. It is his decision. Now go find your commanders, get orders and get rest if you can. They'll be here soon and then there's no telling.' With that he left, the slam of the door spreading silence in the longhouse like rings in a pool. The first noise to breach the quiet was Havar's outraged voice. 'That was unnecessary!' he whined at Runar.

'Yes, it was,' Jorn replied, all trace of nervousness vanished. 'Runar should have left you to blabber to the man with the big axe. He should have let you tell him more about what he can't do. Maybe tell him that he couldn't lop off your fat, yammering head with one stroke and watch him prove you wrong.'

'I'm . . . sorry, Jorn,' Havar muttered, staring at his toes.

'So you should be,' Jorn snapped.

'Still,' Runar piped up. 'You p-p-put on a very con-uh-convincing show. He was f-fuh-furious at the King.'

'For sending a boy,' Birkir rumbled, eyes twinkling. 'A boy who knows nothing.'

'Thank you,' said Jorn. 'Glad you liked it. Now we need to build on this without going too far. We do what Sigurd says, report in and fight with the locals. We hold off these stinking northerners long enough to allow King Olav to get here and trounce whatever is left, by which time I fully expect something accidental to have happened to, say, a third of their grain stores? Just don't get yourselves killed, you idiots.'

'P-p-please, Jorn. Just once. C-can I? Just once?' Runar pleaded as Birkir and Havar smirked.

Jorn frowned in mock annoyance. 'No, Runar. No dying.'

'Wh-what if I get Havar killed?' Runar ventured.

'That's another matter entirely,' Jorn replied.

'Hey! I'm right here, you stuttering little weed!' Havar exclaimed as the four men left the longhouse, grinning among themselves.

### OUTSIDE STENVIK

'ROW! ROW, YOU STINKING, DRIBBLING SHIT BABIES! ROW! COME ON!' Thora screamed at the men, who smiled through gritted teeth. The ships had fanned out and were heading at full speed towards the beach. The other half of the crew was armed to the teeth, ready to jump overboard and hit the defenders hard the moment they touched land. To the north, past Stenvik harbour, Skargrim could see Ingi, Thrainn and Hrafn directing their ships to do exactly the same.

That had been the plan, at any rate.

But the beach was empty. The ships zoomed in, skimming across the water, powered by strong arms and broad shoulders.

Skargrim looked at the collection of huts, the longhouse rising above them. Wooden walkways, deserted. Behind the old town, a fortress rising.

Stenvik.

He smiled a feral smile. 'Not bad, Sigurd. Not bad.'

Thora's scream cut through everything. 'OARS IN!!'

As one, thirty-six oars lifted up out of the water and the *Njordur's Mercy* knifed through the water.

The last thing Skargrim saw before the ships beached at speed was a pole, set in the square by the harbour.

A nag's head was impaled on it, facing out to sea.


### STENVIK FOREST

They'd fought.

Oraekja had ended it, lying on his back on the forest floor. A handful of mud and leaves flung in his opponent's eyes had bought him time enough to get up and close enough to do the knife work. He'd clutched the gangly fighter with his left arm, stabbing repeatedly into the soft belly and twisting the knife in the dying man's guts. His right hand was covered in blood and the stench of the outlaw's innards was still all over the front of his clothes. He reeked, but the fight had shaken Oraekja out of his misery.

He had to find her.

All aches and pains forgotten, he started inching towards the sea.

## STENVIK, THE OLD TOWN

'MOVE!' Skargrim's voice boomed. Three hundred hardened raiders roared an assortment of battle shouts and headed at speed towards the deserted old town. Skargrim ran with them, keeping pace despite his age and bulk.

'Seems a little too quiet,' Thora said, running up alongside him. 'And look. Their southern gate is open.'

Behind him he could hear Egill Jotunn shouting at his men. He stole a quick look and saw the black-clad raiders striding purposefully along, the giant at their point. He shook a massive, slab-like fist in greeting. Skargrim saluted in return.

Looking back at the Stenvik houses, something stirred in Skargrim. He turned to Thora. 'You're right. This stinks.' The command voice boomed again. 'SLOW DOWN, we're walking in! Eyes!'

The men responded at once and slowed to a walk, shields up. On the other side of town Ingi had already called for caution, with Hrafn following his lead. Across the harbour Skargrim saw young Thrainn watch in desperation as a sizeable group of his men disobeyed his order, broke free and set off at a dead run towards the houses outside the wall, screaming obscenities and battle cries. Skargrim also noted that Ingi's contingent made up the rearguard and were slowing down in their approach, if anything.

Thrainn's runaways arrived at the houses and swarmed over the walkways, still shouting.

Nothing happened.

Cutting through into the middle of town, the bloodthirsty raiders hooted and hollered.

Above Stenvik's southern gateway a lone figure stood up, horn in hand. He blew three short blasts, then one long note. The younger of Thrainn's warriors turned and hurled insults back towards the man with the horn.

All around the raiders, walls silently collapsed inwards.

Armed men in twos and threes, shortswords, hand axes. No shields. One cut to injure, two to maim, three to kill. Screams of pain erupted from within the old town.

Then, as swiftly as they'd appeared from the huts, the ambushers were sprinting for their lives back towards the southern gateway, swerving across the southern road in strange lines.

A brace of flaming arrows flew from the top of Stenvik's walls, thudding into wattle walls, wooden roofs. Houses that burst into flame surprisingly quickly.

'No, no, no . . .' Skargrim muttered.

Infuriated, Thrainn's renegades had regrouped and were giving chase with swords raised.


STENVIK

Harald's hand-picked raiders sprinted into town in small groups, their triumphant whoops echoing through the gateway. One of Harald's raiders strode through into the market square and let loose a primal roar.

Valgard called to him across the square from his makeshift aid station. 'Are you hurt? You're covered in blood!'

The powerful young fighter turned and grinned. 'Hah! If so, it's not mine!' A roar of approval went up from the men in the square, soon echoed from the southern wall.

## STENVIK, THE OLD TOWN

Afterwards Thora swore she'd heard the snap as the first man's leg broke. Within a couple of breaths four more of Thrainn's men had run at full speed into the trip holes dug into the southern road, set with vicious barbed spikes to punch through feet and stones at the bottom to ensure a broken ankle. They had been picked off easily by the archers on the wall, their corpses stuck in the road, some buried up to mid-thigh.

Eight raiders dead, another twenty-seven badly wounded.

The remaining men had retreated quickly out of missile range and returned to Thrainn's ranks as the southern gate closed with a dull thump. Now the young chieftain sat at the harbour and looked out to sea, ashen-faced.

'Those men will never fight again,' he muttered.

'No, they won't,' Skargrim replied. 'And not only that – they're still here. The rest of your men can still look them in the eye. They can still hear them whimpering. It won't stop your fighters, but even the hardest ones will be a little less inclined to fight. Sigurd knows what he's doing.'

Of the twenty-seven, only four had life-threatening wounds. The others had been hit just hard enough to take them out of the fight. Sword arms, knees and shoulders. As Skargrim suspected, the houses hit by fire arrows had been liberally clad with kindling to accelerate the fire, heat the blood and encourage pursuit. The rest of the town's houses stood firm. A cautious advance had confirmed that the town outside the walls had been deserted in a hurry.

Hrafn's men had ransacked the houses. One of them had found a leg of lamb that someone had abandoned and taken a chunk out of it. Skargrim and Thrainn could still hear the poor man's retching from where they sat. He'd thrown up everything in his stomach and was now vomiting blood. Thrainn watched, mesmerized, as Hrafn walked over to the man and past the pile of poisoned food they'd gathered up. There was no bounce in the captain's step, not a hint of a smile on his pale face. Just grim determination. Hrafn levered his shoulder gently under the crouching man's armpit and stood him up. A greenish, sickly face with a thin stream of pink spittle stared at them.

Hrafn half-led, half-carried the man into a storage hut by the harbour. He came out alone and walked over to Thrainn and Skargrim.

'Fogroot. A lot of it, too. He won't live through the night,' he said, matter-of-factly. 'Serves him right, thinking with his stomach like that. Although I must say,' he continued, nodding to Skargrim, 'your friend Sigurd has a nice bag of tricks.'

'He always did. We know what he's capable of. Nobody thought this would be easy, did they?' Skargrim looked at Hrafn and Thrainn. Both shook their heads. 'But clever as all of this is, Sigurd will find out that all he's done is separate the boys from the men. Soon he'll find out that he has no water.'

Hrafn grinned at that. 'Lovely. Ragnar?'

Skargrim nodded and smiled proudly. 'He's a wily one, my brother.'

'Always has been,' Hrafn nodded in assent. 'Is she . . .' he gestured towards the *Njordur's Mercy*, at anchor in the bay.

Skargrim nodded. 'She's staying on the ship, out of harm's way. I had four of my men row her out there. She says she won't step on this ground before the will of the old gods is done.'

'Battleground's no place for a woman, anyway,' Thrainn said.

Hrafn grinned. 'I'll be sure to carve that on the forehead of your corpse when the Valkyries come.'

Thrainn smiled back. 'If you plan on hiding in the back, old thing, then by all means do. I'll be up front with the real men.'

'Hah!' The glint was back in the skinny sea captain's eye. 'You could fit Idunn's tit into that mouth, Skargrim!' The big grey-haired raider did not respond. '. . . Skargrim?'

Skargrim faced away from them, looking east.

Thrainn and Hrafn followed his gaze.

Around town the other raiders gradually fell silent as they saw what was happening.

After a while Hrafn broke the silence.

'Who in Bolthorn's name are they?'

## STENVIK

The men of Stenvik were gathered in small groups on the wall, some peering over the edge, whispering and pointing to the east. Others tried their best to catch glimpses of the assembled army to the south. There looked to be nearly four invaders to every Stenvik fighter, and the silent forest loomed with a promise of untold masses of near-invisible outlaws.

Ulfar didn't see Sigurd, but he felt his presence. Suddenly the chieftain was there, walking amongst the raiders of the *Westerdrake*, clapping shoulders, nodding seriously at grizzled old fighters, sparing a smile for the younger men. Sigurd wove through the fabric of Stenvik's defences, bolstering the men's spirits simply by being there.

Sven leaned in and winked. 'He's good, isn't he?' Ulfar could do nothing but nod. The chieftain of Stenvik was dressed for war, red tunic over a bulky mail shirt, round shield on his back, spear in hand and a broad-bladed battleaxe in his belt. Ulfar watched him walk the wall, stopping to speak and share a private moment with every single warrior – and courage followed in his wake. Frightened boys, doubtful fighters and shaken old men now stood up straight, determined and strong. Thinking back, Ulfar suddenly understood something Geiri's father had spent months trying to teach him and Geiri. You can't tell them, he'd said. You have to show them. Looking at the warriors of Stenvik, he realized that Sigurd was not commanding or forcing anything. Walking among them, making them his equals, he simply gave them a choice, a lead to follow.

And they would need it.

After the initial slaughter Skargrim's army had drawn back, setting up camp around the far end of the old town, out of arrow range. Ulfar had tried to count heads but been chastised by Sven. 'We don't need to know,' the old man had snapped. 'There's lots of 'em. Enough for everyone. Leave it at that.' Then, a second later he'd added: 'There's fewer now than there were to start with, though,' and walked away, chuckling to himself.

Now Sven was back at his side, looking to the east.

The fading light made the forest seem alive with movement. From behind every tree, out of every pool of darkness outlaws emerged, black shapes against a grey backdrop. Behind them, shadows flickered in the gloom. Shouts went up along the wall. 'Calm down, boys!' Sven shouted. 'They're just showing themselves.' Most of the mass of outlaws disappeared back into the forest, but a small group broke off and headed towards the invaders' camp, skirting the walls by a wide margin. 'So, Ulfar. Did you count them?' Sven snapped.

'No . . . no, I didn't. Maybe a hundred?' Ulfar stole a look at the old man, who kept his eyes trained on the forest.

Sven's voice lacked its usual note of mirth. 'Eighty. Staggered over a broad line. Twenty more filling in gaps. Possibly another twenty running between trees in the back. They just showed us that they had numbers but made it impossible for us to establish how many they were. Clever,' he mumbled. 'The outlaws are not to be taken lightly.'

Ulfar thought he saw movement around the old town, but

there was no mass mobilization, no onrush of Skargrim's men to meet the forest bandits in bloody battle.

'I hate it when I'm right,' Sven mumbled by his side. 'Somehow that old bastard has rounded up every murdering, thieving bastard around and got them on his side.'

Sigurd approached them. 'So. Got any bright ideas, Sven?' the chieftain muttered under his breath.

Sven snorted derisively. 'Die fast?'

Sigurd looked at his friend. 'I'm sure there's women and children that need looking after if you're scared, old man,' he said gently, a mischievous glint barely visible through the eye guard of his helmet.

'Oh shut up,' Sven said, grinning into his white beard. 'I thought I was destined to rot slowly and take a running leap off the cliff. If we die here we die with honour, defending our town. Can't ask for more than that, can you?'

'Don't reckon you can,' Sigurd replied. 'Keep an eye on them. I'm going to go talk to the rest of our men, make sure they stay awake, alert and as alive as possible.'

'You go do that,' Sven replied.

The last rays of the evening sun faded into night.

## STENVIK FOREST

Somewhere deep inside Oraekja, something stirred. Something called to him, made him feel warm and wanted, pulled at his blood. Made him want to get moving. Skuld was here. He could feel it. She was close and she needed him.

He could almost taste the sharp smell of the pine needles as he hurried through the forest, heading towards the sea. The sounds of the outlaws were all around him, but he didn't care.

He would live.

She'd make sure that he did.


## STENVIK

'So what do you think, son? Should we be lighting torches on the wall?'

Ulfar smiled to himself. This was familiar ground. 'Yes. Definitely, yes.' Sven was about to speak when Ulfar interrupted him. 'If you want to blind your men to the dark and light us up for their archers, then I say absolutely. What you can and will do is light torches down below. We'll be able to use the edges of the light but won't be too badly blinded.'

Sven nodded his approval. 'You're well schooled, boy. I suppose you've learned from your father?'

'Don't all sons learn from their fathers?'

'Some do,' Sven replied quietly.

The two men stood in silence for a spell, listening to the bustle of the town behind them, the chatter of the men on the east wall.

'Geiri's father – my uncle – used to drill me on these things,' Ulfar finally ventured. 'Reading the terrain, talking to the men, considering the outcome of every decision on the battlefield.' Mimicking an aging chieftain, he rumbled: 'That is what makes a good leader, Ulfar. Knowledge.' He snorted noisily. 'Mmm. Knowledge.'

'You're a piece of work, son.' Sven smirked.

'Thank you . . . I think?' Ulfar replied.

'Oh, you're welcome. Now try not to die in the next couple of days, will you? We still need to finish that game. I remember the position exactly.'

'I'm sure you do,' Ulfar said. 'Exactly like it was.'

'How dare you question my honour like that! I'll have your hide—'

'— after your nap and your warm milk?' Ulfar shot back.

'Hah!' Sven exclaimed. 'Here's a free lesson in leadership, son – two, actually, from a wizened old cheat. First – keep doing exactly what you're doing. Keep the mood, the sword and the head up, and we all live to see another day. And last – never underestimate an old man.' Sven grinned wickedly.

Flickering torches in Skargrim's camp illuminated an army moving to the east. Towards the outlaws.

'Looks like Skargrim is going to meet the woodworms,' Sven spat.

'It does indeed,' Ulfar said. The silence lingered. 'You've just slaughtered a lot of livestock, haven't you?' he added after a while.

'Yes. Why?' Sven said, a note of suspicion creeping into his voice.

'Oh, nothing,' Ulfar replied. 'It's just that I had an idea.'


BETWEEN THE OLD TOWN AND THE FOREST

The captains lined up in front of their men.

Thrainn, straight-backed and strong.

Ingi, calculating and assessing.

Wide-eyed Hrafn, grinning manically.

Egill, humming happily to himself.

And Skargrim.

Behind them, over a hundred battle-hardened raiders.

In front, a group of ragged, scrawny men. In the torchlight they looked more like a small band of demons. Gaunt and gangly, clad in green and brown rags. Scattered on the front line were long, thick spears, and the flickering torchlight caught on a variety of edges and spikes, knives and shortswords.

Two lumbering oafs stood out, a head taller than the rest of the motley crew. They looked big enough, but Skargrim had seen and killed bigger. The man in front of them was another matter. His hair was tied in a ponytail and his clothes were ragged, but with folds in the right places for any number of nasty surprises, Skargrim observed. He exuded a quiet physical confidence. Skargrim had no doubt he'd move fast and hit hard. He recognized a killer when he saw one, and this one had killed before.

Skargrim considered his captains and smiled.

That was unlikely to worry any of this lot.

What set the leader of the outlaws apart was his eyes. There was something cold and calculating in them, something . . . baleful.

'So where's the rest?' The outlaw's voice was pleasant and calm.

'The rest of what?' Skargrim replied.

'We were promised two feed sacks full of silver and gold to come here, wait in the forest and kill anything that tried to get through. Now where's my loot?'

'See those walls? Your sacks of loot are in there,' Hrafn chimed in.

'Why don't you take your rag brothers and go fetch?' Thrainn added.

The outlaw leader smiled and looked at Skargrim. 'How lovely. You've taught your dogs to speak. Do they do other tricks as well? I've heard they lick anything that's had a bit of meat rubbed on it.'

Skargrim felt more than heard the hands on hilts and rising blood behind him. Tension rippled through the gathered men. The outlaw leader continued in the level tones of a man negotiating prices at a market. 'I have about two hundred and fifty men in the forest and little time for this. If you don't tell me where and when we're getting paid and fed I'll do one of two things. I'll turn my two hundred and fifty over to Stenvik – there'll be some minor debts of honour, but nothing we can't figure out – or I'll murder as many of you in your sleep as I need to. How does that sound?' Behind him the outlaws gripped their weapons tighter.

The cold shock of the coming fight trickled through Skargrim's spine. He welcomed it like an old friend. Now he'd need to play for time somehow. He puffed up his chest, ready to bellow some manner of nonsense at the man, give his men time to register the change and get ready. In his mind he charted the moves necessary for an attack straight for the leader's jugular. If he hit it in one he might cause confusion and lead them in a rout. A dull pressure built at the base of his spine, pumped fight into his muscles, filled him with murder.

Skargrim reached for the hilt of his knife as the first notes drifted in from the sea.

The song was the yearning for home, the pain of goodbye, the forgotten touch of a long-lost mother. It went straight through Skargrim's chest, tore open his heart and left it bleeding sweetly, yet somehow it filled up the empty black spaces that it found within him, filled them up with life and belief and delicious pain and joy, with pictures of moments with family, with friends, with home. Something blurred his vision and he struggled to stay on his feet.

Then the will to live kicked in and he blinked the tears away, shook the fog from his head.

There was no murder in the outlaws' eyes any more. Instead they all looked up as if watching for the notes to come to life in the air, captivated, like children with a colourful toy.

Skargrim caught their leader's gaze. He was the only other man he could see that was not swept away by the music.

'Skuld,' he murmured. 'I remember. We will do what is needed.' He nodded to Skargrim, turned and walked towards the forest. The outlaws turned with him and followed their leader, disappearing into the darkness as the song grew softer, the notes shorter and the silences longer.

Skargrim watched them leave. 'Imagine that,' he muttered.

When the last note ended the raiders turned and headed to their respective camps, unusually silent. On the way back Thrainn walked up alongside Skargrim. 'That song. Was that her?' Skargrim nodded. 'Was it . . . magic?' the young captain whispered.

'No it wasn't,' Egill Jotunn rumbled behind them. 'It wasn't magic. It was a reminder of what we're fighting for.'

## IN UNFAMILIAR WOODS

The echo of the song mixed with the bitter taste of the mixture and the raw smell of pine needles, resin and morning air. Harald's breath caught in his throat. Those trees were bigger than anything he'd ever seen. Suddenly he felt tiny, shrivelled, like a pebble in a bowl. He turned and Valhalla towered above him, impossibly huge. The doors swung open without a sound and peace filled his heart.

He walked inside.

Light streamed from behind him, cloaking everything in a blanket of soft, grey morning sunshine. A massive table stood in the middle of the packed earth floor, stretching deep into the darkened far end of the hall. Thor and Freya sat on opposite sides. From under waves of luscious blonde hair, Freya glanced at the head of the table, at an available chair.

The hint was unmistakable. Harald sat down.

The gods smiled at him.

'Well met, Harald,' Thor said.

'Indeed,' Freya purred.

'Your hero's heart and skill in battle are the stuff of legend. We are pleased with you,' the red-haired warrior continued. 'Very much so,' Freya echoed. 'The ambush was a masterstroke,' Thor concluded. 'Perfect. Simple, smart and effective.'

Harald struggled to find the words. His tongue felt double the size and his cheeks burned. 'I – I – it went well,' he ended up whispering into his chest.

'WELL?' Thor thundered, banging on the table. 'WELL? It was brilliant! Merciless and swift! You outfought and outsmarted your opponent—'

'It was your idea, wasn't it?' The ever-present hint of a smile drifted with the voice that came from everywhere – the shadows, the darkness and behind him. Harald spun around on reflex, and Loki was there. Not three feet away, leaning up against a support beam, casually picking dirt from under his fingernails with a knife. He looked up and met Harald's gaze. 'Wasn't it, Harald? Wasn't it the idea of a great leader, a man who could be – no, should be chieftain?'

'Leave it, Loki!' Thor growled. 'It could have been his idea. He could easily have made that plan. He could have made a better one, put killers in more huts. Or struck at the bloody forest folk first.'

'He can do anything,' Freya said, winking at Harald.

'I have my doubts,' Loki muttered.

'Well, he could do anything to me,' the goddess whispered, honey dripping off her every word.

Harald's blood caught fire and seared his veins. His heart

thumped and images of Freya's naked body cascaded over him, overwhelming him. As he fought to recover he felt Valhalla fading away behind them. Suddenly he was overcome with grief, with the decay of everything good. He cried then, scalding tears of loss streaming down his pockmarked cheeks as the world he understood slipped from his mind, faded to grey, then black.

When he came to he was sitting on a stone bench, leaning up against the longhouse. It was dark outside, with only faint flickers of muted torchlight illuminating the huts of Stenvik. Harald rose, aching all over, and stumbled home.

## STENVIK

'Why did you pick me for this?' Audun whispered between gritted teeth.

'Because I like your company, you're strong enough to pull the cart,' Ulfar whispered back. 'And we can't use a horse. It's too noisy. Opening the gate quietly was hard enough.'

'So you're saying I'm like a horse, only slightly more quiet?'

'Shut up, you two,' Sven muttered at them. 'This is stupid enough as it is. If we get ourselves killed Sigurd will get very cross.'

'And we wouldn't want that, would we?' The grin in Ulfar's voice was very poorly hidden.

'No we wouldn't,' Sven shot back. 'We wouldn't want that at all.'

Audun rolled his eyes in the darkness and pulled the cart onwards.

## NORTH OF STENVIK

The shimmering half-light made the scout want to whisper and tiptoe. The heath looked like a landscape in a dream, with pools of darkness leaking out from underneath large boulders. The forest had been surprisingly easy going – the outlaws hadn't bothered him at all and he'd got a good idea of where they were camped. Now all he needed to do was follow orders, run as fast as he could to King Olav's camp and deliver the message. After that, his job was done.


## STENVIK

'So when do you say King Olav is coming here?'

'I'd say in three days. Maybe four,' Havar managed between mouthfuls. His chins wobbled as he worked his jaw. 'This is some, mmh, incredible meat! How do you get the lamb so tasty?'

'It's all in the seasoning,' Valgard replied.

'Delicious. De-licious,' Havar grunted as he reached for the bone. 'You must show me how so I can cook for Jorn when the time comes.' Holding it up to his mouth, he looked at Valgard. 'May I?'

A smile and a nod later Havar was tearing into the meat on the bone, plump lips smacking on the fat. Valgard looked at the fat man, barely managing to conceal his disgust.

Three days.

That was all he had.

Three days to force a confrontation between Harald and Sigurd, make sure Harald won, install himself as chief adviser and be ready to welcome King Olav's army.

Something had to happen, and it had to happen right now.

In his mind, he looked at the pieces on the board and remembered something about the game. Something Sven had tried to teach him once. 'Like in life,' he'd said, 'you sometimes have to make sacrifices to get things going.'

Smiling, Valgard reached for a leather bottle.

Einar the town cook looked unusually flustered. 'Too much,' he muttered. 'Too bloody much. Everybody's eating like there's no tomorrow. Too bloody much. The meat's going to spoil, too.' Shaking his head and mumbling into his chest, he scurried between the hastily erected pots around the fires in the longhouse, stirring at random. He turned a lamb carcass on the spit and checked on the supplies. The night watch had eaten before going to sleep and the day watch had eaten before going up on the wall. The long table was littered with dirty crockery.

Ulfar sat at the far end, poking at his bowl of broth. He'd had too much excitement and too little sleep last night, he reckoned.

And still she would not leave his head. Even thinking about her made him feel warm inside, made his mouth turn upwards at the corners, made even the damn broth seem appetizing. Ulfar smiled and shook his head. So this was love.

He sensed more than saw the presence at the table. Turning, he found he was looking at a slight blonde woman – no, girl – with big blue eyes that scanned the room, seeking something. When she was satisfied, she turned to him and half-whispered: 'She would like to see you.'

'She – do you mean . . . ?' She smiled and he realized he must look like a particularly dim-witted puppy.

'Yes of course,' she said. 'Could it be anyone else . . . ?'

'No! Not at all. No.' The words tumbled out of Ulfar in a rush of panic. Then she saw her smile widen and composed himself.

'No,' he said, this time with more authority. 'There is not nor shall ever be any other.'

He saw a playful glint in her eye. 'Shame,' she said, winking. 'From what I remember on the night you arrived, you don't kiss half bad.'

In a flash, Ulfar remembered and turned crimson with embarrassment.

'I didn't – so that's – I mean, I wouldn't – not that we didn't but I hadn't met her – but it's – I mean—'

'It is true, then,' she said, nodding slowly to herself. 'You really do love her.' Ulfar blinked, speechless. 'Then may your love be a true one in joy and in strife, and never forgotten for the rest of your life.'

A draught trickled in from somewhere, chilled Ulfar's bones and made the hairs on the back of his hand stand on end.

'Yes. I mean, I won't.'

Inga blinked a couple of times and her lip trembled for a second. 'Good. If you walk past a house with bearskin on the door and carvings of Thor, Tyr and a dragon, whistle the same tune twice. Then go to the horse pens and wait a while. She'll sneak out if at all possible.'

She turned around and headed for the door.

'Wait! Where's the house?'

'Go east just before the north gate,' she said over her shoulder and was gone.

Ulfar was still looking at the door to the longhouse when Valgard entered. Their eyes met and the healer nodded once before picking his way towards Einar and the pots.

## STENVIK FOREST

A dull throb of hurt woke Oraekja. The branches he'd chosen for a bed last night were digging into his back and hip, sending needles of pain through his whole body. Easing up to a sitting position, he blinked a couple of times and shielded his eyes from the stinging sunlight.

He could not see any outlaws but they were there. He could feel them. They were around him, all around him like an itch. Striving to quell the rising sense of panic, he looked to the south. In the morning light he could see the expanse of Skargrim's camp. It seemed much bigger than he remembered.

Still, that would be where she was. He clambered gingerly down from the tree and started walking towards the camp, skirting Stenvik. He saw the camp guards soon enough, but found he didn't recognize them. It didn't matter.

'Skuld. I need to see her.' His voice sounded unfamiliar to his own ears as he approached, squeaky and wrong.

The two men looked at him with scepticism. 'Why? And who are you?'

'I just need to. She calls to me. I must.' Desperation threatened to overtake him and he had to fight back the tears.

The guards looked at him strangely. 'Hand over your weapons and we'll take you to her.'

Oraekja found it hard to part with his knife and felt naked without it, helpless. Like prey. Visions of the forest, blood and death flitted through his head. Exhaustion blurred his eyes and his knee buckled. A spear butt jabbed into his spine brought him back to the present.

'Move.'

The guard pushed him towards the centre of old Stenvik, back towards the harbour.

## NORTH OF STENVIK

'My King, come quick. Please, hurry!'

King Olav ducked out of his tent. 'What is it, Finn?'

Breathless, Finn gestured for the King to listen. Cries of 'Heathen! Heathen!' rang out from the camp.

Without a word King Olav strode towards the source of the sound, leaving Finn to scurry after him. Soon they came upon a bloodied, scrawny man surrounded by a group of furious soldiers. Finn recognized him. The man's name was Hrutur, a hunter of little skill. His captors hurled abuse and spat at the man, calling him a heathen and a traitor.

'What's going on here?' King Olav asked.

One of the soldiers turned to the King, bowed his head and showed him a thumb-sized Thor's Hammer on a ripped leather thong. 'The bastard was wearing this underneath his clothes, my King. He's a heathen, a supporter of the old gods and an enemy of the White Christ.' Silenced by his presence, the men stared at the King, awaiting orders.

King Olav drew a deep breath.

'Deal with him according to his conduct. You are warriors of the White Christ' – in the circle, Hrutur's face went pale – 'and he is the enemy.'

Finn stood, mouth agape as the King turned and walked away.

The soldiers set upon Hrutur, raining blows on the figure in the middle of the circle.

Finn chased after the King. 'My King . . . they'll kill him!'

'Yes. Yes, they will.'

'Why are you letting them?'

King Olav stopped and turned to Finn. The young man's face was drawn and hard, pain in his eyes. 'Because I'm not just fighting chieftains. I'm uniting a country. Because they need to feel superior to someone, feel right about something. And because conviction, Finn, is worth a thousand swords of good men.'

## STENVIK, THE OLD TOWN

'So – how many for a direct charge, then?' The short fat captain smiled as Thrainn's face flushed crimson.

'Give the boy a break, Ingi. You've sailed long enough. You've had some idiots in your crew. Thrainn has done well to get rid of them,' Hrafn added. Ingi raised his eyebrows and seemed about to answer when Egill Jotunn intervened. 'Who's got the thickest armour?' he asked.

'It seems my men are the best equipped,' Ingi replied cautiously. 'That is why I volunteered them for guard duty.'

'Your men for the shield wall, ours through the holes?' Hrafn suggested. The assembled chieftains lapsed into thoughtful silence.

'Would work, but negates our advantage,' Ingi finally offered. 'There are clearly more of us than there are of them, which would make it stupid to crowd into a tunnel. They could hold the gateways with very few men. I say we go over the wall.'

'They'll see us coming for miles. That wall looks a bastard to climb and we'll be target practice. If we go through the gateway we'll at least be up close and personal,' Hrafn countered.

'I'm not sending my men into that hole,' Ingi replied, full of good grace.

'Nor am I sending mine over that wall,' Hrafn said, equally friendly.

Skargrim cleared his throat and the other captains fell silent. 'Here's what we'll do.'

## STENVIK

Ulfar's mind reeled as he hurried up the walkway towards the north-east of town.

Bad idea. Bad, bad, bad idea.

He really shouldn't be doing this. He should be running to Audun or Sven or Geiri or someone. Someone who could smack some sense into him.

But he didn't care.

Instead he focused on the simple things. Like walking. Because if he ran as fast as he wanted to he might attract attention, and that was the last thing he wished for. He was about to do something forbidden. Something wrong. Something his friends would definitely tell him not to do. Breathing deeply, Ulfar continued walking at a measured pace.

Heading off the north road, he noticed the difference in the houses. This was where the raiders lived, the men who could afford wooden houses instead of wattle huts.

There!

The bearskin on the door. And sure enough, the carvings. Ulfar's heart thundered in his chest and suddenly his lips were too dry to whistle. The only sound that escaped was a pathetic squeak. Panicked, he looked around him. Had anybody seen him? Frustration, fear and tension brought him close to throwing up on the spot.

'You were nearly killed two nights ago, last night you risked your life, and now you're losing your mind because you're whistling badly in front of a house?' Ulfar hissed. 'Get a grip!' He inhaled as slowly as he could, then exhaled and wet his lips. Taking a deep breath, he whistled a couple of notes of a gentle tune, a herdsman's melody from home. Looking around, pretending not to notice the bearskin house, he repeated the whistled melody as clearly as he could. Then he ambled off towards the horse pens, heart thumping in his chest.

He desperately wanted to look back, but didn't.

## THE OLD TOWN

The guard pushed him out onto the docks, the ones he'd run along when he'd set fire to the big ship. He recognized the *Njordur's Mercy*, moored a couple of ship's lengths off the end of the middle pier. 'Is she—' Oraekja began. A jab from the butt of the spear silenced him.

'Right. Hands,' the guard snapped when they reached the end of the pier. Through a dull haze Oraekja summoned up what felt like the last of his energy and presented his hands together, ready to be bound. With practised movements the guard looped a cord around them and tied him up. 'Get in the boat.' He gestured at a small rowboat, bobbing by the end of the pier.

Oraekja clambered down a knotted rope with great difficulty and managed somehow to get into the boat with all the grace of a trussed pig. The guard shimmied down after him, positioned him at the back and sat down on the oarsman's bench.

Soon they were moving across the water towards the *Njordur's Mercy*. Onboard a small group of sailors noticed them and prepared to receive the newcomers. The guard swung the rowboat alongside the sleek, powerful ship and strong hands steadied them on approach. Oraekja was hoisted roughly to his feet and brought across, only just finding his balance. Swaying where he stood, he noticed all the men around him growing quiet.

He sensed Skuld's presence behind him like the sun on his back. Inhaling slowly, he felt something of his old self return. He savoured the moment. He, Oraekja, had returned a conqueror after a successful and daring mission behind enemy lines. He had followed orders, survived on his cunning and guile, and would now reap the rewards.

Turning around, he took one look at her and slumped to the deck, unconscious.

## STENVIK

Audun could feel the tension mounting inside the town. Word floated down from the walls that the enemy was lining up, that they were obviously up to something. Archers had tried a couple of times, but their enemies stayed just outside missile range. For now, Audun thought. Sven had ordered him to fix two broken handcarts and get them to the north and west gateways but park them to the side, out of the way.

Fair enough. He was happy doing anything to keep the hands busy, keep his mind off the violence. Grabbing a handful of bolts, he set to work on the first cart.

The brown horse trained big, accusing eyes on Ulfar. You shouldn't be doing this, they said. It's dangerous, it's wrong and you know it.

'Shut up!' Ulfar snapped, leaning on the fence around the horse enclosure. 'You don't know anything anyways.' The horse snorted, turned away and expressed its opinion by way of a sizeable load of manure. 'Thank you. Thank you very much,' Ulfar scolded the gelding. 'That's a really nice touch.'

'Are you . . . talking to a horse?' Lilia asked cautiously. Heart already hammering, Ulfar whirled. The only thing he saw was her smile, the smile that came from the corners of her eyes, the corners of her mouth, the centre of her very being.

It took his breath away. 'I – I – erm . . .'

Her lips parted slowly as the smile spread wider and wider, revealing beautiful, white teeth. From somewhere within her, giggles bubbled up to the surface. She tried to stop them but failed delightfully. 'You strange, strange man,' she said, eyes alight. 'What did the horse do to you?'

'It shat in the pen.' The words were out before he knew it. His eyes widened in horror as he saw the sentence hanging in the air between them. She looked at the horse, then at him. A moment later she burst out laughing. Waves of relief washed over Ulfar and he found himself laughing along.

Her eyes never left his.

Soon the laughter subsided. Ulfar took a cautious step in her direction, then another.

A tear glistened on her cheek.

Another step, then Ulfar reached slowly for the teardrop. He saw her twitch but she remained still, eyes fixed on him. Her sky-blue shift rose and fell with every breath.

He touched her cheek and he was falling. It all seemed so right and happened so smoothly. How his fingertips traced her red curls, how his hand found her neck and pulled her gently close, how she melted into him.

They kissed, cautiously at first but then with increasing, intoxicating urgency.

'Here. Drink this.'

'I'm not really that thirsty,' Geiri muttered, propped up against the wall.

'Drink it. It will help with your recovery.'

He paused, then smiled a tired smile. 'Thank you. That's most kind.'

241

'Don't worry. It's what I do. I patch you up when you fall on your head.'

Geiri drank. 'It's . . . sweet. Kind of . . .' he blinked. 'Kind of . . . like juniper. I like it.' His words slurred. 'Can I have some more?'

'Of course.'

Geiri took the leather bottle and tried to raise it to his lips again. It fell from his hands as he slumped against the wall, a peaceful smile on his face.

Geiri's heart slowed. Then it stopped.

Slim, delicate fingers picked up the bottle and put the cork in. When Valgard left it looked like the young man was simply sleeping.


## THE *NJORDUR'S MERCY*

Skargrim stepped onboard his ship and looked round, but Skuld was nowhere to be seen. The four fighters he'd set to guard her sat in the prow playing dice. One of them caught Skargrim's eye and nodded silently towards her quarters.

When she'd made it clear that she would be coming with them to attack Stenvik, he'd set aside a little bit of space for her in the stern. He'd erected poles and strung hides to shield her from wind, rain and the gazes of the men. He'd even thrown in his best furs to make her journey comfortable.

Moving towards the hides, Skargrim could hear voices, hers and someone else's. Jealousy flared. Who was she speaking to? Who had she allowed onto the *Njordur's Mercy*? His ship?

The vaguely familiar voice suddenly stopped.

'Enter, Skargrim.'

He drew the hide flaps aside.

Sitting on the soft furs, Skuld smiled up at him. She looked different somehow, as if she'd aged by several years. Somebody lay next to her, resting his head in her lap like a babe. It was the little runt that she'd forced Ragnar to take along for the poisoning. Skargrim's brow furrowed. What was this? When had he returned? Where was Ragnar? Nothing was adding up. At last he managed to stammer: 'What's he doing here?'

The scout made to speak but she interrupted. 'There are things that need to be said, Skargrim.' Fear and guilt flitted over the scout's face.

A chill settled on Skargrim's heart and started to spread, like a lake freezing in winter.

'You know Oraekja. His deeds are heroic and he has shown much bravery. The well in Stenvik is poisoned, and they have no more than three days' worth of water. However, he brings ill news of your brother.'


### STENVIK

'Not bad at all.' Sigurd speared a chunk of roasted pig on his knife, leaned back and nodded at Sven. The smell of cooking drifted across the longhouse and a handful of men sat around the table eating. 'I like it. So you say that was Ulfar's idea?' Sven nodded, gnawing on a leg of lamb. 'Well done. Now all we need to do is send a couple of Harald's men into the holes. Thorvald – we'll need some kindling on the wall.'

'Torches and fire arrows already up with my best remaining archers,' came Thorvald's curt reply.

'Good.' Sigurd's eyes lingered on the scout master's features. 'You're angry, my friend. I can see that. But that damn dale boy is right. We need to get word to King Olav as soon as possible. It might make a difference. It might make all the difference.'

'I know,' Thorvald replied.

'Sigmar was practically born in these woods. If anyone could get through unseen, it's him,' Sven added. 'You say he left yesterday?' Thorvald nodded. 'If he keeps a good pace he should have a decent shot at finding Olav in a day, another two to bring him here. We'll be nearly out of water, but we can source that in the springs at Huginshoyde until the foxbell rinses out of the well. We just need to hold for a couple more days.'

Thorvald turned in his chair and looked away. 'It should have been me.'

Sigurd replied at once. 'And who would then lead the scouts? The fighters on the wall? Who would give commands when neither I nor Sven are around? Who could I trust to plant an arrow in Skargrim's eye at fifty paces?'

Thorvald turned back towards Sigurd, but did not speak. The three sat in silence.

'It's going to be one mother of a scrap,' Sven offered after a while. 'More lamb?'

## THE *NJORDUR'S MERCY*

'So you're saying they surprised you and there was a fight. Ragnar was killed, but you escaped. That my brother fought like a demon, but there were too many.'

Oraekja nodded once, then glanced at Skuld. Skargrim felt her eyes on him but did not turn, did not meet her gaze. The waves lapped at the *Njordur's Mercy*.

'And then you sneaked out of Stenvik, hid in the forest for two days and now you're here.' Oraekja nodded again. 'Where are the plans? The numbers? Guard spots? Strike points? What do the gates look like? How do we break them? Did he not tell you anything?'

'I don't understand . . . The gates are made of wood . . .' Oraekja looked like he was trying to remember something. 'He told me I should have looked up . . .' he muttered.

Skargrim's head felt fit to burst. It just sounded . . . wrong. Ragnar would have collected information, lots of information, anything to help the assault. He would have told the boy. Anything else made no sense. And he would never have got himself caught. How did they catch him? Why? And how was Oraekja the one to escape?

'Your brother is dead, Skargrim.'

He couldn't be. Ragnar was supposed to outlive him, to see his own nephews grow to become raiders.

'Your brother is dead. They killed him. He died in Stenvik. Behind those walls.' Her cold, bony fingers touched his forearm and he turned towards her.

'Avenge him, Skargrim.'

Strength surged through every fibre of his being. Somewhere in the back of his head he heard the chant of a thousand warriors, the hard pounding of pommels on shields, battle cries that sent shivers up and down the spines of those about to die.

'Make them pay.'

Oraekja stared at him and seemed to wilt, to push back into the skins. Skargrim didn't care. He rose without a word, turned and walked off the *Njordur's Mercy* back onto the rowboat. A single thought echoed in his head, thrashed and roared like a trapped bear.

Revenge.

## STENVIK

'This is it.' Thorvald's voice was cold, distant. Skargrim's raiders were lining up by the harbour, behind a protective wall forming slowly as warriors linked their shields.

'It very well might be, yes.' Sigurd looked to the south. 'But you know, my friend, I won't be able to see my enemies for the thundercloud above your head. Why don't you take your anger out on those bastards instead? I challenge you to hit one of their shields from this distance.'

'They're too far away.'

'Come on, Thorvald. You taught all those boys to shoot. No one's ever bested you at the bow. Have you forgotten? Or are you scared you can't hit it from this distance?'

Thorvald wheeled on Sigurd, face contorted in fury. 'They're too – far – away!' he snarled.

Sigurd stepped in close, grabbed the scout master's tunic by the neck and twisted hard, pulling the tall man's face down to his own. Stunned, Thorvald struggled for breath. Quietly and calmly Sigurd whispered: 'Shoot. Or so help me I'll push you over the wall when the first charge comes, make it look like an accident, say you died a hero and use your bloody corpse and stamped-on head to rally the men. Because right now you're absolutely no use to me whatsoever.'

He let go and Thorvald recoiled as if he'd been slapped.

Sigurd just looked at him.

'Well?'

## THE OLD TOWN

Thrainn had picked a hundred of his men, Hrafn another hundred. Some of them carried big iron picks, hammers and wedges to complement their weaponry, tools to break down the gate. Ingi's men stood silently by, all carrying massive round shields for the shield wall. Egill had supplied fifty of his black-clad warriors, all standing to attention and carrying compact recurved bows, ready to provide cover fire. The remainder of their force was arranged in groups led by named and proven men, ready to charge into the breach when the first wave was done. Skargrim's warriors stood by and awaited his command.

He'd stormed ashore barking orders like a foul-tempered northern gale. Ingi had wanted to know what she'd said about commanding the forest people and got a vicious glare in return. Not even Thora dared ask him what had happened onboard the *Njordur's Mercy*. Whatever apprehensions the fighters might have had about charging Stenvik, more than one of them thanked their gods that they were on Skargrim's side today. Wearing his double mail shirt and adorned helmet, he looked like an iron giant.

Pacing between the men, Skargrim was about to sound the charge when the first arrow thudded into the shield wall. Taken by surprise, the shield carrier lowered his guard a couple of inches. The next one tore into his throat, just under the jawbone. He collapsed, gurgling and clutching feebly at the shaft that protruded from his neck.

'LINK UP! MOVE!' Ingi's men adjusted with frightening efficiency, ignoring the dying man and re-forming the shield wall. Alert to the danger, the wall was up when the third arrow buried itself several inches into overlapping shields.

The fourth came from above, only moments later. One of Thrainn's men was unlucky and had his foot nailed to the ground. His screams drowned in the battle cries of the raiders charging.

## STENVIK

Thorvald stepped back and exhaled, sweating profusely. He turned to Sigurd. 'Thank you,' he said quietly. 'I'm here now.'

Sigurd looked back at his scout master and closed his mouth slowly. Two shots in quick succession, the third straight up in the air and the fourth before the last arrow had even reached its apex. 'I'll say you are.' He slapped Thorvald on the shoulder. 'Now get some of your boys shooting like you just did and we might still live through this one.' Turning, he roared at the men on the wall.

'READY!'

## THE *NJORDUR'S MERCY*

Oraekja could not remember feeling this good. He was warm, he was comfortable, and safer than he could ever have imagined. The sea rocked him gently, but he paid it no heed. He had eyes only for Skuld. Nothing else mattered. Even the battle cries seemed muted somehow, like they were filtering through from another world.

He felt his body respond to her presence, felt it shed the fears and horrors of the forest. His strength returned quickly now that he was in his rightful place beside her. Leave the fighting to Skargrim and the animals. He'd be just fine commanding from here. And soon it would be time to claim his prize, the one she'd all but promised before he set out. Right here on these lovely soft furs would do nicely. Still, he could wait a little bit. The anticipation would be at least as sweet as the act itself, he thought.

Her beauty seemed to grow as the fighting intensified. Oraekja leaned back on the furs and gazed up at her immaculate skin, twinkling blue eyes gazing towards the shore, her lips pursed in thought.

Absolutely silent.

In fact, she hadn't spoken or even acknowledged him since Skargrim left for the shore. She'd just tilted her head slightly and closed her eyes, like she was listening to something. Worry lines had scarred her face and made her seem different for a moment. Older than he remembered, somehow. But he wasn't sure. He'd been really tired, and maybe he'd nodded off briefly at that point. He thought he'd heard her mumble some words, but she hadn't woken him. She probably sensed that he needed his rest.

But now he felt ready. It was time to claim his throne.

'What's the plan then?'

She didn't answer. It didn't even look like she'd heard. He giggled nervously. 'Now that I am back, you can tell me everything you want. It is only right, I think. So what's the big plan?'

Still she ignored him.

This wasn't right. This wasn't like he thought it would be. Reaching out, he grabbed her.

'Hey!'

He pulled at her arm, meaning to turn her around so she would face him.

She didn't budge. It was like trying to move a boulder.

Without thinking Oraekja strained against her, pulled as hard as he could. His face turned red and veins throbbed underneath his skin. A faint metallic taste seeped into his mouth and breaths came in spurts. This was not right at all. Her flesh was warm to the touch but he could not move her no matter how he tried.

Slowly, as in a dream, her head turned towards him. She looked him in the eyes and smiled. And with that, she showed him who she really was. What she was.

His grip on her arm grew slack, as did the muscles in his face. He wanted to speak, wanted to apologize, wanted to beg, cry, dive overboard and swim for shore, but his body wouldn't let him. Looking at her, seeing past the surface for the first time, Oraekja was overcome with blind, animal terror.

She smiled. 'Do you love me?'

He nodded, tears streaming down his cheeks.

'Would you do anything for me?'

He nodded again. There was nothing left now but to say yes.

'I need you, Oraekja. The threads are tangled, so we will need you to carry our strength.' He gazed at her, blinking through the tears, understanding nothing. 'But for that you will need rest. Now sleep.' She put her hand on his arm, her touch a gentle autumn breeze.

His world went dark.

## STENVIK

Ulfar sprinted past Valgard's hastily erected healing station, past the groups of reinforcements waiting at the foot of each step, past Audun wrestling a cart into a slot next to the western gateway. He vaulted up the steps two at a time, to find Sven above the southern gateway.

'Welcome back, son. I trust you've spent your time well?'

Ulfar hid his blushes by shadowing his eyes from the setting sun and leaning as far as he could over the south wall. 'Yes. Yes I have.'

Coming towards them up the southern road was an imposing line of metal, shields, spears and swords.

'They'll be going for the gateway,' Sven offered as an explanation.

'Then why aren't all our men down there?' Ulfar said as he turned to look at Sven, who just grinned back.

Movement caught his eye as Harald emerged along with five other *Westerdrake* raiders. They all carried thick spears, half a man's length. 'Time to go fishing,' the captain growled, nodding to Sven. His men sought out the big wooden shields set into the planks, lifted them and disappeared from sight.

Ulfar blinked. Then he blinked again. 'Where did they go?'

'We have a little surprise prepared for our guests,' the old fighter said offhandedly. 'You might want to take cover now, though.' He dropped down to a crouch with surprising ease. Ulfar looked out to the south just in time to see swift, black-clad figures dart between the houses of Old Stenvik.

The first hail of arrows was off the mark but did enough to unsettle the defenders on the wall.

'HOLD FIRM!' Thorvald's voice rang out. 'HOLD FIRM!'

A piercing scream cut through the din and Ulfar peered above the parapet. A black-clad raider stopped between huts in mid-run, an arrow buried deep in his thigh. When the next arrow pierced his armour at the armpit, he stopped screaming and sank to the ground. From the south-western corner, Runar saluted to Thorvald, already nocking another arrow. 'Th-th-they s-sound real nice, d-d-don't they?!' he shouted across the wall with a smile.

'Are you going to let our guests have all the fun?' Thorvald roared at his men. As the scout master's archers returned fire, Ulfar looked over at Sven, crouched behind the parapet. 'So. Skargrim's gatebreakers are approaching and we're trading arrows with archers we can't see. If this were Tafl I would say that we're short on initiative.'

Sven frowned. 'You have a point there, son. Any suggestions?'

Ulfar was cut short by a single voice.

'MOOOOVE!!'

As the word floated on the eastern wind the forest came alive.

## THE *NJORDUR'S MERCY*

Skuld's lips moved continuously, forming words that had not been heard in the world for a long time. Occasionally her hands would pass in intricate patterns over Oraekja's sleeping form as the ship rocked gently on the sea, waves lapping at the side.

On the battlefield an almost invisible, silvery grey tendril of mist snaked and weaved away from every man in death's embrace, towards the *Njordur's Mercy*.

## STENVIK

It looked like the forest itself was closing in on Stenvik. Sprinting ahead, outlaw spear-throwers launched their thick heavy missiles at the walls. A handful of defenders were struck down, falling to their deaths on the ground below as a group of outlaws approached the foot of the wall.

'FIRE!!' Thorvald's voice boomed on the walls. Chosen archers dipped down at once below the parapet, picked arrows specially stuck into the wall by their post and waved them once, twice, over small torches. Touching them to the flame until the bundles of kindling tied to the shaft flared up, they fired the burning arrows straight into the bundles of hay placed strategically in front of the wall. The ground seemed to burst into flame at the feet of onrushing outlaws. The ragged men screamed in rage, danced around the fires and cursed the defenders to death and beyond. The unlucky ones got trapped in the rush and burned badly, writhing in agony at the foot of the wall.

But the charge did not falter. Soon Stenvik's walls were crawling with outlaws, scaling the nearly sheer grass-clad surface from the southern gate eastward to just beyond the northern gate.

'Well,' Sven said stoically. 'If there was at any point a choice, there isn't any more. Get up, son. No more thinking or talking. It's killing time.' Within moments he was gone, a short broadsword in his right, a wicked-looking curved knife in his left.

Ulfar peered over the parapet just in time to see Skargrim's gatebreakers disappear from view underneath a densely packed shield wall firmly placed at the outer gate of the southern wall.

The leading outlaw lunged at the top of the wall on the east side to plant his hand on what he thought was solid earth. Punching straight through the turf, the spike underneath went through his shoulder. Screaming like a stuck pig, the first vagabond over Stenvik's walls was brained with an axe and left hanging as a bar to the others.

The fighting was fierce on the wall, but the warriors of Stenvik matched the onslaught of the undisciplined robbers. In between volleys to keep Skargrim's men in check, archers would pick off climbers, arrows ripping through cloth and flesh. The young and the old on the wall pelted the outlaws with stones, breaking skulls and faces.

Ulfar had his hands full. Equipped with an old, makeshift shield from Sven and a throwaway sword, he found himself dancing along the groove in the top wall, leaping in where openings appeared. As he ran to cover the eastern wall a raider from the *Westerdrake* standing beside him caught an arrow in the neck just as an outlaw vaulted over the corpse of one of his brothers, impaled on the wall spikes. The wiry and bloodied fighter rounded on a young boy with blonde hair. The boy dropped his bow for a knife at his belt.

With few qualms about honour, Ulfar clobbered the outlaw in the back of the head with his shield and watched him collapse like a sack of potatoes.

'Give me a hand,' he said to the boy as he grabbed the enemy. Together they hoisted him up to the top of the wall.

'Wait.' Ulfar stopped in mid-push as the boy drew his knife and slit the outlaw's throat before pushing him over. Ulfar's eyebrows shot up and the boy smiled. 'Makes it slick and harder to climb. Get down,' and the boy dived under the parapet, pulling Ulfar with him. In half a breath, three arrows whistled past at chest height.

Standing up, Ulfar nodded at the boy. 'I owe you my life.'

'We're even. Name's Orn.'

'Well, Orn – you've got good eyes. Thank you for sharing them.' Orn nodded once, smiled and grabbed his bow. Out of the corner of his eye Ulfar could see Thorvald directing reinforcements to where the raider had fallen, while Sven gestured and sent a group of men with bows, long spears and what looked like scythes away from the eastern steps towards the market square.

'THEY'RE THROUGH THE OUTER GATE!'

The men on the wall stole looks towards the inner gate on the south wall. Knowing that Skargrim's raiders were in their gateway showed it for what it was – just a thin layer of timber between their families and death.

'HOLD, YOU BASTARDS! IF THEY COME OVER THE WALL IT'S OVER! HOLD THE WALL FOR STENVIK!' Sigurd roared at the top of his voice, leading by example. The blade of his axe, the front of his tunic and his forearms were spattered with blood and gore.

Ulfar saw Sven look down on the south gate, eyes gleaming.

*

It had been hard work, shifting the chopped timber out from under the shield wall by hand. They'd felt every arrow thudding into the wooden barriers between them and certain death, felt the heat of bodies pushed, crushed together under the shields.

But the gate had given way, they'd hacked through and now they were crowding into the gateway. Outside the smell of war and death had mixed with the screams of dying outlaws to boil their blood. In comparison, the stone corridor seemed hushed. The cold stones were a blessing.

'Fucking tomb,' Thora muttered next to Skargrim, pulling him to the side to let the gatebreakers through.

The gateway was filling up fast. Warriors eager to get out of the hail of stones and arrows pushed in at the back. Soon there was very little room to move.

'GET BACK!' Skargrim roared. 'GIVE SPACE, YOU FOOLS!'

About three feet ahead of him Skargrim saw a little dirt bounce off a raider's helmet. Somewhere in the back of his head Oraekja's words echoed. Ragnar told him he should have looked up . . .

'What the—'

The first heavy spear came down like lightning, smashed a clavicle, punctured a lung and disappeared back up into the hole in the roof as the raider ahead of Skargrim sank to the floor, blood pumping out of his neck. The second struck almost simultaneously on the other side of the corridor, skimming a helmet, carving open a raider's face and punching through his chest beside his sternum. 'SHIELDS! UP! SHIELDS, YOU BASTARDS!' Thora screamed at the top of her voice, but it was too late. The spears struck again and there was no space to move, only the screams of dying men.

Fear and blood gave Skargrim strength. He tore the shield off the back of a man in front, pushed two men to the side and jammed the murder hole. His teeth jarred with the impact as the spear punched into the shield once, twice. Skargrim counted, timed and pulled the shield away at the last moment. The wielder of the spear, expecting resistance, lost control for an instant and the spear slipped out. Skargrim reached up, grabbed the shaft just below the tip with both hands and wrenched with all his might.

The spear was his, along with a very satisfying thud and curse on the other side of the timber.

His victory didn't last long, though.

Piercing screams came from the gate as the front row, the gatebreakers with their tools, all dropped to the floor. Skargrim could see the pools of blood spreading, the hidden holes in the gate where the spears stuck out.

The command made his mouth taste of bile, but there was nothing for it.

'BACK! GO BACK! RETREAT! BACK TO THE HARBOUR!'

He turned around, snarled at the men in front of him and led them at a dead run out of the gateway, through the splintered gate, past Ingi's shield wall and back to the old town. Behind him he could hear the rumble as the south gate opened. The screams of his men, the sounds of murder being done.

Tendrils of shimmering, silver-grey mist streamed with Skargrim, out to sea.

There was no order given that Ulfar could understand. One moment the outlaws were all over their walls, snarling and feral. The next they simply turned around and fled.

Not that anyone complained.

The men of Stenvik roared their approval but got little time to celebrate their victory.

Thorvald, Sven and Sigurd moved among them, commanding a clean-up. Planks were scrubbed, weapons checked and bodies unceremoniously dumped to the foot of the wall after being stripped of anything useful. 'Give them something to clamber over,' Sigurd had growled.

Down in the market square Valgard and Sven were seeing to a surprisingly short line of wounded soldiers. The southern gate was up and the occasional strangled scream from a gatebreaker being put out of his misery rang out.

No one paid them any heed.

The shields up on the wall rose. Harald and his warriors emerged, bloodied but grinning manically. 'Shields! Up! Shields, you bastards!' one of them shrieked, and the others roared. 'Oi! Where's your spear?' Hallmar shouted at one of the fighters. 'Shut up,' the tall raider snapped back. 'Got ripped out of my hands.'

'You got one, though, didn't you?' Harald draped a thick arm around the young raider.

'Yes I did,' he replied, grinning. 'Spitted him like a pig.'

Harald roared and the others joined in.

Moving away from the blood-crazed raiders, Ulfar picked his way down the steps. Glancing into the southern gateway, his stomach churned and his breath caught in his throat.

Corpses littered the stone corridor. There was blood everywhere. The floor was covered, the walls spattered. By the gate a pile of bodies lay, face down, brutally hamstrung. Their throats had been slit. Further down towards the ruined outer gate fighters lay sprawled in various poses, arrows and spears sticking out of their backs.

'I guess we got this round.' Audun stood behind him, looking at the carnage. 'Sven says we're to pile this up and use it as a barrier.'

Ulfar shuddered involuntarily. 'If that's what he says then that's what we do, I guess.' He followed Audun, who was already picking his way through the gateway, feet splashing in pools of blood. Somehow some of it had sprayed up on the wall and nearly to the rough timbers in the tunnel ceiling. Ulfar followed the line with his eyes.

'Murder holes in the roof. There's just about space enough for a couple of men to go down from the top, stand above the tunnel and stab downwards with spears. They sent—'

'Harald and his friends,' Ulfar replied. 'Through the big shields up there. I saw them come out again.'

'And then there's little hidden holes in the inner gate for spears or arrows, and space for swiping a blade down at ankle level. These poor bastards never stood a chance.'

Ulfar cursed softly. 'Sven wasn't kidding when he said he had some surprises for the visitors.' He grabbed a leg and helped drag a lifeless body to the corpse wall Audun was building.

'No, he wasn't. Sven and Sigurd knew what they were doing.'

'Did you take part in building this?' Ulfar gestured at the stone-masonry.

'No, not at all. This is from long before my time. Ten summers? Fifteen? I don't know. Closer to ten, I should think. The story says Sigurd and Sven had raided so much and carried home so much treasure that they needed a fortress to guard it all.'

'Is it true?'

'Might be. I've never seen any treasures, though. I think it's a story and I think they simply wanted to keep the people safe. I—' Audun paused, then pointed at a warrior on the floor. 'This one is alive.'

'Not by much, from the looks of it,' Ulfar replied.

The raider lay on his back, an arrow tip coated in shiny,

brownish black liquid sticking out of his chest. His eyes fluttered.

Ulfar looked at the blacksmith, who nodded once, an odd expression on his face. He then drew his sword and stabbed the man through the heart, a killing blow.

They both shuddered when the light went out of the man's eyes.

After a moment Ulfar spoke up. 'Let's finish the stacking and get out of here.'

'Very good idea,' Audun replied, a shade too quickly.


## STENVIK, THE OLD TOWN

'This really is not going to be as easy as we thought, is it?' Hrafn looked at the other captains sitting around the fire. 'Am I the only one here who expected a real fight?'

Three pairs of eyes trained on Hrafn.

'All right, so maybe not. But we've tested their strength now. There's a fair amount of it.'

'Except in numbers,' Thrainn interjected.

'This is true,' Hrafn acceded.

Ingi cleared his throat. 'Fine. Then let's talk possibilities. We'll have a hard time getting at the inner gate. The outlaws were slaughtered on those walls, so climbing is out. We can hardly sneak up on them from here on in. I say we wait.'

'What? Where's the honour in that? Waiting for them to weaken and die?' Hrafn hissed.

'Think about it. Skargrim said he'd sent men to poison their water. You'll get your fight, Hrafn. But it will be on our terms, when they're weak, thirsty and forced to leave their little fortress. It's safer, it's more efficient and it will be a lot easier.'

No one could really argue with that.

Ingi nodded for emphasis. 'Good. Are we then agreed?'

Hrafn and Thrainn nodded.

'. . . Egill? Do you agree, or would you like to continue to throw men at the walls?'

'We should wait for Skargrim,' Egill rumbled. 'It's not right to decide this when he's not here.'

'Well – where is he then?' Ingi asked.

No one spoke. The answer was written all over the captains' faces.

## THE *NJORDUR'S MERCY*

The waves caressed the sleek hull. A chill breeze stroked the mast, searching for sails that weren't there.

Skargrim knew that he had to report to Skuld, had to tell her what had happened. She would know, of course. There was no doubt about that. But he had to. So now he found himself onboard his own ship, as intimately familiar to him as his own body. Only now it felt . . . different. A little bit colder than the rest of the world.

A small torch mounted on the mast threw wild, dancing shadows at Skargrim as he picked his way to the stern.

'Enter.'

He pulled back the hides and stepped inside.

The first thing he felt was a light touch on his forearm. He turned towards her, looked straight into her eyes.

'Skargrim. Your bravery and loyalty are beyond question,' she purred. 'You have done well.'

'They . . . they slaughtered us,' he managed to stutter.

'Shhh . . .' her fingers seemed to walk themselves up his arm, leaving a trail of goose bumps. Her hand was on his shoulder then a finger found his lips, tracing a line before pressing gently. Her eyes never left his.

'Do not fear, Skargrim. We do not need fear.'

Holding on to the last shreds of self-control, he managed to gently move her hand away from his face. 'We need . . . we need to seal them in. Make sure they're not going anywhere. They'll run out of water. Maybe there's a way to get at the gate as well.'

She smiled, a vision of life, youth and beauty. Then she shook her head, raised herself up onto her toes and gently, softly took Skargrim's head in her hands.

'No,' she whispered. 'No waiting. The gods do not wait. It is not our way. Attack, Skargrim. Attack. No matter what it takes.'

He blinked, his mouth opening and closing.

'Yes,' he finally muttered. 'Attack.'

## STENVIK

The stones in the gateway reeked of death. Every scrape of metal on rock grated on Ulfar's ears, every squelching sound of bodies dragged through puddles of half-dried blood made him shudder. But they were nearly done. He looked on as Audun leaned up against the wall, breathing heavily.

'Are you all right?'

The smith levered himself back up and shook his head as if trying to dislodge something. 'I'm fine. It's just . . . I have a bit of a problem with blood.'

'And that is no bad thing,' Ulfar replied, as they heaved the last body into place. A pile of Skargrim's dead warriors now blocked the southern gateway almost completely. Some had been cut down in the first attack, others shot as they tried to escape. The stone tunnel smelled like a battlefield: blood mixed with sweat and shit.

'This will slow them down some,' Audun offered.

'Or make them all the more furious,' Ulfar replied. He'd seen more death in the last half-day than he'd heard of in his life, just about. His mind wandered back to his father's longhouse years ago, and the feasts for Uncle Hrothgar's return from raiding. When he was a boy he'd admired the massive, scary warrior, pestering him for stories of big raids and the glory of the fight.

Hrothgar would simply smile and say Ulfar would understand when he was older. Ulfar understood now. He understood completely. Three years ago he'd been begging to go raiding, see the world and win his honour, but his father wouldn't let him. Ulfar's fate was supposed to be that of a country lord. He was to manage filthy farmers and count grains until he was grey. One drunken night, one dumb fight, and suddenly he had no alternative. It had taken the intervention of Geiri's father to keep the family of the man whose arm he'd broken from exacting the full debt of honour. Instead they'd settled on a substantial sum in restitution and two years' exile.

Ulfar decided that when they returned home he would give them more. He'd abandon all claims to his father's estate. Give it to Geiri instead. Come here, maybe. Woo Lilia properly, challenge Harald to a duel. Run away with her and explore beyond the north, find a place where they weren't constantly trying to kill each other. Lord? Carry his father's mantle? After what he'd seen here? Not a chance. Not a bloody chance.

'Ulfar.'

Coming from the gate, Sven's leaden voice shook him out of his reverie.

'I'm afraid I have bad news.'


## STENVIK, THE OLD TOWN

'Then so it is.'

'So it is.' Skargrim nodded. 'We attack just before dawn.'

'Why then?' Thrainn asked. 'Why not now? They won't see us coming.'

'And how will you see them, boy? How will you tell your men from their men and my men?' Hrafn asked. Thrainn turned to object but thought better of it. Instead he asked the only man who had been silent since Skargrim came ashore and summoned them to council.

'What do you think, Ingi?'

'What do I think?' The diminutive chieftain looked at them and smiled. 'I think I would like to pitch a battle where Sigurd Aegisson isn't fighting. He knows what he's doing and he can hold that hovel of his for a while without losing many men. Those outlaws will hardly be of great use to us, as you saw on the walls. The gateways are going to cost more than I think we should pay. So if you're going to persist in this, rather than, say, wait outside until they weaken and need to come out for food and drink, you need more than just a desire to attack. You need a plan. And before I say what I think or move a single one of my men to help I'd like to see it. How are you going to crack Stenvik?'

There was a sense of a shift in the dark as Egill Jotunn moved and leaned in, the flickering firelight painting a demon on his face. 'I might have a suggestion or two,' he rumbled.

## STENVIK

Stars twinkled overhead. The moon peered from behind the clouds to cast an eerie silver light over the town. Inside the walls, mounted torches created pools of warm, orange light inside a ring of dancing, jumping shadows.

'Let him go.' Sven's voice was calm, reassuring. 'He needs time. I don't know if he's lost anyone close before.'

Audun watched Ulfar as the young man headed north, away from them. He looked listless, head hanging and shoulders slumped. Audun nodded, slowly. 'It's a shame. Geiri seemed a good man.'

'No doubt.'

'How did he die?'

'He fell asleep and his heart simply seems to have stopped.'

Audun shook his head. 'No way for a young man to go. No way at all.'

'No.' The two men stood and watched as a cloud drifted across the moon.

Darkness.


## VALHALLA

'What's on your mind, Harald?'

Freya ran her fingers through his hair, slowly and tenderly, touching him just right. He felt weak with desire.

'I . . . I'm just not sure.'

'What do you mean? You follow your chieftain's orders, do you not?' Thor leaned forward, looking concerned. 'Is he unfit to rule?'

'Or do you want to do it yourself? Give the command? Lead the troops to glory?' Loki did not grace him with a look, devoting all his attention to a twig in his hands. Deft flicks of the knife carved impossibly small runes into the wood.

'No. I follow Sigurd's orders, he's the chieftain. We've been through that. It's just . . .'

'. . . just what, my brave warrior?' Standing behind him, Freya leaned on his shoulders. He could feel her firm, heavy breasts pressing into his back and thought his heart would burst.

'I . . . I don't know how much Sigurd respects the old gods.' Harald looked around nervously. 'I mean – all of you. You and the all-father. I don't think Sigurd is all that faithful. He just wants to keep all of us alive until we die in our sleep. I think he's growing craven in his old age and I think Sven is at least partly to blame. If there was any sense in them we would be allying with Skargrim and the outlaws and then taking on that upstart king.'

The three deities all looked at him with renewed interest. Harald could have sworn that even in the darkened end of the hall somebody had suddenly started paying attention. The deep shadows seemed to be . . . listening.

'You're saying that Sigurd Aegisson is no longer loyal to us?' Loki asked quietly.

Thor smashed his fist on the table. 'WE SAVED YOU!' he thundered, face suddenly flushed with anger. 'We held the dark at bay! Sent you weather for crops! Kept you safe from hunger and death! You built this town for us, and THAT is why you're ALIVE!'

Freya's face was hard. 'We gave you the gift of children, and we gave your children the gift of life. Do you know how easily we could take that away? Fill your town with barren women?' She looked down on him, cold and knowing. 'You know how that feels, don't you? Would you wish it upon all your kin, Harald?'

'See?' Loki said to Thor and Freya. 'I told you. I was right all along.' Neither of them answered him, so he turned to Harald. 'How long since the last sacrifice, my friend? How long since the last ceremony?' Somehow Loki, suddenly calm and amicable, was the most terrifying of the three.

'I – I – don't know,' Harald whispered. 'I've been sailing. A year? Maybe . . . two?' At the edge of his senses he felt the vision slowly start to unravel. 'No! Don't go! Tell me! What do I do?'

Thor, Freya and Loki moved into the centre of the longhouse. United, they looked very much like a family.

'Set your town to rights, Harald,' Thor said.

'For us. For me,' Freya whispered.

'I have given the men of Stenvik a chance to live your lives the way we intended. Take it . . . or face the consequences,' Loki added, still smiling.

The gods turned their backs on him, walked into the darkness and disappeared. Harald clenched his fists painfully hard as Valhalla faded from view.

## STENVIK

Ulfar was numb.

The packed earth wall at his back was cold to the touch, the grass he sat on was soft . . . but he knew it. He didn't feel it. He had nothing but cold and detached information, from somewhere outside and above himself. It didn't matter. Nothing really mattered.

Geiri was dead.

Ulfar leaned back and looked up at the stars. The steps up to the wall were just a few yards away, and for a moment he thought he might go up there, walk amongst the men on the night watch and try to make himself useful.

And what good would that do?

They were overmatched. Sigurd knew it, Sven knew it. They were going to get overrun tomorrow and that would be the end of that. He'd seen death enough times by now, sure – but he always thought of it as something that would happen to other people. And still he felt nothing.

He stared out into the middle distance, numb to the world.

It took the heat from her body, the smell of her, the feel of her hair as she nestled against him, to make him react. As her arms pulled him into a soft embrace their bodies twined together instinctively, seeking strength in each other.

Ulfar took a deep breath.

Inside, emotions welled up. He clung to her and trembled silently, shook with the intensity of it as scalding tears flooded down his face. Her hands were on his head now, clutching him to her breast, stroking his hair, murmuring words that didn't exist. Ulfar struggled to regain control, but everything he'd been a part of since arriving in Stenvik collapsed on him at once, demanding to be let out. And holding on to Lilia was so painfully sweet. He was equal parts proud and happy, mortified and ashamed to be crying in front of her, frightened and small and safe and loved.

'Everything will be all right,' she whispered. 'It will all be right. We will live. Together. It will be all—'

Three yards to their left, the body of a wall guard landed with a thud.


## ONBOARD THE *NJORDUR'S MERCY*

Oraekja felt strange. Cold.

Cold and heavy.

His muscles did not seem to respond like they used to and his skin felt wrong. It felt almost like that time he'd been frostbitten on a hunting trip. Nothing but lumps, blocks of flesh.

Her hand on his chest burned and stung, the feeling of it pumping through his veins. He could feel himself . . . swell . . . all over. Panic coursed through him and he wanted to thrash about, but couldn't. Instead his eyes fluttered open.

She sat beside him, eyes fixed on Stenvik. Her hand passed over his chest and she muttered under her breath, the words indistinguishable to his ears.

He could feel something drift towards them from the shore, over the sea, into the boat, closing in on him.

It flooded into his eyes, ears and mouth, filled him. Oraekja screamed as the silver shimmer encased him. No sound escaped his lips.

### STENVIK

The wall was crawling with outlaws.

Ulfar took the last steps three at a time and jumped straight into an uneven fight. Four scrawny men in rags surrounded a young, blond boy swinging an axe in a panic. Ulfar's borrowed sword took the first forest man in the neck, dropped him at once. Two more snarling heads could be seen emerging over the parapet so Ulfar took a step in towards the dying man's falling body and hoisted it over the wall, taking the climbing invaders by surprise. They cursed loudly as they tumbled backwards under the weight of the corpse.

The remaining three on the wall turned towards the new threat. One of them had his face shattered by the blade of the youth's axe for his troubles. Ulfar ducked a quick lunge by the nearest fighter and shouldered him in the sternum. Quick slashes, thrusts and a cut, and the two young men were the ones left standing.

'That makes two, foreigner,' said Orn.

'You're welcome,' Ulfar replied, swiftly grabbing a bag full of small stones and throwing it with all his might at the face of a climbing outlaw. 'TO THE WALL! ENEMY ON THE WALL! ALL TO THE WALL!' he screamed at the top of his lungs. All he could hear from the darkness was grunts and metal clashing on metal. 'TO THE BLOODY WALL!!' Orn echoed. The door to the longhouse slammed open and Sigurd was visible in the pale torchlight. 'NORTH!' Ulfar shouted and watched the chieftain set off at a dead run towards them. Raiders piled out after him, carrying an assortment of weapons.

A blood-curdling cry erupted from the outlaws, reverberating around Stenvik.

They were all over the walls.

Orn and Ulfar turned back to back and fought the onrushing invaders. A menacing brute brandishing a thick spear advanced on them from the east, two axe-wielding warriors from the west.

On instinct, Ulfar nudged Orn. 'I've always liked two better than one. What do you think?'

'Agreed,' the scout muttered under his breath.

'GO!' Ulfar shouted, spinning around to Orn's side. Taken by surprise, the axemen hesitated for a moment, adjusting to the situation.

They died quickly.

Retracting his bloodied sword, Ulfar felt a firm shove take him off balance, nearly throwing him over the outer wall. The spear passed just under Orn's arm where Ulfar's ribcage had been a moment ago. Infuriated by the slip-up he spun around. The spearman behind them had gambled on the lunge and was pulling his spear back when he saw Ulfar's face. He had managed to drop the spear and draw a dagger when the sword punched through his stomach and upwards into his heart, gutting and killing him instantly. Ulfar used the momentum to toss the man over the wall, where curses and shouts told of more climbers.

Screams drew the two men's attention, and Ulfar turned to scan the walls.

Raiders of the *Westerdrake* were charging up the western and southern steps from below, but the outlaws were not giving way as easily this time around. With the high ground and an assortment of spiky weapons, they did not yield an uncontested inch to the defenders.

Only the eastern wall seemed to be won.

Sigurd and a handful of raiders had beaten back the forest people, moving steadily outward, re-manning the wall. Suddenly the outlaws found themselves pinned between advancing blades.

'STENVIK!'

Pushing his own men aside, Harald stormed up the western steps. A ragged, slim fighter threatened him with a spear, but the captain batted it effortlessly away and brained the attacker with a hand axe. Within a couple of steps he was in the enemy's midst, snarling and ferocious. He was a sight to behold. Every movement had one purpose and one purpose only: pain. Judging by the rapidly thinning ranks of outlaws on his part of the wall, Harald was doing well.

'Ulfar!'

The urgency in Orn's voice tore him away from the hideous spectacle. Another wave of attackers was climbing up the north wall with murder in their eyes.

### NORTH OF STENVIK

'Ready the troops.'

'At once, your highness.' Finn was already moving through the makeshift camp, making up a mental list of the chieftains he'd need to find. The scout had staggered into their guards in the middle of the night. Finn had to admire the man's toughness: he was short and stocky, looked more like a sailor than a woodsman and breathed like he'd run all night and possibly all day, but he still insisted on delivering the message to King Olav in person, muttering something about orders from his captain.

There had been a strange expression on the King's face when he'd emerged from the tent. He'd only told Finn to ready the troops and bring the commanders to him. With chieftains and warriors of note in tow, he turned back to King Olav's tent to find the King waiting and ready.

'We waste no time on big words. Stenvik is under siege. Rouse your men and move out now – we march to their rescue in the name of the Lord.'

Chieftains from the entire eastern half of the country turned silently and set about following the orders of the King.

The army was on the move before sunrise.

## STENVIK, THE OLD TOWN

Skargrim was almost invisible in the shadow of the old longhouse. He stood stock-still and listened to the sounds of battle: clashing swords, screams, dying men.

Egill Jotunn approached him from behind.

'It seems strange to hold back when there's killing being done.'

'I know.'

'Still, I think you're right. We can't see in the dark, we don't know each other's men on sight and we'd lose more than we'd gain.'

'The night is good for many things, but not for this. Not now.' They stood together in silence for a spell. Then Skargrim spoke again. 'It sounds like the woodlice are giving them a proper fight this time.'

'That it does. As for tomorrow . . .'

'Yes?'

'I'd like you to come take a look at something,' Egill said.

Skargrim turned, looked up at the looming giant and nodded. They walked away from the walls, towards the campfires.

## STENVIK

The ravens circled lazily overhead, specks of cawing dark in the first rays of the morning sun.

Bodies lay strewn on the trampled grass at the foot of the wall, sometimes piled two or even three high. Women and children moved with purpose on the parapets, scrubbing and cleaning where they could, throwing straw over pools of blood where they couldn't.

In the market square Valgard worked on. The sounds of last night's slaughter in the dark had nearly driven him mad at first, but soon even they had faded into ugly background noise. He'd been at his post throughout, with three warriors nominally supposed to assist him. He knew what it was about, though. They thought he was so weak that he would not be able to defend himself if a single outlaw were to get over the wall.

The line of wounded had seemed endless.

He had men with clean wounds, blood flowing freely from gashes in their shoulders, arms or sides. Others came in with broken forearms or limping on one foot. It was an endless parade of horror, pain and suffering.

And through it all Valgard had worked.

Bandages and water. Salve and ointment. Binding, healing, sometimes even passing a hand over a nasty wound and mumbling something incomprehensible if he thought it would make the man feel better. Some he could heal, some he could save. Some were beyond helping.

'You've done well, son.'

His heart skipped a beat. He hadn't heard Sven come up behind him, didn't know how long he'd been there. Somewhere in the back of Valgard's throat a lump started slowly dissolving.

'Th-thank you. I've done what I could,' he stuttered.

'How does it look?'

Valgard reeled off numbers. 'Fifty-six wounded as far as I can gather, of which forty-two are out of combat. I've lost twenty.'

Sven nodded. 'It's been hard to get a head count. There are a lot of men missing, I fear.'

Valgard trembled. The blood came back to him, the endless wounds, the gritted teeth of the men trying their hardest not to scream. 'Bjorn . . . Bjorn came in . . . he held his stomach in like this . . . with the right hand. I looked at the wound . . . but it was too deep. I couldn't do anything, Sven. And he . . . he knew.' Valgard swallowed hard. A single spasm raced up his spine and smashed into his skull, showering the inside of his eyes with stars. With every muscle in his face tightening, he breathed deep before he continued.

'He looked me in the eye and smiled. Then he very slowly changed so he was holding in his guts with his left hand . . . drew his sword and went back up on the wall.'

'He killed four of the bastards before they got him,' Sven said quietly as he put an arm around Valgard's sloping shoulders. 'You've done well, son.'

Valgard blinked and gritted his teeth until he felt they would explode in his mouth.

'Thank you, father.'

'Sigurd!'

'What?' the chieftain snapped.

'You might want to come here and have a look,' Sven replied.

Something in his voice halted Sigurd's stride across the market square.

'What's so important?'

Sven nodded towards a corpse that had been thrown to the side of the square and covered with sackcloth. Sigurd raised a questioning eyebrow. 'This is the dead poisoner, is it not?' Sven nodded. 'Well, unless he's about to stand up and dance, I couldn't care a handful of lamb shit about him. Sven, I've not slept for a while now. I'm going to catch some rest. Why are you of all people bothering me with this?'

Sven didn't answer.

'What? What's so special about him, then?' Sigurd asked, annoyance rising.

Without a word, Sven walked to the body and pulled the sack-cloth away.

Sigurd looked at the face, greying features contorted by death into a frosty smile. His eyes widened as recognition hit home, and he took an involuntary step backwards, as if to distance himself from the corpse.

Sven looked Sigurd straight in the eyes. 'I don't know about you, but I reckon this will mean a little bit of extra trouble.'

Recovering, Sigurd looked down at the corpse, then back at Sven. 'That depends.' A sudden flicker of a smile danced in his eyes as he drew his knife. 'That depends entirely, my friend.'

There was not much left to do.

Audun worked the whetstone, trying to clear his mind of the grisly clean-up in the tunnel. The closed space, the heavy stones and the smell of the blood-sodden earth had almost overwhelmed him.

Almost.

It had taken all his willpower. Pushing the thoughts away, he worked on the sword. Despite the circumstances he could not but marvel at the thing he held in his hand.

It was a fine weapon.

Sometimes he wondered about the metal and exactly how much he controlled it. This one had turned out longer than he'd wanted it to be, so he'd had to make it slimmer to compensate. It would need a good edge which would have to be maintained, and it would not be useful for anything but killing. Its wielder would not need to be strong, but if he was fast and agile he would be deadly. He'd known for a while whose sword it was.

The sounds of axes hitting wood drifted in from the raiders' camp and echoed across Stenvik, regular and rhythmic.

Sigurd stood over the south gateway, looking down. The grassy walls were now coloured a dull reddish-brown with outlaw blood. Corpses lay strewn at the foot of the wall like a giant's scattered toys.

Beyond, the old town was buzzing with activity.

'What are they up to?' asked Thorvald. He scratched his greying head, the toll of the night visible on his face.

'Whatever it is, they're going to need to sharpen their axes again before they're done,' Sigurd replied. The sound of wood being chopped was punctured by shouted commands. A woman's voice cut through the noise and some of her words reached the men on the wall.

Thorvald looked at Sigurd and raised his eyebrow.

'I never knew you could fit a hatchet up there,' he said.

'I guess you can do anything if you're determined enough,' the chieftain replied. 'I'd like to know what exactly they're chopping.'

'Could they be building a fire?'

'Hardly,' said Sigurd. 'I don't know what they'd burn. It'd take ages to burn down any of our gates and they'd have a tough time getting the kindling in place.'

'And there's not that much wood in the houses, really,' Thorvald added.

'This is not good,' Sigurd declared. A thundercloud was forming on his face. 'This is not good at all.' He turned to Thorvald. 'Get Sven. Get Ulfar and Jorn too. And then I need you to ready and equip every single man in the village who can hold a bow.' The scout master turned and set off.

'It's a damn shame about that Swedish boy,' Valgard said after a while.

Sven snorted as he rolled up bandages. 'You know what, son? I can actually think of more pressing problems.'

'I guess. But where does this end, though? I mean . . . His next of kin should be pressing for honour, but there's none of them here. And who would they prosecute? The two fools who started the fight both seem to have vanished – I drank with them a couple of days ago but haven't really seen them since. I guess . . . when it comes down to it Harald is at the root of this, isn't he? Has the pig farmer come forward?'

'Hand me the poultice jar, will you?' Sven glanced at Valgard without stopping his work. 'I suppose he is. But the situation doesn't exactly lend itself to tribunals, does it? With the two fools gone and all. I saw that farmer yesterday and asked him whether he would be claiming his rights; he was surly as a boar and told me to piss off. I just don't see it happening. Ulfar would have to make a claim on Geiri's behalf, Sigurd would have to agree, and we'd somehow have to survive long enough to deal with it without getting massacred by bloody Skargrim and his monsters.'

'Mm,' Valgard replied. 'I see what you mean. Still, it's a damn shame.'

'SVEN!' Thorvald's voice rang out. Sven was moving before he'd finished the word. Before he left he turned to Valgard. 'Don't die. I'll be very angry if you do.'

Valgard mustered a smile as the old man hurried towards the scout master, but his head was in another place altogether. He stalked around the table in his mind and threw the board against the wall. Pieces scattered across the floor.

Curse it. Curse it all.

King Olav was on his way, bringing with him the end of hope. When the King's army occupied Stenvik, Sigurd would be permanently installed as chieftain, Harald would get older and worse and his idea, his plan to occupy a place as the chieftain's trusted adviser and second in command, would be blown to the winds. His back ached, but he ignored it. Until now he'd tried to be gentle and pull.

Maybe it was time to push.


As Ulfar ran towards the stairs to get to Thorvald, Audun closed in and grabbed his arm. Ulfar started to speak, but something in the blacksmith's eyes stopped him.

They stood together for a moment in silence.

Then Audun handed Ulfar a sword in a strange old scabbard.

'What's this? I have a sword already.'

'Have a look at this one,' was all Audun said.

Ulfar grabbed the handle. It fitted his hand exactly. 'Hm. Feels good . . .' he drew the sword. 'Whoa. Long.' He moved his hand experimentally, swung a couple of times. Then he fell silent, turned and looked at Audun.

After a long spell he bowed his head and said simply: 'Thank you.'

Audun nodded in return. 'Note the inscription.' Ulfar looked at the hilt, at the runes for vitality and speed. 'Be quick and live, Ulfar Thormodsson,' Audun said quietly.

'I'll remember that,' Ulfar replied.


## ONBOARD THE *NJORDUR'S MERCY*

Voices.

Screaming, screaming at him. Ordering, begging, cajoling, cursing. Telling him to let them go, leave them be. Like the talons of a bird raking his bones, they were making his blood go cold. A sickly smell filled his nostrils, a smell of dying flesh.

Oraekja's eyes flew open. Hides above him, above them blue sky. He tried to move his head, to look around, but nothing happened. The world felt like a block of ice: cold, translucent, immovable. Floating on memory, absolute terror possessed him. He screamed, ears ringing, blood pumping pure fear through his body.

She leaned over into his field of vision and looked at him, a soft, tender smile on her lips. 'No one can hear you, you know.' She looked down at his chest, towards his legs. Then she smiled and nodded. 'Not yet. But they will.' She turned towards Stenvik. 'They will.'

She faded from view as he passed out again.


## STENVIK

Shadows danced on the wall, following Sven's every move. Pacing back and forth, the energy in the steps belied the age of the body.

'He's taking his time with that timber, our Skargrim,' Sven muttered.

'He wants us to brace ourselves until we're tired,' Sigurd answered. 'Then he'll hit us with whatever he's working on just as we're hoping the night will shield us, and he'll hit us hard. This is him fighting with us in here.' Sigurd pointed to his head. 'This is where he wants us to be soft.'

Sven did not break his stride. 'I'd not mind him here on this wall. Then we'd see who's soft and who's hard.'

'Not a bad idea at all,' Sigurd said. 'Let's smack the hive and see what flies.' With that he walked towards a dirty sack stowed away on the south wall just above the gateway. Grabbing it, he stepped up onto the outer wall.

'SKARGRIM!' he shouted.

Nothing happened. The axes didn't even slow down.

'SKARGRIM! THIS IS SIGURD AEGISSON! I HAVE SOMETHING THAT BELONGS TO YOU!'

The sounds gradually diminished as one by one, the axes stopped. A tall, broad-shouldered man in a thick bearskin cloak walked out onto the south road and stood silently facing Stenvik.

Sigurd reached into the sack and pulled out Ragnar's bloodied head, holding the hair by the roots. Two swings and it sailed in a silent, majestic arc through the air, spinning slowly as it travelled. It landed roughly six feet in front of Skargrim and rolled towards him until it stopped by his feet.

The big man looked at the severed head of his brother for a few moments. Then he looked back up at the walls.

'FOR THAT YOU DIE, SIGURD,' he shouted back.

'EVENTUALLY,' Sigurd bellowed. 'BUT I KNOCKED YOU ON YOUR HAIRY ARSE ONCE AND I CAN AND WILL DO IT AGAIN. SO COME ON, YOU BASTARD! I'M BORED!' Skargrim retreated silently in between the houses of the old town. Sigurd turned to Sven, Ulfar and Thorvald, who looked back at him with varying expressions of astonishment. 'If we get to him he might think he should go in before he's ready.'

Sven shook his head. 'Couldn't you have got him to think we've got five thousand men instead? That way he might consider not going in at all.'

'We're better at fighting than waiting, Sven. Look around you.'

Sven did. The planks on the wall were stained with the blood of outlaws and far too many defenders. They'd gone some way towards replenishing stones and refitting spikes, but the night had taken its toll. Death lay heavy on the air and the men of Stenvik felt it.

The old fighter frowned. 'I still think we should have played for time rather than force his hand. But maybe he's not done with whatever they're building in there. Maybe he'll hold off until tomorrow. Maybe—'

'We have movement. They're coming.' The certainty in Thorvald's voice chilled Ulfar to the core. 'Bows!' the scoutmaster shouted. 'BOWS! NOW!' Within moments Sven was off to gather the reserves on the ground. Sigurd set off to fire up the defenders on the wall.

Ulfar was left standing alone with only his new sword and shield for company.

'Hello again, foreigner,' said Orn. 'Are you going to hold the south wall on your own?'

'Might as well,' Ulfar shrugged. 'There's no mead to be had and the women are all looking after the children so I have little else to do. But I wouldn't mind some conversation.' All around them weary but determined men lined the walls, bows in hand. It looked like they'd scrounged every single ranged weapon in the town; some men stood by bundles of javelins; others had even pulled spears out of dead outlaws.

'Good,' the youth replied. 'There's this one thing I've seen though. Can I tell you?'

'. . . Yes?' Ulfar replied, puzzled.

'It's kind of . . . strange. And I'm not sure if it's . . . I don't know.' The young man suddenly seemed embarrassed. 'I don't think my eyes are deceiving me. They never have before. It's just that I've been—'

A furious roar went up from the old town.

'— I've been seeing . . . erm . . . I'll tell you later.'

'You'd better, boy. You've got me all curious,' Ulfar added. 'Maybe you'll tell me her name as well?'

Bowstring already drawn, Orn grinned as he sighted the area in front of the outermost houses. 'Maybe I will. She's – what is that? Are those . . .'

Long, flat wooden structures were emerging from the old town, bouncing unsteadily.

'The bastard . . .' Ulfar's voice trailed off in awe. 'He's . . . he's cut them up! They're going to run up the bloody wall!'

The walkways of old Stenvik had been made of slim logs tightly barred with planks. Now the same logs and planks were being carried upside down towards the walls by men hiding under the wood, shields at their sides. Arrows from the wall were already harmlessly thudding into the cover.

'Aim for the feet!'

'I am! Where are you going?' Orn shot back, firing and drawing at speed.

'I have to go get something!'

With that Ulfar broke away and ran down the steps.

## STENVIK, THE OLD TOWN

Egill Jotunn's plan was simple. It was the same as their first one, only faster and harder. He'd shown Skargrim what he wanted to do, how he'd wanted to rip up the walkways, how they should be carried. Then when the walkways had been dug up – they only needed about four strips, forty feet each – he'd grabbed an axe and cut grooves into the planks with ease. The men had followed his lead. Ingi had volunteered his men for shield-wall duty again – improbably, the stout chieftain had counted his losses on one hand after the disasters of yesterday. Ingi's men would block missiles, then team up with Egill when the time came.

In Skargrim's head, Skuld's voice repeated the same word again and again. Attack. Attack. Attack. The image of his brother's severed head flying through the air filled him with white-hot murderous rage. Only the tenuous thread of the battle plan unfolding in front of him kept Skargrim from charging Stenvik by himself.

Hrafn and Thrainn's men were doing a good job carrying the four ramps; two towards the east, two towards the west. The arrows hardly slowed them down. They were twenty yards from the wall and moving steadily . . . fifteen yards . . . ten . . .

'NOW!' Egill's voice bellowed. As one, his black-armoured warriors sprinted forward, drew and fired. A hail of arrows rained on the Stenvik wall, and Skargrim grinned to see a handful of defenders fall. Another flight of arrows was already on its way, and then the black warriors were safe behind the cover of old Stenvik's huts. As the archers on the wall ducked out of sight the ramp carriers burst into action. The men closest to the wall dropped their end. At the back, the strongest of the raiders started pushing.

Slowly the wooden structures rose into the air.

Stenvik's archers emerged and saw what was happening. Immediately arrows and javelins thudded into undefended raiders, felling a brace of them – but the ones pushing up the ramps were covered by their burden.

'MOVE!' Again, the giant roared. This time a small group broke free of the houses, hit the south road and ran at speed towards the southern gateway.

Egill ran in front, carrying a battering ram. With him ran a group of twenty men in animal skins.


## STENVIK

'Harald! Man the holes! They're coming through the south gateway again!' Sigurd barked.

Harald gestured to his helmsman. 'Leifur! Take three and go!' A big raider nodded his acknowledgement. Soon the shields were up and four warriors disappeared down into the tunnels leading to the murder holes. 'ARROWS TO THE SOUTH!'

Runar rose from behind the parapet, an arrow nocked to the string of his bow. It flew true, pierced a thick piece of bear hide and thwacked into the shoulder of one of Egill's runners with a thud.

The man screamed but did not stop.

Around him arrows and spears were finding their targets, but nothing seemed to even slow the runners, whose screams rose louder with every hit. Coming up on the broken south gate, Egill spotted the barrier of dead warriors. He lowered his shoulder and charged.

The impact scattered the bodies of Skargrim's men. The

runners followed him and disappeared under the archers, into the tunnel.

Spears flew towards the defenders on the wall, followed by Hrafn's men sprinting towards the base of the walkway. Some even started climbing before the top of the wooden structure slammed into the outer wall. Within moments, hardened fighters were launching themselves at the raiders of the *Westerdrake*.

Some were picked off by bowmen, others by thrown javelins. Yet others were hewn down before they'd managed to find their feet on the wall.

But one got through and held off the defenders long enough for two of his men to carve out some space on the western side. Soon the fighting raged along the wall, and despite their efforts the defenders were running out of room.

In the south-east corner Sven slipped between bodies, a knife in each hand. Like a viper he would appear, find a gap, stab, twist and slink away. By the other ramp, eastwards, Sigurd and Harald held their side. Sigurd's axe drew deadly arcs in the air before him, splitting armour and crushing heads. Beside him Harald fought with cold precision, filling all spaces that Sigurd didn't, blocking blows and meting out punishment to those who hesitated for a moment. All around them warriors were locked in deadly combat. By the foot of the stairs large groups of men waited to fill the gaps on the wall or face the attackers when they came down.

One of Thrainn's fighters was a fraction late with his shield. The blade of Sigurd's axe passed neatly through his throat, severing his jugular and spraying shimmering red life over the wall. As the man went down Sigurd turned and shouted down to the ground: 'Jorn! The gate! Bring men!'

Moving quickly, Jorn gathered Birkir and Havar with him. Together they rounded up a fifty-strong group of fighters. Jorn picked one spearman for every three blades and then rushed them towards the south gate.

Leifur had barely had time to get in position. They'd dropped down under the shields and squeezed through the tunnel that led to the murder holes in record time. It was horribly cramped for a big man like him and sometimes he wondered whether Harald sent him down on purpose, just to torture him. Put him in his place. He'd had to hold his breath while he squeezed through and dropped down into the tiny chamber above the gateway. Inside the wall, away from the clamour of battle, the silence was deafening. Leifur had to work hard to still the thumping of his heart.

Now he had his feet braced in the foot stands, spear in hand, eyes trained on the log that slid aside to open the hole. He reached for the handhold on the pole and moved it.

The moment the murder hole opened a metal-tipped boat hook shot through from below, twisted and descended, burying itself into the timbers in the ceiling. An involuntary shout escaped Leifur's lips and he slammed the log back into place, heart thundering.

Too late.

The hook had bitten into the timber and now someone was pulling, straining, working to wrest the floor from underneath him. Leifur watched as the woodwork started to shift. With each straining pull, the timber groaned.

A single thought pushed all others out of his head.

He needed to get out.

Now.

As he was clambering up, his handhold slipped. Heart thundering, he cursed his sweaty palms and tried again.

Below him, the wood cracked and snapped.

There.

He could just about lever himself up into the tunnel that would take him back up to the wall. The spear was in the way. He fumbled with it, threw it down. Groping for a handhold, he started his ascent.

As his feet left the footholds he felt more than heard the timbers groan, split and give way.

Pushing himself back into the tunnel, Leifur scrambled away on his hands and knees, eager to get as far away from the hole as possible.

Ahead he could see the chamber where he'd be able to stand up, get onto the wall and fight these bastards properly. Pain lanced through his knees but he didn't care. He just needed to keep moving. Keep moving. Keep—

A cold, bony hand latched onto his ankle and pulled him down.


Ulfar moved like liquid, like smoke before a strong wind. Running up the steps, he danced along the inner wall. He had to jump, skip and swerve to avoid being gutted by swords and axes swung by friend and foe.

Seeing his first target fighting on the south-east wall, he shouted as loud as he could: 'SVEN!!'

The grizzled old warrior's head snapped round at the familiar voice.

'WHAT?'

'CATCH!'

Two fist-sized leather pouches flew towards the old warrior, who switched both knives into his left hand and plucked the bags out of the air with ease. A puzzled expression crossed his face.

'FROM EINAR!' Ulfar mimed a gesture and nodded towards the walkways, holding two more bags. Comprehension dawned, and with it an impish grin. The old man barked a laugh, turned and dived back into the fray.

Ulfar spun and headed towards the walkways on the south-west side.


No gate, armour or shield was thick enough.

The screams from the gateway cut through everything.

Howls of rage and hunger were soon mixed with genuine terror and pain. Blood leaked from under the gate in a mesmerizing, slowly growing pool. Someone cheered half-heartedly. 'That's it! Get the bastards!'

No one joined him.

Standing behind Jorn, Runar hissed into his ear: 'Y-you ha-ha-have to say something!'

'Any suggestions?' Jorn snapped back.

Runar's eyes blazed with frustration. 'No! Just say anyth-th—' He squeezed his eyes shut and forced a deep breath. 'Just . . . say . . . anything but say it like – l-l-like you bloody mean it! Go!' With that he pushed the Prince of the Dales in front of the men waiting by the gate.

Jorn looked at the soldiers. The faces before him were exhausted, frightened, and well on the way to losing their nerve altogether. He opened his mouth to speak and a spine-curdling wail from the gateway drowned his words, his actions and his thoughts. Completely unbidden, a bubble of mirth burst out of him and Jorn laughed. He shook with laughter. The men by the gateway stared at him like he was mad, but Jorn ignored them.

When he finally recovered, he stood up straight and faced the men. '. . . I think someone might have sat on something sharp,' he added by means of explanation.

The effect was instant.

The idea of a fearsome raider howling in pain and holding his arse bounced between the men, leaving smirks and sometimes even smiles. 'Now I don't know what's in our gateway,' Jorn continued. 'But I've not yet encountered anything living that doesn't die when you cut it.' Grins turned cold and knowing around him. This, they knew. 'So I say embrace it, hold fast and take whatever comes through that gate, cut it and cut it hard, and then cut its head off and stick it on the fucking wall! STENVIK!!'

'STENVIK!!' The men roared in response. Behind them Runar nodded approval.

A thunderous boom shook the gate.

## ONBOARD THE *NJORDUR'S MERCY*

Her voice was almost like touch, leading him in and out of consciousness. Words melted into each other and became sounds, devoid of language but full of meaning. Inside him the screams of the others had subsided. She had made them go away because she loved him. Oraekja was at peace now. He was full of the life of warriors. It didn't feel different or wrong any more. He just wanted to do what she would ask of him. But she said he was not strong enough. Not yet. There was one strand missing, she said, one thread still uncut. He drifted off again, an ugly, warped smile on his blue-tinted lips.

## STENVIK

Two moves. That was all he needed.

Ulfar wrong-footed an attacker on the wall and ran him through. The sealskin-clad raider tumbled over the inner wall. Dodging a javelin thrust, he slammed his one remaining pouch down at the top of the walkway.

One.

A lithe raider sprinted up the walkway and leapt over him, aiming a savage sword blow downward. In one fluid motion Ulfar sidestepped and ducked, placed both hands under the man's foot and heaved upwards as hard as he could. The sword sliced the air in front of his face as his opponent squealed in surprise and sailed over the edge of the inner wall. A scream of pain followed by the reserves' roar of approval told Ulfar he was free to continue. He drew his sword and brought it down hard on the bag.

Two.

White, clear liquid gushed out over the ramp, dripping down towards the ground. 'Is that it?' Orn shouted from his position further to the west.

'Just wait!' Ulfar shouted back. A big, burly mail-shirted raider armed with a shield and a vicious-looking axe moved up the walkway, sure-footed and well balanced. He looked almost graceful until he got to the first foothold covered by the white liquid, where suddenly his legs slipped from under him. He crashed into the planks. With both hands full and nothing to halt his fall he slammed down face-first on the wood, sending shudders through the structure and knocking him unconscious.

Then he started sliding downwards.

The men on the wall cheered, but Ulfar was not done. 'TO ME!

FOUR STRONG BASTARDS TO ME!' he shouted at the top of his lungs. In an instant a handful of *Westerdrake* raiders gathered around him. The big raider continued sliding down, picking up speed as he went along. The ones after him tried to jump over, but found that the surface they left was not the surface they landed on. The walkway that had moments before been a passage for fierce and deadly warriors over the walls of Stenvik was suddenly like an icy slope in winter.

'PUSH!' The defenders on the wall went after the suddenly unencumbered walkway with gusto. Lifting and twisting, they seized control of the wooden structure, throwing it down to loud cheers. Suddenly the attackers on the wall found themselves without reinforcements and fighting reinvigorated men of Stenvik who looked less like fighters and more like demons in human form. Cheers from the eastern wall and loud curses from the ground told of Sven's success on the other side.

'My dad always said working is fun if you have the right tools,' Ulfar said to Orn with a grin.

'What was in the bag?' the youth asked, open-mouthed.

'Water and lard,' Ulfar replied, grinning from ear to ear. 'Einar had a pot full of it. Now make sure those bastards leave those bloody sticks lying where we've dropped them.'

Smiling, Orn reached for his bow and watched Ulfar head to the ramp on the west wall.

'Spears!'

Ten men stepped forward, all armed with the outlaws' broad, thick hunting spears. They set them in the ground and braced, tilting them forward.

'Bows!'

Another five men took their places to the side, bows at the ready, arrows notched.

'Blades!'

Two lines of axes and swords formed beside the javelin wall. Birkir's head rose above the others; on the other end of the line Havar's cheeks wobbled nervously. The gate shook again. Stones broke loose from the wall.

'HOLD YOUR LINES.'

Earth and grass gave way as the gate creaked and leaned forward. Jorn darted in front of the gate and turned to face the men.

'REMEMBER! IF IT BREATHES, IT LIVES! IF IT LIVES, IT DIES TODAY!'

The men roared back at him, determination etched in their stances, in their faces.

Something heavy hit the gate from inside. A voice bellowed 'NOW!!' and Jorn just got out of the way before the big slab of wood came crashing to the ground.

Through the arc of the southern gate came the biggest man any of them had ever seen.

The last walkway tipped over and crashed to the ground. The few of Hrafn's men that remained on the wall were overmatched and overpowered. Warriors were thrown over the edge, dead or dying. The remaining raiders shuffled back to their camp, some dragging wounded comrades, others limping on their own. The defenders cheered and shouted insults after them.

Then the south gate came crashing down.

As one, the men on the wall turned to look down on a living legend. Egill Jotunn strode into Stenvik wielding the log he'd used as a battering ram. Ten scrawny, filthy bearskin-clad warriors came with him, screaming garbled obscenities. Roaring, the small team charged the fifty defenders. Those on the wall watched in horror as the first volley of arrows slammed into the berserkers and didn't even slow them down. Egill threw the log at the spearmen, took out three men and obliterated the first line of defence. In an instant the market square turned into a boiling, heaving mass of bodies, blood and pain.

Sven turned away just in time to see the first murder hole shield rise silently on its hinges, soon followed by the other one. Without thinking he took a running jump and landed on the shield closest to him, slamming it down. Below his feet a howl of rage turned into a feral scream. 'ENEMY ON THE WALL! TURN AROUND, YOU BASTARDS!!' Sven yelled.

The shield exploded upwards, sending the old warrior stumbling off. A snarling wild-eyed man in animal skins crawled up out of the hole, foaming at the mouth, keening and howling.

## ONBOARD THE *NJORDUR'S MERCY*

Oraekja opened his eyes and saw only cold. Stars twinkled above him in a sky turning from day to night. She leaned in, looked down and smiled a kind smile. He watched her hand on his chest, felt the freezing, scalding feeling in his heart, felt it spreading through his veins. Felt his body spasm, shake, unfamiliar weight in his legs, in his arms. Felt himself scream again, his throat raw. He watched her mouth move.

> *'Sleep now, faithful*
> *Fury's servant*
> *Cloaked in starlight*
> *Sheathed in darkness*

293

*Feel the thunder*
*Taste the lightning*
*Legend is your*
*Destination.'*

And Oraekja was no more.

## STENVIK

The heat in the smithy was suffocating. Everywhere he looked he saw sharp, jagged edges. Swords and axes. Spearheads. Blood. Audun leaned on his worktable, head spinning. There was too much blood. Too much death. It was in the air, he could taste it. He'd come to Stenvik to hide, to stay away from the blood, but he wasn't safe, not even here among his tools.

A wave of old, dark thoughts swept him away.

Sven barely dodged a murderous swipe from the berserker's rusty sickle. Up on the wall around him the sounds of weapons clanging mixed with grunts and groans, screams of pain and spine-chilling howls from the men in animal skins.

'DIE, YOU BASTARD!' the old warrior screamed as he pivoted and rammed the dagger in his left hand to the hilt through the wolf-skin and into his opponent's ribcage. 'DIE!' Sven kneed the grunting man savagely in the crotch for good measure. Blood spurted along the dagger's blade as he pinned the berserker's weapon arm between them.

The stocky, thin-haired berserker did not go down. Instead he turned, looked at Sven and grinned, his face full of broken and yellowing teeth. The wounded man's head came at him so fast that Sven barely got his nose out of the way.

'OW! LET GO, YOU GOATFUCKER!'

Sticky, scarlet blood streamed out of the fighter's side as he pummelled Sven with his left fist, firmly hanging onto a clump of the old man's big, bushy beard and pulling downwards, trying to dislodge his weapon arm.

'Oh no you don't,' the old warrior grunted as he twisted the dagger savagely and yanked it upwards and out. His opponent coughed and staggered back, bleeding freely from his side. Face contorted in rage, he growled. 'I know I've said to some people that their mother was a bitch, but in your case it might actually be true,' Sven snarled back at his opponent. Never taking his eyes off the invader, Sven drew a battered old shortsword in his right hand to go with the bleeding dagger.

Paying no heed to the gaping hole in his side, the berserker charged, screaming and foaming at the mouth, madness in his eyes.

Sven stood still.

The sickle swung back, muscles flexing in the madman's arm. Then he unleashed a killing blow at his target.

Which wasn't there.

Instead Sven stepped towards the berserker at the very last moment, putting all his weight into the impact, driving both weapons clean through the onrushing attacker. Dagger through the chest, sword through the stomach.

Impaled by the strength of his own charge, the berserker sputtered and coughed. Sven braced against the dying man's last gasps, feeling the life pour out of the insane fighter. 'Now stay dead,' the old warrior snarled through gritted teeth, shoulder to the dying berserker's chest, head resolutely turned away.

His blades made a wet, slurping sound as he withdrew and a last shove sent the corpse over the wall.

Sven turned around and surveyed the scene. On the east wall Harald and Sigurd were holding their own, but the sheer ferocity of the berserkers' attack had taken the Stenvik defenders by surprise. Already exhausted, some of the men on the wall had simply been overwhelmed. Their dead bodies had been thrown like rag dolls over the wall or sprawled on the walkway, broken and mutilated.

Down in the market square, things looked no better. The defenders were putting up a brave fight, but they were no match for the sheer brutality of the onslaught. Egill Jotunn had drawn a massive, two-handed sword that he swung in broad arcs, shattering armour and sending sprays of blood sky-high. A circle had formed around him as defenders sought to get out of the way of the killing blade.

And now something seemed to be barrelling into the defenders from behind, from within the town, pushing and ploughing into their ranks, towards Egill.

An axe thudded into the wall next to Sven. A frustrated roar followed too close, way too close and the old warrior jerked to his left as a skinny, scrawny fighter, shaking with fury, yanked the axe back and swung to face him.

Shoot and run.

Runar fired again, an arrow thudding into the back of a berserker. The man did not turn, did not seem to notice. Instead his fist went into a defender's face once, twice, three times, turning it into a bloody pulp. In an instant the vicious warrior was away again, seeking his next target like a starving dog. Something warm spattered Runar's cheek. He turned to see the crazed light wink out in a berserker's eyes not an arm's length away, a serrated knife falling from his limp, lifeless fingers. Birkir pulled hard on his hand axe, working to dislodge it from the bearskin around the dying man's neck. He managed on the third pull.

'Move faster, you scrawny fucker,' Birkir shouted. He smiled and Runar watched as the blood-lust swept him away. 'COME ON THEN, YOU STINKING DOGS!' the big man roared as he turned towards the giant in the square. Stepping over the bodies of many defenders and few berserkers he waded into the fight, axe in hand.

Egill spotted him, turned and moved to meet the new challenger. Runar drew and shot but the angle was wrong. The best he could do was pierce the half-giant's shoulder. Without breaking his stride Egill pushed at the end of the arrow until the head came through on the other side, then pulled the bloodied shaft out and threw it away.

Birkir screamed as he charged the half-giant.

With frightening speed, Egill danced away.

Turning to readjust, Birkir stepped in a pool of blood and lost his balance. Moving in, Egill took the big fighter's head clean off with a simple powerful sweep. Time seemed to stand still as Birkir's body fell to the ground. All eyes were trained on the impossibly large frame of Egill Jotunn, the speed with which he moved, the force in the blade that went through the big man's neck.

The spell was broken by a loud wet crunch, and then another. At the perimeter two berserkers dropped dead, heads no longer a recognizable shape.

A barrel-chested man moved into Egill's field of vision. The front of his shirt was rust-coloured and blood dripped off his sleeves. On his head, a mop of blonde, unruly hair. Two big blacksmith's hammers in his big calloused hands. His blue eyes blazed. His mouth contorted in a cold, fierce smile. The man who had answered to the name of Audun howled, a fierce, primeval sound. Foaming at the mouth, he charged Egill Jotunn.

## STENVIK, THE OLD TOWN

Skargrim watched the fight on the wall, heard the screams from inside the town. He did not move. Thora stared at him, eyes ablaze. 'Do we charge? The men are ready. Give the order!'

'No. Ingi is right. They've retaken the wall, we can't get up there quick enough and the gateway is a death trap. Running in would be just the same as murdering our men.' Thora looked over at Ingi, calmly assessing the situation, unmoved by the spectacle. She looked back at Skargrim and spat on the ground.

'You dickless fucks.' She stormed off.

Somehow he knew that now Skuld wanted him to stand rather than fight and that she was pleased with the day's fighting as it was. That it was right.

It didn't make him feel any better.

## STENVIK

Alone in the dark, Lilia remembered. She saw how her mother clutched her baby sister to her breast, saw her cry, saw her scream when her father was cut down by the raiders. In the moonlight they looked like creatures from horror stories; demons come to kill and eat them all. Through cracks in the wall she saw Harald, their leader, calmly cripple and murder men and boys she'd known all her life. Moments later he kicked in their door, grabbed the baby from her mother and bashed it against the wall until it stopped screaming. He threw the lifeless body away like a rag doll, punched her mother in the mouth and threw her outside.

He kept Lilia for himself.

She clutched the dagger and stared at the door.

They'd not take her so easily this time.

The massive sword carved the air over Audun's head, but he didn't flinch. Didn't care. It was just metal. He knew metal. On the edges of the blood fury he remembered metal. His hammers were metal. They belonged on swords. Audun put all his weight behind the blow and smashed his hammer up into Egill's blade.

The smooth arc of the sword was broken. Egill's eyes flew open as he struggled to regain his balance. He stared at the blacksmith. 'You . . . you're him. The Third Seven. But you're . . . different.' The massive fighter regained his balance and stood firm. 'Come on then, blood fiend! Show me something I haven't seen.'

Audun roared, a man on a cliff in a storm, braving the elements, swept away on the tide of blood, the smell of it, the irresistible flow of it. In one fluid motion he launched a hammer at the half-giant's knee. With stunning speed the sword came down, blocking the blow with a loud clang. Undeterred, Audun swung the other hammer.

Egill screamed in pain as the bones in his left forearm turned to pulp under the metal. A leather boot came up and caught Audun in the chest, sending him sprawling halfway across the square. The smith clambered up again, covered in blood, grinning manically. Around him the men of Stenvik rounded on Egill's berserkers. Audun didn't notice. Snarling, he launched himself back at Egill. The blacksmith's hammer met the half-giant's sword in mid-air. Grunting with effort, arm hanging limp at his side, Egill roared.

'You will die like all the others! No one can stop me! I am Egill Jotunn!!'

Audun blocked a powerful swing with the hammer's head and aimed a vicious stomp at Egill's shin. His heel landed with a satisfying crunch on top of the half-giant's foot. Audun followed up with a shoulder barge delivered with all his might to Egill's chest.

The half-giant doubled over and staggered back. Coughing, he struggled to rise. 'You cannot defeat me! You cannot—' A violent cough drowned the rest of the sentence.

'DIE, YOU TURD-FACED MOTHERLESS RAT BASTARD BITCH-FUCKERS!!' An incredible shriek cut through the noise. A fresh wave of black-clad warriors streamed through the southern gateway, led by a tiny woman wielding two daggers.

As the last berserker on the wall met his match, the defenders hustled down the steps to meet this new enemy. Across the market square Egill Jotunn limped away, swinging weakly at Audun; the blacksmith batted the sword away without hesitation and moved in.

The hammer connected with the half-giant's right knee, smashing it. Aloft again almost at once, it smashed into his left knee.

Tendons, knee cap, joint.

Snapped, shattered, broken.

Egill Jotunn roared and fell.

Audun's hammer split his face and caved his skull in, killing him instantly. The black-clad fighters screamed and cursed, redoubling their efforts.

The sun set on blades rising and falling, the dying screams of warriors and a town fighting for its life.

## ONBOARD THE *NJORDUR'S MERCY*

Skuld stood in the prow, sniffed the air and looked towards Stenvik as day faded into dusk.

'Come to me,' she whispered. Weaving its way towards her on top of an almost invisible carpet of shimmering, grey-tinted air inches above ground came a thread so thick as to appear almost solid, silver sparks dancing within.

Her hands moved silently, summoning the life-forces of the newly departed warriors, calling them to her. Letting them deliver her prize.

The last thing she needed.

The final thread.

The soul of a legend.

## STENVIK

The market square was littered with bodies. Pools of blood soaked slowly into the ground beneath the stones. Smells mixed in the air and assaulted Ulfar; entrails and death, mostly. He knew those smells now. In the middle of the square Sigurd leaned on the haft of his axe, blood splattered across the front of his tunic. Sven and Valgard were moving towards him, probably to receive further instructions. Ulfar had watched across the square as the last brace of black-armoured warriors retreated through the tunnel with the tiny woman, driven back by two old men and a handful of *Westerdrake* fighters. He'd been too tired to cheer.

At the far end he saw Audun slink away, unnoticed by the exhausted fighters.

Ulfar followed.

'We would have been massacred,' Sven said.

'And we should have been,' Sigurd growled. 'I still don't understand why they didn't follow through. Why didn't Skargrim come over the wall?'

'Does it matter?' Sven shot back. 'We're alive. We're alive and they' – his gesture took in a square full of bodies in black armour – 'are not.' A rag-tag group made up of the old and wounded was already picking its way through the corpses, shifting one here, rolling another over there, searching for any useful equipment. 'Their own fault for running that many people through a hole, the bastards,' the bearded old warrior added.

'I don't like this, Sven. I don't like it at all.' Sigurd paused, brow furrowed. 'Set some men to barricade the bloody gate. Use whatever you can. Send Thorvald to round up the women and children. We're keeping them in the longhouse until I say so. Where the hell is he going?'

Sven and Valgard turned around to see Harald stagger off towards the west gate, stumbling in between houses and out of sight. 'He's been on his feet for a long time,' Valgard ventured. 'He's probably just going home for a rest while he can get it.' He knew exactly how Harald was going to get his rest, but kept that to himself.

'Well, he's going in the wrong direction,' Sven spat. 'Bloody useless at times, that man. He's been acting strange in the last week, more so than usual.'

Valgard shrugged. 'People have their bad days, I guess. Sometimes they come in weeks.'

Sigurd snorted. 'They do, don't they.' He turned to Sven. 'Get on with the barricade, old man, unless you'd like to walk down to Skargrim's and get your throat cut immediately.'

'Might save me dealing with upstart puppies like yourself,' Sven shot back and smiled.

Valgard rolled his eyes and moved towards the healing station. There would be no shortage of work for him there.

Ulfar heard it before he saw it.

Coming around the corner he found Audun on his knees, vomiting hard. Spasms shook the blacksmith's massive back and shoulders, delivering the contents of his stomach onto the grass behind a small storage hut.

Audun, Stenvik's mender of iron and hammer-wielding hero in the battle of the market square, was down on his knees, face red, neck veins throbbing, tears streaming down his cheeks.

Words did not come to Ulfar.

Instead, an image of Lilia gently insinuated itself into his head, left a lingering trace, a touch, a suggestion. Drawing the blade that Audun had made for him, Ulfar swiftly cut a piece of his tunic, folded it twice and made a rag. Then he knelt by the blacksmith's side, held the cloth to his friend's forehead and waited for the bad time to pass.

In the aid tent some of the lucky ones, those with minor wounds, knocks and scrapes, were trading insults and jibes, talking about who had done more damage to the raiders, who'd fought like a girl, who'd been knocked out before he could hurt himself. Valgard listened to their patter as he prepared more bandages. Stars twinkled overhead; the air was cold and crisp. The night was almost over. And what had happened? He had been forced to quietly end the lives of seventeen raiders with his knife, warriors who would never rise again, proud men who would just have become shamed cripples, extra mouths to feed. The dead bodies had been unceremoniously dumped in a pile that would stink of battle if the whole town didn't already. Valgard spat and tried to breathe with his mouth. They could try and hide the fear if they wanted, try to cover it with bluster, but in the end they'd been lucky. The black warriors had easily been a match for the raiders of the *Westerdrake* and their prowess could have overcome the situation, coming two and three abreast through a hole in the wall. The Stenvik archers had wounded at least half of them before close combat had even begun.

And even so, the defenders would still have struggled if it

hadn't been for Audun. That man had kept them alive. There was no doubt about it. The stories would probably vary, but by last count he was thought to have disposed single-handed of about twenty black warriors and five berserkers, not to mention the giant. Sven's duel with the knife bitch had been something to behold too: she'd been murderous quick and taken out many good men, fat Havar among them, but the old dog had stepped in and simply refused to die. Instead he had seemed to read and anticipate all her moves, parrying and countering, pushing her slowly back. In the end she'd retreated into the tunnel with eight of the black-clad warriors, running to the safety of their own camp. No doubt she'd be telling some nice tall tales about the Stenvik men's numbers and fighting ability. That would be good for making them think twice about the next assault, but it would probably still not be enough.

Someone moved in behind him. 'Go get some sleep.'

The thin, pale healer snorted. 'Sleep? Sleep is for—'

'Now, son.'

Valgard smiled to himself. He knew better than to argue with that voice. He turned, nodded at Sven and walked off, past three women moving towards the longhouse, when something occurred to him. Slowing almost imperceptibly, he changed course and headed towards the west gate.

Ulfar wandered aimlessly through Stenvik. Audun had not wanted to talk to him. Instead he'd grunted and wiped the vomit off his chin, stumbled to his feet and staggered home. Every bit of his own body screamed for sleep, but his brain would not let him. Images of murder on the wall flashed in his mind, throats opening and blood gushing from gaping wounds, light leaving warriors' eyes.

He saw Valgard slink away from the wounded, saw Sven sit down and start working by candlelight, rolling up bandages and preparing for the next wave of the wounded.

'Not very nice, that,' he commented casually as he ambled over to where the old man was sitting.

'What?' said Sven, taken aback. He peered out into the darkness, trying to locate the source of the voice. 'Bloody light. I'm blind. It's Ulfar, isn't it? What's not nice?'

'Leaving a feeble old man all alone like this,' Ulfar said with a smirk.

'Oh go kiss a cow, you bastard,' Sven replied cheerfully. 'The bloody lard was inspired. It's a good fighter's head you have on your shoulders there, son.'

'Thank you.' Ulfar blushed in the darkness. 'I just – I did what I thought I needed to do, I guess.'

'You did well is what you did,' the old man said. 'Now, would you do me a favour and do the rounds? Have a look in on the lads. Some of them are sleeping. Some of the others are in a bad way. See if anyone needs help.'

Ulfar nodded and turned towards the rows of wounded men laid out on pallets. As he walked he found to his horror that these were no longer strangers. He recognized faces and remembered names. A chill passed through him.

'Ul . . . far . . .' A soft voice whispered from the pallets.

'Coming,' he answered on reflex. Looking over the rows of wounded men, he could not see any movement. 'Where are you?'

'. . . Here . . .' the voice sounded again, along with a flicker of movement halfway down the row of sleeping bodies. It was Orn. The young fighter he'd left on the wall was now a boy with a shattered collarbone, four broken ribs, a fractured skull and a badly twisted leg. Someone had smashed his right shoulder for good measure.

'Here I am.' Ulfar took Orn's hand and mustered a smile. The boy's face was pale and drawn, making his eyes all the more remarkable. All his strength seemed to shine out of them, blue and sparkling in the faint moonlight.

'I need to tell you what I've seen.' His grip on Ulfar's hand tightened.

'Ah! Yes you do,' Ulfar replied. 'What is it?'

'I didn't know who else to tell it to. All the others always tease me because I'm so young,' Orn said quietly. Ulfar said nothing. 'I may not be full grown yet but I see well,' Orn continued. 'I'm named after the eagle and I've inherited his sight. Everyone knows this.' Strength and determination crept into his voice. 'And I've seen things in the last couple of days that I've not told anyone. Magic. Every time someone dies on the wall, a little grey spark or cloud or something seems to leave them and slide towards the harbour. I think – I think someone onboard the ship that lies anchored there is harvesting their souls.' Orn looked at Ulfar, then looked away. 'You don't believe me, do you?'

'I have no reason not to believe you, my boy,' Ulfar said. Orn relaxed back onto his pallet. 'I'm just not entirely sure what you've seen or what I'm going to do with it. Is it . . . what? We've already seen the strange army of outlaws, we've seen a union of bastards from the north, apparently – what can I do about some grey mist?'

But Orn was fast asleep, an exhausted smile on his lips.

## VALHALLA

Empty.
Hollow.
Dead.

There was not a single soul in the mighty hall. There were no stools around the great table. No echo of fighting men's songs. It felt like it had been empty for some time, and Harald could already see it falling into disrepair.

'Thor . . . ? Freya . . . ?'

The words bounded around the wooden box, sounding weightless and stupid. What the hell was he doing? Calling out to . . . who? To what? He felt his anger rise. He was being a fool and he didn't like it.

'This is all cowshit. This never was. I'm dreaming,' he spat into the darkened far end. Shivering, he suddenly felt absolutely certain that if he walked towards the darkness it would draw him in, surround him, gradually slow him down and then, when at last he stood still, it would kill him.

He would never find the far wall.

Shaking, he forced himself to look at tangible things, rotting wooden fixtures barely visible in the dusk.

He blinked.

How had he not noticed that?

Lying on the floor in front of the massive table, standing out like a bloodstain on a white shift, was a piece of wood.

Loki's voice whispered in his ear.

'Take it, Harald. Set things right.'

Startled, he spun around.

Nothing.

Heart thumping in his chest, he turned back to the table and the piece of wood.

He caught his breath.

It was stunning.

An exquisitely carved wooden dagger, edge and point sharpened to perfection, intricate runes set on the hilt. The work of

Loki. Harald sheathed the dagger in the folds of his tunic with
great care and left the hall.

## EAST OF STENVIK

Two logs stood in the middle of the eastern road, midway between
the forest and the wall. Diagonally crossed, they leaned back onto
a third for support.

The scouts on the eastern wall peered out into the morning
gloom. Something seemed to be tied to the logs.

Not something. Someone.

A man hung on the frame. He was naked from the waist up,
arms tied to the rising 'V', legs spread and nailed to the logs. His
head was pulled back.

As the first rays of the morning sun rose over the forest, light
played on the ravaged body on the frame.

Broken ribs protruded from his back, shaped like blood-stained
wings. Sigmar stared at Stenvik, his eyes wide open and lifeless,
mouth frozen in a silent scream.

## STENVIK, THE OLD TOWN

'He's gone. Ingi's gone.' Skargrim felt sick to his stomach.

Gone.

He looked at the other two captains standing around the
cooling campfire, warriors rising around them.

'I knew we shouldn't have—' Thrainn began.

'No you didn't.' Hrafn cut in. 'No you didn't, and that's a bad
road to go down. You didn't, I didn't and Skargrim didn't. So we
all take the blame for this and we carry it like men. Unless this
is part of some master plan that I am unaware of. I for one was

happy when Ingi suggested that his men take watch for the night because he'd missed out on the action. I have . . . I had nearly a hundred wounded men, and put some of them out with him. Their throats have all been cut. Clean, neat and silent. He launched over twenty ships last night. Next to our heads. And none of us knew, or noticed, or woke up.'

Gone. A third of their force was simply gone. Skargrim still couldn't get his head around it.

Hrafn continued. 'So what I would like to know is what we do now. I've not run away from a fight yet. What do you say, Skargrim? What do we do?'

Bile rising in his throat, the grizzled old captain turned without a word, set his sights on the *Njordur's Mercy* and half-walked, half-stumbled towards the pier. Neither the wooden boards nor the familiar gentle roll of the waves lapping against the ferry boat calmed him down. He clambered onboard, moved to the hides and swept them aside. 'You knew. You knew he would betray us,' he snarled. 'You – you . . .' As his voice trailed off Skargrim blinked, shook his head and swallowed.

She looked up at him, sizing him up. 'Yes, I did.'

'Wh— why? Why didn't you do anything?' he croaked, unable to look.

'I couldn't. It was foretold.'

'But you're – you can . . .'

'If it is in the web I cannot change it.' Her smile was tinged with regret. 'I can only . . . add to it. That is why I summoned the people of the land to stalk the forests, the shamed and the desperate, the cruel and the wicked. That is why I've called on the gods to help us. Behold the Einherji.' Skargrim stole a glance at the body lying at her feet and an involuntary shudder rattled through him. 'You were right about Ingi. He knows how to avoid a fight he thinks he can't win. He was always going to leave at the first sign of real trouble.' She paused and cocked her head, as if listening to something on the wind. After a little while she turned her eye back on the Viking captain, standing rooted to the spot, gazing at her. 'Rouse the men. They fear you, they love you and they'll follow you. Make ready to storm Stenvik.'

He stared at her, dazed.

'Have faith, Skargrim. The gods are pleased with you. You are a man of great honour. If you sacrifice, if you give to the land, the gods will be good to you. Now go.'

And if you refuse, they will not.

Skargrim nodded, turned and walked towards the prow.


STENVIK

His face was drawn and his shoulders slumped, but there was no give in Sigurd's voice. He turned to his hastily summoned war council, standing in a tight circle just outside the chieftain's longhouse. 'How many fighters do we have?'

'About a hundred, give or take. Some more wounded, weak or old,' Sven shot back. Jorn stood next to him, face grey with fatigue and a thick bandage wrapped around his upper left arm.

'They'll overrun us if we try to hold the wall,' Thorvald said. His voice was flat, distant. Sigurd had led him up onto the wall, showed him what they'd done to Sigmar. The lanky scout master had taken a deep breath and nodded once. He'd stayed for a long-drawn-out moment, eyes fixed on the frame, on Sigmar. Then he'd exhaled, turned and walked away. Now he stood by the door to the longhouse, opening it mechanically to admit women and children, back straight, eyes looking out through the walls and to somewhere else.

'I agree,' said Sven. 'Ideas?'

A timid voice broke the silence. 'M-m-maybe I c-c-can . . . ?'

## STENVIK, THE OLD TOWN

'Tell the men we're moving on Stenvik.'

'What?' Thora rounded on Skargrim, incredulous. 'Is your brain wrapped in seaweed, captain? NOW you're moving? NOW you're charging? You could have HAD them last night! If you'd followed me – if you'd gone in – Egill Jotunn would have been alive. A lot of his men would have been alive! All you do is wag your fucking tail when she says so! You're nothing but a dog to her! She whistles and you come calling, like a spineless, dickless lily boy!! How the fu–'

Skargrim grabbed Thora by the throat with incredible speed, the massive fist closing around her windpipe. Almost gently he inched his hand up until her jaw was resting on it. Then he lifted her off the ground. His arm did not tremble.

Thora struggled in his grip, clawing at his arm, kicking out, trying to reach the ground with her toes. Skargrim looked at her impassively.

'Tell the men. Now.' He let go. Thora collapsed on the ground, coughing, spitting and swearing. Around them, wide-eyed fighters turned on the spot and ran to follow Skargrim's command.

## STENVIK

Harald moved through the streets of Stenvik in a stupor. The wooden dagger by his breast felt hot and heavy like a stone from the fire, cold and light like an icicle. It pulsed, it sent his heart racing. It threw images at him. Images of power. The old gods, the knife in the stomach, muscles and sweat. Fighting the sea and winning, flying with the wind at their back. Taking pleasure, loot and women.

'Harald.' Someone appeared in his field of vision, blurred and shifting like a mirage on the horizon. He blinked and tried to focus. 'Harald. Are you well?' True concern in the voice. The figure moved closer, seemed to smell him. Muscles tightened, fists clenched. A cold smile spread on Harald's weathered face. He could almost taste the blood about to be spilled.

'Have you seen Lilia?' the thin man asked. Harald recognized Valgard's voice, but only just. With great effort he banished his dark thoughts. 'I thought I saw her walking down towards the longhouse,' Valgard continued. 'She would be safer in your house, wouldn't she?'

Harald growled and set off towards the middle of Stenvik.

Valgard smiled at his back.

## ONBOARD THE *NJORDUR'S MERCY*

Wisps of grey smoke curled around the still body of Oraekja, twisting sinuously over and across each other in dizzying patterns. Looking down on him, Skuld closed her eyes and began to move her hands in waves and lines that matched the strands of grey, weaving and forming.

When she spoke, her voice was no more than a whisper.

> *'Blood and body*
> *Given freely*
> *From the gods*
> *The words are spoken*
> *Threads are woven*
> *You have woken*

*Rise, immortal*
*Odin's warrior.'*

At her feet something stirred.

## STENVIK

Clutching his forehead and squeezing his eyes shut didn't help. Harald's head was full of fog. He growled in frustration.

Nothing made sense.

Why wouldn't she be at home? She should be there, where she was supposed to be. She should be waiting for him. Why wouldn't she be? Long, powerful strides took Harald to his house, past men running in different directions completing tasks he cared nothing about.

He pushed the door open. Nothing.

All at once the last days of waking, walking the walls and fighting to control his temper blended together and crashed down on his shoulders. The yearning for the sea took hold in a maddening rush. All the muscles in his body felt taut and tensed. He struggled to breathe. What had Valgard said? He hadn't been sure where she was. He'd been pissing himself, the little weasel. He'd not wanted to tell him about Lilia and that skinny fucker from the south. But he had, eventually. Or as good as.

Where was she?

Where the hell was she?

## STENVIK, THE OLD TOWN

Skargrim cursed.

Only a third of the men who had landed two nights ago stood

lined up by the jetty, eyeing him with distrust. He stared back at them, scowling. He looked over at Thora, who refused to meet his eyes.

Be honest. That's what Ragnar would have told him.

He cleared his throat.

'I did not choose this.' A battle-hardened army of warriors, brawlers and murderers looked at him warily. 'And you do not answer to me,' he continued, the words trickling out of him, flowing through him. He started walking in front of the men. 'When the skalds sing of this day, they will NOT call it the Ballad of Skargrim!' Months of strain and fear came loose inside his chest and crashed like a breaking iceberg into the cold, dark sea. He rode the wave of it. 'You have seen brothers and friends fall! You have watched the men of Stenvik fight back, hiding behind their walls and inside their holes! And you've asked yourselves why are we here? WHY?' Suddenly he felt strong again, in power, standing in the bow of the ship in the van. 'Because we fight for our lives! We fight for the right to live as WE choose! We fight to be free men, to decide for ourselves what we do!' He stalked the square in front of Stenvik harbour, willing the men to see what he had seen, understand what Skuld had made him understand. Showing them the only way forward and the only reason to move. It was suddenly so clear. 'We fight them here because the next fight will be closer to home and the next fight closer still, until we're fighting them in our towns, standing over our children's bodies. All because some upstart king wants to tell us our gods are wrong, our world is wrong, our understanding is wrong, our fathers and our fathers' fathers are wrong. So now we turn on Stenvik for the last time. Their south gate is broken. They cannot man the wall for long. Then they will fall and the old ways will stand.'

He looked at the crowd before him. The seven hundred looked back, and none of them spoke. Then a loud bang broke the silence.

Metal on metal.

Hilt on shield boss.

Another. And another. Quicker.

The men on the beach parted for Thora.

Buckler strapped to the left arm, she banged the hilt of her shortsword on the shield again – and again – and again. One by one the men picked up their weapons and joined in.

Overcome, Skargrim looked at her. She looked straight back at him, eyes flinty.

'I'm sorry,' he mouthed. She moved towards him, shortsword in hand. Seven steps. Five. Three.

She stepped into range. 'Shut up, you thick fuck,' she said, keeping her voice low. 'You're a cock and a fool, but you're not . . .' she paused and cricked her neck. 'You're not a bastard. Never have been. And someone has to stay with you to keep you alive.'

Fighting back emotion, Skargrim nodded.

Without warning, Thora rammed the buckler into his chest, just below his sternum. As he doubled over, fighting for breath, she leaned in and whispered, her breath hot on his ear.

'I don't care whether she's just a regular bush witch from up north or the ruler of fate reborn, though – I *am* going to kill that bitch when this is over. Don't get in my way. Understood?' He coughed hard. 'Good. Now stand up straight and lead the charge, you old boil-arsed bear,' Thora said, smiling an unpleasant smile.

## STENVIK

There. Just down the road.

Harald lengthened his stride to catch her, grabbed her arm

and twisted her around to face him. She screamed in surprise. 'You're coming home with me,' he hissed between clenched teeth.

Lilia stared at him but dug her feet in.

He glared at her, showed his teeth and squeezed her arm.

'Harald. Harald . . .' Someone talking. Woman. He shook his head, tried to make the sound go away. 'Harald . . . they said we were to go to the longhouse. You can't take Lilia.'

The fire started in the base of his skull and spread from there throughout his body in the blink of an eye. It was in his veins, in his eyes, in his bones. He threw Lilia to the ground and whirled on the source of the sound. 'What did you just say?' he snarled.

Inga recoiled from him. 'I just . . . I . . .' she started whimpering.

'Say it again. Say it again, you little bitch. Say it.'

'You are a coward, Harald Jormundsson.' The voice was quiet, insistent, intense . . . and familiar. 'Look me in the eyes. Look at ME.'

It didn't make sense. He turned, peering out of the depths of himself. 'What . . .?'

Lilia stood straight and proud, red hair glowing in the morning sun, blue eyes blazing and trained on him. 'I know you. I know that you are less than a man, Harald Jormundsson. You are a cruel boy, a horror and a fiend. I hate you and I never wish to see you again. I demand that our so-called union be broken, and if you try and drag me home I'll wait till you fall asleep filled with that foul mixture' – she stepped closer to him, so close that he could smell her – 'and then I'll stab you in the heart until you die!' She snapped her teeth at him.

And he hit her.

Fast and hard.

She crumpled to the ground, blood flowing from her cheek. Mindless with rage, he reached down and grabbed a fistful of hair in his left hand, yanked her up until she was almost sitting and prepared to hit her again.

Then he stopped, fist raised.

A hand had snaked under his left arm and grabbed hold of his shoulder. A slim dagger's point pressed uncomfortably hard at the base of his spine.

'Let go of the woman, son,' a voice behind him said, almost conversationally. Harald released his grip on Lilia, who collapsed onto the street. She pushed away from him and struggled to rise. Inga came out of her stupor and helped Lilia to her feet. The two men stood stock-still, entwined in what looked almost like an affectionate embrace.

'You need to calm down, my boy,' Sven said. Harald saw Inga look at the man behind him and then set off towards the longhouse. Lilia stood still, watching him. Looking at him, into him and through him. He tried to turn, tried to stop her seeing the dagger by his breast, the door to Valhalla. But it was no use. Sven had him pinned. Harald cursed.

'Yes, and your mother too, a couple of times,' Sven replied levelly. Lilia turned and walked away. 'Now, after she's gone I'm going to release you. I don't think Sigurd would appreciate it if you got angry with me. We need to kill the others, not each other. Do you understand?'

'Yes,' Harald grunted after a few hissed breaths.

'Good.' Sven eased the arm back, maintaining pressure on the point of the knife. Harald could feel a drop of blood trickle down his spine. Behind him the old fighter stepped back. Harald turned. Sven watched him intently, relaxed but quite clearly in a fighting stance.

The dagger went cold next to Harald's skin. Not now, it told him. Not now. Loki and Freya and Thor would have told him that too. Not this fight. He smiled at Sigurd's adviser and nodded. 'I don't know what I was thinking,' he said, and mustered a smile. 'I must be tired or something.'

'We're all bone-weary,' Sven said. 'And I know you have your black moods every now and then. But save them for Skargrim. He's coming, and he's coming soon.'

A rising clash of weapons banged on shields carried on the breeze from the old town. Around them men ran towards the south gate, women to the longhouse. Still watching him as one would a cornered animal, Sven grinned and inclined his head towards the sounds of battle.

And suddenly everything made sense again. Harald had seen enough warriors prepare for war to know when the rules changed. And these rules he knew. Fights were simple. He smiled back, and Sven relaxed. As Lilia's words echoed in his mind the burly sea captain's smile broadened.

He knew the rules, sure enough. But the rules for this fight would be slightly different.

The door to the longhouse slammed shut and the thick bar scraped across the inside, settling in place with a heavy thunk.

Like a layer of night snow, an eerie silence settled on Stenvik.

On the wall Thorvald commanded his best remaining archers. His face was pale and drawn, his jaw clenched. He had only spoken a handful of words since Sigmar's death. Beside him Runar finished sticking a handful of arrows in the earthen wall, looked down and signalled to Jorn.

In the market square, nearly seventy fighters quietly checked their armour and equipment. Sigurd and Sven inspected the scene. They had done all they could. To the south, a makeshift barricade of timber, stone and the corpses of their enemies blocked the gate.

319

Harald stood by the remainder of his men and smiled.

Jorn nodded to Sigurd and moved to his post.

In the smithy, Audun sipped the last drops of stale water. Then he reached for two mallets, hooking them to his hip. Grabbing a big two-handed sledgehammer, he moved towards the door.

Ulfar returned from his assignment and whispered to Sven, who nodded and shook his hand.

Valgard watched from a distance and smiled.

Thorvald's voice rang out. 'NOW!' The archers on the wall started firing at an unseen enemy. Then, with more urgency: 'SHIELDS!'

Death fell on Stenvik.


Skargrim was out of options and it filled him with primal, savage joy. He'd explained the plan to Thrainn and Hrafn in moments. Now orders were flying back and forth, groups were being marshalled and shields were up. Like cold water down his spine, bloodlust awoke in the old chieftain. He looked across the line at Thrainn to the west and Hrafn to the east. Then he nodded to Thora, who drew a deep breath.

'MOVE!!'

Arrows punched through knee joints and arms, stuck in shields, glanced off mail jerkins. Sprinting, roaring, Thrainn Thrandilsson's raiders rushed to the fallen walkways on the south-west side and started to raise them, hand over hand, straining and cursing. The men who could not help threw themselves at the wall and started scaling, kicking at the packed earth for footholds, inching upwards. With swords on backs and knives in hand they climbed on faith, looking straight at the wall to shield their faces from arrows and stones.

On the other side Hrafn's warriors launched deadly javelins at single targets with precision born of years of raiding together. More than one Stenvik archer would see the first spearman, duck down only to stand up and be thrown off the wall by the force of the second spear, launched moments later. This covered a sustained effort by Hrafn's strongest men, and the first ramp rose quickly into place.

Hrafn was the first up the planks, cackling madly.

Runar stood, drew a bead on him and loosed. Whooping, he knew the moment it left the string that the arrow flew true. The cheer turned into a shriek as Hrafn, running at full speed, somehow shimmied past the line of the deadly missile that should have punched clean through his throat.

He hardly even slowed down.

Firing three quick shots in succession at the waiting warriors, Runar put two fingers in his mouth and whistled. Thorvald's head whipped round, sweat pouring off the old man's face. He read the situation in a flash.

'BACK! BACK!!'

As one the archers turned and fled for the steps. Hrafn jumped up onto the wall to see the last of them disappear with surprising speed down towards the ground. He got to the top of the stairs just in time to see the warriors on the ground remove the planks that the archers had used to slide down.

The stairs had been smashed.

Instead of regular steps, a treacherous, uneven, rocky slope and grim defenders with long, thick spears awaited the raiders. Hrafn grinned and ducked as two arrows flew over his head. 'Not bad, Sigurd Aegisson. Not bad,' he chuckled to himself, seeking cover behind the inner wall.

Back in the embrace of stone and blood.

Skargrim's nostrils flared as he tried to ignore the stench of death. All around him his warriors were clearing out the corpses of Egill's men, each grabbing a fallen raider and dragging him out of the tunnel.

Looking up, Skargrim noted the broken murder-hole covers with some satisfaction. Stenvik was going down hard . . . but it was going down.

'WE HAVE THE WALL. SEEK COVER!' Hrafn shouted. Two of his fighters had already fallen to well-placed Stenvik arrows – their archers had been swift to find where the invaders' heads would be briefly visible above the parapets. Now the groove between the inner and outer wall was slowly filling with Hrafn's men, crawling on hands and knees. 'KEEP DOWN!' he shouted again, grinning. Plans were all well and good, but it wasn't a proper scrap unless they changed a little. 'STAY WHERE YOU ARE!' he bellowed. Crouching down, he made eye contact with his warriors and motioned for them to start crawling, head down, following the groove towards the north side of the wall.

Skargrim's blood boiled. The silence in the gateway was oppressive, broken only by the grunts of the corpse-bearers. One of the men pulled a body from the top of the pile and rays of light leaked through the barricade.

Stenvik.

Sigurd.

'COME ON, YOU BASTARDS! WORK FOR IT!' Thora screamed, setting off a chain reaction of growls, shouts and insults through the entire tunnel. As four more corpses were pulled away the last obstacle came into view. A wooden cart filled with rocks and turned sideways across the opening. Roaring, Skargrim waded over the corpses and barged into the cart.

It didn't move.

Cursing and slipping on the blood-slick stones, he pushed again. Nothing.

He found a foothold, bent his knees and pressed for all he was worth. The cart moved, but rocked back. Skargrim pushed harder. This time the wood creaked and the cart moved further. All around him he could sense more space as the corridor cleared.

One of his men joined him on the cart, and then another. Together they pushed and the cart rocked. As it balanced on a wheel, more people joined and pushed. The cart fell with a loud crash, shattering and spilling stones over the road. Skargrim charged roaring into Stenvik.

Three of the arrows missed him, another four thudded into his shield. The last one grazed his elbow. Blood oozed slowly out of the wound as Skargrim's men poured through the southern gate, spreading out.

A chill of foreboding filled him. He looked down at the blood, already thickening. A drop fell off his elbow.

If you give to the land . . .

The drop hit the ground and a blast of cold air swept in from the harbour, followed by an inhuman scream.

Something was coming.


Audun could feel it. After yesterday's events everything had changed. Or everyone, rather. No one knew how to talk to him after he'd shown what he was capable of, after he showed the people of Stenvik that he was a berserker. They hadn't asked him to hold the line with them but had hinted that his presence would be welcome. Just before they hurried away.

He felt sick. There was death all around him and he could feel the murder in his blood like a disease. His body didn't feel right;

didn't feel all his after yesterday's killings. Audun tried his best to quell the rising bile, but found himself wanting to vomit, drink water and hide under a pile of furs for a week. But for some reason he couldn't quite comprehend he was here instead. Hiding behind some huts at the edge of the square, observing from afar.

The men in the market square looked uneasy and as sick of killing as he was. Thorvald's archers were retreating, firing at the raiders coming over the wall. From his vantage point to the side he followed the fighters' eyes towards the barricade he'd helped assemble.

The cart was moving, rocking back and forth.

It was a good cart, he thought wistfully. He could maybe have been a bit more generous on the wood on the aft axle, but despite its flaws it had done what it had been made to do. Audun smiled to himself.

The cart tipped but did not rock back. Instead it kept tipping until it was tipping over, falling and crashing to the ground.

Skargrim charged into Stenvik.

All eyes were on the big, grizzled captain as Runar and a handful of archers let fly.

When they heard the strange sound Audun looked at the men in the market square. Faced with Skargrim on the ground, raiders on the wall and possibly something unknown like the berserkers, they exchanged worried glances.

All of them, except one.

Harald smiled a hunter's smile as he slowly inched from his position with the raiders of the *Westerdrake* and towards Ulfar.

Audun cursed and moved into the market square, following Harald's path.

Harald watched as another arrow thudded into Skargrim's shield. The big captain's hand closed on the hilt of the sword. Roaring, he charged the defenders' ranks. His men followed and the Vikings flowed into Stenvik.

The square was battle, blood and chaos.

He grinned. This was good. The dagger by his breast pulsed hot and heavy. This was how it should be. From the blood the strong should rise and serve the gods. He spotted an opening and stabbed hard, his sword piercing the throat of an unfortunate raider and sending him down. One more for Valhalla.

They'd been right to meet them this early on – the invaders couldn't use their numbers yet, but he could see the defenders would be pushed back. To his left Sven shouted: 'They're coming over the wall!' The old bearded fucker was still alive, fending off two of Skargrim's men with good footwork. He was a hard man to kill, Harald mused, but the battle wasn't over yet. 'Ulfar, go help to the east! Slow them down!' Sven shouted. Ulfar broke off at once from the group and set off towards the east wall. Harald grinned, banged the pommel of his sword on a raider's helmet and stepped from the front line to follow Ulfar. The rules for this fight were going to be different.

Sigurd wrenched his axe from the broken head of the dying fighter before him, never taking his eyes off Skargrim. A circle had formed around them, roughly the reach of their weapons. Many warriors had died already inside that circle.

Skargrim nodded at Sigurd and smiled. It was not a friendly smile.

'Sigurd.'

'Skargrim.'

Without warning the huge Viking captain launched himself at the chieftain of Stenvik, swinging to kill.

\*

Hrafn motioned silently to his fighters crouched behind the inner wall and watched them pass the signal on. It was time.

He held his breath for one moment . . . two . . . and when the first warning cry sounded from the north side of town he climbed over the inner wall and dropped the twenty-five feet to the ground. All over the eastern Stenvik wall, from the southernmost point to the northern one, fierce raiders in sealskin coats did the same. Landing lightly, Hrafn saw the faces of the poor archers that had been set to watch one point on the wall, only to be faced with their field of vision filling with enemies. Not long now, he thought. Not long . . . there.

'RETREAT! BACK TO THE LONGHOUSE!'

Echoes of panic.

Hrafn smiled.

Runar didn't give himself time to think.

Move, stop and shoot.

Move, stop and shoot.

He vaulted a fence, turned and squared his feet. Like he'd been taught long ago, he took the moment to control his breath, size up the onrushing warrior, draw and shoot.

The arrow glanced off the nose guard, punched through his enemy's left eye and dropped him dead.

Move, stop and shoot.

Back to the longhouse. That was the idea.

'How are we doing?' someone shouted just behind him.

Runar turned. 'I'm f-f-f-fine,' he replied, adding, 'He's not,' as he pointed to the collapsed man with an arrow sticking out of his skull.

'I can see that,' said the tall young man and smiled. Suddenly someone cannoned into him from behind and felled him to the ground.

Move, stop and shoot.

Runar turned and ran for cover. He had orders; they were to get back to the longhouse. Some people had to learn the hard way that you shouldn't stop to talk in the middle of a fight.

The first blow knocked the wind out of Ulfar. It was followed by a flurry of hard punches. A meaty hand grabbed his hair, turned and twisted hard. Lying on the ground, Ulfar found himself staring at Harald's face, bright red with rage.

'She's mine!' he screamed. 'Mine! Always!' Stunned, he looked into the furious sea captain's eyes. There was nothing human there any more. Ulfar tried to roll out of the brute's grip. No luck. Harald had him pinned and he knew it. A triumphant smile spread on his ugly face. 'No you don't. And when I'm done with you she won't like you at all. Because you won't be pretty.'

The straight right broke Ulfar's nose easily. As his head snapped back, Harald let go of his hair and grabbed his throat with the left hand, squeezing hard. Pain shot through Ulfar, veins pumped in his throat. He couldn't swallow. Couldn't breathe.

'Mine,' Harald hissed. Black spots appeared in Ulfar's eyes. 'She's mine and I can do what I want and you're not going to—'

Harald's eyes rolled up into his head and closed. He went limp. Instinct brought Ulfar's hands up to ward off the big man's falling body.

Harald's weight shifted off Ulfar. Big hands grabbed him and lifted him up. Through a haze he sensed he was being helped to stand by strong arms. He coughed hard and sucked the life-giving air back into his lungs. 'We can't stay here,' Audun said. 'The fight will come to us and that bastard will wake up sooner than later. Follow me.' Dragging Ulfar, dazed and coughing, he headed for the broken steps. All around them man-shapes darted between houses and huts; retreating archers and spearmen, fierce raiders giving chase.

A ring of blades tightened around the longhouse.

The battle raged in the market square.

Skargrim knew his men were as tough as they came, but the raiders of the *Westerdrake* were fighting for their lives, their town and their chieftain. The two groups were locked together in the confines of the town, refuting the invaders' greater numbers.

Sigurd stood in the middle of the line blocking their path to the longhouse. They had traded murderous blows, delivered hits that would have floored lesser warriors. Bleeding freely from a cut in his left arm, Sigurd ducked a swing and instead kicked at his opponent's shield, throwing him off balance. Recovering with stunning speed, Skargrim avoided the sweep of Sigurd's big battleaxe.

A sudden bellowing roar echoed through the southern gateway. The raiders' rearguard rushed into town, not looking forward but over their shoulders.

And Skargrim saw fear on Sigurd Aegisson's face for the first time.

'We have to run. There's too many of them,' Audun said. Standing on the south-east corner of the wall they could see the warriors closing in on the longhouse from all sides, weaving through Stenvik, moving between houses, chasing the archers and spearmen. 'We can't win this fight, Ulfar.'

'Wait.'

The roar echoed through the gateway and caused a commotion in the market square. Sigurd's line broke and retreated towards the longhouse, but Skargrim's men did not give chase and turn it into a rout. They were too busy getting out of the way.

A warrior walked into Stenvik.

His skin was blue and grey. The torn chain jerkin he wore was crusted with ice and blood. He wielded a sword in one hand and a big wooden shield in the other. Moving stiffly, he staggered towards the soldiers defending the longhouse.

Ulfar shook himself, blinked and looked at the fighter. At the air around him. He looked away, towards the pier. Then he turned to Audun. 'Come with me.' And with that Ulfar vaulted up onto the raiders' platform, heading down.

'Run, you bastards!' Sven shouted.

Sigurd's men did not need to be told twice.

When that . . . thing had emerged from the gate even the most hardened of warriors had stepped back. Now the men regrouped in a tight circle around the longhouse as Thorvald's archers climbed up onto the roof. So far everything was going as they'd expected.

Apart from this, whatever it was.

It looked only marginally human. The eyes glowed icy blue, the hair hung limp on the skull. Purplish-green bruises, cracked skin . . . it looked like a corpse left outside in winter. It moved like one, too. However there was no mistaking its intentions. Bellowing again, it staggered towards the longhouse. Skargrim's men followed at a safe distance.

Behind Sven bowstrings sang and arrows flew towards the abomination, burying themselves in its body, neck and arms.

It didn't notice.

Warriors emerged at a safe distance behind the creature. Some came down the roads from the gates, others from between huts and houses.

The longhouse in the centre of Stenvik was surrounded.

## STENVIK, THE OLD TOWN

The sleek ship lay at anchor a few boat lengths off the pier. There was no guard in sight. 'Whoever was here seems to have left in a hurry,' Audun whispered.

Ulfar put a finger to his lips, and then bent down. He felt around by the ground until he found what he was seeking. 'Come here,' he whispered back. Audun knelt next to him. 'Here – feel this.' He moved the blacksmith's big hand over . . . nothing.

'Are you . . . well?' Audun muttered, concerned. 'Did you hit your head when—' He stopped talking. Ulfar looked at him and nodded.

'You feel it too. The air is colder just . . . here. Orn told me he'd seen something that suggested witchcraft, and I'm willing to bet that the source is on that ship.'

Audun frowned. 'What do you mean by witchcraft?'

'I don't know,' Ulfar said. 'But I saw that thing coming into Stenvik and I don't think they'll stop it without our help. If you want to chop down a tree you don't go for the branch – you go for the root. Are you with me?'

Audun looked at him, rose and moved towards the ship. Together they found the rowing boat. 'Something smells a bit strange here,' Audun offered.

'That would be the last passenger, I guess,' Ulfar replied. The stocky blacksmith shuddered and put his energy into rowing. They were at the ship's side in moments, boarding easily. 'Keep in mind that whatever is on this boat will be . . . evil . . .' His voice trailed off when he saw her.

A woman stood by the mast.

Tall, blonde and exquisite, she was the very picture of beauty. There was a faint, shimmering silver light glowing around her. 'Welcome, Audun Arinbjarnarson. Well met, Ulfar Thormodsson. I have been waiting for you.' The stocky blacksmith and the tall young nobleman exchanged puzzled looks. The woman continued. 'It was foretold that two mighty warriors would stand after Stenvik. The weave said one would be quick to think and swift on his feet, the other full of anger and the strength of many men. Together these warriors would defeat a mighty foe. So I chose five of the fastest and strongest Vikings I could find and went to war against King Olav. I thought two of them would fit the description, one way or another.' She walked towards them, picking her way over the polished planks of the *Njordur's Mercy*. 'But Stenvik has proved more . . . stubborn than I'd expected. They've forced me to call on an Einherji – the souls of the dead come to fight in the body of a willing sacrifice. The brave men of Stenvik will try, but he cannot be slain by mortal hands. All souls released in battle will make him stronger. And now I will make you an offer.'

She smiled and looked them in the eyes. 'Join us. Join Skargrim's host, the warriors of Finnmark, the brave men of Trondheim. Stand with us and the Old Gods against King Olav. Stand . . . with me.'

Audun looked at Ulfar, then back at the woman. 'That would mean that the men of Stenvik would be killed.'

'Their souls would live on in Valhalla and drive on my Einherji against King Olav.'

'What happens to the Einherji if you die?'

The woman paused, looked to the sky and seemed to listen for something. Then she turned her attention back to them. 'The threads say two warriors will walk away from Stenvik, and I cannot change that. But I can tell you this. If you slay a weaver you shall be cursed to walk the earth, men of war for evermore. You will never rest, never know the peace of death. You will live with pain.' She took one more step towards them, smiling, hands held out in supplication, her voice soft and soothing.

> 'Strong, the living
> Drawn to struggle
> Weak men's champions
> Live in dying
> Ever losing
> Soul and spirit
> Changers, movers
> Starkad's brothers.'

She moved a step closer. 'I have woven the thread of Skargrim. I have cut the thread of Egill Jotunn. I have spun the Einherji into the great web.' Another step. She gazed at Ulfar and Audun. 'What would you have me do with your threads?' Close enough for them to smell, she reached out and touched the two fighters.

The ship swayed gently.

Audun reached for the leather thong that held his mallet to his belt. He loosened it, grabbed hold of the heavy iron hammer and hit Skuld in the head with all his might, just as Ulfar ran her through.

The body collapsed as life disappeared, withering before their eyes. At once the ship felt warmer. Ulfar was already making his way into the small boat.

Audun looked down on the dead woman, reached for her white shift and wiped the blood off the hammer with it. 'I don't know about the boy,' he added quietly, 'but you're a bit late to curse me, woman.'

## STENVIK

Thorvald died quickly. Sven had seen him snap; seen the rage take over and banish the fear. He'd known the scout master was dead before he'd taken his first step towards the monster. Credit to him, he still moved well and fought like a mountain cat. He'd even landed a few blows with his axe as he rushed out, some of which would have crippled a normal man.

But the beast was not to be slain. Instead it seemed to grow stronger. Every move was faster than the next; every swipe more horrendous.

The fourth swing had connected and split Thorvald in two at the waist.

Blood had pumped out of the scout master, spattered the monster's face, flowed freely towards the rest of the advancing force. The monstrous creation hadn't even seemed to notice.

'Blow the horn,' Sigurd snarled.

'We can't! That beast will kill us all!'

'If we're going we're going together. DO IT!'

Sven took a step back to comparative safety, reached into the folds of his tunic and pulled out a small horn. Putting it to his lips he blew three short, loud blasts followed by a long one.

The defenders started shouting and banging weapons on shields, making all the noise they possibly could. Some even took a couple of steps towards the encircling attackers, intent on making this a last stand.

A scream of pure pain cut through the din.

The blue-grey warrior dropped his weapon and shield. He

staggered to his left, then to his right, all the time wailing with the voice of a hundred dying men. Then the light went out of his eyes and he toppled over, hitting the stones with a crash.

The noise was such that no one noticed the people silently emerging behind the raiders. At the sound of the horn every resident of Stenvik that could still stand, the old and the young, the weak and the sick, those wounded in battle; anyone who could still wield a weapon had stepped out of the huts and houses at the edge of town. Led by Jorn of the Dales, they fell on the invaders from behind.

Beside Sven, Sigurd roared.

'ATTACK!!'

The defenders charged, and Stenvik was no longer a town. It was a seething mass of blood, fury and death. Suddenly numbers did not work to the attackers' advantage; the people of Stenvik knew their home inside and out and would come at the raiders from all angles, chipping away, fighting with reckless abandon.

Sigurd cleaved through seasoned, hardened fighters like wheat on a field. His axe seemed to move constantly, carving and cutting, slicing and slashing. Sven moved with him and covered his back.

Skargrim looked all around, trying desperately to make sense of the situation. Suddenly they were set upon from all angles. Those of his men that had been forced in between the houses for lack of room were disappearing in a rising wave of screams and clashing steel. On the other hand not many of the raiders of the *Westerdrake* seemed to be falling at all. He turned to Thora, grabbed her with both hands and brought her face to his. 'Take care of him for me, Thora. Please. Make sure my son lives to avenge me.' She stared blankly at him for a moment, awash with bloodlust. 'Go.' She blinked, nodded, turned and headed towards the southern gate, weaving between the fighters. On the west side cries of 'Thrainn is dead! Thrainn is dead!' and 'Jorn! Jorn of the Dales!' went up, along with sounds of heated battle. In the square south of the longhouse Skargrim's troops suddenly found that they were fighting on equal terms. The big, grizzled sea captain dispatched a pesky defender with a brutal downward blow. Retreat was not an option. They'd never get the ships under way.

Sigurd Aegisson stepped into the gap, axe in hand. He swung and connected with Skargrim's shield, taking the top off it with the first stroke. Fighting to stay alive as the chieftain pressed the attack, Skargrim moved out of the deadly arc.

And then, suddenly, he understood.

He saw Hrafn, saw the mad raider cackling, thoroughly in the grip of battle frenzy, fighting three of Sigurd's defenders. Two fighters charged at his men from the south gate; the stocky one wielded a hammer, the tall one a slim longsword. On the roof of the longhouse a scrawny boy was aiming and firing, killing with nearly every arrow.

In the end the gods didn't really care who won. They didn't want the head of the King. This was all the Old Gods wanted. Blood, chaos and fury. Souls to Valhalla.

Several horns sounded, along with more screams and sounds of fighting. The moment it took Skargrim to realize that they were coming from outside, from the east, was the moment he couldn't spare.

Sigurd's axe smashed into his shield arm, breaking bones, splitting skin and shattering links in his armour. Furious, Skargrim screamed and launched himself at the smaller man, but the chieftain of Stenvik had anticipated the move. He'd spun, staying on the side where the shield hung limp and strapped to the big raider's broken arm. The blade of Sigurd's axe sang as it sealed Skargrim's fate.

Lilia awoke with a flash of pain. The hut was dark. She must have passed out after she staggered home. A coarse, rough hand held on to a fistful of her hair. She fumbled for her knife, but something heavy landed on her wrist. 'No you don't,' a deep voice growled.

She was pulled to her feet and dragged out of her home.

## OUTSIDE STENVIK

King Olav's army had combed the forest, flushed out the outlaws from the positions indicated by Ingi's scout, and killed them all. Approaching Stenvik, they looked upon what had no doubt once been imposing town walls. Now the last rays of the evening sun fell upon a mound of grass strewn with corpses, stained with blood, steeped in death.

When they rode in through the south gate they fell silent. There were bodies everywhere. Old men, boys, warriors, women. They rode through a big square with what might once have been market stalls. Piles of corpses had been stacked to the side; many men had died here.

'Clear the way!' Finn roared. At his command a group of twenty soldiers moved ahead and started shifting bodies out of the King's path.

The road led north, to the longhouse.

And they started seeing the people left alive. Tired, bloodied, wounded people. Some were limping towards a makeshift tent where a thin, pale man seemed to be dressing wounds; others were struggling to open the doors to the longhouse. Again, bodies everywhere. Some of the people were walking around, spears in hand, occasionally stabbing at prone forms on the ground.

A column of King Olav's most devoted warriors followed Finn, with the King riding in their midst. A handful of bloodstained fighters started forming a line between the King's advancing soldiers and the longhouse.

They did not look friendly or overjoyed to see them.

'Who is your chieftain?' Finn shouted.

An old, weary and grey-haired man moved to stand in front of the line. He nodded silently, leaned on the haft of his axe and fixed Finn with a cold look. Finn stared back into the eyes of a killer and had to curb himself from taking a step back or going for his sword. Instead he dismounted and offered a hand.

'Well met, Sigurd Aegisson.'

'Well met,' the man replied without moving. Surprised and embarrassed, Finn stumbled into the speech he had prepared. 'King Olav Tryggvason wishes you to know that it is a great honour—'

'Yes. I'm sure he does,' the man replied. 'I do not wish to interrupt, but could you maybe put some of your men to work helping us? As you may see we have a town full of dead bodies, no water and little food. I have already spent time on one of your messenger boys and am in no mood to spend any more on you.'

Finn stared at the old man, and for a moment he thought he saw a flicker of something in his eyes.

Contempt?

'I don't know if—' he started. Then he stopped, because the greying man with the big axe wasn't listening. He was looking over Finn's shoulder.

'Thank you, Finn,' said King Olav. 'I will talk with Sigurd.' Red-faced, Finn retreated and took his place behind the King. Around them the people of Stenvik had slowly stopped what they were doing and were gathering behind their chieftain. The doors to the longhouse opened and a woman peered around them, shouting for someone named Lilia. She disappeared back inside. Soon a handful of other women emerged and then the doors were shut again. Archers were climbing down off the roof of the longhouse.

King Olav dismounted and stood face to face with Sigurd Aegisson. The King nodded towards the chieftain. 'Your actions this day are those of a hero, Sigurd.'

'Hero . . .' The chieftain smiled wearily. 'There are a lot of heroes in this town . . .' He looked at the man in front of him and added: '. . . my King. Most of them are dead.' Picking himself up, the chieftain continued. 'But welcome to Stenvik. This is what we have to offer. We have a lot of roasted meat that will go bad if no one eats it. We have no water. We have many wounded, children without fathers, houses that need repair and two smashed gates.'

As he looked around, King Olav's eyes followed his. Behind them, the King's army filed in.

'On the other hand, we have recently come into possession of quite a number of longships,' Sigurd added with a feral grin.

King Olav nodded slowly. 'I can see where you stand, Sigurd, and there is no doubt that your alliance with me has brought this on the town. As Christians' – Sigurd grimaced; the King ignored it – 'we are bound by the word of the White Christ to help one another in times of need. We will soon have—'

'WARRIORS OF STENVIK!'

A booming, gruff voice rang out over the town, interrupting King Olav. Heads turned, seeking the source.

'THIS – IS – WRONG!!'

## STENVIK

Home.

This was not good at all.

Home. Get home.

Valgard rushed through Stenvik as fast as his breath would allow, tears streaming down his cheeks. He could see any number of ways that this would play out, and none of them looked good.

Now he had to put his trust in the contents of the box.

Tired, shaking, and trying his best to remember words in a foreign language, Valgard hurried home.


Confusion spread like a ripple in a pond.

The voice was a man's, but coming neither from the people amassed behind Sigurd nor the army behind King Olav.

It came from the top of the eastern wall, where a burly man stood, lit by the rays of the evening sun. His arm was wrapped around a woman, his hand in her hair. She seemed to be struggling to escape.

'You cannot give this town away, Sigurd Aegisson! You cannot just hand it over to that upstart puppy king and his White Christ!' the man on the wall roared. Finn sensed the tension rising around him and saw some of Stenvik's warriors glancing at each other. 'I've watched you and Sven destroy my town. I've watched you piss on my father's legacy, on his father's legacy. BUT I WILL REDEEM US!' The big man reached into the folds of his tunic and pulled out what looked like a piece of wood. There was no glint of metal to suggest it was a weapon. 'You are about to sacrifice my town, so I must sacrifice that which is most dear to me.' The woman kicked and struggled, but to no avail. He had her pinned. Out of the corner of his eye Finn recognized Runar, sitting on top of the longhouse with an arrow nocked. Finn traced Runar's glance to a tired and bloodied Jorn, who was signing for him to hold.

'STENVIK BELONGS TO THE OLD GODS!'

Staggered roars of approval from the men of Stenvik turned to shocked cries as the man on the wall jammed the piece of wood into the side of the woman's neck and tore through her windpipe. He grabbed her by the hair, jerked her head back as he held her body over the wall and let blood stream from her cut throat down onto the ground.

King Olav and Sigurd Aegisson turned to face each other.

Over the King's shoulder Finn saw the spark of realization in the grizzled chieftain's eyes, saw the fluid motion as he stepped back and the axe that swept up to block the King's sword. As one, the King's soldiers drew their weapons and Stenvik descended into chaos. Wading over dead bodies, the King pressed the attack against Sigurd. The chieftain parried the first three blows. Then the arrow took him in the shoulder. Up on the longhouse roof, Runar was firing indiscriminately at Stenvik's fighters.

A bearded, scrawny and furious old man rushed at the King, screaming at the top of his lungs and wielding a knife in each hand. Finn drew his sword and stepped in to cover the King's flank. The old man struck like an adder and Finn had to retreat in a panic. There was no doubt – the whole town was bewitched, under some kind of mad blood-spell. Finding power in the purity of his belief, Finn struck back faster than he thought possible, slashing across the old man's chest.

The fighter coughed and blood spattered his beard. Taking two steps back he sized Finn up. 'Not bad, son. Not bad at all. You hit hard for a fat little seal,' and quick as a flash he threw his left-hand knife underhand at Finn's leg.

Finn felt the point slam into his thigh just above the knee, just below the edge of his mail coat. Something ripped.

He brought his sword up on reflex to block the old man's assault but he would not hold out long on one leg.

'HELP!' he shouted.

'And you sound just like your mother too,' the old man snarled. Three arrows punched through the old warrior's hand, knee and shoulder in quick succession. He snarled as he fell. Limping, Finn turned to the longhouse.

Runar waved at him. Finn saluted weakly. Turning, he was just quick enough to see Sigurd Aegisson stumble and fall. King Olav levelled the point of his sword at the chieftain's throat.

Ulfar had only one thought in his mind.

Harald would die.

Bounding up the broken steps, he drew his sword. When he reached the top of the wall he turned and moved towards the hulking sea captain, stepping carefully on the blood-slick planks. Harald turned, saw him and dropped Lilia's body. Ulfar watched her topple over the wall and fall silently to the ground. There was no scream of pain. There was no crash. Instead she landed with a dull thump and lay still, a discarded carcass.

Ulfar recovered just in time to deflect Harald's first blow. The burly fighter was on him, slashing and hacking madly with a big, heavy sword. Ulfar danced and dodged Harald's frenzied onslaught. 'YOU RUINED IT!' the big man shrieked. 'This is ALL YOUR FAULT! If you hadn't come here she wouldn't have died! You killed her! You did! You did!' The words melded together into a torrent of wide-eyed snarling insanity, followed by blows that grew ever heavier. Ulfar stepped backwards into a pool of blood, his foot flew out from under him and his head smacked into the wooden fortifications.

*Blur*

*Ears ringing*

*Something walked over him.*

*Something big.*

*Couldn't see.*

*Sword.*

*There.*

*Get up get up get up*

*Someone on the walkway.*

*Fighting.*

*Hammer.*

*Audun.*

*Embracing Harald.*

Ulfar shook his head and blinked furiously. Harald and Audun were locked in a crushing embrace. The point of Harald's sword jutted out of Audun's back. Audun's head was smashing into Harald's face. The big sea captain buckled. Audun had him in a crushing hold and head-butted him again. And again. And again. Harald seemed to sink into himself, his face a bloody pulp. The point of his sword disappeared into Audun, who staggered backwards. The big sea captain fell to the ground and lay still.

Audun seemed to struggle for balance. One step forward, then one step back. He turned and looked at Ulfar.

'I . . . can't follow you around all the time . . .' he wheezed and smiled.

'You idiot,' Ulfar muttered, voice shaking. 'You bloody idiot.'

Audun's eyes rolled up into his skull.

Ulfar rushed forward and caught the blacksmith before he fell. 'No. No no no no no.'

Audun died in his arms.

Supporting the weight of the stocky blacksmith, Ulfar looked over the inner wall. Beneath him King Olav's soldiers were busy rounding up the people of Stenvik, stripping able-bodied men of weapons, forcing proud warriors to their knees. To the north and south archers clambered up the broken steps, but no one seemed to take notice of them.

Audun's face looked surprisingly serene in death. Ulfar adjusted the body so he could lay his friend down to rest.

He felt the first thump as Audun's heart started beating again. The blacksmith's eyes flew open. He gasped for air, face contorted in agony. Ulfar saw King Olav's archers take up positions on the wall on either side of them. He saw the sun dipping below the horizon in the west, casting long shadows across the land. Then he dragged Audun to the outer edge of the wall and found a spot where the spikes had been broken. Holding on to his friend, he let himself fall.

# Epilogue

'You are an asset, my good man.'

'Thank you, my King.'

King Olav nodded graciously and leaned back on the high seat in the longhouse. 'It was an absolute pleasure to find you here. It pained me to discover that the old ways were still alive in Stenvik. It gave me no choice. I had to fight and subdue Sigurd Aegisson, a man I respected.'

'As did I, my Lord. But he was no man of Christ.'

King Olav nodded. 'And my judgement turned out to be correct. It was shocking to find that he had poisoned a significant amount of the grain stores; no doubt what he intended to feed to my men. His punishment will be suitable.' He looked thoughtfully across the longhouse. Tapestries taken from Saxon monasteries hung on every wall except the one behind the dais. There, wall mountings for some sort of weapon stood empty. 'I still remember my soldiers' surprise as they brought you before me. They found you in your little hut, kneeling, they said, cross in hand, praying to the Lord. In Latin! He truly is a hidden gem. Isn't he, Finn?'

Slumped in the right-hand seat on the dais, Finn spoke slowly and measured every word. 'He most certainly is, my lord.'

'It is only my duty as a Christian,' their visitor replied.

'And the Lord thanks you. Before you leave, however, I would like to thank you for the work you've done for poor Finn here. No doubt his leg will heal fully. He says that mixture of yours is very good for pain relief. I'm sure we can find a place in our ranks for a man with such skill.'

'You're too kind, my Lord. Too kind,' Valgard replied.

Outside, banks of grey clouds drifted across the moon.